**He turned his head, bringing
his lips just over hers.**

"Now, you can kiss me, Cupcake."

Unable to resist the invitation, Faith rested her hand on his chest, stretched her chin up just a little, and put her lips on his. He reacted immediately, turning his body toward hers, sliding the arm that wasn't wrapped around her shoulders to her back, and pulling her in. His mouth slanted over hers, his tongue pushing past her lips. She drank him in, making out with him for long minutes, savoring his flavor and the way he kissed her. Controlled yet wild. She'd never been kissed the way Connor kissed her. His lips were perfect, sealed over hers but parting to let her take in a breath, preventing her from getting too far away.

ACCLAIM FOR
JESSICA LEMMON'S NOVELS

BRINGING HOME THE BAD BOY

"Clever, romantic, and utterly unforgettable."
—Lauren Layne, *USA Today* bestselling author

"4 ½ stars! A sexy gem of a read that will tug at the heartstrings…A heartfelt plot infused with both emotionally tender and raw moments makes this a story that readers will savor."

—*RT Book Reviews*

THE MILLIONAIRE AFFAIR

"Fast paced, well written, and impossible to put down… Jessica writes with humor infused generously throughout in a realistic, entertaining way that really helps to make her characters realistic people you'll want to know…You won't be disappointed!"

—HarlequinJunkie.com

"Landon and Kimber's banter is infectious as their chemistry sizzles. Smartly written with a narrative infused with humor and snark, this modern-day romance is a keeper."

—*RT Book Reviews*

"I have always loved Jessica Lemmon's books and have enjoyed reading this series. She has again captured me with her magnificent writing and characters."

—NightOwlReviews.com

HARD TO HANDLE

"[Aiden is] a perfect balance of sensitive, heart-on-his-sleeve guy who is as sexy and 'alpha' as they come...A real romance that's not about dominance but equality and mutual need—while not sacrificing [the] hotness factor. A rare treat."
—PolishedBookworm.com

"Lemmon's latest is a pleasant example of living in the present and celebrating second, and sometimes third, chances."
—RT Book Reviews

"[Aiden is] a fantastic character. He is a motorcycle-riding, tattooed, rebel kind of guy with a huge heart. What's not to love?...I really enjoyed this book and I think readers will find it entertaining and heartfelt."
—RomanceRewind.blogspot.com

"I smiled through a lot of it, but seeing Aiden and Sadie deal with all of their hurdles was also incredibly moving and had me tearing up more than once as well...I can't wait to see what Lemmon will bring to the table next."
—HerdingCats-BurningSoup.com

"Aiden has all the characteristics of a bad boy but with the heart of that perfect hero...Their gradual spark leads to some well-written steamier scenes."
—RosieReadsRomance.blogspot.com

CAN'T LET GO

"I loved Sadie and Aiden in *Tempting the Billionaire*, and I was waiting for their story to finally be told. I love that this novella [lays] the groundwork for what will come in their book. I look forward to seeing how their story unravels in *Hard to Handle*."

—HarlequinJunkie.com

"This novella was long enough to get me hooked on Aiden and Sadie and short enough to leave me wanting more… The chemistry between the characters is fan worthy and the banter is a great addition. The writing style draws readers in. I can't wait for *Hard to Handle*."

—BSReviewers.blogspot.com

TEMPTING THE BILLIONAIRE

"A smashing debut! Charming, sexy, and brimming with wit—you'll be adding Jessica Lemmon to your bookshelves for years to come!"

—Heidi Betts, *USA Today* bestselling author

"Lemmon's characters are believable and flawed. Her writing is engaging and witty. If I had been reading this book out in public, everyone would have seen the *huge* grin on my face. I had so much fun reading this and adore it immensely."

—LiteraryEtc.wordpress.com

"If you are interested in a loveable romance about two troubled souls who overcome the odds to find their own happily ever after, I would certainly recommend that you give *Tempting the Billionaire* a try. It was definitely a great Valentine's Day read, for sure!"

—ChrissyMcBookNerd.blogspot.com

"The awesome cover opened to even more awesome things inside. It was realistic! Funny! Charming! Sweet!"

—AbigailMumford.com

A
Bad Boy
FOR
CHRISTMAS

A *Bad Boy*
FOR
CHRISTMAS

JESSICA LEMMON

FOREVER

NEW YORK   BOSTON

Copyright © 2015 by Jessica Lemmon
Excerpt from *Bringing Home the Bad Boy* copyright © 2015 by Jessica Lemmon
All rights reserved. In accordance with the U.S. Copyright Act of 1976, the scanning, uploading, and electronic sharing of any part of this book without the permission of the publisher constitute unlawful piracy and theft of the author's intellectual property. If you would like to use material from the book (other than for review purposes), prior written permission must be obtained by contacting the publisher at permissions@hbgusa.com. Thank you for your support of the author's rights.

Forever
Hachette Book Group
1290 Avenue of the Americas
New York, NY 10104

www.HachetteBookGroup.com

Printed in the United States of America

First Edition: September 2015
10 9 8 7 6 5 4 3 2 1

OPM

Forever is an imprint of Grand Central Publishing.
The Forever name and logo are trademarks of Hachette Book Group, Inc.

The Hachette Speakers Bureau provides a wide range of authors for speaking events. To find out more, go to www.hachettespeakersbureau.com or call (866) 376-6591.

The publisher is not responsible for websites (or their content) that are not owned by the publisher.

To the brave men and women who serve our country.
Thank you for your sacrifices.

ACKNOWLEDGMENTS

Connor's book wasn't always a Christmas book. In fact, its first inception years ago (albeit, only halfway written) took place in the spring! But, oh, how my ex-military landscaper fit beautifully into the chillier months, despite his dislike for the season. I blame Faith for changing him for the better. I admit, I really, really wanted to hate her (just a little) for her bodily perfection, but she ended up one of my favorite heroines.

Thanks to Lauren Plude, who suggested we make this a Christmas book. You worked through the synopsis with me, making sure we had the characters right before I ever set fingers to keyboard. You also went the extra mile to make sure the cover was *perfect*.

Thanks to everyone at Grand Central/Forever, including and not limited to Julie, Jodi, Leah, and Jamie—you keep the plates spinning at a dizzying speed. You all rock!

Thank you, Nicole Resciniti, for lending an ear whenever I need one.

Thank you, readers, for sending me your photos and comments and e-mailing me your praise. You're the lifeline to this whole writing thing. With no eyes to read my words, where would I be? (Let's not ever find the answer to that question.)

xo,

Jess ☺

A
Bad Boy
FOR
CHRISTMAS

CHAPTER 1

*G*litter.

Glitter *everywhere*. Lining the seams of the car's seats, sprinkled liberally across the floorboards, and at this point, probably a part of Faith Garrett's DNA.

She had spent the day gluing pink glitter onto the surface of one hundred pumpkins in various shapes and sizes for a Breast Cancer Awareness dinner. The woman in charge of said dinner had *oohed* and *ahhed* over the dinner's bedazzled centerpieces, going as far to throw her arms around Faith's neck and sing the praises of Make It an Event. As well she should. Faith and Sofie had busted their butts to pull together the last-minute dinner, which was why Faith had taken a sudden interest in arts and crafts. There wasn't time to hire out the task.

With the heel of her pump, she kicked off the shop vac and blew out a sigh. This was not working. Maybe she could use tape. She ran the back of her hand over her forehead, feeling a dab of perspiration there. The crisp October weather she loved had yet to make an appearance in Evergreen Cove. Instead, the temperature was in the high seventies, and there was not a prayer of a breeze blowing through the colored leaves still clinging to the trees lining the mansion's drive.

She leaned back into the car, snagged her fountain Coke from the cup holder, and took a long, delicious, sugar-laden sip. While she stood basking in the noonday sun, she admired her home away from home. The quartz blocks twinkled and the gold turrets stood regally against a blue sky filled with puffy white clouds.

The mansion looked more like a fairy-tale castle than a house, but then it was the host to Sofie's fairy-tale romance, so that was not an inaccurate description. Since Sofe had closed the doors on her business downtown, Faith was lucky enough to get to spend her workdays here, planning events in the library-turned-office, drinking coffee in the gorgeous kitchen, or helping set up the massive ballroom for the occasional fundraiser.

Maybe it was her way of having a slice of fairy-tale life for herself. Because face it, after the epic mess with Michael last year, a fairy tale was clearly not in the cards for her. Had she listened to her mother about "the curse" (legend had it the women on the Shelby side of the family "couldn't marry"), maybe Faith could have saved herself the heartache.

Then again, maybe not.

The last thing she needed, the very last thing she *wanted*, was a relationship. Been there, done that, cleaned the toilet with Michael's T-shirt. No, what she wanted more than anything was not a man. What she wanted—

what she needed—was to find her independence. She wasn't going to rely on a man any longer. She was moving on. Her life had taken a turn, but not for the worst. For the *better*. She'd see to that.

In the meantime, she was content to be happy for her friends. Sofie and Donovan seemed to have found their happily-ever-afters, and Evan and Charlotte had found theirs. Freed of her fiancé and, finally, freed from living with her mother for way too long, Faith was on a different path altogether. The path to find her inner strength.

Had to be in there somewhere.

She strode toward the front door, past thick, neatly trimmed hedges, flowering mums, and decorative rocks interspersed in between. The saplings out front stood strong and tall, accepting their new homes in the dirt like they'd been there from the start.

The beauty of the grounds never failed to amaze her. As someone who couldn't grow a plant if her life depended on it, the fact that one man and Mother Nature were responsible for this blew her away. The door opened, and she turned her head expecting Sofie to come strolling out, cell phone to her ear.

Instead, Connor McClain walked her way, and Faith's tongue promptly welded to the roof of her mouth. Broad shoulders molded by a long-sleeved henley, wide frame in perfect proportion, thick legs pressing against worn, soft-looking denim...The only other thing that amazed her more than the grounds was the way this man's muscular thighs filled out a pair of well-worn jeans.

He moved with purpose, not quite a stride but more of an amble. All those large upper-body muscles—perfectly outlined by his fitted shirt—moved fluidly, which was unexpected. A guy with that much girth should be a little less graceful.

He might be easier to write off if he was only made up of the physical attributes, but no such luck. The guy was ex-military, worked tirelessly for his friends, and had a flirty sense of humor that almost threatened to break down the barrier she'd so firmly erected since Michael had raided the Cookie jar... so to speak.

Her hand went to her hair as Connor brought that amble over to her. Since she was very tall, five-ten to be exact, she guessed him around six-one. She couldn't be sure, unless she was within kissing distance of his incredible mouth, which he'd stopped just shy of. But kissing that incredible mouth wasn't going to get her any closer to her independence. So she shouldn't consider it. *Not even for a second*, she reminded herself as he grinned at her. Her heart thrummed.

Around his penetrating grin, Connor spoke the words, "Afternoon, Cupcake."

She was sort of known for her sugar addiction. After a recent stressful workday, he had caught her devouring a bakery box full of Sugar Hi cupcakes. It wasn't her proudest moment. But showing weakness had its perks, because he'd ribbed her good-naturedly ever since. She recalled lamenting to Charlie some time ago (who Evan referred to as "Ace") that she'd never had a nickname. Now she did.

Truth was, she liked it way too much to ask him to stop.

"Good afternoon to you, Beefcake."

His smile didn't budge, proving he liked her nickname for him, too. And maybe that's all this was for both of them. A few teasing nicknames and prolonged glances. It was better than nothing. His eyes left hers, narrowing and traveling her face. Self-consciously, she smoothed the hand over her forehead where she felt her hair tickling her skin.

He stepped closer, until her vision was filled with broad muscle and golden-flecked hazel eyes. One rugged, working-man's hand, so different from any hand that had ever touched her, raised and brushed her hair away from her eyes. Then he dragged his fingertips over her forehead. She tried to keep her eyes on his, but for a scant second they went to his mouth again. Firm lips. Stubbled jaw.

Yum.

"Maybe I should start calling you Sprinkles instead?" He held his hand up for her to see. Pink glitter dotted his fingers.

It took her a second to reroute her thoughts. His touching her had sent her brain on a one-way vacation to Neptune. She traded the Coke from one hand to the other, scrubbing her hand along her skirt, which she noticed was covered in glitter as well.

A low chuckle echoed from Connor's throat.

"Laugh it up," she said, but did a pretty good job of laughing with him. "Now it's stuck on you, too."

"Damn." He backed out of her personal space and spread his palm. Thick fingers, blunt nails. A callus here and there. Even his hands were insanely attractive. "How am I going to explain looking like I had a run-in with a stripper when I go on my date tonight?"

She felt her face blanch as her blood raced from her cheeks to her toes. He had a...a *date*? She tried to reel her emotions in, but the effort was too little, too late. No doubt he'd seen the abject disappointment flit across her face.

Misplaced. *Misplaced* disappointment. She reminded herself she did not need or want a man. It didn't matter if he was going on a date. Connor was ridiculously attractive. And insanely, ridiculously attractive men with great senses of humor went on dates. But she also silently acknowledged that she preferred not to think about who he dated. Or what they did on those dates...

She forced a smile. Even though she'd justified everything to death, it took a lot of effort to get the words, "Ohh, a date. Have fun!" past her lying lips.

"I plan on it." His eyes jerked to one side, a strained silence settling between them. "I should get started so I can get out of here on time." He lifted a tool belt full of garden trowels and other implements for digging in the dirt.

"Yeah. I have to get back in there." She showed him her pink-glittered palm. "Try and clean myself up."

His grin returned and she had to remind her knees to stay strong. Her entire body seemed to forget it was one cohesive unit whenever he was around. One by one, parts of her turned to jelly. Kneecaps oozed, her spine melted, and the part between her legs... Well, she just wasn't going to think about that part.

Being alone was best. She had spent three years believing she was half a unified whole and had spent three seconds learning otherwise. No. Regardless of the way the landscaper's pectorals tested the strength of the henley he wore, Faith was an independent woman. Hear her roar. Or meow.

She might be able to rustle up a hearty purr.

"Have a good day," she told him, finalizing her decision to stop ogling him and get back to work. Deglittering herself was at the top of her to-do list.

"You got it, gorgeous." He stepped past her, not sending another look over his shoulder, not giving her a flirtatious wink, not saying another word. Just a brief interaction before he walked to the far side of the house and vanished around the corner.

What her friends Charlie and Sofie had was fine, and Faith was happy for them, but it wasn't something she wanted personally. A relationship with a man from the Cove was not in her future. No man from *anywhere* was in her foreseeable future.

Things were better this way.

* * *

Connor sneaked a glance over one shoulder as he walked away from Faith. Legs. Heaven help him, legs up to her neck. How he'd encountered a woman who looked like a Victoria's Secret model but was as down-to-earth as they came on a daily basis and not begged her to go to bed with him was an epic accomplishment on his part.

Admittedly, parts of him had wanted parts of her since he laid eyes on her for the first time. Not that she remembered him from back in those days. He understood why. Back then he'd been a too-smart, skinny kid with no direction and an on-again off-again girlfriend who was way more "off" than he'd ever dreamed.

Faith, with her recent engagement implosion, had more

in common with Connor now than ever before. It may have been years and years ago for him, but he knew what it felt like to be cheated on. Knew the sting of that pain—of being lied to, of being discarded for someone else. He may not have caught Maya in the act, but he had caught her *after* the fact.

Way after the fact.

He pulled the gloves from the back pocket of a pair of stressed jeans. At least he didn't marry Maya. And Faith didn't marry the dickhead who screwed her over. Bullet dodged for both of them.

That last thought hit him square in the chest. Maya wasn't the only bullet he'd dodged. Toward the end of his tour overseas, he'd dodged several of them. Literally. And a few of them had his name carved on them.

Closing his eyes, he pulled in a deep breath, counting down from five. He concentrated on the feel of the breeze on his skin, on the sounds of the birds, the rustling of leaves. Then he reopened his eyes. The anxiety didn't happen often anymore, but when it did, that was his way of dealing with it.

That and his friends. Faith had become his friend, he supposed. They didn't hang out, but they talked. Gorgeous as she was, he responded to more than just her looks. There was something fragile yet tough about her at the same time. He'd locked eyes with her on more than one occasion and had seen the pain there. With her height, she often looked him damn near dead in the eye when they were face-to-face, and he thought if he looked long enough he might uncover all her secrets.

But they had an unwritten rule—an invisible boundary line they'd silently agreed not to cross. She for her own reasons, probably having to do with her idiot ex, and he because, well…Sleeping with the girl who was his buddy's girl's best friend was the jewel in the crown of Stupid.

He and Faith worked together often, on projects both personal and professional. Getting intertwined—which made him think of her legs around his waist—with her was a high risk. If something went wrong, the fallout would be brutal.

So, Cupcake was a demilitarized zone. He wasn't going to date her. Hell, he hadn't seen her date, or talk about going on a date, since her breakup. Understandable. After the shit that went down with her ex, he guessed it'd be some time before she was interested in crawling into bed with anyone.

Damn if the thought of her crawling didn't insert an image into his head of her tiny, pert ass in the air, those elegant, long legs…

He blinked out of the image, blaming her outfit today: dark blue dress that matched her navy eyes, and a pair of shoes that made those long legs even longer. Was she actively trying to kill him?

So, yeah, it hadn't escaped him she was beautiful. And it hadn't stopped him from teasing her to get those pink lips to part into a smile as often as possible. He was a sucker for a cheap laugh, and in spite of what she'd been through it'd been fairly easy to get her to laugh. Which swelled the head on his shoulders almost as much as the one in his pants.

She hadn't been laughing a moment ago when he mentioned his "date" though, had she? He'd been shamelessly fishing. Despite his reasons to keep his distance from her, part of him was curious to see if she'd pursue him after all these years. His "date" tonight wasn't a date, anyway. It was an appointment with his sister, Kendra. Ken was having trouble with her car, and he offered to come over and take a look. One of the many services he provided since he'd moved back to town. Not that he minded. He'd do anything for his older sisters.

Their family was tight. His father owned McClain's Handyman Services, a business that had served the town of Evergreen Cove since before his oldest sister Dixie was born. A few years after, they had Kendra, and five years later, Connor was born the baby of the family. Roger McClain had been overjoyed. A boy to take over the business.

When Connor grew up and showed zero interest in fixing anything, save for himself in front of a science project, Roger began applying pressure. The pressure kept coming, driving Connor right out of the house at age eighteen, where he'd met Donny Pate and the two of them had shared an apartment and made some spectacularly bad decisions.

He guessed it was a belated rebellious streak that made him behave like the kid he was. He'd spent most of his childhood being way too grown up for his own good, and then after he enlisted, spent his years longing for the idea of "grown up" the way he used to know it. Serving his country was the highest honor, but war was hell on earth.

A few months ago, he hadn't been sure his friend would keep his inherited house, but Donovan had stayed in the Cove after all. The mansion loomed in the light, her clean windows shiny, gleaming. His buddy belonged in this town, and he belonged with Sofie. Claiming his seat as "heir of Evergreen Cove" was the right fit for him.

Connor dug out a pair of garden shears from his tool belt before dropping it into the plush, green grass. He lowered to one knee and started on the scraggly lavender bush at the side of the house. No matter what he did to save it, the thing was determined to die. Part of him wanted to dig it up, toss it in the fire pit, but another, more stubborn part of him refused to give up on it.

As he clipped, he felt a slight streak of envy he couldn't explain away. Maybe because Donovan, after living a no-madic and detached lifestyle in New York, had found his home in the Cove. Connor grew up here, still had family here, but ever since he had returned, Evergreen Cove felt more foreign than Afghanistan. She hadn't quite wel-comed him back with open arms…Proof was piled in his apartment. He'd been back for nearly two years and the cardboard boxes he'd hauled out of his parents' house and into his own place had yet to be unpacked.

The patio door opened and Donny and Sofie's big white and brown mutt, Gertie, strolled out. Sofie followed close on the dog's heels. Soon the furball was standing way too close, big black nose sniffing his face.

"Hey, Gert." He ruffled the dog's fur. Another soul in the Cove who'd found an unlikely forever home. He hoped the pooch knew how good she had it.

Donovan's fiancée, cell phone in hand, gestured to him. "Mrs. Anderson called and asked when you'd be over to set up for the Harvest Fest."

"On the docket for this week." Like he'd told Mrs. An-derson already. *Twice*. Persistent little old lady, he was learning. And tough. He'd attempted to backtalk her once

and suffered her wrath. She was not a librarian to be tri-
fled with.

"Sorry, she can be kind of a pain." Sofie wrinkled her
nose.

"Kind of?" he asked with a smile.

She chuckled. Sofe was a catch and a half. Bright,
adorable, and would do anything for anyone. She was exactly what Donny needed at a time when no one—not
even Connor—had been able to reach him. She brought
Donovan back to life, and then together, they brought the
mansion back to life. He never would have thought Donovan Pate could have been domesticated, but it was nice to
see his buddy fall into line.

Lucky bastard.

Connor pushed to standing and patted Gertie one last
time. The dog had showed up here skin and bones last
spring and had put on plenty of weight. Her coat was
glossy, her pale blue eyes bright. "Good girl. Yes you are."

Gertie wagged her tail and leaned against his leg, smiling up at him.

"Tell you what," he said to Sofie. "I have a few hours
to kill this afternoon, why don't I stop by there and make
sure Mrs. Anderson knows I'm on top of things." It was
an inconvenience, but not a big one. Like he'd do anything for his sisters, he'd do anything for his friends, too.
And now that included Sofia Martin.

"Really?" She looked relieved with her hand pressed
flat against her collarbone.

"Really." He gathered his tool belt and shears and am-
bled toward the driveway where he'd parked.

Before he made it to his work truck, she called out,
"Faith said you had a date tonight."

Did she, now? He turned and Sofie raised an eyebrow. He wasn't the only one fishing for information this afternoon. Yeah, he wasn't giving the brunette anything.

Before he climbed into his truck, he waved. "See you tomorrow."

"Tease!" she shouted as he reversed out of his parking space.

Yeah, let that get back to Faith. He didn't mind stoking her jealousy. Not at all. Maybe she'd be filled with jealousy over his "date" and openly pursue him. All he needed was an opening, and then he'd charge in like a bull.

In town, he passed Cup of Jo's, Fern's Floral Shoppe, and the now vacant storefront that used to be Sofie's event-planning company. His company, C. Alan Landscaping, had no home base. Not technically. Right now billing was done on his phone and in his head, and there was a box of receipts overflowing on his kitchen table. Probably he should do something about that.

When he'd first started taking the occasional odd job he hadn't needed a fancy accounting system. But with all the referrals he was getting from Make It an Event, business had picked up and he found himself dogged by paperwork. Organization was not his forte.

The only upside to the influx of paperwork was that every referral was an excuse to thank Faith for sending a new client his way. Which he did daily and twice on Sunday. He smiled to himself remembering the way she looked today. Trussed in a tight dress and high-heeled shoes, and decorated with pink glitter. Yeah, being around a creature as gorgeous as Faith Garrett was not a hardship.

He pulled around the back of the library and shut off

the engine. Mrs. Anderson shuffled in his direction wearing orthopedic shoes, her wrinkled mouth pulled taut, determination in her deep-set eyes.

Thoughts of Faith and his libido vanished into the atmosphere.

CHAPTER 2

Thunder rumbled long and low in the distance, briefly causing the lights in Faith's new apartment to flicker. She paused, take-out container in one hand, serving tongs in the other, wondering if she should light some candles. Even if she and her friends had to eat and drink by candle-light, by golly they were having Girls' Night Out in her kitchen.

She opened the lid and plated what was inside: sweet and spicy chicken drummettes from Salty Dog. The local bar had great food, and the chicken wings were among her favorite menu items. Procuring another square serving platter, she plated the evening's crowning glory next.

Three shiny, glistening, glorious Devil Dogs. Tall, rectangular, chocolate cream–filled cakes, dipped in dark chocolate, each topped with whipped cream and a cherry. She would like to say she'd had the wherewithal not to scarf one down before her friends got here, but the truth was she'd ordered four of the cakes from Sugar Hi. The fourth one was gone before she got home. It was *perfection*.

She had no regrets.

A roll of thunder rattled her picture frames, but this time the lights remained steady. She wasn't quite used to the sounds in her new place yet, and oh, how it made her miss her old apartment. Being here was like having to break in new jeans. Uncomfortable. Foreign. And given this place had two hundred less square feet, a little tight.

Her old apartment was at ground level rather than the top of a long flight of stairs, with a big, beautiful oak tree and a picture window looking out over the golf course. After giving up the place to move in with Michael, there hadn't been any hope of getting it back. Whoever had moved in was smart enough to stay rather than give up the prime real estate.

Which left her renting in Shady Pines. She was able to score a second floor with a balcony, and she'd admit it was nice not to have anyone stomping around above her this time around. The new building wasn't as fancy as Oak Grove, but it was private. Freestanding, the six-unit building had small homes on either side, but not too close, with a patch of pines on one side and a parking lot with a basketball court on the other.

She was lucky to find it, really. Given the touristy draw of this town, most places were rented out to vacationers looking for some lakeside R&R. When one didn't own a house, one was left to rent whatever was available.

Shady Pines was available.

Her immediate neighbors living in the building were

elderly and friendly, aside from the guy downstairs who worked nights and rarely spoke to anyone. Faith didn't mind having older folks nearby. It wasn't like her friends were going to get "wild" or anything.

She arranged a number of bottles on the counter, frowning at the selection. She couldn't get the one wine she wanted most. Layer Cake Primitivo was hard to find, and her favorite wine to drink in the fall. Packed with flavors like cherry, espresso, and white pepper, the red was great by itself, but with chocolate, it was *to die for.* In her former profession as the wine and beer girl for Abundance Market, she had special-ordered and kept in stock anything she liked. Primitivo was always stocked if the shelves had space for it. And if not, she kept a stash for herself in the back of her cabinet.

Recently, she'd run out.

She let herself run out, vowing to face her demons, specifically Michael and Cookie, who now also worked at Abundance. But in the end, Faith had chickened out (again), popping a Uey in the parking lot and driving to the small, under-stocked wine shop on Belinda Avenue. It was quaint, and she loved the staff, but alas, no Primitivo. The woman behind the counter politely offered to order it for her, but Faith had turned her down.

She'd compromised so much—she'd *lost* so much— the wine had become a sticking point. The next bottle of Layer Cake would be purchased from Abundance Market, so help her God. She couldn't avoid the market forever. She could go. She had to go. And soon, when she found her courage, she *would* go.

You realize how ridiculous you're being, don't you?

Yes. She was being ridiculous. Unsurprisingly, that last

thought reverberated through her head in her mother's voice. Linda Shelby had always been critical of her eldest daughter, and learning Faith's fiancé was no longer her fiancé had only stoked that flickering flame.

To be fair, that voice—her mother's or not—was not wrong. Abundance Market wasn't exactly Mordor. There were no gates, no mouth of Sauron, no leagues of orcs to battle her way through. All she had to do was park in the lot, walk through the automatic doors, and straight back to aisle fifteen.

But when she pictured Michael at the service counter, or Cookie uncorking bottles for samples as the new wine girl, Faith's insides seized. The potential of running into the woman who soiled Faith's future—and her favorite rug from IKEA—was too great a risk.

C'est la vie.

With a wave of her hand, she swept the worries aside. She arranged three wineglasses near the bottles just as chattering outside drew her attention to her front door. Charlie and Sofie had arrived.

Faith brushed her hands over her slim capris and simple blue T-shirt, ran a hand down her long ponytail, and pulled open the door.

Her friends squealed when they saw her as if they hadn't all just seen one another earlier this week for lunch. She had no idea how she would've gotten through the Michael/Cookie disaster without them.

Charlie hustled in and wrapped her arms around Faith's neck. "You look beautiful."

"Oh, thank you. So do you." Charlie wore an orange dress—Charlie could almost always be found in a dress—with a floral pattern on it. Faith's newly married friend could also almost always be found in flowers. Her hair, honeyed blond rather than Faith's near-platinum, had recently been cut. The shoulder-length style suited her round face and huge, hazel eyes.

"She always looks beautiful." Sofie entered behind her with a grocery sack in hand. She winked as Faith relieved her of the handled bag. Sofie—Ms. "I Don't Do Weddings" Martin—since she'd met and become engaged to one Donovan Pate, now *did* do weddings. Charlie's nuptials had been her first climb back into the saddle, and soon, though she hadn't announced a date, Sofie would marry her mansion-owner.

It was times like these when loneliness threatened to overshadow Faith's happiness. And, at times like these, she reminded herself that she was independent now and would do just fine on her own, thank you very much.

Sofie unloaded the crab dip and pita chips she brought while Charlie searched the cabinets for another plate. Faith reached the serving platter on the top shelf and handed it over. She was taller than both of her friends, Sofie being the curvier of the two with a sizable backside her fiancé, Donny, couldn't get enough of. Every chance he got, the man wrapped his hand around Sofie's rear end and gave it a squeeze.

"I have wine. I have food. I have Devil Dogs." Faith gestured to the breakfast bar in invitation.

"Be still my heart," Charlie commented, eyes widening at the sight of the cakes. She used to claim not to be much of a "sweets person," which was impossible to understand, but after her first Devil Dog, she reassessed her position on sugar.

"I don't know why you say you don't like this as much

as your old apartment," Sofie said, taking a tour of the tiny living room. "This place is cute. Quaint."

"That's just a nice way of saying small." Yes, her new place was smaller than her old apartment on Bent Tree Avenue, but she *did* like it. Sofie was right. It was quaint, and quaint was fine. It would take some getting used to. She'd only been moved in for a week.

"How much space do you need, really?" Charlie asked rhetorically as she walked into the living room and dropped her purse on the sofa.

Charlie meant that supportively. At one point, right after finding Michael in the snares of Cookie Monster, Faith may have been sensitive to the fact that Charlie's statement could imply Faith *didn't need* that much space since she was now alone. She didn't feel that way now. Sensitive, reading into every little thing. She knew her friends had her best interests in mind. Losing her ex was a blessing. One she wouldn't have wished for at the time, but things had turned out exactly as they should have.

Healing was a beautiful thing.

The trio settled down to eat, filling their wineglasses, chewing on chicken wings, and eating the crab dip Sofie brought. Faith moaned in ecstasy as she took another scoop and chewed. "Oh man. I forgot how much I liked this stuff."

"Second best thing Abundance carries besides their potato salad," Charlie agreed, scooping some dip onto a toasted pita.

Faith couldn't be happier as she watched Sofie chew merrily away. The last couple of years, Sofie had lamented the few extra pounds she'd gained. She was not fat, not by any stretch of the imagination, but since she'd been single, her body was a constant source of stress. Then Donny Pate, the man Sofie swore she hated, came back to town, invaded her space, and those issues had gradually dissipated.

Evidently, copious amounts of sex with a man who thought Sofie walked on water could cure many body hang-ups. Faith couldn't say she knew from experience. While she and Michael had sex when they were together, "copious" never described their love life. More like a light drizzle than a monsoon. Scheduled. And he had his own prejudice for the way a woman's body should look. Faith hadn't met his "requirements." She felt her face pinch in disgust.

"Abundance has the best anything-salad," Sofie said, dipping another chip. "Have you had their Waldorf? To die for."

Faith slapped a smile on her face when she realized she'd been grousing over Michael, of all things.

Her best friend, who had probably been reading her mind this entire evening, asked, "Still can't go in there?" Sofie's brows bowed into a sympathetic bend. "You know I can pick you up something whenever I go. We *do* work together. It's not like it would be hard to get it to you."

"I don't think about it, actually." Minor lie. A lie of necessity. An affirmation, really.

Her friends smiled, tight-lipped, letting her have the lie. This was why they were her friends. They knew when to intervene and shake sense into her, but they also knew when she needed her space.

"I have three horror movies." Faith held up the sleeves containing movies she'd rented at a kiosk outside the wine shop. Since the Cove's local video rental closed, there wasn't anywhere else to rent good movies unless she bought them. And horror movies were seasonal—not something she wanted in her permanent collection.

"It is almost Halloween, and—" Out of nowhere, thunder shook the house, making them all gasp, then laugh. On the end of her laugh, Faith finished, "*And* it is our duty to watch some scary, twisted stuff."

"So the Devil Dogs are kind of in theme." Charlie winked.

Snatching a bottle by the neck, Faith spun the wine and showed off the label. "So is the wine."

"Blood Bath?" Sofie wrinkled her cute nose. "I assume that's a red."

"With notes of mania." Charlie nodded.

Sofie grinned. "Finishes in the trunk of a car."

Faith laughed. "Come on, let's see how many we can watch."

* * *

An hour later, the three of them were crammed onto Faith's sofa, each covered in their own afghan. Faith sat with her knees to her chest, arms wrapped around them. The Devil Dogs had been obliterated, and so had the Blood Bath.

Sofie was at the far end of the sofa, lounging on one arm, a half smile on her face. Charlie was in the middle, properly alarmed at the madman stalking a group of teens at a lake, but her scared shrieks often dissolved into hearty laughter.

Faith did not feel like laughing. She had underestimated her ability to handle this kind of a movie while living alone.

Yes, it was campy. Yes, it was ridiculous. Yes, the blood was fake. But something about having a huge, un-killable man near a lake was freaking her right out.

Not that she'd admit it. She wondered if she should open another bottle of wine, but worried if she drank more, she would end up awake in the middle of the night, heart pounding like a kettledrum, panicking over every subtle noise…

That would not be good.

If she still lived at Linda Shelby's house she could dig a Valium out of her mother's medicine cabinet to help her sleep. As it stood, she'd just have to go it alone.

The credits rolled and Charlie stretched. "One of my favorites."

"Really?" Sofie asked. "I prefer the *Scream* movies. Good, old-fashioned, terrifying fun."

"What's next?" Charlie asked.

Next? Faith gulped in fear. She'd been very, very brave when she'd picked movies at the kiosk. What with the sun shining and no danger of anything lurking around corners. Now that it was nighttime, she'd gone yellow.

"Yeah, I'm ready for more wine and more horror," Sofie said, rubbing her hands together. "Faith?"

"Oh. Yeah. Bring it on." She wiped her clammy hands on her blanket.

Sofie narrowed one eye. "You sure?"

Faith pulled back her shoulders and grinned. She was done being a fraidy cat about every freaking thing in her life. Tonight, she'd finally watch a *Saw* movie, and tomorrow, she'd finally set foot into Abundance Market. And, hell, may as well have more wine.

"Heck yes! We can't leave the bottle of Demon Seed

unopened." Pushing herself off the couch, she went to the kitchen and grabbed the corkscrew. Outside, the rain pounded and thunder rumbled in the far, far distance. The storm had blown through and the night was once again quiet.

Charlie and Sofie started talking about shoes and Faith felt herself smile.

She was with friends, in the safety of her sweet little apartment. There was nothing to fear. No madmen. No men at all, actually.

Just the way she liked it.

* * *

The sky growled in protest and Connor jolted awake. Disoriented for a few seconds, he blinked at his surroundings.

White walls. Wood floors. Bare windows.

His apartment.

He reached for the handle on the side of the recliner and dropped the footrest to sit up. He had a bed but rarely slept in it. More often than not, he left the TV on to keep him company, then fell asleep to whatever show he watched last.

Tonight, he had attempted to do the same until the electricity went out. He saw now that the digital clock on the stove blinked the wrong time. 12:02. Must've just clicked back on.

Swiping a hand down his face, he abandoned the recliner and went to the refrigerator. He stood in the open light, tipped an orange juice container, and drained the end of it down his throat.

Unwanted images seeped through the cracks of his mind.

He lifted the carton, blinking sleepy eyes. *Tropicana. 100% pure.* Focusing on the words, he read the side panel. Anything to keep from thinking about Afghanistan.

It was no use. Whenever he woke in the middle of the night, his brain kicked up his worst memories like dust and threw them in his face. They weren't exactly nightmares; he never woke up in a sweat or a panic like some of the guys in his unit had, but when he woke in the dark, in the quiet, it was with a picture in his head.

The picture was always the same.

A mother's face frozen in a look of terror as she clutched the toddler against her leg, one arm wrapped around his dirt-streaked face and the other over his back as she cradled him against her skirt.

He squeezed his eyes closed and in the process crushed the cardboard container in his hand.

Five, four, three . . .

When he got to one, he let out the rest of his breath in a long, even exhalation. Another clatter of thunder shook the windowpanes. Flashes of light bounced off the stacked cardboard boxes in the corner of his living room.

For some reason, the boxes made him think of his buddy. How Donovan had faced his fears, stopped running. He'd come back to the Cove permanently. Let a woman into his house, his life. Meanwhile, Connor was awake, facing down the skeletons of his former life, the packed boxes their bones.

He walked over to one pile—stacked three high—and rested his hand on the top. He could tear open the tape, find out what's inside. Even as the thought occurred, a sardonic smile curved one side of his lips. He'd been telling himself he would unpack since he came home two years ago. He'd yet to listen to that internal voice.

What was inside was the life of a man who'd left the Cove angry with Maya, fed up with his father for trying to strong-arm him into the family business. What had come back was a man who had survived a spray of machine gun fire at the expense of a mother and her child. In a weird way, that moment mirrored Maya and her pregnancy. He hadn't been able to save her and the baby from an asshole, either.

Tossing the orange juice container into the trash, he stretched his arms, pulling his palms over his chest, then opened the refrigerator again, this time pulling out a plate of leftover roast chicken, mashed potatoes, and vegetables Sofie had sent home with him. He put the plate in the microwave, hit a button, and stared blankly at the stile turning his dinner.

He'd eaten a lot of meals with Donovan and Sofie over the last year. He'd crashed at the mansion more often than not. In fact, he'd probably stayed there more than he'd stayed in his own apartment over the last six months.

Recently, even in a thirteen-thousand-square-foot house, Connor had begun feeling like he was in the way. Not that Donny or Sofie would ever make him feel unwelcome, but it was clear they had made the mansion their home and were starting their life together there. It made him take a hard look at his own life and realize he hadn't moved on much. He cast a glance over at the shoebox full of receipts on his kitchen table. Hell, maybe he hadn't moved on at all. He'd sort of ... frozen in time.

They were moving forward—both of them. And in

a weird way, Connor felt like he was hampering their progress. The last thing he wanted to do was freeze his friends in place with him.

As he ate, he wondered what the hell time it actually was, whether he should lift weights before going back to sleep. Or hell, maybe he'd try sleeping in bed. That would be one step toward making this place feel more like home. The very first step.

But as he scraped the last bite into his mouth, he knew he was lying to himself.

He wasn't going to sleep at all.

$\mathscr{C}$ HAPTER 3

Well, that was embarrassing.

"Thank you, Officer."

Incredibly attractive, blond, full-lipped Officer Brady Hutchins gave Faith a smile. "Ain't no thang, Ms. Garrett."

He capped his comment with a wink and turned for the door. Brady and Faith had known each other since grade school, and though they hadn't kept in close contact, Evergreen Cove was a small enough town, and Brady a good enough looking cop, that he was hard to miss. A few years back, before Donny had come back to town, Brady had gone on a date with Sofie, but Sofie said there wasn't a spark. Faith got that. She was beginning to wonder if she had any spark left in her. Especially since, faced with this man right now, she felt nothing.

An appreciation for long, dark blond eyelashes, gorgeous green eyes, and a nice, firm build, sure. But on a personal, *oh-baby* level?

Zip.

Good Lord. Maybe she was broken.

No, you're not. Because: Connor.

True. Connor made her eyes bulge out of her head and her tongue stick to her palate like she'd glued it there. Made her voice go quiet, her skin tighten. There weren't so much sparks between them as there was an explosion—like a rogue firework igniting a tanker truck.

She purposefully shook her head to dislodge the thought. Didn't matter if she wasn't *feelin' it* for Brady. He hadn't come to her house at four a.m. to flirt with her anyway. He'd come because she'd called 911. And she'd called 911 because she heard noises.

She opened the door to see him out, but he faced her in the threshold, his smile gone, concern evident. "You sure you don't want me to stick around until sunlight?"

"That's really sweet, but I think I've embarrassed myself enough for one night." She gave him a tight smile.

He ducked his head and met her eyes with those gorgeous eyes of his. Faith was tall, but Brady was taller. Especially since she was standing here in a robe and slipper socks.

"Long as you're sure," he said. "I don't want to scare you, but I feel like you should know that the window locks aren't as solid as I'd like. And a deadbolt on a door can be busted."

She tore her eyes away from his uniform—dark blue with a badge, insuring safety for every resident of the

Cove—and studied her windows. Windows that suddenly didn't look as safe as before. Her breath went shallow. The idea of someone busting in here was... terrifying.

"But..." he started, and she met his gaze. "If I had found evidence of anyone tampering anywhere, there's no way I'd leave you here by yourself. Fact is, you're on a second floor, surrounded by neighbors. A burglar probably wouldn't bother. Unless you have enemies. Piss anyone off recently?"

Faith laughed and Brady grinned. He knew her. She was too nice to have enemies.

He palmed her shoulder in a friendly way. "Unless you have a stash of valuables in here, or a ton of cash, it'd be a lot of trouble for a random burglar. The patio doesn't make for an easy getaway. Maybe whoever tried gave up and went on to an easier take."

"Maybe." Arms wrapped around her torso, she hugged herself, remembering the stone-cold fear that had radiated through each and every one of her limbs when she woke to the sound of scratching outside her balcony door. In that moment, she felt very small and fragile, her only weapons a knife from the kitchen and the cell phone in her shaking hand.

Afraid she was overreacting, she sat for a good five minutes and listened. The rain made one sound, the thunder made another, but the scratching on the balcony door? That sound could only be one thing.

An intruder.

Then Brady got here and started poking around outside. He found nothing. Now Faith was left believing it was an animal outside her window, and she had overreacted thanks to back-to-back-*to-back* movies she had no business watching if she was going to continue to sleep by herself.

And she was.

"Really, I'll be fine. I'm sure it was a case of my overactive imagination combined with way too much red wine."

His startlingly attractive grin returned, this time with a sexy pair of smile lines bracketing his generous mouth. His palm on her shoulder squeezed.

Nothing. Not a single tingle anywhere.

What was wrong with her?

Doesn't matter. You're going to be single forever.

Oh. Right.

"I'm a call away," he said as he stepped out of her apartment. "I'll be patrolling the area for the next hour or so. I'm sure whoever it was won't try anything else with me nosing around." He smiled reassuringly and she had to admit, she did feel safer knowing he wasn't leaving right away.

"Thanks."

She didn't go back to sleep after Brady left, choosing to stay up, drink a cup of coffee, and watch TV...as long as what she watched had *nothing* to do with anything scary. She settled on an infomercial channel and watched the screen with little to no interest. The announcer was jabbering about super-absorbent towels and was not a madman bent on murdering innocent people, so the program met her requirements.

By eight a.m., she was on her way to work, her bag thrown over her shoulder, keys in hand. She had forgone the sunglasses this morning. There was no need given the fact the sky was heavy and gray, the same color it was when the sun had come up, but not out.

Inside the mansion, the front door opened to a huge foyer and a curved staircase leading to the second floor. When Donny had first inherited the mansion, he'd planned on cleaning the place out and selling it to a buyer who would turn it into a bed-and-breakfast. Then he met Sofie, and any plans he had to stay away from Evergreen Cove fell by the wayside. Sofe had changed him for the better. Faith had watched it happen. It was encouraging, hopeful. Beautiful.

Proof that true love did exist.

"Just not for me," she grumbled to herself as she dropped her keys into her purse.

"What's that?"

Donny strolled into the foyer dressed in worn jeans and a plaid button-down shirt cuffed at the elbows. His long, ink-black hair brushed his cheekbones on the sides, and his collar at the back of his neck. Tattoos decorated both forearms and one hand. He was attractive when they all worked together at the restaurant years ago—in a dangerous, intriguing way. Now, he was attractive in a sexy, grown-up way. A way that showed his dark edges were still there, only less ragged since he'd met Sofie.

Her eyes ran the length of the tattooed tree on his arm. "Hey, new ink."

He twisted his forearm, examining the trail of blowing leaves. "Yeah. Evan added them."

"Nice." Sofie had told her the meaning behind the many tattoos decorating his arms, shoulders, and torso. The sad fact was they didn't mean anything. Donny had endured injuries at the hands of his abusive father when he was a child. His many tattoos covered the scars. Faith wondered if the orange and red leaves were significant of anything, but didn't want to pry.

Tipping his chin, he asked another version of his initial question. "What'd you say when you walked in?"

She threw a hand. "Pfft. Just talking to myself. I had... sort of a ridiculous night."

"I thought we had a great night." Sofie stepped out of the office on the right, grasped the doorway, and rested the toe of her knee-high suede boot on the floor, knee bent. Her shoe collection was enviable.

Covering, Faith exclaimed, "Are you kidding? I had an awesome night!"

Donny turned to his wife-to-be, satisfied. Sofie didn't let her off the hook quite that easy. "What was ridiculous? Did something happen?"

At his fiancée's urgent tone, Donny snapped his head around. *Great.* Faith had been hoping to keep this quiet. Brady wasn't a gossip, and he was the only officer who showed up at her house. Then again, Donny and Sofie were her friends. People she trusted.

She pushed her hair behind her ear. "It's really kind of embarrassing. About three o'clock in the morning, I woke up because I thought I heard something at the balcony door."

"Something like what?" Brow furrowed, Donny took a step closer to her.

Faith may be tall, but Donovan Pate was *tall*. He hovered around six-four, a lean, formidable, towering man. And right now, he looked like he'd added suspicious and protective to that list of adjectives.

"Sounded like scratching." Shrugging, she played down her fear. "Probably a raccoon. Or possum." She chewed on her lip in thought. "Or is it opossum, with an *O*? I never know which one's right."

"That last movie we watched would give anyone nightmares," Sofie chimed in, ignoring Faith's vermin conundrum.

He briefly snapped his attention to Sofie. "Yeah, we talked about that. Never, ever watch a movie like that unless I'm here to come home to."

"You were here." Sofie smiled gently.

Faith watched as the pair exchanged looks she thought might be secret sex looks. What would she know? She had been in a sex wasteland for approximately fourteen months. The wilderness.

She hated the wilderness.

Before she could excuse herself to the office, Donovan stopped her with a request. "Describe the scratching."

"Well…" Her eyebrows went up. "You know. Scratching. Like"—nerves jumped as she remembered—"okay, when I first woke up, I thought maybe it sounded like someone was trying to break in. But when Brady got there, he didn't find evidence of tampering."

"You called the cops?" Her best friend's surprise was evident in her tone.

"Good girl." Donny dipped his head in encouragement. He turned to Sofie. "You better do the same if you ever think you hear anything anywhere in this house. If I'm not here, and you hear tampering or what sounds like tampering or what you *think* might sound like tampering, you call the police."

"Baby, I hardly think—"

"End of discussion."

Wow. He was absolutely wonderful, gentle, and perfect with Sofie. This side of him—this protective, warrior side of him—wasn't exactly new, but it was intense. Faith had never seen him quite this intense.

"I'll come check out your place tonight." He nodded as if the decision had been made. "I want to make sure you're safe."

Faith weaved her fingers together, clasping her hands and remembering what Brady said. Mostly remembering that he'd pointed out her windows weren't secure and her door was completely penetrable. Still, she didn't want to put out her friends, especially when Brady had told her he'd found nothing. He'd done a thorough search. She trusted his judgment.

"That's really sweet," she said, "but I'm going to have to get used to the things that go bump in the night if I hope to get used to living by myself."

"What's going bump in the night?" Connor came from the direction of the kitchen, a sandwich in hand. He took a bite and chewed and waited for an answer.

Great. The gang's all here.

Donovan jerked his head in her direction. "Faith heard someone tampering with the balcony door."

"That's not…" She held out a hand like a stop sign as she turned to Connor. No sense in calling in the troops…literally, in his case. Everything was handled. "I *thought* someone was tampering with the balcony door. According to the police—"

He swallowed the bite he was chewing, his eyebrows slamming down over narrowed eyes. "Police?"

"I overreacted. That's it." She held up both hands in

exasperation. "Ask Sofie. We watched some crazy scary movies, and then I went to bed. I haven't slept in a house alone for a very long time. I'm sure—"

"Does she have a security system?" Connor directed this question to Donny.

Arms folded over his flannel, he shook his head and frowned. "Not unless she got one since I helped move her in."

"I'm standing right here," Faith said.

Connor turned his attention to her. "Do you?"

Her turn to frown. "No."

"Let Donny take a look," Sofie encouraged from the other side of the room. "It wouldn't hurt to have a second set of eyes on your place."

"I'll do it." Every head in the room swiveled to Connor. He polished off his sandwich in one big bite, chewed, swallowed, and said, "I have tools to reinforce your locks. I also know how to break a lock."

"You do?" Faith and Sofie said in tandem.

Connor didn't answer.

"That's a good idea," Donny encouraged.

Faith looked from one man to the other. "No, it's not a good idea. You are both overreacting as much as I did last night. Brady said..."

"Who the hell is Brady?" Connor's brow furrowed.

"The police officer," Faith answered.

"I would rather overreact than under-react," he said. "No matter what *Brady* said. I may see something he missed."

Faith gestured to the big-shouldered landscaper, who had clearly gone insane, but Sofie didn't back her up. Not even a little. She stepped closer to Donny in a show of unity, her brow wrinkled with concern. "I think he's right. What if it's the old owner who knows the quirks of the place? He or she would know how to get in if they had to."

"The old owner is dead," she blurted, then paled as a dart of fear shot down her sternum. That did not make her feel better. A haunting was scarier than a corporeal body trying to get in.

"It's settled, then." Donny dipped his chin to Connor.

"Hello?" Faith waved both hands in front of her, feeling invisible. "I said I don't—"

But the topic was already dead. Donovan leaned down to kiss Sofie good-bye. "I'll be at the Braxtons' place until dinner. Love you."

Faith was aware of the "third wheel" tension stretching across the room as Sofie tipped her chin, said, "Love you, too," and then kissed Donovan for a long, long, *long* time.

When the kiss went on longer, Connor cleared his throat.

Correction: fourth wheel…

Donovan raised his head inches from Sofie's mouth. Then a completely wicked smile overtook his face, and he grasped her butt with both hands and stuck his tongue down her throat.

"And that's my cue." Faith looked away from the couple fused at the lips and met Connor's gaze. His eyes snapped to the floor as a small smile curled his tempting mouth.

"Yeah." He palmed his neck and turned for the dining room while she ducked into the sanctuary of the office.

At her desk, she thought of that gaze more than once.

There was a dose of heat beneath the protectiveness. And damn if it didn't occupy her thoughts for most of the afternoon.

* * *

By six that evening, the sun was low in the sky. Connor had put in a full day preparing for Harvest Fest at Library Park. He returned to the mansion, satisfied when he found Faith there. Good. She'd listened to him. He wondered after she had argued earlier.

He shut his truck door, strode to the porch, and let himself in, encountering the leggy blonde in the foyer. She pulled her purse onto her shoulder, keys in her palm.

"Where do you think you're going?"

Her slim, fair eyebrows slammed down. Okay. Maybe she *hadn't* listened to him. She seemed prepared to leave without him tonight. Not gonna happen.

"Where am I going?" she repeated. "I am going to get in my car and drive to my apartment and open a bottle of wine and watch something on my television." As if he didn't get by her intentionally slow inflection she was angry, she capped that statement by marching to the front door.

He opened it for her. "Right behind you."

She spun to face him, fanning her subtle floral perfume into his face. It mirrored her: soft, delicate. A scent he couldn't quite pick out. And he knew flowers. Maybe it was the way it mixed with her skin that muddled his mind, but damn. Angry or not, he wanted to haul her close and have a closer inspection. "Connor, I appreciate this. I do. I would just rather forget about it."

Can do. He shrugged. "Forgotten."

"Thank you." Her shoulders sagged with what he guessed was relief.

"Still following you home, though."

Those shoulders went rigid and she growled low in her throat. Then she walked out the door and clopped down the cobblestone drive.

Grinning, he shut off the light in the foyer and followed the trail of flowers and sass out the front door.

$\mathscr{C}$HAPTER 4

$\mathscr{F}$aith watched in her rearview mirror as Connor followed her home. So much for blowing him off tonight. She parked on the curb as she normally did, hooked her purse on her shoulder as she normally did, and walked up the stairs like she normally d—

"Whoa."

A firm hand wrapped around her upper arm and tugged her back. She was now close enough to Connor to feel his body heat at her back. In the cool autumn air, his heat felt nice. Not to mention he smelled incredible. Some earthy, natural, spicy smell that was at once clean and manly.

Tone low and serious, he said, "I'm going first." Before she could argue, he stepped in front of her and took the stairs. And then she forgot to argue at all.

Connor McClain's ass had not missed her radar.

In her world, where men were amoeba at worst

(Michael) or where she noted passing attraction with zero sparks (Brady), noticing this man was unnerving. And so far she'd noticed nearly every detail about him. Yes, her permanently single, spark-less radar had still picked up on the incredible backside now hovering a step or two above her.

His jeans were snug, not too tight—just tight around butt and thigh area. And, oh yeah, she had seen this pair before. They were distressed, faded along the seams and the bottom of the pockets, and contoured his body perfectly.

Unfair really, she thought as she followed him up the stairs. Why did he have to be this painfully good-looking when she'd banished herself to a land of Singledom?

He reached her front door and bent, studying the lock on the knob and the deadbolt. She crossed her arms, losing patience. For one, she had to pee. For another, she didn't want him here anyway.

"Can I go in now?"

He didn't answer, simply walked past her to inspect the balcony. The balcony wasn't connected to the landing, so there was a space. A considerable amount of space. There was also a concrete ledge. A ledge he climbed onto and balanced on while resting one palm on the side of the building.

"Oh my God! Get down before you kill yourself!" Seriously, it was two stories. He might not die but he could break his leg.

He ignored her. No surprise there. Giving the gutter a solid tug, he rested his hand on it as he leaned forward. Then he gauged the distance between the ledge and balcony, crouched, and in one smooth jump, breached the gap. Like a cat—or a super-buff Spider-Man—he landed on his feet and pushed himself to standing.

She let out the breath she didn't know she'd been holding. "You know, I could've let you in and we could've walked through the house together."

Silent, he inspected the lock on the balcony door with the light on his phone.

Talking to herself now, since she was the only one who would respond anyway, she got her keys out and shoved them in the lock. "Fine. I will just let myself in."

Inside, she flipped on the light in the kitchen, illuminating her small space. By the time she set her purse on the kitchen table, she heard the balcony door slide open.

Connor wore a scowl as he prowled over to where she stood. "I'm in your apartment."

Startled, her eyes went from him to the ajar balcony door. "I see that."

"Whoever was here last night didn't succeed in getting in, but I did." His scowl remained. "I don't like that."

Well. She didn't like that, either.

"I'm staying."

"You're . . . staying?" She blinked. "Here?"

"You have a couch."

"I . . ."

"Faith. I'm in your apartment."

Yes. He was.

"If I can get into your apartment, so can someone else." He looked more concerned than smug.

And now that he'd proven what Officer Brady Hutchins had already eluded to—that gaining entry to her apartment was not at all difficult—she found herself in agreement with Connor's plan to stay.

She nodded. "Yeah. Okay."

After she used the restroom and changed into a pair of yoga pants and a baggy T-shirt, she walked into the kitchen to pull a bottle of wine from the cabinet. Connor was perched on the sofa, digging through a black bag he had retrieved from his truck.

"Do you always travel with an overnight bag?" she asked.

"Yeah."

She waited for him to expound. He didn't. "Would you like some wine?"

Without looking over his shoulder, he said, "No."

Of course not. He was a beer-from-the-bottle-kind-of-guy if she'd ever seen one.

"Well, you should have some. It's delicious."

He stood and she heard a clicking sound, and she nearly dropped the bottle in her hand when she saw the gun in his. She set the bottle onto the countertop with a little too much force, alarm evident in her voice. "What's that for?"

"Protection."

"You can't be serious."

Gun safely tucked into the back of his waistband, he crossed to the kitchen and stood close enough to her to muddle her senses. He really did smell good.

"Cupcake, I'm not going to stay here with you unarmed. Not without a security system in place and not when anyone could walk through your balcony door."

A shudder rattled her spine and she forcibly tried to hide it. She didn't like the idea of anyone walking through her balcony door.

He pushed the sleeves of a pale gray henley over his

elbows and took the wine bottle from her hand. Then he lifted the opener from the counter and had the bottle open in a matter of seconds. He tossed the wrapper from the neck of the bottle into the trash and stood the cork on its end next to the bottle. Wordlessly, he walked back into the living room and sat down on her couch.

She blinked at his broad back. "I thought you didn't drink wine."

He didn't even turn his head. "I'm not drinking it tonight."

Alrighty, then.

She poured herself a glass, and after debating whether she would behave differently with him in her space, decided not to. He was the one who wanted to stay here. He was going to have to make his way around her.

At the counter, she paused. He looked good in her living room, big arms laid across the back of her couch, leg crossed, ankle to knee, and that masculine way she'd always admired. More important, she *did* feel safer with him here. There was an ease, a confidence, about him that set her at ease, too.

Pulling her shoulders back, she tried to act casual as she strode into the living room and plopped down onto the opposite end of the couch. "So. What do you usually do in the evening?" She took a sip of her wine.

When he didn't answer right away she turned her head to the left. Elbow propped on the couch's arm, he rubbed his bottom lip with the side of his index finger. "Not much."

Even in the long-sleeved shirt, she could make out the bulge of his biceps and rounded, muscular shoulders. No wonder she felt safe with him. He could snap an intruder in half with one hand.

"What do you usually do in the evening?" He was still staring at her, his mouth kicked up into a small smile on one side. He was also still rubbing his lip with his finger, which was beyond distracting.

"I…um." She jerked her eyes away from his mouth and looked down at her glass. "I usually drink a glass of wine, watch some television, and then take a bath." When he was silent for too long, she looked up at him again.

"I am down with that plan." His small smile widened into a grin.

She allowed herself a smile. "You are not following me into the bathroom. You can protect me from out here."

He leaned farther into the corner of her couch, looking totally at ease. "I'm not sure about that." His grin persisted and she felt her head shake.

This was the way it normally was with him. Not the closed-lipped military badass silently inspecting every inch of her living quarters, but the easygoing, super-flirtatious, drop-dead gorgeous man teasing her right now.

Amazing she'd been able to resist him at all. But then that hadn't really been on either of their agendas, had it?

She cleared her throat. "How was your date last night?" Eyes on her wine, she tried to sound mildly interested, not pathetically nosy. She wasn't sure she pulled it off.

"Fine."

Fine.

Twisting her lips, she flicked her eyes over to him. "What did you do?"

"Fixed her car."

"Oh." Well, that didn't sound very romantic.

"Why do you ask?"

"Just making polite conversation." Nervous now, her gaze bounced around the room.

"Wasn't a date," he said next, and she snapped her head around to meet his eyes. Mischief danced in his expression, his tempting mouth lifting into another sexy, distracting curve. "Just told you that to bother you. I was at my sister's house."

Flustered, she shook her head. "I'm not bothered by who you date."

But his smile suggested he knew she was fibbing.

Wine in hand, she leaned forward and grabbed the remote from the coffee table. Maybe what she needed to do was stop talking. "You have to watch what I watch, and no complaining."

"Wouldn't dream of it, Cupcake." He produced a water bottle from that black bag of his and leaned back against the couch, re-crossing his leg. "Flattered you asked about my date," he mumbled after he took a drink.

She pretended not to hear him and flipped through the channels.

* * *

Faith didn't make it to the bathtub. After the sleepless night he guessed she'd had the night before, it didn't surprise him when her eyes grew heavy and she rested her head against his shoulder.

It did surprise him she'd poked at him about his "date." She was interested, which automatically made this venture with her more interesting.

Sometime in the middle of whatever reality show marathon they were watching—some sort of desperate housewife type of thing—he had gone to her tiny, open kitchen to make a snack. He settled on microwave popcorn, bringing the bowl back to the couch to share. He sat on the center cushion. Faith had scooted closer. Which meant when she nodded off, the side of her head conked onto his shoulder.

He didn't have the heart to move her. He did, however, have the sense to sneak the remote out from between their legs and turn the freaking channel. *Good God*, he thought as the channel winked away from the puffy-lipped, smooth-faced woman currently swearing her hair extensions off. He'd never seen so much plastic surgery in his life. How did Faith watch this crap?

After settling on the Travel Channel, on a survival show—a show, unlike her choice, that could prove *useful* in life—he settled back into the couch. The woman leaning on his shoulder migrated south, reaching for the afghan on the back of the couch and covering herself as she settled a cheek onto his lap.

Faith Garrett in his lap. He had imagined this a time or three. But never like this: because she was too tired to go to bed and he was watching over her. More because she'd whispered something treacherously dirty into his ear and then pulled his pants open with her teeth.

He pulled a hand down his face and blinked at the television. Yeah, he really needed not to think about that right now. Not that he minded being here—he wanted to protect her. But he would prefer she didn't need protecting from anything. He didn't want her in danger, period.

Outside her front door and balcony earlier this evening, he had noticed scratches around the locks. Scratches either Officer Brady Hutchins had missed, or new scratches that had occurred today while Faith was at work. Curious to see how hard it would be to get into her apartment, he produced a small pick from his pocket and found himself standing in her living room within seconds. Not good. Not good at all.

Sometime around two a.m., a motion sensor light went off in the parking lot, snapping him out of the television's drone. His spine straightened, his senses sharpened, his breathing went shallow. Faith slept deeply. Keeping as quiet as possible, he sat stone still and listened.

After a few seconds the light clicked off, and he grabbed a pillow from the couch, gently lifting her head and extracting his thigh in the process. Her hair felt like silk against his fingertips, her lashes fluttering ever so slightly as she slept. A surge of protectiveness swelled in him stronger than before.

She snuggled deeper into the sofa. He liked the idea of her warm and safe. And the idea he'd given her both those bare necessities. He watched another few seconds in case she woke. She didn't.

Good. She needed her rest. Faith may be trying to play the tough girl, but he could see she'd been scared. She'd agreed pretty quickly to let him stay. Not that he would've taken no for an answer.

He crept to the balcony door, slid it open, and slipped outside. The light out here had no bulb. Which was not safe. Shaking his head, he vowed to replace it tomorrow, then kept close to the wall before tentatively poking his head over the balcony.

Tingling at the back of his neck—a premonition similar to when he was at war—alerted his senses and drew his attention to the grass. He allowed his eyes to focus on the dark, get acquainted with the sights and sounds of the night. Crickets chirping. Trees blowing, their deadened leaves rustling softly.

A shadow stretched across the grass—visible even in the dark. Connor's spine snapped straight. His own shallow breaths filled his ears. Muscles flexed, he pressed to the side of the building to be sure he wasn't seen. The shadow belonged to a man, he guessed. That shadow shortened as dark clothing came into view, and a jacket with a hood looked in his direction.

Then that dark shadow was running. Not bothering to stay silent any longer, Connor darted back into the apartment.

"What's going on?" Faith was sitting up now, eyes wide open.

"Stay put." He threw open the front door, pausing to instruct her. "And lock me out." He waited while she hustled to the door, and when he heard the snick of the deadbolt, he ran down the stairs three at a time, holding on to the handrails so he didn't get a face full of concrete at the bottom. He may have lost the chase in those few seconds he'd waited for her to lock herself in, but protecting her was his mission. If she had any prayer of sleeping soundly in the future, it hinged on him catching this dirtbag.

Once his feet hit the grass, he took off at full speed in the direction he saw the figure vanish. After sprinting for about thirty yards, he came to a stop, hands on his hips. Catching his breath, he looked around but saw nothing.

Nothing. Whoever had been sneaking around her apartment was gone. He walked back to the building, still on high-alert, eyes peeled in case the guy was hiding around a tree or behind a car. Frustration at the fruitless chase had him growling in the back of his throat. So close. So fucking close.

He crossed the parking lot and angled a glance up at Faith's balcony. She stood, wrapped in the blanket from the couch, her hands holding the railing, elbow-length fair hair blowing in the soft breeze.

Delicate. She was so delicate. Just seeing how vulnerable she was made it hard for him to take his next breath. What could have happened if he hadn't been here tonight? She'd never know, he thought, rage clenching his fists. He hadn't felt that surge of protectiveness since Afghanistan. No moment had come close to the moment when a hot blast echoed over his skin and sent him running straight for the helpless mother and child huddled in a doorway. He hadn't succeeded. This time, he would.

"Everything okay?" Faith called down to him. He saw the worry lighting her fragile features—even from two floors down. No way would he leave her on her own until he was sure she was safe.

"Everything's okay," he confirmed, the final dab of adrenaline ebbing from his bloodstream. Everything *wasn't* okay. But it would be. As soon as he handled it. Until then, she was gonna stick to him like peanut butter on the roof of his mouth.

"What happened?" she asked as he walked toward the building.

"Dog." He hated lying to her, but he guessed she wouldn't get much more sleep tonight if she knew he'd run after a dark figure into the woods. Again his anger surged, but he held himself in check, not wanting to worry her.

"Told you that you were overreacting." She laughed, at his expense he guessed, but it was good to see her relaxed, so he let it go. Upstairs, she let him in, then flipped the lock. "I guess I should get to bed. Sorry I crashed on you."

He wondered if she knew she had literally crashed *on* him, and decided to let that go, too.

"You snore," he told her instead.

Her mouth dropped open. "I do not."

"Don't get me wrong, I appreciate it. It helped me stay awake."

"To protect me from the big, scary dog?" She arched an eyebrow in that cute smartass expression she'd perfected.

"Yeah."

He removed the space between them, drawn to her by some unseen force. A force that had no business radiating between the two of them. Especially since he had no business hitting on a woman who trusted him to keep her safe. He wouldn't take advantage of staying here with her. Even as the thought crossed his mind, he found himself grasping the blanket around her shoulders and pulling it tightly around her.

"You're welcome," he said, his voice low. That sweet, floral smell lifted off her skin again.

Her eyes left his to study a spot on the floor. He heard her swallow in the quiet air between them. "I really wanted to succeed at being on my own. I need to be on my own. I relied on Michael for way too long. And after, I relied on my mother. Started feeling like a kid again, you know?"

He didn't know, but he dipped his chin in agreement anyway.

"It's important for me to rely on myself." She lifted her

eyes and met his again. The expanse of those navy blues broke his heart in two. She didn't need to be strong for him.

"This isn't a toughness contest, Faith. I came here because you need someone here. When the danger's gone, so am I."

It was a good reminder for both of them. One night on her sofa, and he had already decided time in her company was a hell of a lot better than the terrible visions attacking him on his recliner at home. The warmth of her homey space much more welcoming than his blanched walls and sparse, impersonal furnishings. She took hold of the blanket and he moved his fingers away, brushing her hand as he did.

"Go to bed, Cupcake. I'll be here when you wake up."

Her eyes turned up to him, but she didn't speak. She simply nodded, then walked down the short hallway into her bedroom and closed the door.

CHAPTER 5

$\mathcal{S}$ince it had long ago been determined that Faith couldn't cook, she picked up takeout from the local Italian restaurant the next evening. The smell of buttered garlic bread, fettuccine Alfredo, and spaghetti Bolognese drifted from the bag as she unloaded each container and placed it on the counter.

Connor had followed her to the restaurant, like he followed her everywhere, save for the hours she spent in the mansion working with Sofie. Despite only finding a dog outside last night, he seemed extra worried about her. And while yes, she would like to foster her independent streak, she wasn't staying here by herself when it was so easy to gain entry to her place.

Upon entering her apartment tonight, the first thing he had done was go out to her balcony and replace the bulb, then lecture her on the safety of having a working light. Now he was paying a visit to her neighbors, asking if they'd seen or heard anything suspicious in the last few days.

As she pulled plates from the cabinet and began arranging their food, she thought back to last night. He had not only been protective, but he'd also been funny, flirty, and almost—dare she say it?—sweet. In the morning when she woke, she'd been acutely aware of a man wandering around her house outside her bedroom door. She heard him clattering around in the kitchen, listened as the shower stopped and started. Part of her wanted to poke her head out after the water shut off just to see what he looked like fresh out of the steam. Instead, she lay in bed, covers pulled up to her neck, and waited until she was sure he was completely clothed before she left her room.

She heard a key in the door, and a moment later he walked in, yanked the key out of the lock, and dropped it in his pocket. The sound of him letting himself in, the idea that he was already at home and familiar to her, was both heady and terrifying. Heady, because they fit in the same space easily. Terrifying because . . . well, for the same exact reason.

"So?" she asked, sliding a bowl brimming with dressed salad to the center of the table.

He shook his head.

That's what she thought. If her upstairs neighbor, Al, or her neighbor, Phyllis, had been home, she doubted—unless their hearing aids were turned up to ten—they'd heard a thing aside from the game shows blaring from their televisions.

"You said the guy downstairs worked nights?"

She shrugged as she put the Alfredo and the Bolognese

on the table. "I'm guessing. I've never met him before. He leaves at dark and comes home in the daylight."

Connor frowned. Whatever thought he was turning over in his head, he didn't share it with her. He pulled out a chair for himself and sat while she poured herself a glass of wine. "I have water and Diet Coke."

He made a face. "Diet Coke? Shit'll kill you." Lifting his chin in the direction of her wine, he asked, "Can I taste?"

"Oh. Of course." She handed over the glass.

Then she stared.

There was something about the way his large, work-worn hands looked grasping her delicate crystal. Something about the way he tipped the glass, pursed his lips, and drank a bit of the liquid down. When his tongue darted out to catch a stray drop of red, her head got light.

Right. Breathing is good.

He handed over her glass, a certain knowing smirk sitting on his lips. She was so totally busted. With a grin, he said, "I'll have some."

"Well, well. Look who likes wine after all."

She tried to play cool with her thoughts dancing around the idea of sipping from the side he sipped on. At the cabinet, she retrieved a second glass, poured his wine, and sat down to their dinner. Suddenly, things were intimate. She should've put on some music or something to cut the silence.

"Um. Dig in," she said, clearing her throat.

Connor reached for one kind of pasta, then the other, dumping a gratuitous amount of each onto his plate. Watching him dig in with gusto made her wonder if he dug into life in a similar fashion. What was she thinking?

Of course he did. He'd dug his heels in right here in her apartment.

When he bypassed the salad, she couldn't resist giving him a hard time.

"Come on, plant man, eat your veggies." She filled a smaller plate with greens.

"Salad is my dessert." His brow lifted in challenge.

She stabbed a few pieces of lettuce with her fork. "Salad is not an acceptable dessert. Devil Dogs on the other hand..."

He shoved a meatball in his mouth in one huge bite. After he had chewed it down to a reasonable size, he spoke out of one side of his mouth. "Yeah, I know how you feel about dessert, Cupcake." He licked his lips and winked, and for a second their little dinner felt a whole lot like a date.

She snuggled in, liking sharing dinner with someone other than her mother—who normally ate not much more than the olive Faith was chasing around her plate now. If he was going to be here, she may as well enjoy the banter.

"How did the Harvest Fest setup go? Sofie said Mrs. Anderson is being a pill."

"You mean being herself," he said with a grunt, winding pasta around his fork. "It's good. Straw, pumpkins. Scarecrows. That haunted house she insists on setting up every year."

"The one where she dresses the skeleton in pink." She wrinkled her nose. So silly. And not scary at all.

In a look of equal befuddlement, he scrunched his brows. "Why does she do that?"

"No one knows." She started in on her pasta. "You need to get us your invoice so we can pay you."

"I'll get it to you."

He would, but it always came months after he'd completed the work. She guessed the paperwork part of his business was his least favorite. Connor wasn't the pencil-pusher type.

"I can dummy one up for you if you tell me what you charge," she said. "I brought a stack of bills and invoices home with me to work on anyway."

Lifting his wineglass—which again she thought of as sexy in his manly grip—he ran his tongue over his teeth before taking a drink.

"I'll get it, Cupcake. But thanks."

She cut her noodles. He scoffed.

"Wind. Don't chop." He demonstrated spinning the noodles on his fork.

"I can't take a bite that big. I'll get sauce on my chin."

He grinned. A flash of straight teeth against suntanned skin.

"I'll help clean you up, Cupcake."

She jerked her gaze to the salt and pepper shakers between them, her face heating. He went back to eating, comfortable to let her stew in the gathering sexual tension. Faith drummed her fingernails on her wineglass, wishing she could think of a subject change.

Her mind was a void.

Giving up, she put down the glass and finished eating. After he appeared done, sitting back in his seat and stretching his palms over his taut, flat stomach, she stood and reached for his plate.

His hand wrapped around her wrist. "What are you doing?"

"Cleaning up." She felt her eyebrows rise.

"She who makes the dinner does not clean up the dinner."

"Sorry to disappoint you, but when I went into Viva Italy, it was to pick up this lovely meal you just enjoyed. I didn't *make* any of it."

The warmth looping her wrist remained even after he let her go.

"You know what I mean." He took her plate and stacked his on top.

She watched in wonder as he tracked to the sink. "You're going to do dishes?"

"Yeah. And you're gonna do your homework."

Faith sent a frown over at her laptop bag. She didn't mind bringing work home with her, and really, wouldn't have minded doing his invoice for him—if he let her— but it would be challenging to work with company. Especially company like him...

She slid a gaze over at the very well-built man who looked as if he should be stacking logs against a cabin in the woods, not squirting dishwashing liquid into her stainless steel sink.

Her eyes trailed over his big arms. Well. He was distracting, to say the least. She wasn't sure if she could concentrate with him here.

Apparently she didn't have a choice.

During the years she and Michael lived together he never washed a dish. Sure, he might rinse out his coffee mug in the morning, or dump food into the disposal, but mostly he'd left every plate, bowl, spoon, and cup in the sink, crusted with whatever food item was on it previously.

She carried over the salad bowl, disposing of the leftover lettuce, and handed it to Connor who sloshed his hands into several inches of soapy water. He took the bowl, water dripping onto her arm during the transfer.

"No helping, Cupcake. Not a mess I can't handle." He grinned again.

She'd bet there weren't a lot of messes he couldn't handle. Her eyes went to masculine hands sliding in the bubbles as he scrubbed, her pulse thrumming against her neck. Gosh, he made it hard for her to think. How could he stand there, looking all domestic-like? The man was a completely hot, totally built military guy taking up space in her tiny galley kitchen. His standing on a pink rug and scrubbing her delicate dishware was in total opposition of who he was.

She licked her lips, debating whether she should ask or not. Then she blurted, "Can I ask you something?"

Not turning in her direction, he scrubbed, not the least bit worried. "Go."

"How long are we going to do this?"

He sent her a sideways glance, his scrubbing interrupted for a quick beat before he started in again. "You mean me follow you around, watch over you every night?"

"Yeah. Don't you have something to do? Wouldn't you like to sleep?"

"I sleep." He rinsed a plate and rested it in her wooden dish drainer. "A little."

"I mean in a bed." She couldn't imagine trying to sleep in a strange place. She'd only been in her apartment a little while, but at least she was in her own bed, surrounded by her own things. "My couch is passable, but it's not as nice as a mattress."

"Surprised you'd offer, but I accept. I'll sleep in your bed. Safer for you if I stay close."

For a second, she wasn't sure if he was kidding. Then she spotted that twinkle in his eye, drew her hand back, and swatted him in the arm. "That's not what I meant!"

"Be clearer when you speak, Cupcake." His low laughter that did funny things to her stomach.

"You know what? You make creating a spreadsheet and answering fifty e-mails sound appealing."

"Never know," his low voice rumbled as he dried a dish and put it into the cabinet in front of him. "You might like sharing your bed with me."

He held her eyes for a second or two...maybe three, as her heart pounded relentlessly against her ribs. As she considered what that very scenario might look like. As she imagined the feel of his roughened hands on her subtle curves. Just as her mouth went dry and her mind fuzzy, Connor looked away.

"On the other hand, your snoring would keep me awake, so I wouldn't get much sleep anyway."

She let out a grunt of disapproval, restating how she'd be working at the kitchen table if he needed her, but on the inside, she was giving a lecture to her hormones, which had all lined up for a turn to gawk at the man in her kitchen.

Shaking her head, she punched her password into her laptop, determined to forget that last conversation. She peeked at him one final time and he winked.

He frustrated her in every way.

Sexually, most of all.

* * *

Connor finished the dishes while Faith tapped away on her keyboard. Tonight, he would pay her nocturnal downstairs neighbor a visit.

She said the guy drove a blue car. That's it. A blue car. When Connor asked what kind of car, she'd said, "I don't know. The kind with doors. And wheels." When he sarcastically asked if it had a windshield she'd replied, straight-faced, "Front and back."

God, she was cute. Made him smile.

After he cleaned the kitchen, he walked over to the table where she was sitting and leaned both fists on the surface. "I'm going to ask Donny if Gertie can come stay with you."

Donovan and Sofie's very big Saint Bernard mix would sooner chew her own paw off than attack anyone. But a nice loud bark might be enough to deter anyone wanting to get inside.

"Hmm?" It took her a second to come out of her concentration. She leveled him with a gaze before blinking up at him. So freaking cute.

"Having a dog at your place would alert you to an intruder before you and I ever hear a thing."

"No dogs allowed." Her long hair brushed her arms and the laptop keyboard as she shook her head.

"And? The important thing is that you are safe. I'll talk to your landlord if it comes to that."

"I am safe. I have you." She smiled up at him prettily.

Ah, hell. That got him. Dead center in the chest.

"Besides," she said, eyes going back to her screen, "Sofie would never give Gert up. That dog is her baby."

Well. He'd see about that.

"I'm going to talk to your neighbor. See if he heard

anything." A small fib. He wanted to see if the guy downstairs was the guy he spotted in the grass.

Her brows lifted. "Okay."

"I'm just downstairs. Gonna watch the house from my truck for a bit, but I'm not taking my eyes off you." It was important she understood he wasn't running out on her after vowing to protect her. But it was hard to watch for anyone suspicious from behind these four walls. "If you need me, call my cell. I'll come back up right away."

She touched him, just a light graze of her fingertips, and his entire body ignited under that soft press. If he ever had her in his arms, they'd be nuclear. He just knew it.

"I'm not worried." She pulled her hand away and that radiating heat receded. "Not with you around."

Damn if she didn't make him feel ten feet tall. He straightened away from her, slid his keys off the edge of the counter, and walked outside. Before he pulled the door to, he poked his head back in and said, "Lock this."

"The deadbolt, too?" She rose and came to the door.

They shared a heated, lingering look that made him not want to leave. "Deadbolt, too."

* * *

After a conversation with Faith's downstairs neighbor, Connor determined that the overweight manager of a local Kentucky Fried Chicken, who was likely in his mid-fifties, had not scaled the side of the building, hurdled the balcony wall, and jimmied the lock on the patio door.

Knowing it wasn't that guy didn't make Connor feel much better since he still didn't know who was trying to get into her house.

After watching the lot for a few hours and seeing nothing suspicious, he'd come back to the apartment and crashed on her couch until sunup. He was awake first, pouring coffee into his go-cup. Faith shuffled into the kitchen, looking incredible, as usual. Even in the morning. That was something.

"I need you to pack a bag, Cupcake."

She poured a cup of coffee for herself and asked around a yawn, "Why?"

"Because it's Friday and I have somewhere I gotta be." He didn't miss his Fridays with Jonas. "You'll be safe at my place."

"You want me to stay at your place?"

"I want you safe. My place is safe." He screwed the lid on his cup and gestured for her to hurry. "Cupcake. Bag."

She made a meager attempt to thwart him, but finally agreed. They carpooled to the mansion, then she went her way: to the library, and he went his: to the indoor greenhouse behind the utility room.

After a restless night and the frustration mounting from not finding his prey, Connor needed to unwind. Last year, Donovan agreed to let him use this space for growing his patented, prize-winning lavender. Since the local florist had begun requesting it on a regular basis, he'd been tinkering with a way to grow it faster and thicker so as to keep her stocked. The space, filled with old shelves and furniture he'd repurposed, was just what he needed.

Entering the space filled with the heady, spicy, earthy scent of lavender, as cliché as it sounded, instantly relaxed him. And made him sleepy.

Stifling a yawn, he drank down some more coffee and strolled through the space, past the shelves lined with various seedlings and starter plants he would nurture through the winter months until spring, then past a pair of antique doors separating the massive box of lavender under the grow lights overhead.

Then he got to work.

* * *

Sofie was leaning on her elbows on Faith's desk in a threatening manner. "I swear if you do not tell me..."

Faith laughed. "There is nothing to tell! We had dinner. He drank some of my wine. That's it. Honestly, he hung out in his truck more than he was in my apartment."

"Oh." Sofie straightened and folded her arms over her chest. "Well, that's not very fun."

"I'm not looking for a fun time with Connor. He's there to make sure I'm not attacked in my sleep."

Her best friend canted an eyebrow. "Yeah, well I wasn't looking for a fun time with Donny, either." She smiled sweetly and then returned to her desk. "I meant to ask...when he and I travel to New York in a few weeks, you sure you'll be okay with the business?"

"For the fourteenth time, *yes.*"

"I've never been to a Thanksgiving that lasted an entire weekend." She screwed her mouth to one side. "And at Alessandre D'Paolo's mansion. I'm going to have to take my best shoes."

Faith smiled. Alessandre was Donovan's mentor and very close friend, the closest thing Donovan had to family, and yes, ridiculously wealthy. "Relax. You have the shoe thing on lock." Sofie had a million pair. Give or take a few.

"Well, even though it's a holiday, I'll be available if you need me."

"I will call if I need you." Faith looked up from the list she'd been diligently checking off. "I'm sure our clients will be enjoying their own families as well and won't need much from their event planners."

Sofie chewed the side of her mouth. "But the Kauffman dinner..."

"I've got it." Kauffman Enterprises was having a fairly small shindig over at the conference center for their employees. "I finished sending the confirmation e-mails last night, finalized the caterer, and had the decorations delivered to the venue."

Her friend let out a breath. "What would I do without you?"

"You'll never have to know."

* * *

By the end of the day, Faith was beyond ready to go home. She'd had a few unpleasant phone calls, a virtual e-mail apocalypse over balloons—of all things—and had stayed at the mansion two hours later than she expected to.

It was now after seven, and her stomach was rumbling. Sofie and Donovan had dinner plans, so they'd cut out an hour or so ago. Faith had promised to be out the door right behind them, but she'd stayed to finish up one thing... that had turned into eighteen other things.

Connor was around here, she knew. He'd vowed to stick to her like Teflon. But also, she swore she could feel him nearby. It was like a weird sixth sense. The air didn't exactly tingle, but parts of her did.

Your pheromones.

Yikes. That was concerning.

She hadn't seen him in a while, though. He'd poked his head in the library earlier, cell phone pressed to his ear, and saluted her. Which was beyond sexy. After he sauntered back into the foyer, she'd blinked at the doorway for a few seconds while attempting to unscramble her brain.

Finished with her last phone call for the evening, she tossed her own cell phone onto the desk, collapsed back on her chair, and blew out a breath.

About that time, Connor strolled back into the library. "Gonna be much longer?"

"You don't have to wait on me. Go if you need to go."

"Cupcake, what did I say?" His clenched jaw and stiff posture suggested he was peeved.

Yeah, she didn't think that would work. There was more to do, but nothing she couldn't do from her laptop. She was just being difficult because the idea of sleeping at Connor's house—with him in it—was making her twitchy. What if... what if...

She closed her eyes against the images of his mouth on hers and whipped her hormones back to their corner.

"You don't go anywhere without me," continued the brute in charge of her safety. "That includes staying in a big-ass mansion with only Gertie to protect you."

"I thought you said Gertie was a good protector?" she countered.

A low sigh echoed in his broad chest, but when he stepped into the office, his body showed none of his earlier signs of agitation. In that easygoing stroll of his, he approached her and loomed over her desk. "I have a security system in my house. You'll be safe there."

So he kept saying.

"And quite frankly, I need to sleep. The last two nights I didn't get much."

She stood, ready to give in. She was starving, and more arguing would only further delay her dinner.

"I need to be sharp so we catch this guy."

"Guy?" What was he talking about?

He came around to her side of the desk and got close. Facing him full on, she got a sense of how broad his shoulders really were. She was slim and small-boned, and Connor was a contrasting wall of muscle; his presence was nothing short of commanding.

Gently, he took hold of her arms with both hands and frowned. "I didn't chase off a dog at your house. It was a person. Not sure who. By the time I got out to the grass, he was gone."

"A...person?" She felt her heart rate ratchet up, her blood go cold.

"It's why I wanted you at my place tonight. Yes, I need to get some sleep, but I also need to know you're somewhere no one will look for you. I know for a fact someone is lurking around your building."

"My gosh."

"Don't want you there without me in case he comes back." Strong hands squeezed her upper arms in an attempt to comfort her.

"He?" Even though he was calm and being so careful with her, she still felt as if everything moved around her at warp speed. There was a man—who Connor had seen—trying to get into her apartment. And maybe even trying to get to her. Suddenly, she was taking Connor's extreme measures much more seriously.

"If I could skip tonight, I would. But I have to go, Faith."

She didn't have to tip her chin much to look into his hazel eyes. They were right there, almost level with hers. She swallowed thickly. He'd called her by her name instead of Cupcake, and that made her feel the direness of her situation.

"Tonight, you're bunking with me." His face softened, and he gave her a wink. "Up to you whether you want to bunk with me literally or not."

Her shoulders dropped as she felt herself relax. He was intentionally lightening the mood. "This isn't some elaborate scheme to get me into your bed, is it?" Flirting with him eased her tension in an instant.

"Come on, does that even sound like me?" The corner of his mouth hitched.

"Yes."

His grin remained. "Pizza tonight?"

"And Devil Dogs. Have you had one yet?"

"Not yet. But you're the one with the sweet tooth around here, aren't you, Cupcake?"

And he was back. She grabbed her purse and pulled it onto her shoulder, deciding to leave her work for later. Even if she had to work the weekend, it would be worth it to have a break tonight.

"Mark my words," she said as they walked into the foyer and shut off the lights, "I'll convert you yet."

At the front door, he stood right behind her, his low voice rumbling in her ear and sending shivers down her spine. "I think you might."

* * *

The drive to Connor's place wasn't far. He lived just on the other side of the lake, in a building that had several apartments, all on one floor. They walked down the sidewalk into the U-shaped area, each dwelling partitioned off by its own six-foot piece of privacy fence. His was in the back right corner, and behind the privacy fence was a square of concrete with a grill, and the front door.

"It's not much," he commented, echoing her thoughts. He popped open the door and she followed him in. Beyond the threshold, she saw boxes stacked against every wall. His furniture consisted of a recliner, a television . . . and not much else.

"I was under the impression you had lived here a while."

"Going on two years."

Two *years*? He hadn't unpacked, hung up any pictures, or amassed any more furniture than this in two years? Looked like temporary housing. A small dinette set stood against the wall next to the compact kitchen. Maybe he had a severe minimalist style.

"Not expecting to be here long?" She put her purse on the countertop, the sparkling-clean countertop. And not just because it hadn't been used. There was no dust. The floors were clean. His place may be sparse, but it was also spotless.

"I'm not here much." He walked to the front door and pointed out a number pad for the alarm system. "Three-two-eight-four. Key it in, press Enter. Do not let anyone in. I'm not expecting company, and neither are you."

He gestured for her to try, and she entered in the code and pressed Enter. The screen read ENGAGED.

"I'm the only one who knows this code. When I get

home, I will let myself in. Hang out, help yourself; I'm going to stay until the pizza gets here. After the pizza's here I'm gonna run my errand. Be back within an hour. Do not let—"

"Anyone in," she finished for him.

"You're safe here," he said, his hard tone softening. "Call me if you hear anything, or even if you think you do."

She thought of her apartment. Of the scratching sound she'd heard when she'd been in her bed, covers to her chin, alone. Dread pooled in her stomach, and she wrapped her arms around her waist.

"Cupcake, you hear me?" He ducked his head so they were face-to-face, but he didn't have to duck very far.

She nodded, focusing on his concerned hazel eyes. "I hear you."

Once the pizza arrived, Connor scarfed down three pieces in record time. "Engage the alarm behind me. Do not let anyone in. Call my cell if you hear anything."

He was so serious, she said nothing as she followed him to the front door.

"I have cable. I'll be back in an hour."

In other words, sit down, watch TV, and try not to freak out about the fact that someone was possibly stalking her, and may know where she was right now.

A shudder crept up her spine and shook her shoulders.

Unfortunately, it didn't escape the attention of her protector. He dropped his hand from the doorknob and came back to her. "Look at me."

She did.

Rather than grasp her upper arms this time, he palmed her neck, threaded his fingers into her long hair, and tipped her chin with both thumbs.

"You are safe. If this alarm sounds, the cops will be called automatically, but they will call me next. Yes, I am being overly cautious. No one followed us here. It's highly unlikely you'll have to contend with the alarm." His eyes warmed the longer he looked at her and he continued to hold her face. "I'll be back in one hour. You're safer here than anywhere else."

Okay. He was probably right. And she had no reason to doubt him. She nodded to let him know she understood.

"Cupcake. Breathe." He gave her a soft smile.

She blew out a stuttered laugh. "I am a coward."

He didn't laugh with her.

"No, you're a woman who is dealing with an unknown intruder. You are not a coward." He held her eyes a moment longer. Long enough for her to notice the flecks of gold and green mingling in his. "Set the alarm." A second later, his hands were gone, his body walking out the front door.

She engaged the alarm, watched out the window as he walked to his truck, and then stood with her hands knitted, wondering how she would make it through the next hour without losing her mind.

CHAPTER 6

*C*onnor wouldn't miss a Friday night with the man who saved his life no matter the circumstances. That included leaving a scared woman at his house right now. But if he'd thought for a second Faith wasn't safe in his house, he never would have left her. Plus, his buddy wasn't one for company. He didn't think Jonas would appreciate his bringing a girl around. Or Faith for that matter, who would have had to sit on a dilapidated couch and listen to the two of them shoot the shit.

Jonas answered the door, beer bottle in hand, enormous television blaring behind him. He'd started without him. Not surprising.

Connor stepped inside. Like him, Jonas lived alone. And, like his apartment, Jonas's place had that not-quite-lived-in look. Boxes lined the hallway, and the only furniture in the living room was the eighty-inch TV and a treadmill behind a lumpy sofa handed down from his sister.

"What's on par for tonight?" Jonas asked, making his way for the fridge. "*The Avengers*? *The Hangover*? Or do you feel like playing Call of Duty?" The latter was a joke, and he made that clear by flashing a smile. Neither of them had any interest in playing war. Not after seeing so much of the real thing.

Jonas was older than him by ten years, divorced about three years ago, right around the time they were both in Afghanistan together. His wife and young daughter moved across the country, unable to handle him being gone so often.

It was a reminder to both of them why relationships were so hard for military guys like them.

Jonas had come back the last time different, quieter. Sadder. Connor always thought his friend was the man he would've become if he didn't have a supportive family. Yeah, he may bitch about his dad, about the family handyman business he didn't want any part of, but the truth was Mom, Dad, and his two sisters had been what kept him sane.

Not to say Jonas wasn't sane, but there was an open wound that hadn't quite healed yet. Any man would have an open wound after the trauma of Afghanistan, but his wife poured salt into it when she left with his daughter. He may have been contented to morph into part of his sofa and never leave his place, but Connor refused to let him sit here and rot. He came by every Friday if for no other reason than being a physical reminder that Jonas was a hero. If it wasn't for his friend, Connor would've died that day in the desert.

"Or, hey," Jonas said, "we could always go for something scary." He handed over a bottle of Miller and Connor accepted with a smile.

"Actually, I only have time for a beer or two. Then I gotta bolt."

Jonas's eyebrows lifted in surprise. "Shit. You got a date or something?"

"Not exactly. Faith is being stalked by someone I haven't found yet."

"The model?" Jonas waggled his eyebrows in appreciation.

"Easy," he warned.

They both knew she wasn't a model, but after Jonas had been by the mansion once and caught sight of her, it was the only moniker he referred to her by. She looked like a model so it wasn't a far-off description.

"She's at my place now. Her apartment's security consists of a deadbolt."

Jonas plopped down onto his lumpy sofa and tipped his beer bottle. After he swallowed a drink, he shook his head. "And you're here with me? That's fucked up. If I had a woman who looked like her at my house, I wouldn't leave her to come see some sorry sack of shit like me."

"Yeah, well if that sorry sack of shit saved your life, I bet you'd make time to have a beer with him." Connor sat on the opposite side of the couch staring blankly at the TV.

"Tell me about the intruder." Jonas had a mind for puzzle solving. And since he didn't get out much—had taken to computer programming from home rather than work outside the home—Connor knew he was probably itching for a puzzle to solve. So he told him the whole thing. The scratches on the locks, the shadowy figure disappearing into the trees, and the fact that Connor didn't like the idea of Faith staying there by herself.

Jonas stared through his beer bottle, now forgotten on the battered coffee table littered with magazines, his elbows on his knees as he listened intently. Like Connor, he had a side of him that was all military. That side snapped into place almost audibly when someone—Faith, in this case—was in danger. Frown lines deepened his forehead. "I don't like it."

"Neither do I."

"You did good by taking her to your place. Stay at her place tomorrow night. Sounds like the bastard is getting braver. Wouldn't surprise me if he was someone she knew."

Connor sipped his beer. "I thought maybe a relative of the former owner. She said the guy died, so maybe a grandkid wanting to find a secret money stash in the walls. Prescription meds they kept hidden."

But those didn't add up, either. Because the person trying to break in had been careful. Really careful. Like he was testing his limits and seeing how much closer he could get.

In agreement, Jonas shook his head. "I don't think so, man. Is there anyone she might know who would want to break into her place?"

"She says no. But I'll ask her again." He couldn't imagine Faith having enemies, though.

"You should." Jonas reached for his beer and leaned back in the corner of his sofa. He drained the bottle and gestured to the door with the neck. "I were you, I would get my ass home before my supermodel girlfriend conked out on me."

"You a love expert now?" Connor stood from the sofa

and finished his beer. "I don't see you with any girlfriends in your house." He started for the door.

"That's because I'm a dickhead. You're a nice guy. Nice guys always get the girl."

For some reason, that made him think of Maya. They didn't always get the girl. "Sometimes the dickheads get the girl."

"You find that girl, you send her over." Jonas dropped their empty bottles into the recycling bin in the kitchen and bent into his refrigerator to get a refill. "Expect a full report next Friday, Sergeant."

Rather than answer, Connor saluted, smiled, and shut the door behind him.

Back at his place, he keyed in the code and let himself inside.

"Just me," he announced.

But Faith didn't hear him. And the reason she didn't hear him was because of the headphones plugging her ears, connected to a tiny mp3 player on a band around her arm. The TV sound was muted, but she was bent, ass in the air, following the moves of the women stretching on-screen. He was suddenly a big fan of yoga.

Watching her move in those skintight pants, he couldn't help staring. There were a lot of places to rest his eyes. Where her slender thighs met the swells of her perfect ass, for starters. And the way her legs tapered to delicate ankles. The way her ponytail practically touched the ground as she deepened her stretch.

How the hell was he supposed to concentrate on protecting her with this sort of distraction?

From her position upside down, she caught sight of him beneath her outstretched arms and gasped. Standing abruptly, her long blond ponytail swung behind her shoulders. Her navy eyes were round, perfect pink lips matching in a frozen "O" beneath flushed cheeks.

God. Cute.

She rested her hand over her chest, her small breasts lifting and falling with her hectic breathing. The tight tank top she wore wasn't leaving a whole helluva lot to the imagination. And those pants...Every yard of stretchy fabric clung to her long, long legs.

"You scared me." She tugged the headphones out of her ears and looped them around the mp3 player she tossed unceremoniously on the chair. She flicked off the television next.

"Me?" He shut the door behind him. "Those pants nearly gave me a heart attack." Faith may be lean, but those graceful, slender limbs curved in all the right places, thickening in the thighs, rounding at her perfect butt.

"Thanks. I think."

"Welcome." Reluctantly, he dragged his gaze from her body to her face and found her eyes had gone from round to narrow.

"How was your errand? Your *mystery* errand since you didn't tell me where you were going. Have another hot date?"

"Wouldn't you like to know?" He liked having secrets from her. Mainly because it forced her to ask him questions. "Left you here afraid; thought I would come home and find you curled up on my chair, a blanket over your head."

"I work out when I'm nervous."

"Lucky me." He strolled to the refrigerator. "Get you something to drink?"

"I have wine. I packed it."

"You packed wine?"

"Yeah. I packed wine. Don't start. I don't have a problem."

No, he had a problem. The problem was somewhere in the vicinity of the front of his pants, and it was growing into a bigger problem the longer he was in the room with her. The woman was decked out in Lycra.

God help him.

Bottles of beer lined the bottom shelf of the fridge and he bent to grab one, musing over her question about a "hot date." It had been a while since he went on a date, actually—a real one—not fixing his sister's car. Had been some time since he'd stayed overnight with a woman, or had a girl here. He uncapped his beer and frowned in thought. How long *had* it been? He chewed on the side of his lip, calculating.

Man. A while. He seemed to remember it being cold… Snow on the ground…

Shit.

"I can take the recliner tonight. Really, I don't mind. You need your sleep."

He snapped out of his thoughts and refocused on Faith, who was walking toward him. She was graceful. Each elegant step like a dance move. Normally, she was in her work clothes whenever she was at the mansion—streamlined pantsuits or dresses that fit as if they were tailored to her. But tonight, her hair was in a sloppy ponytail rather than flowing over her shoulders, and a few stray strands had come down around her face. Her fair skin was free of makeup, her cheeks slightly pink from exertion.

"How are you this beautiful after you work out?" He had not planned on saying that out loud.

Her dark blue eyes opened wide, then blinked at him.

Pull it together, man. He cleared his throat, averted his gaze. "I get done working out, I stink like a pig. I'm a sweaty mess."

"That's not a bad thing. You forget I've seen you land-scaping the grounds at the mansion." Her mouth opened like she might continue, then those cheeks tinged a little pinker and she fell silent.

Oh really?

And here he thought he was the only one suffering from a bout of errant attraction.

"Do not smile at me." But she smiled at him as she gave the order.

One hand around his beer, he slid his other hand into his front pocket and took one step closer to her. She didn't back away. A good sign. "And what do you see when I'm landscaping the grounds at the mansion?"

She rolled her eyes, but her mouth twitched. Yeah, she was about to lie to him. The cute kind of lie. A lie to save her from embarrassment. But she didn't lie. Rather than answer, she changed the subject. "Like I was saying, I will be more than happy to sleep on the recliner."

Not contented to stop teasing her, he dipped his head in the direction of his favorite chair. "Recliner's my bed most nights. You can sleep in my room. That's against a lot of rules I have, one in particular being if there is a woman in my bed, I'm in there with her."

"You really don't give up do you?"

"You want me to?"

Her face fell.

Too far.

She was okay with the flirting and teasing until it went the direction of serious. Then she backed off. He watched as her shoulders tightened and her arms crossed, her entire body going rigid. "I admit, it would be fun..."

Well, that was not what he expected her to say. He tried not to let the surprise he felt show. He kept his mouth shut and ignored the stir below his belt buckle.

"Really fun," she said, almost to herself.

Fun. Hell yes, Faith in his bed would be fun.

She blinked out of her thoughts. "But where would it go, you know? You and me? I'd like to think we're friends and—"

Yeah, this, he couldn't do. Before she continued down a list of why she would not be crawling into bed with him tonight, he put a hand on her shoulder. He gave her a squeeze, grounding himself at the same time. "You don't have to dump me, Cupcake. I wasn't being serious."

Not all the way serious, anyway. Though, if she had replied in the positive, he'd have her flat on her back in his bed right this very minute. He took a long pull of his beer.

Then another.

Down, boy.

"Sorry. This may sound pretentious, but I'm used to turning men down..." She cringed. "Now I sound like I'm full of myself."

"Stop apologizing, Cupcake. You forget I know you. I know you're not full of yourself." The opposite, actually. Besides, he had no doubt, not a single one, that she turned down men by the dozen. She had been single since Michael dumped her for a cheap thrill, and looking the way she did, all that blond hair and lethal body... Hell, Connor knew men were probably lined around the block the second word got out she was no longer engaged.

"Open your wine, and don't apologize for wanting that, either." He gestured to his recliner. "I'll be in here if you need me."

* * *

Well. Maybe she should have kept her mouth shut.

Connor's teasing had gotten a little *real* all of a sudden. Or maybe it was just her. She'd been under a lot of stress lately, and being in close quarters with the man who looked as fantastic as the man she was temporarily living with could really mess with a girl's head.

She focused on the task of opening her wine, turning over the memory of him calling her beautiful.

How are you this beautiful after you work out?

"Beautiful" was something she'd heard a lot over the course of her life. And it wasn't that she didn't appreciate the compliment, but sometimes she wished people would see her as more than pretty.

Then again, recently, she'd been wondering if she *was* anything other than pretty. Her identity used to be wrapped up in Michael. Wrapped up in the idea of being half of a whole. Wrapped up in the idea of proving her mother wrong, of proving the Shelby curse to be a silly old wives' tale in their family.

Now she wasn't really sure who she was. She had successfully moved out of her mother's house to live on her own, and no sooner was she there than she was being ushered out of that house and into Connor's. And yes, she understood why. She even approved it. She had no desire to be on the receiving end of whoever was trying to get into her apartment for whatever reason.

Still, it kind of made her feel like her road to self-discovery had come to an abrupt end. A dead end.

With a juice glass full of merlot—Connor, not surprisingly, did not own a wineglass—she went into the living room. The recliner, the television, the boxes. He stood and gestured toward the chair. "Have a seat."

"I'm not kicking you out of your seat. Although"—she took a look around the barren space—"you could use another piece of furniture or two. I guess you don't have company very often. I mean, except the girls you insist on joining you in your bedroom." She batted her lashes.

Something flashed in his eyes, something dark. She couldn't quite read his expression. Rather than have a snappy comeback, rather than look as if he were full of confidence, he looked almost chagrined. Or pained.

"Well, Cupcake, you could always sit on my lap." Ah, there it was. The teasing was back. And quite frankly, she preferred the teasing. Teasing was much easier than the darkness that settled between them for a fraction of a second, or the tense energy she'd felt firsthand moments ago.

"Tempting. But I doubt you're as cushy as your bed. You seem to be made up completely of rock-hard muscle." Oops. Did she say that out loud?

He crossed his big arms over his chest, not taking her seriously. "Now you're teasing *me*."

She lifted a shoulder into a careless shrug. But it was not careless. The shrug was meant to disguise the sexual tension radiating between them. Right about now, on a scale of one to one hundred, it was cranked up to eleventy million.

They watched each other for a few moments, and then he came a step closer. Then one more step. "I like how tall you are. If we ever make out, neither one of us would have a sore neck afterward."

Subconsciously, she wet her lips, her eyes going to his mouth. His bottom lip was full, capped with a perfect top lip, and at once she wondered what the beer would taste like on his lips. Good, she'd bet.

Really good.

"Too bad neither of us is interested, huh?" he asked.

The question was rhetorical, she knew, but she still had to blink a few times to reset her brain. "Right."

He grinned. "Right."

"Well." She took one step away from him just in case she spontaneously pressed her lips to his. "It's better to have friendship, don't you think?"

"I do." Brushing by her, he crossed the room, hooked a kitchen chair with one hand, and dragged it to the living room. He turned it around and threw his leg over it, straddling it and folding his arms over the back. "I get to pick the first hour." He snapped up the remote and flicked the channel. "And during your hour, I get a veto. You are not watching that housewife shit tonight."

Like that, they'd gone from flirting to friends, making it over another hurdle.

She sat down on the recliner, curled her legs underneath her, and sipped her wine. But she didn't watch the show on television as much as she watched the flickering television highlight the planes of Connor's handsome face.

* * *

Faith woke in the morning wrapped in navy-blue sheets. She was a little disoriented, if not a tad hungover. Normally, she didn't make it a habit of finishing an entire bottle of wine, but the more she drank, the more relaxed she felt. The more relaxed she felt, the more fun it was to argue with the man of the house over what to watch next.

How many shows about catfish hunting could a girl endure, anyway?

She stretched, enjoying the sunlight sifting through the simple venetian blinds covering the two bedroom windows. Then pulled on her yoga pants and strolled out into the hallway. After a quick trip to the bathroom, she pulled open the door to find Connor standing in the threshold.

Wearing a white towel.

Wearing *only* a white towel.

She couldn't keep her eyes on his face. Her gaze snapped from his mussed, still-damp, sandy-colored hair, trickled across broad shoulders, and landed on an even broader bare chest covered in a smattering of light hair. For a little too long, she inspected the tribal tattoo circling one bicep.

Then there was the matter of the towel. Tucked in just over one hip, it appeared to be hanging there by not much more than a prayer.

"You done? I still need to shave."

"I—um."

Earth to Faith.

Before he could catch her drooling over his near-nakedness, she slipped by him in the doorway and hustled for the living room. And yes, she grazed the terrycloth covering what she could only imagine was underneath.

And boy, did she imagine.

She imagined it all the way through pouring herself a glass of water, through nibbling on a piece of toast, through climbing into his truck, and during the ride to the mansion.

For some reason, he didn't mention her finding him almost nude. And that made her wonder more. It wasn't like him not to tease her about something. Unless he really didn't find it a big deal to wander around in the nude. Maybe he thought the towel was enough of a barrier between them.

If so, he'd be wrong. Yes, she'd lived with a man who had exited the bathroom in only a towel. But Michael didn't have that chest. Those shoulders. Or the thighs straining against the—

"I'm going to reinforce your windows and door until you can get a decent security system installed at your place. We can stay there tonight," Connor said, driving up the long lane and into the driveway of Pate Mansion.

She turned her head and her visual of him this morning was replaced with the way he looked now. Long-sleeved waffle-style henley, jeans, boots. No less attractive covered up. How about that. "I thought you were my security system."

"Even so. Not leaving you as bait without me." He winked over at her. "You're stuck with me, Cupcake."

There was an idea.

"I think whoever's been trying to break in might come back if they haven't already," he said.

She felt her eyebrows lift. "And you want to be there when they do?"

"Yes. I would like to catch this person so you can sleep soundly in your apartment."

She wanted that, too.

"Do you have any enemies?" he asked.

She snorted. Brady had asked her the same question when he stopped by, but she couldn't think of a single person who wanted to do her ill. Except for maybe… "Cookie?"

"Did you have words with her when you caught her and Michael together?"

Oh, how she had wanted to, but the shock of what she was seeing had tied her tongue.

"No." Faith shook her head and looked at her lap. "I just slunk away like a coward."

He parked the truck and shut the engine down. The next thing she knew, he was facing her fully, his index finger crooked under her chin. Her eyes met his concerned expression.

"Promise you're going to stop referring to yourself as a coward, Cupcake. I don't like it. And it's not true. What that rat-bastard did to you was wrong. What Cookie did to you was wrong. Make no mistake, what they did? That was done *to* you. No one knows what to say in a situation like that."

He spoke like maybe he'd experienced a similar situation. She wondered if he had. They never talked about his past relationships. They didn't talk about much of anything other than his work or hers. What they had was a little bit deeper than "how is the weather," but not by much.

A small smile pulled her lips. "Okay. I promise." It was high time she stopped reacting like a kicked puppy. If she was supposed to move on with her life, she better start freaking moving *on*. "My house tonight."

"That's my girl."

He let go of her chin and turned to get out. She sat there for an extra second or two letting the words "my girl" roll around inside the cab of the truck. Something about being Connor's girl was really appealing.

And really scary at the same time.

$\mathscr{C}$HAPTER 7

$\mathscr{B}$y five o'clock, the mansion's kitchen smelled like cinnamon.

He'd been in the kitchen having a beer with Donny when Faith appeared, practically floating in, her nose in the air.

"My mouth is watering," she announced.

"Cinnamon rolls," Connor said.

Her blue eyes grew in circumference.

"A pan of pinwheel heaven," Sofie said, strolling into the kitchen via the utility room. "You two staying for dinner?"

Connor looked to Faith who nervously looked to Sofie. "I…"

"We have time, Cupcake." He could use something not takeout, that was for damn sure.

"I can't turn down dessert," Faith told Sofie.

Donovan put on a faux expression of authority and said, "After you finish your dinner, young lady."

Table set, and food piping hot and plated, the four of them sat down to eat. Connor had been eating Donny's cooking since his brief stint working at the Wharf. At the seafood restaurant, his buddy sneaked him food so he didn't have to pay for it. Now that he thought about it, not all that different from now.

Ever since he'd been back in town, Donovan had been cooking one thing or the other. Tonight it was Chicken Marsala, rice, broccoli, and those cinnamon rolls baking away in the oven apparently torturing Faith.

"How much longer?" she asked, her fork digging forlornly into her rice.

"Eat your broccoli," Donovan teased.

Connor laughed.

Faith glared at him. "You leave me alone."

"Forget it. I'm all over you until we find your intruder."

"Sounds kinky." Donovan took a sip of his beer.

"Yeah, what'd you two do last night?" Sofie asked, narrowing one eyelid.

Unable to resist, he blurted, "Tantric sex. Faith is really flexible."

That earned him a swift kick to the shin. "We slept in separate rooms."

"After." He slid his foot away before she could nail him again.

Despite the fact it wasn't true, her cheeks reddened.

"I don't want details." Donovan cleared his plate and swiped Connor's. "More?"

"Three plates is my limit." He pulled his palms over his stomach.

"Nothing happened," Faith continued arguing.

"It's fine if it did," Sofie said through a giggle.

Happy to watch her flail, Connor chimed in, "Come on, Cupcake, secret's out."

"There is no—" Then she shut up and rolled her eyes, realizing everyone was smiling at her. "Okay. Fine. Everyone tease the ditzy blonde."

"Shut up and eat your cinnamon rolls." Donny rested the pan on the top of the stove. "Anyway"—he tossed aside the oven mitt—"we don't think you're ditzy."

"The opposite." This from Sofie. "We know you're too smart to get involved with Connor."

Faith quirked her lips. "Hmm. Good point."

He saw her try not to smile. He liked her teasing him. Dishing it out. That was good for her.

"Two please," Faith ordered as Donny came to the table with a plate of piping-hot cinnamon rolls. "And that's not nearly enough frosting."

* * *

"I'm going to die."

Connor chuckled as Faith collapsed on her couch. He'd been busy reinforcing the latches on the windows and installing a second deadbolt on the door while she showered and slipped into yoga pants and a tee. Frankly, pants with an elastic waistband were the only pants likely to fit her after the amount she'd eaten for dinner.

Now, with her elbow-length hair piled at the back of her head in a messy bun, and without shoes or a stitch of makeup, she was too miserable to care that she looked like death warmed over.

"I ate too much," she groaned. She had. Donovan's cinnamon rolls were legendary. And not normal legendary, more like *legen*—wait for it—*DARY*. And after too much Chicken Marsala, rice, and veggies—that Sofie made her eat, she might add—Faith pounded down two and a half cinnamon rolls. "Shouldn't have eaten that last half."

Laughter from the other side of the couch shook the cushions.

She held her stomach. "Hold still."

"Yeah, because that half a cinnamon roll really put you over. I'm impressed, though; you don't look like you can hold it, but girl, you can eat."

"I'm blessed with high metabolism." She raised her head and leaned on one hand. "What's your excuse? You inhaled three thousand calories, at least."

"I do a lot of physical labor."

His comment made her peruse the length of his henley-covered arms, this one maroon, but still tight enough to show off those drool-worthy biceps and pecs and—

"Faith."

She redirected her gaze and feigned sick again. She wasn't as full as she was letting on, but it was helping quell some of the lust that'd settled into her apartment the moment they returned home together.

When she met his gaze, his lips twitched, his eyes snapped to her mouth, and just as quickly, he turned his body away from her and faced the television. "What's your pleasure?"

So many answers.

"Food Network."

"Thought you were stuffed."

"I am, but I figured it was something we could agree on."

"Your funeral," he said, flicking the channel.

After a *Diners, Drive-Ins and Dives* marathon, Connor had gone to the kitchen for more food. *More food.* Although, she had followed. Here she thought she'd been too full to eat ever again. But her stuffed tummy was no match for the various dishes full of epic awesomeness Guy Fieri dished up. So far she'd had potato chips, cheese and crackers, and was now attempting to steal a bite of Connor's ice cream.

Clasping her hands together, she begged, "One bite?"

"Hot fudge." He moaned in pleasure and gestured with his spoon to the bowl of melting ice cream.

"I know what it is. It's *my* hot fudge."

Another bite. "Mmm." He swallowed, licked his lips. "You should have gotten yourself a bowl. It's amazing."

"I don't want a whole bowl! I want a bite. One bite."

His eyes narrowed. Lips quirked.

Ruh-roh.

"Trade ya."

"Oh no, you don't."

He lifted a spoonful and held it over the bowl. Fudge dripped from the edge of the spoon, and she swore her nether regions tingled. If she couldn't have sex, she damn well would have sugar.

"A kiss," he said.

"Kiss!" The idea of it bounced around in her brain and grabbed on to parts of her she didn't want to acknowledge.

He shoveled the bite into his mouth, leaving a pitiable amount in the bowl. One bite to be exact. *Her* bite. He licked his lips and she stifled a whimper.

"Just let me have it." She tried giving him her best

Puss in Boots expression. "I'm the one fearing for my life, here."

He remained unfazed.

"Sorry, Cupcake. Kiss for the rest." He tipped the bowl slightly. "That's the deal."

"I could get my own bowl."

He dipped his chin in agreement. "You could."

Damn. Nothing was working. He really didn't budge. On anything. And she didn't want her own bowl. She'd have to get the ice cream out, and a bowl, and scoop it, and then microwave the hot fudge...

She bit her lip and thought about it for another second. Time was precious. Her ice cream was melting. "No tongue."

Shrugging, he said, "Your playground."

One quick peck was a small price to pay for the deliciousness at the bottom of the bowl. But when she crawled onto her knees and brought her mouth closer to his face, she was ultra-aware of his smell, that earthy, spicy smell she'd grown to associate with him. Aware of the barely there stubble pressing through his normally clean-shaven jaw. Aware of his eyes darkening...

Well. What the hell. She closed in and pressed her lips to his.

His mouth was cool and he tasted of fudge and sweet, cold cream. She meant to pull away, honest to God she did, but he not only tasted of sugar, he also tasted of Connor, and the taste had her leaning in for more. So did he. Before she knew what'd happened, he hooked her jaw with one rough palm and her hand was resting on his denim-clad thigh. They were almost making out. *Almost.*

No tongue. As promised.

Dammit.

Her and her big mouth.

She pulled away abruptly and was pleased to find his expression dazed. The smile wasn't far behind, and neither was her reward.

"You earned it," he said, his lips tipping.

Oh, right. So hard won.

"Thank you," she said primly, taking the bowl and spoon and eating the rest in one bite. She even scraped down the sides. Anything to keep from meeting his unwavering gaze. It was locked on to her like a heat-seeking missile. She could feel it.

She also ignored it. "Mmm. That was good."

"Good enough to make you want more," he murmured, his low, low voice rumbling between them.

Breaking her rule, she looked up and saw the dark intent in those seemingly harmless hazel eyes. In the daytime he was easygoing, sandy-haired, I-should-be-on-a-sexy-fireman-calendar Connor. But in her apartment, lazed onto the arm of her couch, sideways smirk cocked just so, he was...dangerous.

In the most delicious way possible.

"I'd better get this into the kitchen." She unfolded her legs and stood, scuttling out of there and thinking she should stick her head under the faucet while she was at it. At the sink, she rinsed the bowl but watched him. He sat there, arms splayed as per his usual, a safe and comforting presence.

He'd gone out of his way for the last several days to make sure she went nowhere alone, make sure she was safe, and she'd done nothing but snipe at him. Playfully, sure, but still.

Drying her hands on a dishtowel, she walked over to the side of the couch where he was leaning. "Thank you, Connor."

He looked surprised, eyebrows raised, as he turned his head and looked up at her. "For the ice cream?" Heat infused his eyes. "Or the kiss?"

She smiled. Twisted the dishtowel she'd carried in with her. "For watching over me. I appreciate it. And I don't mind kissing you, even though I should." She really should. But now that she watched his mouth, she couldn't remember why. Something about independence . . . but the excuse sounded lame now.

"I don't mind kissing you, either, Cupcake. But I have to tell you, you think it's something we shouldn't do, I respect that." He slapped the cushion on the couch. "I promise not to make you get within six inches of this mouth for the rest of the night."

Her shoulders slumped in disappointment. She was a head case. But he didn't need to know that. "Deal."

She sat down next to him and he wrapped an arm around her shoulders. He felt so good, she snuggled into him.

"And you don't have to thank me," he said at the next commercial break. The low timbre of his voice reverberated along his ribs. "I'd watch over you no matter what."

"Thank you," she repeated anyway. Then she rested her face on his chest and watched Guy enter another restaurant and tease the chef.

* * *

A shadow moved outside the patio door and Connor's shoulders went tight. The movement jostled the woman snoozing against him and she made a soft grunting noise. His arm tightened protectively around her.

He'd turned off the television an hour or so ago when she had gone to sleep, but he kept watch for lights or movement outside in case the intruder came back. Turned out he was going to get his wish. Jonas was right. The bastard had come back.

The figure outside of the window was dressed in dark clothing and scaling the old, half-dead tree outside the patio window. The largest branch was hollowed from decay, and that was the same branch the idiot crawled onto right now.

So that was how he'd been accessing Faith's balcony. Connor didn't figure anyone would be stupid enough to climb the crumbling tree. He was wrong.

He couldn't see the other man clearly, but could tell it was a *him*, if height and stature could be counted on. The guy's face was covered with a ski mask, and since his hands were busy clasping onto the wide branch as he crawled toward the balcony railing, he didn't have any visible weapon.

"What's going on?" came a sleepy question from his right shoulder.

He lowered his lips and put them to Faith's forehead. "Shhhhh. Be still."

She turned her head and started to gasp, but swallowed it a second later. "Oh my God," she whispered.

"Still, Cupcake."

She complied but he could feel her body go stiff and the slightest shiver overtake her slender body. His protectiveness mixed with a fierceness he'd honed in the army. No way would he allow an intruder to cause Faith fear in her own home.

Slipping out from beneath her, he kept his eyes on the dipshit who might fall to his death before Connor could get to him. This would not be good. Not because he cared about the criminal's well-being, but because if he succumbed to a broken bone, Connor would be the one to break it.

Just as he started to step away from the couch—hopefully the intruder wasn't wearing night vision goggles—Faith clutched his shirt in her fist. "What are you doing?"

He turned away from the balcony briefly, but only to put his finger to his lips in a shushing motion, disentangle her hand, and kiss her fist. "Gonna break that guy's legs."

She didn't smile. "Do you want me to call the police?"

"Not yet." First he wanted the guy to know that Faith had someone looking out for her. Someone who might not heed the governing laws of Evergreen Cove.

She curled in on herself and huddled into a corner of her sofa, wide eyes latched onto the figure outside. Even more reason to snap the jerk in two, he thought as he crept to the door.

He'd have to move fast. Not like the patio door was silent when it slid open. The wooden pole usually lying across the gap wasn't there, so once he disengaged the lock, nothing would keep him from throwing the door wide. He unlocked the door now, pressing his back to the living room wall and hoping to stay out of the guy's field of vision.

He looked to Faith to get a read on whether or not the

intruder noticed. She nodded her head in a silent "okay." He nodded back. Sweat prickled his temples and under his arms. In an instant he was back in Afghanistan under the cover of night, staking out a suspicious vehicle in the hundred-degree, stifling nighttime air.

But this wasn't Afghanistan. There was no bomb waiting to blow him to kingdom come, no small cell of terrorists anxious to behead him. This was one man on a very shaky tree limb. Arguably, not a very smart man.

Figuring he had another second, Connor used it to close his eyes, take a deep breath, and then, he moved into action.

With one hand, he slid the patio door aside and exited onto the balcony. He got lucky. The guy was scrambling over the railing as Connor reached him. He looked up, discovering his bout of bad luck a second later. Then his bad luck got worse. Startled to find a man barreling at him from the doorway, the guy's arms pinwheeled as he pitched backward over the railing.

Reflexes lightning fast, Connor snatched him by the front of the shirt, hauled him over the railing, and slammed his back to the concrete. He anchored the guy with a knee to the chest, hearing a pained "Ahh!" as the dipshit's arms came up to swat him away. Adrenaline pumping through his veins, the guy's hands bounced off his arms like gnats.

Connor wrenched the mask off and revealed light brown hair, a fairly large nose, and thin lips that peeled back and shouted, "Get the fuck off me!"

He didn't miss the fear lining the guy's voice. He'd heard a lot of men scream in fear. This dickhead was no exception. A bit melodramatic for the situation, but still.

He knew fear when he heard it. Hauling the guy to his feet, Connor backed him to the railing and leaned him over the edge.

"Who are you and what the fuck do you want?" he demanded, twisting the other guy's shirt in his fists.

Ignoring him, the man wailed, "Get off me! Help!"

Then Faith's voice rang in the air. Disbelief outlined two softly spoken syllables.

"*Michael*?"

CHAPTER 8

*S*he was not seeing this. She was not seeing the man she was once going to marry dressed in a head-to-toe black outfit standing on her balcony because he'd climbed a tree and tried to break into her apartment.

But she was seeing it, because there he was. Michael continued pawing futilely at Connor's ironclad grip. Yeah, like he had a chance of overpowering the soldier. Her ex wasn't going anywhere.

"Faith! Help! Get this gorilla off me!"

"Don't talk to her," Connor demanded.

"Yeah, don't talk to me!" She strode out onto the patio and Michael stopped flailing.

"Inside, Cupcake."

"Cupcake?" But Michael's laugh sounded like it may be coated in terror. "Faith, wait, I can explain."

"I said don't talk to her," Connor repeated, this time shaking Michael to get his attention. He still had her ex bent awkwardly over her balcony. She didn't think he'd throw Michael over, but Michael did. And to be honest, a tiny, evil part of her found it kind of fun to watch.

"Now should I call the cops?" she asked Connor.

"Do it."

"Please! The ring," Michael said as she backed into her apartment.

"Talk to me, not her, dickweed." Connor twisted his fists into the hoodie with renewed vigor.

Michael obeyed, holding his hands up in front of him in surrender. "I just came for the ring." Desperation replaced the terror in his voice.

Ring?

"It was my great-grandmother's and m-my mom was asking about it. Told her I was having it cleaned. She wants it back."

"The engagement ring?" she heard herself say.

"Y-yes!" Michael turned his attention to her, a nervous smile splitting his sweating face.

"Did I say you could talk to her?" Connor gave him another brief shake.

"And you think I have it?" she asked, perplexed.

"Dammit, call the cops, Faith." This from Connor who took his eyes off Michael for a fraction of a second to spear her with an irritated glare.

"Wait. I do have it."

"See?" Her ex-fiancé smiled. "She has it. That's all I want. I wanted to get it and get out."

"You could have called." Her frustration reaching a peak, she considered suggesting Connor toss him over the balcony and save them the trouble of this conversation.

"You changed your phone number." Michael sounded

hopeful now. "I knew you'd refuse to talk to me if I came by."

Valid point.

She narrowed her eyes. "How did you know where I live?"

"Your mom."

Of course. Linda Shelby strikes again.

"Let him go," she told Connor.

"Forget it."

"Police!" came a voice followed by a knock from her front door.

"Someone beat you to it," Connor said, then keeping his eyes on Michael, instructed, "Get the door."

One of her neighbors must have called. And Michael was making enough noise out there to raise suspicion— even from her hard-of-hearing neighbors.

"Wait," Michael protested.

"Sorry, asshole. Too late." Connor grinned as he hauled Michael away from the edge of the balcony. He jerked his head in the direction of her living room. "Faith, honey, get the door."

"Honey?" Michael's voice went high. "Are you dating this caveman?"

Dragging him into the house, Connor dropped her ex into the armchair. "I said stop talking to her. Faith. Door."

"Fine!" She threw her hands wide. "I'll get the door."

"Police!" Another shout followed by a series of sharp knocks. She pulled open the door to find Brady, hand on his weapon. The moment he caught sight of her, his expression shifted from alarmed to concerned. "You okay?"

"I'm okay."

Brady barreled into her living room taking in the situation: Connor, arms crossed, standing sentry over Michael, who was straightening his hoodie and looking perturbed, if not like he might piss his pants.

"Who are you?"

Michael sat up straight in the chair, eyes wide with terror, but Brady's question was not directed to him.

"This is my friend, Connor. He caught my ex-fiancé breaking into my patio door. Michael, you remember Brady."

Michael never liked Brady. Probably because Brady was ridiculously attractive. Once or twice, he'd caught Brady in Abundance Market chatting up Faith about wine and had freaked out. Never in front of the officer, however. Only in private, whining about her lack of couth. Seemed Michael had been sensitive to the potential of her cheating. Probably because he was the one who was cheating on her.

Bastard.

"McClain." Connor stopped seething over the armchair long enough to extend a hand.

After hesitating, Brady shook it, his mouth turned down disapprovingly at the sides. "You staying here, McClain?" His eyes swept the room.

"Who called you?" Connor's arms again crossed over his chest.

"Downstairs neighbor. Are you staying here?"

"I am."

Brady assessed him a moment longer, then turned to Faith. "Didn't know you had a boyfriend."

Before Connor could say whatever he'd opened his mouth to say, she spoke. "He's a friend. He offered to sleep on the couch since I was nervous."

The two men stared each other down, Michael temporarily forgotten. That is, until he spoke up. "Can you get the ring, Faith? I'll get out of your hair."

Slowly, Brady and Connor turned their heads to face him. Now he had two frowning badasses standing over him instead of one.

"You need to start talking," Brady informed him.

"And don't leave out the part where I dragged you in by the neck," Connor added.

* * *

"You're sure you don't want to press charges?" Brady asked.

She found the ring in the drawer of her jewelry box. Honest to God, she'd forgotten she'd tossed it in there. Michael had never acted like he cared to have it back, and she'd been so focused on moving on, she didn't give it any more thought. It'd been there for over a year. Why he wanted it back now was beyond her.

She nodded her answer, looking into Brady's green eyes. "I'm sure."

He started to put a palm on her shoulder, but Connor took a step closer to her and slid his arm around her waist. "I got her, Hutchins."

Cocking his head to one side, Brady narrowed his eyelids. "You need to know your place, McClain."

"And you need to know yours. Your concern is the perp behind you. Not me. Not her."

"I'm not an enemy you want to have." Brady's attention was solely on Connor now. The officer wasn't as wide as Connor, but he was as tall. And the guy was no slouch. She could tell there was plenty of firm muscle beneath his uniform.

But the Popeye and Bluto thing was ridiculous.

"Okay!" Faith's raised voice gathered both guys' attention. "You two need to stop acting so possessive. I'm fine. Michael has the ring, which he should have. It's his. I admit, he went about getting it back in a moronic way." She angled a glance at her ex, who pursed his lips and, wisely, remained silent. "But no harm, no foul. I don't think he'll be back here trying to break in anymore."

"He does, call me," Brady said.

"She can call me," Connor interjected.

Good Lord.

"I have an idea. Why don't all of you go home?"

"No way," Connor said first.

"I mean it. Out. All of you. Mystery solved. Damsel no longer in distress. *Out.*" She pointed to the door. Connor and Brady stood stock-still, but Michael took his leave, scampering out the door and throwing a brief glance over his shoulder.

The two men who were left watched him go, then returned glaring at each other.

She crossed her arms and tapped her foot. "Thank you, Brady. Good night."

Connor smiled. "Yeah, Brady. Good night."

"That's Officer—"

"You too, Connor. Or I'll have *Officer* Brady Hutchins escort you out."

The soldier tipped his head and watched her for a beat as if trying to discern whether or not she was kidding. She was not. She wasn't a piece of veal to be fought over. And there was too much testosterone in her house.

"Good night. Both of you." She walked past them and popped open the door, holding it open so they could exit. They did, Brady waiting for Connor to go first, which he did, reluctantly.

Once Brady filed out, he turned around to speak. She shut the door in his face.

* * *

It'd been three weeks since Michael had reclaimed the ring from her jewelry box. Faith would think after he had what he needed and she was out of danger, she was free to resume her new life of independence.

Her two man-guards did not agree.

If Connor wasn't following her home and watching from his truck to see she got safely inside, then Brady was patrolling her apartment's parking lot. She really didn't believe Brady had any romantic interest in her, just assumed he was doing his job.

While Brady did his job, she was contented to do hers. And Connor did his. His job put him at the mansion most days. He was working on several projects at her behest, plus his indoor greenhouse was there, so he checked in often. Things were not tense between them. The pattern was thus: He continued insisting on watching over her, she would argue, then he would do what he wanted anyway and follow her home.

He'd insisted on having a security system installed in her apartment, and as much as she wanted to claim independence and tell him she could handle it, she let him oversee the company who installed it. If there was one thing she trusted him with, it was her safety.

And they never brought up the kiss over the ice cream bowl. She assumed he believed what she believed. The kiss was a fluke. At least that's what she'd started telling herself. He still flirted as per his usual, but he didn't push harder and she was glad. That's what she'd started telling herself, too—that she was glad—though she was pretty sure it was a lie.

It was true she didn't need a complicated entanglement with a man, but she still would like to steal another smooch or two from the man. Not that she'd ever admit it aloud. Only in the quiet, dark of her bedroom where things no longer went bump in the night.

With things set to simmer, she found herself loving her apartment and embracing her newfound freedom more and more. She really did feel better now that the security system was installed. So much so, maybe she should push herself to overcome another fear and enter her former workplace for the first time since she walked out…

From the parking lot at the bank, she watched across the street as shoppers entered and exited Abundance Market.

Today was the day.

She would walk in those sliding doors, saunter back to her familiar playground in the wine aisle, and pilfer the rest of the Layer Cake Primitivo they had in stock. Then in celebration, she could swing by Sugar Hi and pick up Devil Dogs and eat and drink her spoils.

She navigated her way to the market's spotless lot, parked, and took a deep, steeling breath. Then she got out and headed for the entrance.

Here we go.

The doors slid open to the familiar smell of freshly

baked bread and freshly ground coffee from the stand at the front, staffed by a smiling barista dressed in one of Abundance Market's signature orange aprons. As wonderful as it smelled, caffeine was not on the menu. She turned down an espresso when the young girl behind the counter offered, then glanced to the right and blew out a breath of relief. Michael wasn't at the Customer Service counter. Maybe he was in the back. Or maybe, she thought with a burst of hope, he wasn't here at all.

Either way, she was on a mission, and the mission was—

"Oof!" She turned and smacked into a woman in the produce section and sent an array of oranges rolling off the stand to the floor. "Oh my gosh! I'm so sorry."

Both women squatted down to clean the mess, and that's when Faith looked up and her smile froze.

Cookie's eyes widened with recognition before she pushed a lock of dyed blue hair away from her face and tucked it behind her ear. When she did, Faith spotted a ring. *The* ring. The same ring Michael had attempted to break into her house to steal back.

And it was on Cookie's left hand.

* * *

Now late November, there was nothing alive outside, or not much anyway, since the season's first frost killed the plants last week. This was Connor's least favorite time of year. Everything was in the process of dying or dead. The ground would soon be buried in inches of snow, then eventually, frozen solid.

The entire reason he gravitated toward his landscaping

business was because having his hands in the dirt, creating something that lived, grew, and thrived, was paramount to keeping him sane. Maybe not literally, but... yeah, maybe literally.

Hands on the eight-by-six box of lavender, he drew in a deep breath and shut his eyes. As counterintuitive as it was, the winter months reminded him of Afghanistan. The landscape was painted all one color—there dusty brown, here dim gray. Nothing grew green and lush. His nasal passages and throat were dry in both places. He'd noticed that more than ever last year. Part of the benefit of coming into his greenhouse was getting some much-needed moisture into his head.

The back of his neck prickled and he turned, finding Faith standing by the antique doors acting as a divider. He'd salvaged them from this room, leaving the chipped paint and blurred glass as he found them.

Her face was slack, eyes down. She carried a white bakery box in her hand, and his memory briefly returned to the day she'd carried a box of cupcakes into this room. The day he'd found her, she looked equally distraught— and attempting to bury some work crisis in a box of Sugar Hi. He'd hated seeing her sad and, determined to make her laugh, started calling her Cupcake. Since the nickname lit her face with an irresistible smile, he decided not to stop.

"Hi," she said now.

"Hi."

"I thought you'd be in here."

So she had sought him out. He liked that. After weeks of pushing him away, or reluctantly letting him watch over her, she had finally come to him. She sat in a chair in front of the lavender, opened the bakery box, and pulled out a donut hole.

He watched her chew morosely before taking the folding chair next to hers. "Faith?"

"Hmm?" she asked, picking through the assortment and coming out with an éclair. He peered into the box and saw frosted chocolate chip cookies, brightly colored mini-cupcakes, donut holes, and a chocolate-dipped cake with whipped cream and a cherry on top. Devil Dog. Her favorite.

"Talk to me, Cupcake."

"I have some of those, too," she announced, abandoning the éclair and pointing out a pink confection with rainbow sprinkles on top. "But I don't want one." She lifted the Devil Dog, took a massive bite, then sent him a look as glazed as the donut she'd just eaten. "Do you?"

He reached for a donut hole instead and popped it into his mouth.

"Flowers look pretty." Her voice was flat. Robotic. "Nice to have this here in the winter. Almost winter."

He ran his tongue along his teeth, sugar coating his mouth. "There a reason you're eating a box of Sugar Hi?"

"Yes." Her eyes were focused on the window across the room. It was cold today, the wind blowing what leaves remained across the yard. She took another bite of the Devil Dog and chewed, looking as unhappy as he'd ever seen her.

"Well at least enjoy yourself." He grabbed her hand and steered the cake to his mouth. He took an enormous bite, cramming as much of the monstrous chocolate cake in his mouth as he could fit. When he got to her fingers, he took a bite and left her with a smashed pile of crumbs.

Chewing, he rolled his eyes into his head. "Muh," he moaned. "Uhmmm." He chewed, aware of the frosting on his lips, the whipped cream on the tip of his nose. "Mmmph."

His reward wasn't far behind. A smile parted her mouth. She dropped the remaining bits of cake into the box and laughed, eyes shining with tears as she took a breath and laughed some more. There she was. He knew she was behind that mask of sadness somewhere. With some effort, he finally finished chewing the cake and swallowed, then licked his lips.

She cleaned her fingers with a napkin, then used it to swipe the cream from his nose. Her eyes moved from his nose to his mouth, where she watched his lips with interest, her smile fading. Rather than using the napkin, she swiped the corner of his mouth with her fingertip.

Something between them shifted. The air crackled with anticipation.

Taking her arm, he steered her finger to his lips, and, keeping his eyes on hers, sucked the chocolate off, swirling his tongue around before slowly sliding her finger from his mouth.

Her mouth dropped open, her small chest lifting then falling as she took in a nervous breath. She blinked as if snapping out of the trance and stood up, closing the bakery box and abandoning it on the chair.

He let out a breath, attraction filtering through every pore in his skin. *Damn.*

Now facing the lavender beds, she leaned over them and took a deep breath. He walked over and stood behind her. Almost to herself, she said, "Lavender. Of course."

"Pardon?"

"You think I'd have figured that out by now. This is what you smell like all the time. I thought it was cologne or fabric softener..." She took another inhalation and exhaled, saying quietly, "God, that's been driving me crazy."

Directly behind her now, mere inches separating their bodies, he stroked his palm up the side of her arm, anchored the other on the lavender box next to her hand, and said into her ear, "How crazy?"

She answered with a soft moan, and he took the opportunity to nip her earlobe and suckle it gently. Abruptly, she spun within the cage of his arms. He tried to back away from her, so they could both steady themselves, but before he evened out his weight, her mouth crashed into his.

Connor was a big guy. It took a lot to knock him off balance. So when the delicate, slender blonde fused her lips with his and took another step closer, he was surprised to feel his equilibrium tip. Before he toppled backward, he grasped her hips for balance and instinctively squeezed his fingers into her flesh.

Damn. He knew he was right about her curves. They were there. Hips filled his palms. Palms he had to concentrate to keep from wrapping around her sweet little ass.

Unlike the kiss over the ice cream bowl, he felt her wet tongue tease the seam of his lips. He opened for her and let her in, tasting the chocolate frosting and the salt of her tears. Looping one arm around her narrow waist, he kissed her back, pressing her delicate curves against him. A groan sounded in the back of his throat when two small but perky breasts smashed into his chest.

She didn't stop there, nipping at his top lip and dragging her fingers along his scalp. He backed her against the lavender beds, needing to anchor her, to anchor himself, to get a handle on what she'd unexpectedly laid on him.

The faint taste of chocolate lingered on her tongue, and he made it his job to remove every last remnant of it with his. When her hands snaked up his chest, for a second he thought she might push him away. Then she molded her hands along his pecs and ran them down his torso until her fingernails teased along the hem of his shirt.

Right about now, he was having a hard time staying upright. *Hard* also being the perfect adjective for the head not located on his shoulders.

She drew away first, eyeing him through wide, dark pupils while he fought to regulate his breathing. Good God, this woman knew how to use her mouth.

He didn't have far to bend before he was taking her lips under the will of his again.

$\mathscr{C}$HAPTER 9

$\mathscr{H}$ad a kiss ever made her feel so good?

Not ever.

Connor knew the angle to tip his head so his lips welded to hers, and when he drew back to angle his head the other way, he grasped the back of her skull to tilt her so she went with him.

It was. *Amazing.*

Helping was that he tasted like a Devil Dog. Sweet and delicious. Also helping was the fact that he'd taken that huge bite of her favorite dessert to get her to smile. It'd been so long since a man made her smile.

Correction: since a man other than this man made her smile.

She didn't know what came over her. Maybe the memory of their first kiss. It wasn't like she'd forgotten. She'd thought about the ice cream kiss many, many times over the weeks, lamenting she hadn't gotten a French kiss.

She'd wondered just as many times what his tongue might feel like against hers.

Marvelous. As it turned out.

A grunt sounded across the room, followed by, "Uh, never mind."

Donovan. The man of the mansion. Inside, she felt herself wilting. Almost as humiliating as being caught by a parent.

Connor, still holding her head, pulled his mouth from hers and tightened his hold on her hip. "Don't move, Cupcake. I walked in on him and Sofe a number of times. Serves him right." Hand still warm against her scalp, he kept his eyes on hers.

From her peripheral, she watched Donovan cross long arms over his chest. "You didn't see anything."

Connor's lips lifted into an impish smile. "S'mores."

Faith turned her head to see Donovan blanch. That was new. His lips pressed into a firm line. "Find me when you're done." He stalked out of the room.

"Do you need to go?" she asked Connor who'd yet to release her.

"No." He pulled her close, pressing her body closer, which was saying something considering they were already touching from chest to thighs.

She'd started something here—something she realized, admittedly too late, that couldn't continue. Placing her hands on his chest, she applied a bit of pressure. "I shouldn't have...Um. I'm not really in a position to be kissing anyone."

"Not true," he said, his lips over hers. "You are in the perfect position to be kissed."

Before she could argue, his tongue traced her bottom

lip before he kissed her top lip. He continued for a while. Slow, drugging kisses using his tongue, his mouth. All the while keeping his hands off her erogenous zones.

Except she felt as if every part of her body was now an erogenous zone. Like her lower back, where his palm burned. Her hip bone where his other hand rested. Even her cheek where his nose brushed as he slanted his mouth over hers again.

"Mmm." That was her. Oh Lord, she was humming against his mouth. A breakdown. She was probably having some sort of breakdown caused by running into Cookie at the market.

"Connor," she managed to get out before his lips covered hers again.

He paused long enough for her to get out her request.

"I didn't come in here to make out with you."

He grinned, lips temptingly close.

"I mean it," she said, sounding very much like she didn't mean it. "I came in here to relax."

He leaned closer so his mouth moved on hers when he asked, "This isn't relaxing?"

Hell no. She was revved up, throbbing in places that had no business throbbing. But she couldn't tell him that. She couldn't say "yes," either, because they'd end up kissing some more.

Oh, that would be nice.

His mouth pursed again and she said, "Don't you want to know why I bought an entire box of empty calories?"

He backed off some and his eyebrows lowered.

She didn't want to talk about it, either, but talking about what happened was better than the alternative. Losing herself in his mouth.

"Not if it makes you sad to talk about it." He smiled. "Like you like this. Better than you crying."

Wow. That was sweet.

With a sigh, he released her. "Tell you what. I'll give you a break, then after you tell me your story I get one last kiss."

Him and his bets.

"No deal," she grumbled.

He pulled her closer. "Then I'll take as many as I want now."

Fingers over his lips, she acquiesced. "Fine. You get one. *Just* one."

"Tongue?" he teased.

How could she say no after she went at him tongue first a minute ago? "One kiss. With tongue."

Straightening, he gestured to the chairs. She sat primly on the edge of one and he handed over the bakery box before having a seat himself.

She pulled open the box and tasted a chocolate chip cookie. Sugar. Blessed sugar. Sugar never let her down. Sugar understood.

"I have been avoiding Abundance Market since I quit. You know that's how I came to work with Sofie, right? I walked away from my job. I couldn't stand being around Michael."

"Understandable," Connor growled.

"Seeing *Cookie* every day was not good for me, either. I guess that probably gives the both of them too much power."

His fingers sifted into her hair to brush the strands away from her face. "No, Cupcake. It makes you smart. There's nothing wrong with getting away from the person who is causing you pain. Nothing good comes from silently taking it."

Again she wondered what his story was. Everyone had a story; everyone had a background. Sometimes they were pretty stories, but most of the time they were stories of pain. The kind of pain that changes a person—makes them the person they end up becoming. She wondered what pain was locked away inside Connor's heart. But asking was too much like starting something deep, wasn't it?

He spoke, then, bringing her thoughts back on track. "So you went in there today." He dipped his chin at the box of treats. "And then you went to Sugar Hi."

"Coping mechanism."

"Death by sugar coma."

How was it he always made her smile? Even when she didn't want to. "I went in there to get wine. But instead I found Cookie...wearing the engagement ring Michael came to collect."

Connor's upper lip curled. "Should've thrown the bastard off the balcony when I had the chance."

She gripped his wrist, smiling bigger, because seriously, who knew he was this sweet? "Thank you."

His head dipped into a tight nod.

"The idea of a curse sounded silly when I first heard it, but after my failed engagement—after seeing a woman wearing the ring that used to be mine...Crazy as it sounds, I'm starting to think it's real."

"Curse?"

"Crazy."

"This I gotta hear."

She took a deep breath. Lavender and Connor. A heady mix. "My mother, Linda Shelby, is...eccentric."

"Famous, too," he supplied.

Yes, that, too. Twenty-five years ago, she wrote a sweeping historical romance followed by ten more books in the series. To readers, she was a legend. To her daughters, sometimes eccentric, sometimes an embarrassment, sometimes controlling. To love Linda Shelby was to accept the fact that she thought of herself first.

"She believes none of the women in our family get married because of a curse. Weddings have been planned, brides have been dressed and have walked as far as halfway down the aisle, but for one reason or the next, they never wed." Faith grunted. "She's nuts." Then she shook her head, feeling mean-spirited for talking about her mother that way. "I don't mean to sound ungrateful. I am happy for everything she's achieved. It makes me proud to see how she's made a life for her, and my sister Skylar and me."

"But…" His eyebrow lifted.

"*But*, life has always been about her. Yes, she gives Skylar and me money, and we never want for anything… Except for maybe normalcy."

"I can imagine. I hear she has several…male friends."

Faith cringed. "Boyfriends. And they are not independent in the least." She was *so* not going to talk about her mother's parade of male models. "Linda shies away from anything traditional. For example, this time of year. Thanksgiving." She paused for a moment. "I've never told anyone this before."

He leaned in, interested.

"I have never had a traditional Thanksgiving dinner."

"Not ever? Not when you dated? No friends inviting you over?"

She shook her head. "I always told them we went out of town for a big family reunion. Truth was, my mother would go out for sushi and give Skylar and me pizza money. She doesn't cook as it is, but Thanksgiving for her is too mainstream to participate in. Christmas, too."

"And your ex?"

She could tell he hadn't wanted to ask, but was flattered at the same time that he had.

"Michael's family lives in Minnesota. He invited me out every year, but I always got the idea he didn't really want me there. So, I let him have the reprieve, telling him to go without me and I'd spend the holiday with my mom and sister." She didn't, though. Skylar was usually with her boyfriend du jour and Linda was doing her own thing.

The excuse worked. Michael didn't have any interest in hanging around her mother or her sister, so year after year, he'd book his flight and leave to visit his family without her. That should have been a clue he wasn't a keeper. She'd been so blinded by the idea of breaking the curse—of being a part of something meaningful, she'd ignored the warning signs of him not being The One. She'd assumed once they were married, she'd visit his family, but until then...

It was an out, she realized, frowning. He'd been backing away from her for a long, long time.

"I can relate to not enjoying the holidays." Connor was trying to side with her. But he totally missed the mark with that assumption.

"It's not that I don't enjoy them," she argued, feeling her eyebrows draw in. "I love them. I watch all the old black-and-white movies: *Miracle on Thirty-fourth Street*, *It's a Wonderful Life*. I still keep a book of Norman Rockwell paintings under my bed. Tradition was something I always craved."

"You should be around my family. They'd cure you. Traditional to a fault." He laughed dryly. His eyes went to the plants around him. "This is my least favorite time of year. Everything dies. And it always reminds me of..." He trailed off.

"Reminds you of what?" she pressed after the silence lingered for more than a few seconds.

"Nothing." He stood abruptly, slid his hands into his back pockets. "You came in here to have a minute, collect yourself. I should give you that."

She stood, too, confused by the sudden change in atmosphere.

"Connor?"

He kicked the white box on the floor with the toe of his boot. "Done?"

"Yes."

He lifted the box and turned to leave the room. "I'd better see what Donovan wanted."

"What about your kiss?" she called after him.

He paused at the antique doors and gave her only his profile when he said, "Later."

* * *

"Let's have it. No making out in your mansion? That something only you and Sofie get to do?" Connor called to Donovan as he entered the great room.

He'd left Faith, and the promise of her mouth, to come in here to track down his cock-blocking friend. But it wasn't all his buddy's fault. It was the mention of "this time of year" that turned him off. This time of year was when he'd watched the horror unfold before he took his last leave and came home to the Cove permanently.

Nothing squashed libido faster than the stench of death he'd narrowly avoided—and the mother and child he'd failed so spectacularly.

"Something else entirely," Donny answered. Palms flat on the surface of the table, he was examining a stack of papers spread out in front of him.

Connor glanced over pages of details for houses in the area. Small houses, nothing close to the mansion's size. "Downsizing?"

After what he and Sofie went through to keep this place, he hated to think of them moving. This was Donny's childhood home. Not one with good memories, but in a way—in every way—his birthright.

"Nah, man," he answered with a smile. "Scampi would kill me. She loves Pate Mansion. These are comps for the cottage in the back."

Ah. The cottage. Connor knew it well. He and his buddy Anthony had been out there clearing brush this summer. Connor had also done some landscaping at Donny's request. The entire place would be lined with tulips come spring. He'd planted bulbs not long ago.

"You selling it?" He looked over the comps again.

"Thinking about it. If guests come to stay, not like they won't have any privacy in the mansion."

Good point. This place had thirty-some rooms. At least a dozen of those were bedrooms, at least ten bathrooms. Privacy was not an issue in *Chez Pate*.

"That back two acres could be parceled off, sold," Donny said. "Make a great home. Plenty of woods separating the properties, so whoever moved there wouldn't be in our way."

"That's true." Connor kept the brush cleared and the grass from getting out of control, but he hadn't touched the trees. There was plenty of coverage, and a private lane with a separate entrance from the road.

Donovan elbowed Connor and lifted his eyebrows.

Connor frowned. "What?"

"The cottage. What about you?"

"Me? I have a house."

"You have a crash pad." Donovan straightened from the table. "Not unlike the pad I crashed in for seven years in New York."

The idea of a home—or the fact that he'd failed to make one—made Connor uncomfortable. So he deflected. "You just don't want to bother listing it."

"True. I did try offering it as a space for Open Arms, but Ruby said they were better suited in modern digs."

"Yeah. Guess abused kids and solitude aren't really a good combo."

"No. They're not." Donny's mouth tightened and Connor felt the pull of his friend's dark emotions in the center of his chest. Donny had been to hell and back as a kid. Then sent himself to purgatory when he left here years ago. Determined to live out his penance in New York, Donny thought he didn't deserve any good in his life.

Until Sofie knocked him out with those bright green eyes and her killer curves, and Donny, who'd already loved and left her, fell ass over teakettle for the brunette. Best damn thing that had ever happened to his friend. He'd better keep the mansion for his girl, Connor thought to himself. She deserved nothing less.

"Anyway," Donny said, back on task. "I almost hate to ask you this, because I know you're a landscaper not a handyman…"

And his buddy knew how much Connor didn't enjoy being Mr. Fix-it. "You want me to make sure it's up to code," he guessed.

"I can double whatever you'd normally charge. You've worked on the mansion. You know my style. Know how to keep it in sync with what we have here. If we don't end up selling, maybe we can rent it or something." Eyes back on the comps, he sighed. "I don't know."

"Makes sense." Like he'd leave his friend high and dry. "I'll start this week."

Gratitude was shared with a curt nod. "Just had the electric turned on and the hot tub out back needs attention. Entire place needs winterizing, but there is a backup generator in case the power ever goes out." Donny continued talking about the details of the house while Connor logged them in his head.

Much as he hated to admit it, he was looking forward to splitting his time between working on the cottage and his landscaping business. This time of year was slow, and he was not good at sitting idle.

Busying his hands with the cottage was just the pastime he needed.

* * *

Sofie, hands filled with papers, looked up when Faith walked into the office. "Oh, hey. I'm so glad you're here. I need to talk to you about the toy drive I mentioned last week."

Maybe that's what Donny was talking to Connor about. It better be important for Connor to have sped out of the room and not kissed her again. Not that she was being petty.

The toy drive Sofie spoke of was her latest brainchild. She was holding a super-fancy Christmas soirée here at the mansion, to be attended by the wealthy residents in the Cove. Guests were asked to bring gifts for children without, and volunteers would wrap, deliver, and follow up with the families after the new year. Faith thought the charity was a perfect idea. And it gave her a chance to play Santa when her Santa moments were few and far between.

"Yes!" she exclaimed. "I am so excited."

Sofie's face fell.

Faith twisted her lips. "Aren't you? This is going to be so fun."

"I would be excited if we didn't have to go out of town for Thanksgiving." She chewed her lip and gave a forlorn look at her computer screen. "Maybe I shouldn't go."

Faith came to the edge of Sofie's desk and pressed her palms into the wood. "You have to go. This is Donny's family. Essentially." The members of Donovan's actual family, who had left him this mansion, were no longer alive—not that they were worth considering anyway. "This is your chance to spend a holiday with your future family." She thought back to what she'd confessed to Connor in the greenhouse about her never having a Thanksgiving. Then she thought about Connor's reaction to the holidays—the opposite of her excitement. "How is Connor taking the news that he will be preparing for Christmas at the mansion?"

Sofie's confused expression said it all. Then she said it out loud. "What do you mean?"

With a sigh, Faith turned and sat at her desk across from her friend's. "Connor said he didn't care for the holidays. That his family loved them, but they weren't for him."

Concern dented Sofie's brow. "Really? Every time I have ever come to him for help with an event, especially if it's a holiday, he has taken it on without complaint."

That sounded like Connor. He put others first more often than not. He put Faith first, too...like when he stayed at her house, getting little-to-no sleep so he could catch the man—the *amoebae*—who was trying to get in through her patio door.

"Do you know what happened to him? Anything about Connor's past?" Concerned that she sounded as if she was prying, Faith covered with, "I mean, I'm just curious... About him."

"Mm-hmm." Sofie smiled a knowing little smile. "Yeah, I heard how 'curious' you were a few minutes ago when Donny walked in on you two. I have to say, I'm a little shocked you're visiting Cougartown." She winked.

"Cougar...what?"

"Connor." Sofie relinquished her papers and leaned back in her office chair, smugly folding her hands over her waist. "You know he's a lot younger than you. And I know how you feel about bedding younger men because of your cougar mom."

Sweat beaded Faith's brow. She hadn't given much thought to how old or young Connor was. Now that her friend was teasing her, however, she found "denial" was not just a river in Egypt but a river she'd like to float down, blissfully unaware of any facts or figures.

The best way to deter her friend would be to bring up one thing Sofie had never shared.

"Tell me," Faith said, a smug smile of her own as she crossed her arms over her chest. "What did Connor mean when he said something about you and Donovan and s'mores?"

Sofie's smile erased from her face. She sat up, fluffed her mahogany hair, and cleared her throat. "We were talking about Connor's past. What did you want to know?"

She would have to get that story out of her bestie eventually.

"What's his damage?" Faith leaned her elbows on her own desk and waited for a story. She didn't get much of one.

"Well...to be honest, I don't know a ton." Serious now, Sofie raised her eyebrows and looked to the ceiling in thought. "I know that he was deployed for about four years, that he finished his tour of duty before returning to the Cove for good. Donny said he first went overseas after a split from his girlfriend. But he didn't say much else about her. I guess it was pretty painful for him."

Hmm. Faith considered this. A painful split from a girlfriend. She wondered if he was engaged as well, or maybe if he was cheated on. That would explain his reaction to Michael, the dirty, rotten, cheating bastard.

"I get that." Faith reached for a pen and drew squiggles on her planner. "After catching Michael and Cookie together I felt like leaving the country." Which brought her to her next confession. She blew it out on a breath, hoping the speed with which she announced it might cut through the pain. "They're engaged."

Nope. Still hurt. She forced herself to hold her chin up.

"No!" Mouth dropped open, Sofie resembled a gaping carp.

"Yes." It also occurred to Faith that she had gone to Connor first, not Sofie. What did that mean? She decided to float down her river of denial on that topic as well. "Guess why he wanted the ring back?"

"What! He most certainly did not propose using the very same wedding ring!"

"He most certainly did." Faith filled Sofie in about her trip to Abundance Market, the way the oranges rolled off the display, and the way she had found Cookie wearing Michael's grandmother's wedding band. "She has a blue streak in her hair."

Clapping her hand over her mouth, Sofie's eyes crinkled at the corners in a concerted effort not to laugh.

"Brave," Faith kept her expression deadpan. "If my name was Cookie and I was a monster, I would not dye my hair blue."

Sofie lost the battle and threw her head back and laughed. Faith joined her. It felt good to laugh. Even if it was over a blue-haired Cookie monster. They sobered a minute later.

"I needed that." Faith swiped a finger under her eye to catch a stray tear. "So. Now that's done. Like, *done* done. There's no going back after he tried to commit a burglary and then got engaged to The Other Woman."

Not that she had seriously considered taking him back last year, but for a second, she had begun to believe they could exist as friends. He'd proven to be as bad, maybe worse, than he was back then. The friendship door? Officially closed. Closed, locked, armed with a security system.

And guarded by an ex-military landscaper with deliciously large biceps.

She smiled to herself. Hey, it was her fantasy. May as well make it worth fantasizing about.

"Anyway," Faith said, done talking about the topic. "When do you and Donny leave?"

"Two days." Sofie studied the piles on her desk. "I'm going to have to take some of these things with me."

"No, you are going to have to leave me really good notes. I will take care of whatever needs taken care of here so you can enjoy your vacation."

"It's your holiday, too." Sofie rolled her eyes. "I mean...as much as your mother does holidays."

"I forgot you knew all my secrets." Faith should have thought to exclude Sofie from the people she had "never told" about her Thanksgiving past. Sofie was her best friend, had been since they worked together at the Wharf. Her best friend knew her better than she knew herself at this point.

"Like you could've kept them hidden from me for long."

She was right. And Sofie had Faith's back. Which also meant Faith had hers. "Leave good notes. And tell me everything you need for the toy drive. I'm not going to let you go to New York to spend the holiday relaxing and have work hanging over your head while you're there."

"Thank you." She could see Sofie meant it, and trusted her, which was just as important.

"Besides, Thanksgiving is only one day, it's not like I'm missing out on much."

While Sofie went on about how true that was and the types of foods she was better off not eating if she did miss a Thanksgiving dinner, Faith smiled politely. Because she did not believe what she had just said—not really. Thanksgiving wasn't only one day to Faith. Thanksgiving was the culmination of all the days that came before it, all the days that came after it, and led up to the holiday of ultimate togetherness: Christmas.

She'd missed out on so much. A dart of pain stabbed her in the chest. With effort, she brought her mind back to present, and paid attention to the notes she was taking on her planner. Writing down everything Sofie said, she vowed again to make her best friend's holiday as stress-free as possible.

If Faith wasn't able to have a Thanksgiving for herself, she may as well gift her friend with one.

CHAPTER 10

*W*ith Donovan and Sofie out of town, the house felt big and lonely. Yes, Connor was there on occasion, but since he had stopped dogging her every step, she hadn't seen as much of him. Which meant he hadn't collected on the kiss she promised him the day in the greenhouse.

Which bothered her.

And it shouldn't.

Faith left the office and headed through the house in the direction of the kitchen. She'd been personally e-mailing invitees to the toy drive and it had taken all of her brainpower to remember to change the name at the top each time she copied/pasted the body of the message, as well as remembering to include a personal note about why the person was being invited.

Eyes blurry, the only thing she could think about was the Sugar Hi box with two frosted carrot cake cupcakes inside. A stray from her traditional Devil Dog, but it was autumn and autumn called for carrot cake.

She came to a halt at the threshold of the kitchen, her breath clogging in her throat.

Part of it was shock over the fact that Connor was leaning over the countertop inhaling one of her cupcakes. The other part, and the part she was having trouble reconciling, was the fact that there was a tear beneath one of the pockets of his jeans, and the slash of skin she was currently staring at was his bare ass.

He stood, chewing and smiling with his lips closed. She knew because she hastily redirected her gaze to his face. The way he licked the frosting off the corner of his mouth and lifted his brow suggested he may have caught her eyeballing something she shouldn't.

"Tore them on a nail on the fence this morning." He turned to look over his shoulder, splitting the tear with his fingers to show her a faint red scratch on one chiseled butt cheek. "Hurt like a bitch." His eyes found hers and he gave her a sly smile. "Don't suppose you'd be willing to patch me up."

She choked on her laughter, shaking her head for effect. "I don't think so," she said, trying to sound disgusted and not turned on.

His smile erased as his brow went down like she'd hurt his feelings. "You would deny me medical care in my moment of need?"

Flustered, she stepped past him and snatched the small white box off the counter, determined to change the subject. "I hope you know you owe me a cupcake."

"*Cupcake*, I took that in payment for the kiss you never gave me."

So he didn't forget.

"You'd rather have a carrot cupcake than a kiss?" Her pulse pounded against her neck. She knew which one she would prefer, and hoped she was doing a good job hiding it.

"Hmm..." He made a show of craning his neck to look at the remaining cupcake in the bottom of the box. "It was a pretty good cupcake."

Her mouth opened in argument, but the argument never came. And the reason it never came was because Connor covered her lips with his, launching his tongue into her mouth. She tasted sugar, cinnamon, and nutmeg from the frosting, and his mouth, which tasted wonderful because it tasted like *him*. The smell of lavender filled her senses, that earthy, spicy smell mingling in her nostrils and making her lean into him. Cupping the back of his neck, she tilted her chin, continuing their sparring session with fervor.

Noses bumped, his unshaven chin scraped her jaw, and his hands—his big, manly, rough hands—grasped her at the waist and pulled her flush against him.

This went on until finally, she had to pull back to inhale or suffocate. Not a bad way to go, she'd admit. Now she was panting and trying to recalibrate her brain cells, which had apparently oozed right out of her ears since Connor put his mouth on hers.

He looked as dazed as she did for a second before his smile snapped into place. "Nope. That was much better than the cupcake."

Since she was warmed by his compliment as well as that toe-curling kiss, she laughed. Light and effervescent, the giggle rolled around her chest for a few seconds. She hadn't stepped away from him yet, so she rested her arms on his big shoulders and looked him in the eye, which was not hard to do considering she had on high heels today.

"And here I thought you forgot. Since then your mind seems to have been elsewhere."

His gaze fettered to the side, his face going a little too serious for the light moment. He recovered quickly, flashing her a smile that was a bit disingenuous.

"Been busy." He straightened, but his hands stayed on her hips, warming her skin through her skirt. "Want to see what I've been busy doing?" He tipped his head in the direction of the utility room standing behind him.

She felt her teeth scrape her bottom lip as she looked in the direction of the washer and dryer. He meant the door leading beyond that room. Where he kept his greenhouse and the patented lavender that had soaked into her brain—a smell she would forever associate with Connor McClain.

"I don't know. The last time we were in there…" she started. He ducked his head and kissed her lips, just a peck, and embarrassingly enough, when he pulled back she found herself leaning into him, lips pursed, wanting more.

"Yeah, I'm not really seeing any argument about what happened in there."

There was part of her warning she should probably stop kissing him altogether. Granted, he didn't seem to be throwing her onto the ground and devouring her; it was only kissing. But only kissing would lead to more.

Her eyes traveled the expanse of his sure shoulders. She wanted more. Was it possible to have more without having "all"? Because if more was an option, she was *so* in. She'd mentioned before to Sofie and Charlie how she had no interest in permanence. That her next relationship would be a one-night stand. She had even joked that the man standing in front of her now might be the one-night *standee*.

She wasn't in any position to be in a relationship. He knew that. And he hadn't argued the fact when she said it before. Sure he told her she was in the "perfect position to be kissed," but he hadn't said anything about them being anything to one another. They were friends. They had now kissed three times, give or take a few small smooches. And they were still friends. She didn't feel an overwhelming urge to put a label on it.

So she wouldn't.

Tugging her hand, he led her through the utility room, down the hall, and into the indoor greenhouse. Willingly, she followed. He popped open the door, and Faith pressed a hand to her chest, her mouth dropping open in awe of what was before her.

Poinsettias. Poinsettias everywhere. "Oh my gosh, they're beautiful."

"I cleaned out several local florists. Takes ten weeks to grow them from scratch. Didn't have that kind of time since the toy drive is in three weeks. Although"— he dropped her hand and walked over to one of the plants, gingerly stroking the red leaves—"I couldn't risk waiting until the week before the drive and not being able to find any."

"How long do they stay in bloom?"

"Typically? Month, month-and-a-half, longer if you baby them. Which I have been."

She'd bet. He was good at caring for things. People. *Her.*

"It's seventy-eight degrees in here, and needs to stay right around that. Basically, if you are comfortable, the poinsettias are comfortable." He gestured around the room to the grow lights, a fan blowing gently, and a large white square thing she assumed was a heater.

She couldn't help smiling at the idea of this big, rugged man pampering these delicate red-leaved plants. She'd never kept a plant alive in her life. She didn't have a green thumb, more like a black one. Assisting plants to their imminent demise... like a horticultural grim reaper.

"How is it that you are a complete badass, who carries a gun, hurdles my balcony, protects me from my ex-fiancé, and yet you have a gentle enough touch to care for dozens of fragile plants?" she asked.

The heat in his eyes intensified as he prowled over to her, his big body moving fluidly. He was a case study in opposites. Hard but gentle, big but agile.

"That sounded like an offer," he said when he stopped in front of her.

Sputtering, she tried to laugh that off. "Hello? Ego. I was paying you a compliment. I didn't mean anything more."

He crossed his arms and tipped his chin up, looking down his nose at her. "Oh yeah? Your 'compliment' included the words *badass*, *protects*, *gentle*, and *touch*. Are you honestly telling me none of those descriptors dampened your panties?"

On the inside, his brash words shocked her, and yeah, okay, did in fact dampen her... well... whatever. On the outside, she gave him a smug look and offered a smooth comeback.

Folding her arms much in the same way he had folded

his, she said, "Well, I would ask you if I had the same effect on you, but you don't wear underpants."

The zinger didn't make him laugh or argue. He came closer. Arms still crossed, he leaned down and got in her face. "That sounds like an offer, too."

She thought she might get a kiss again, but he straightened away from her, his lips twitching. "Need you to do something for me."

"Ohh-kay." She had no idea if he was going to stick to the topic or veer from it. There were plenty of things she could think of to do "for" him, and none of them would require underpants.

"Come to Thanksgiving dinner at my family's house."

Her eyebrows rose. Last thing in the world she'd expected him to say to her.

"I may not be into the holidays like I used to be, Cupcake, but everyone should experience a traditional turkey day. You've missed out for a while now. That's not right. My mom would love the company. She makes enough to feed twice as many people as are there anyway."

"I couldn't..." What she *couldn't* do was finish her sentence. Already, her mind was whirring with images she'd seen on television and movies, paintings, and advertisements. Dressed turkey. Beautiful side dishes. Family and friends gathering to pray, laugh, and share stories of holidays past.

"Not only can you, you will."

"Oh, I will, will I?" She narrowed her eyes at him, hoping to convey defiance, but in reality downplaying a deep, dark longing left over from her childhood.

"Thursday, six sharp." His eyes cut down her shirt and skirt combo and back up. When he reached her face, his eyes were heavy-lidded with desire. "It's pretty casual around there, but I gotta tell you, I like you in a dress."

Now she was grinning. "You do, do you?"

"Legs, Cupcake." Then he winked and left her standing among many, many potted poinsettias. As she approached one of them to check the dirt as Connor had done, she felt a small smile curl her lips. Finally, she would get to experience a real family dinner. The idea made the pit of her stomach ache, and her heart beat extra fast. Her first real Thanksgiving.

And she would be spending it with Connor McClain.

* * *

Downright assaulting cold air kicked off the lake in the winter. This being the end of November, Thanksgiving evening was no exception.

Connor offered to pick her up at her place since she hadn't worked at the mansion today. The day off was at Sofie's insistence. When Faith called to ask a quick question about a forthcoming event, she'd also mentioned going to Connor's family's house for dinner. Sofie had insisted— well, first she'd shrieked "*squee!*" then she'd insisted—on the day off.

So far Faith spent most of her day planning what to wear. Shallow, maybe, but if Linda Shelby taught her one thing, it was she only had one chance to make a first impression. Connor had said to dress casually but he liked her in a skirt. Since it was about fifty degrees outside, she was not excited to wear her new charcoal gray skirt... unless she paired it with the thick pair of plum-colored tights she'd dragged out of her drawer.

Her shower had been an ordeal and a half. She applied a hair mask to get her extra fine locks to lay smooth and soft, and then spent an hour blowing out her hair with a dryer set on low to ensure *smooth and soft* lasted the entire evening.

Undergarments were easy. She'd invested quite a lot of money in her underthings over the years. Pretty panty sets with matching bras were her staple. Another lesson from Mom: no matter what, if a girl looks good under her clothes, she feels good.

She pulled on a pair of pink lace panties and matching bra before consulting her closet one final time. She had laid out the skirt, cream-colored sweater, and tights, but now, in spite of shaving her legs to smooth perfection, she was not feeling this particular ensemble.

She hung the outfit back in her closet and debated on dress pants next. But this wasn't a family meeting. A pair of distressed denim draped over a hanger and she tugged those off, choosing an olive green button-down shirt with a faint floral print on it. Once she had that on, she looped a leopard print scarf around her neck and chose gold hoops for her ears and one ring, also gold, made to resemble a belt, complete with buckle. Her waist-length green-brown peacoat with large brass buttons and knee-high brown flat-heeled boots capped off her wardrobe.

A last look in the mirror had her feeling mighty pleased with herself. Maybe because on the outside, she looked comfortable and casual, but beneath she was a sexy siren. Linda Shelby was right.

Yet again.

She thought of the curse, but only for one fleeting second. Didn't matter how cursed she was, her choice not to get married was an easy one to make after Michael had added his nuts to Cookie's dough.

She snorted at her lame joke, then her smile faded as it often did when she thought of the way things had happened. Once, Faith told Sofie she wondered if she said yes to Michael's proposal because she was curious to see if the curse was real—a sort of test. When she considered it now, it seemed true. But in her gut, in the pit of her heart, she knew it wasn't. She'd been overtaken by the notion of someone wanting her. Wanting her forever.

No man had wanted her mother forever. Faith had a hazy recollection of her father, and her mother claimed not to know his whereabouts. He could be in Tahiti for all Faith knew. Albuquerque. Mars. He was, according to Linda, "a man who couldn't take the pressure of being with a woman who was so independent." And in that moment, standing looking at her peacoat and her carefully selected outfit, Faith wondered if that mantra hadn't been pounded into her brain from birth.

In an effort to not be left behind by a man, had she tried to be less independent than her mother? Had that kept her from becoming a lawyer, or a doctor, or a CEO? Was the reason she'd frittered away her twenties as a waitress, bartender, and clerk in countless retail stores in the Cove to appear more approachable?

No, she decided, getting angry at the direction of her thoughts. Not everyone was born knowing what they wanted to be when they grew up. She learned a lot as the beer and wine buyer for Abundance Market, things that had helped her immensely as Sofie's assistant. (Partner, Sofie would argue.) Faith enjoyed what she did, loved where she worked, and was glad her best friend could count on her when she was away.

The sound of a key in her door made her smile at her reflection as chills chased down her arms. Of course he'd let himself in. She liked the sound of him letting himself in.

She strode to the door and keyed in her alarm code to unarm the system. Connor was dressed in his signature style of jeans and a tight, dark-colored henley. He wore a jacket, old bomber-style brown leather, and a pair of laced boots in brown as well. He looked . . . wow. Incredible. Sure and strong and casual and damned sexy.

He pulled the key from the lock, and the smile that found his face was like the rest of him: warm and genuine.

"I went with jeans," she explained needlessly. And maybe because this suddenly felt like a date. A very intimate, meeting-the-parents kind of date.

"Nice." Given the way his eyes traveled the expanse of the denim to the boots and back up again, she guessed he approved. "Ready to go?"

She nodded, unfolded her hands, and reached for her purse dangling on the back of her kitchen chair. The bag was a wide-strapped leather, rust-orange with gold metal accents. Matched her fall outfit perfectly.

As she went to slip it onto her shoulder, he took it from her hand and dropped it onto the back of the chair. Then his hands were on her jaw, tilting her face up to meet his.

"'Bout to ruin your lipstick," he announced before he smashed his lips into hers. She put her hand over his, her other clutching the cold leather of his coat, and kissed him. He smelled of lavender, and a faint but noticeable cologne, one fragrance complementing the other.

When he pulled back, there was a slight pink sparkle to his lips. She wiped the glitter away with her thumb.

"Sprinkles," she said, her voice choked with lust.

"Sprinkles." He brushed the side of her lips as well, holding her eyes in heated challenge. She wondered how this would go tonight, him and her, his family...

As if he read her mind, he said, "Everyone knows I'm bringing you. They assume we're dating. I never bring women home."

"Never?" She gulped.

"Not since Maya. Haven't told you about her yet."

She flinched, even though she didn't mean to.

"You know?" His eyebrows raised in interest.

"I asked Sofie...about you. She didn't know much." Her lips stabbed her teeth, worried she had invaded his privacy.

His chin dipped in simple agreement. "It's not a secret, Cupcake. I'll tell you about her sometime."

Fair enough. But there was a question she had for him. "How do you want me to behave tonight? I mean, around you. If they think we're dating, or have been."

He shrugged big shoulders. "However you like."

She took her hands from his body to fold them together again. "I didn't know if I should try not to touch you, or..." Or if his family would expect her to cling to him.

"You feel like touching me, Cupcake, touch me. That rule's the same wherever we are." He grinned, and the warm lighting in her living room made the traces of red stand out in the dark blond stubble dotting his jaw.

And what about kissing him? She didn't ask. Surely, she could get through one dinner—a family *holiday* dinner—without sucking face. But as his firm lips closed in to steal one last short kiss before they left, she wondered if maybe she couldn't.

CHAPTER 11

Outside Evelyn and Roger McClain's two-story clapboard, Faith wrung her hands, gloved fingers laced together in what appeared to be nervousness.

Connor figured nerves were to be expected in this situation. Faith had a tight, close circle of friends from what he'd seen so far. Her family was just her mom and sister, and whatever younger man her mother was courting at the moment.

Eccentric did not describe his family in the least. Traditional, now there was a word. Simple. Well-meaning, but open-minded. His two older sisters were overprotective and fussy, his mother was almost as manly as his father, and Roger was a real man's man, who drank Budweiser from a can and preferred fish on Fridays.

Faith chewed on her lip and bounced on her toes as Connor lifted a fist to knock. Cute that she was so anxious. He couldn't resist teasing her more.

Lowering his arm without knocking, he said, "Fair warning. My mom can be cold at first. Takes a while for her to warm up to people. When you meet her, it's best to shake her hand, and politely thank her for the invite. After dinner, she may engage you in conversation, but at first she'll watch you like a hawk."

Her breath was visible in the cool night air when she blew out the word, "Okay."

He lifted his fist and solemnly knocked. "Here for you, Cupcake."

Faith nodded, serious, and more nervous than before. He almost felt bad about it. Until his mother appeared in the doorway. Then, he didn't.

Evelyn McClain threw open the door, apron on, flour in her hair, and a huge smile on her face. Gleaming golden eyes latched on to him, and she leaped onto the porch and hugged him against her, thumping him hard on the back.

"Hi, Mom."

"Five pies. We have *five pies*." She held him at arm's length. "Have you ever in your life?"

He held out an arm in introduction. "Faith Garrett."

She turned to Faith and he watched as his date stood taller and extended a hand. "Nice to meet you, Mrs. McClain."

His mother's head jerked on her neck. "Nice to meet—" She huffed, then clasped Faith to her bosom. "Nice to meet me! You're the prettiest thing I've ever seen!"

Faith's eyes were wide, her chin on Evelyn's shoulder while his mother patted her gruffly and continued to tell her how gorgeous every part of her outfit was. Finally, Faith caught on, and gave him the evil eye. Like he expected, her smile curled into a treacherous warning that said she'd get him back for that.

He looked forward to it.

Evelyn held her at arm's length as well, admiring her some more. Connor couldn't blame his mom. Where Faith was concerned, there was a lot to admire. "We are so, so glad to have you here, Faith. And please, call me Lyn." She turned and bustled back to her kitchen, stating again there were "five pies."

Connor took Faith's hand and led her inside.

"Any other lies you'd like to tell me before I go in?" she asked.

Smiling, he shook his head, glad he brought her. Glad he insisted she come. "No, just that one. My sisters are the same, but they'll be curious. Like, twenty-questions curious. Only answer what you want. They can be... aggressive."

"Aggressive?" Her steps faltered in the foyer as he shut the front door.

"In a nice way."

* * *

Rapid-fire conversation shot around the McClain dinner table at a rate Faith could scarcely follow. First there was the prayer, led by Roger and chimed in by Evelyn. Then Connor's sisters got the giggles during. Faith sat between Dixie, the oldest—her brown hair like her father's and golden eyes like her mother's—and Connor, holding their hands over the table. Her hand was thrust up, then down when Dixie snorted.

Evelyn—Lyn, she'd insisted—shushed her eldest and

Dixie pulled it together, but Faith and Connor's other sister, Kendra, were pressing their lips tight to keep more laughter at bay. Kendra resembled her father, with her dark eyes and pronounced nose, but her hair was a fairer shade of Connor's, blond hair she wore in an asymmetrical cut at her chin.

Dixie's style was professional, her dark brown hair pulled into a tight ponytail, her expression and manner suggesting she took *no shit* from *nobody*.

And the food. *Oh-em-gee*, the food!

Lyn basted the turkey in what Faith guessed was a bath of butter and heaven. Angels' tears themselves had to be responsible for the moistest piece of poultry she had ever put on her tongue. The entire table could have been a scene from the Norman Rockwell book she'd kept under her bed. A colorful tablecloth and cloth napkins, fine china and the "good silver" as Dixie kept referring to it as she rounded the table and put down place settings.

Every side dish was as beautifully presented as it was delicious. And there were a lot of them: mashed potatoes, sweet potatoes, green bean casserole with crunchy onions on top, Nan's (their grandmother's) cranberry sauce, and stuffing with loads of sage and thyme, all immaculately plated and, shortly after, efficiently devoured. What wasn't consumed was packed away in individual containers to be sent home with everyone.

Then there was the matter of the five pies.

Apple, traditional pumpkin, rhubarb, chocolate silk, and even though it didn't fit the season, tart lemon meringue. Faith soon learned that the lemon pie was for Connor, who preferred it over the others. She had a small slice of the apple and rhubarb, and yes, even the chocolate. Connor fed her a bite of the lemon, which drew curious glances from his sisters. Since the pumpkin wouldn't fit into her stuffed belly, Lyn promised to send a few slices home with her. Surprisingly, there was enough pumpkin left as everyone else had either skipped dessert (appalling!) or partook in the chocolate silk and lemon meringue.

After dishes Faith was told she wasn't allowed to do—not by Connor this time but Lyn, wonder where he got that from?—she wandered into the family room where a football game she couldn't care less about played on the TV, and Dixie's sons, Drew and Corran played with a toy racetrack Dixie had brought from home. Her husband, Tad, sat watching TV with one eye on his boys.

"You survived. I'm impressed," he said as she walked in.

She chuckled, bypassing the boys crashing their cars into a set of coasters in a stand they'd pulled from the end table, and sat on the opposite end of the couch with Tad, a glass of wine in hand.

"Well at least they let me drink," she joked.

He smiled over at her. Tad Finlay was of average height, red hair hinting at an Irish or Scottish heritage (she was afraid to ask which and inadvertently offend him), and he was attractive in a way that was very different from Connor. A lawyer, Tad was less rugged. He and Dixie lived in Pennsylvania and had been married seven years. Drew, their oldest at six, and Corran, their "last" according to Dixie, was four.

"The McClains are incredible." He lifted an auburn brow at her. "Overwhelming at first, but incredible."

She let out a breath and realized she'd been anxious most of the evening. "They're great..."

He lifted his beer can. "But overwhelming."

She tapped his can with her wineglass, wondering if he was overwhelmed for a similar reason she was. For years, life had been Linda, Skylar, and Faith. Sure, there had been a rotating door of various boyfriends for Mom, and sometimes Skylar, but for the most part their family was small, fairly quiet, and kept to themselves.

After a few hours at the McClain house, Faith determined this was not the case. As evidenced by what happened next.

Dixie blew into the room, a force to be reckoned with like her mother. After a quick check on her redheaded boys, she latched on to Faith and dragged her out of the family room. "Borrowing her," she announced to Tad.

Tad did not argue. Neither did Faith, hustling out of the room and concentrating on not spilling her wine.

She was led through the house, up the stairs, past the bedrooms, where they met Kendra who was standing in the middle of the hallway, arms stretched overhead. She pulled the string and dropped folding ladder-style stairs leading to the attic.

"Welcome to the McClain sisters' Thanksgiving tradition." Kendra smiled, then flicked her eyes over at Dixie. "Even though technically, she is a Finlay."

Dixie Finlay led the way into the attic, followed by Faith, and last, Kendra. Then Kendra pulled up the attic stairs, which would've ensconced them in darkness if Dixie hadn't been across the room flicking a switch. Twinkle lights strewn around the room lit the space in pale light with long shadows. It was warm up here, with vents blowing heat into the storage area, telling her this was more of a spare room than an attic. From what Faith could see most of what was up here was from when the girls were young—boxes marked BARBIES and KENDRA'S BOOKS among the others.

"We don't bring all of Connor's girlfriends up here, you know," Kendra said.

"Not that we've met many," Dixie chimed in.

Faith wanted to argue she wasn't his girlfriend, but she remembered him saying the family had assumed as much, and she didn't want to cause any trouble. "So I'm lucky?"

"Remains to be seen," Kendra answered, reaching behind her. She came out with the package, but Faith couldn't tell what it was. Ken tore apart the cardboard in the plastic covering, and held up four V-shaped... somethings.

"Wishbones." Dixie took one and handed it to Faith. "Synthetic. Our old tradition included the actual wishbone from the turkey. But there is only one, and you have to dry it out overnight or it won't snap properly. So I found these about ten years ago, and ever since then, we get more than one snap, and this year we are sharing this tradition with you."

She examined the piece of breakable plastic in her hand. Shaped like a wishbone. Clever.

"Typically," Kendra said, tossing the package behind her, "you would wish on a wishbone. We don't do that."

"No we do not." Dixie accepted her wishbone. "We play a game we like to call You Wish You Didn't Have to Tell the Truth. Because after you split the wishbone, the person with the biggest half gets to make the loser tell the truth about whatever topic is on the table."

Kendra nodded in unity. "You are probably going to want to win. Because you realize our questions are going to be about Connor when we win."

Faith looked at the wishbone in her hand, trying to think if she had any secrets about him she couldn't share.

"To be diplomatic, and because you are new here, we are giving you two wishbones. One to snap with each of us. So you actually get an extra chance to demand the truth from us." Dixie gestured to herself, then to Kendra.

Kendra handed over the last of the fake turkey bones and Faith accepted it with reluctance. She didn't want to play this game at all.

"Ken and I will go first," Dixie stated. Kendra held up her wishbone and Dixie grabbed the other half. They counted to three, and then snapped it in two.

Dixie won. "Perfect."

"Crap."

"You know how lucky I am in this game, Ken, you are just going to have to take your medicine." Dixie smiled a pretty but evil smile that belonged on a Disney villain. This was the side of her that scared Faith a little bit.

"What really happened between you and that guy, Grady?" Dixie asked, eyes narrowing to intimidating slits.

"Can you be more specific?" But Kendra appeared to be stalling, more than she needed Dixie to expound.

"After you dated him for three weeks, and handed over your virginity without a second thought," Dixie stated plainly, "did you come to your senses and dump him, or did he leave you?"

Ken's mouth twisted. "You have been saving this question for a lot of years."

"I am a patient woman."

And scary, Faith thought again.

Kendra took a deep breath and slid a glance over at Faith. "Sorry you have to hear this." Then to Dixie she said, "Grady left me. He said I was too inexperienced, and he liked that red-haired girl who was two years older than him. You know, the one who shared our bus stop in elementary school."

With a gasp, Dixie said, "Britney Fuller?"

"Yup."

Dixie shook her head. "Obviously, Grady was an idiot. Britney was nasty."

And with that they moved to the next wishbone. Dixie and Kendra gripped either side of the V. This win went to Kendra. Kendra asked the truth about a math test from the tenth grade that Dixie always claimed she aced. Dixie accused Kendra of also saving up a good question, and admitted she cheated on the test.

"I knew it! If Mom ever found out..." Kendra paused and looked over at Faith. "Oh, we should tell you, Mom will never find out. And Connor will never find out. They know we are up here and might know what we are doing, but they also know what happens in Wishbone Attic stays in Wishbone Attic."

"Good news for you." Dixie gestured at one of Faith's wishbones. "When you lose and I get the truth out of you."

Great. Here went nothing.

"One, two, three," Faith counted and Dixie pulled, and won, her half the bigger one.

She held it up in triumph. "I don't want sex details about my brother, but I want to know what you two have done. Kiss? Sex? Do you have a casual affair going? Have you talked about marriage? Children? You know, that kind of thing."

Dixie Finlay did not beat around the bush, as it turned out. Faith shook her head. "That sounds like more than one question to me."

"Smarter than Maya," Kendra stated.

Dixie chuckled. "Not a compliment."

Connor had mentioned Maya, but only briefly. Now Faith's interest was newly piqued. "Who is this Maya I've heard about?"

"What have you heard?" Kendra narrowed her eyes.

"Connor mentioned her, but didn't say much," Faith answered.

"He mentioned her?" Dixie exchanged glances with her sister. "That's impressive."

"Guess you'll have to win our break to find out," Kendra said with a quick lift of her eyebrows.

"But I didn't get my answer yet," Dixie interrupted, and Faith got the idea she was never one to be deterred. She tapped her chin. "Hmm. Now to narrow down to one question."

Faith fiddled with the broken wishbone, half worried Dixie might ask what base Connor had gotten to, or if either of them had done anything below the waist. Hard telling with her. But, Faith could rest in the knowledge that other than a few incredibly hot kisses, she and Connor hadn't done anything.

Dixie's eyes popped wide. She'd decided on a question. "Has Connor spent the night at your house and/or have you spent the night at his house?"

Oh no, the one question she had to answer honestly

would make them sound like they had done way more together than they had. She bit her lip, deciding how much to say.

"Interestingly enough, he has spent a few nights at my house, and I have spent one night at his." Faith held up a finger when Dixie's eyebrows crawled up her forehead. "But we have not had sex."

"You got a bonus answer anyway," Kendra pointed out.

"Maybe I should reiterate you have to tell the truth in this place," Dixie said, gesturing around the dimly lit space. "We do not take kindly to liars around here, Faith Garrett." She leaned forward and whispered conspiratorially, "If that is your real name…"

"It's the truth." Briefly, she filled in his sisters about how long she and Connor had known each other, about her ex-fiancé trying to break into her apartment, about Connor's insistence to stay at her house, about her holing up at his apartment for a night while he ran a mysterious Friday errand.

"That sounds like him," Kendra remarked. "So protective."

"He likes you," Dixie stated in the same sure tone she used with everyone—like Connor liking Faith was the simplest, most obvious of truths.

Kendra held up her hand. "My turn."

Faith counted off and broke the plastic bone, thrilled when she ended up with the bigger half.

"Oh boy, I bet I can guess what's coming." Kendra smirked, but didn't seem the least bit upset by ratting out her brother. "Ask me anything; Connor is an open book."

Dixie's cackle suggested this might only be true in Wishbone Attic.

Now for Faith's question. Did she want to know more about Maya? Or about where Connor disappeared to on Friday nights?

Since he'd promised to tell her about Maya in his own time, she went with, "Where does Connor go on Fridays? I know he has some sort of mission, an appointment he will not miss."

Dixie went uncharacteristically quiet. Kendra pressed her lips together as if deciding how much to say.

"You have to tell the truth," Faith reminded gently.

"Easy answer, but not a very easy explanation." Dixie tipped her chin. "Might want to refill your glass."

"Oh, I didn't—" Faith started, but Kendra produced a bottle of red wine from behind her back. She refilled Faith's glass, and hers, then Dixie's. Wow. Equip the girl with a Devil Dog and she and the middle McClain could be new best friends.

They sipped in silence for a few moments. Kendra elbowed Dixie and, taking on the challenge of answering Faith, it was Dixie who spoke. "What I am about to tell you has come from two years of infiltrating my brother's force field. I don't think it's any betrayal of trust that I'm telling you; it's just not something he talks about. And after I tell you you're going to understand why."

"If he asks," Kendra interjected, her brown eyes going wide, "and you expect the relationship with him to go anywhere, you're going to have to rat us out and tell him that we told you."

Dixie nodded sagely. "It's true. He wouldn't like it if you lied to him and pretended to know less than you do. So it's best to come clean. Are you still sure you would like to know?"

Oh boy. If that wasn't the proverbial can of earth-worms. But she'd come this far... "Tell me."

After another quick glance at one another, Kendra nod-ded and again, Dixie spoke. "I'm better with facts. I'll unload the facts on you, and then Kendra can hit you with the feelings stuff."

Hands gripping her wineglass so tightly she feared she might crack it, Faith felt herself lean imperceptibly closer.

Dixie crossed her legs and sipped her wine. "Connor and Jonas were stationed in Afghanistan, in a small vil-lage, when an IED meant for the troops went off. Insur-gents swarmed the area, but most of them were taken down. Three men in the unit were severely injured; two died in the blast. While the rest of the men were tending to medical care, Connor noticed, hunkered under rubble about to collapse, an Afghan woman with a toddler cling-ing to her leg. Both were bleeding, both injured."

Faith felt her stomach turn as she pictured the terrify-ing scenario. And she could tell Dixie had only paused. The story wasn't done.

"Before he thought of his own safety," Kendra chimed in, "Connor ran across the street to pull them out from un-der the unstable building."

"That was when Jonas grabbed his arm and pulled him behind their vehicle." Dixie's pallor went from pink to gray. "An insurgent was running down the street, machine gun at the ready. When Jonas pulled Connor out of the way, the bad guy shot the woman and her child."

Faith lifted a fist to her mouth. The scene Dixie painted was not a pretty one. In fact, it was a nightmare.

"He would've died." Kendra toyed with the stem of her wineglass. "Jonas killed the terrorist after he saved our brother's life. You can guess how Connor feels about this. And why he goes to hang with Jonas every Friday. Connor feels almost responsible for that mother and child losing their lives. He wanted to protect them."

"He's been in a similar, first-world situation. Here in the Cove, when he was young and confused," Dixie put in. "Oddly, it mirrored what happened overseas."

"Another time he tried to protect a woman and her child," Kendra said. "But failed."

Faith knew they meant Maya, and her stomach lurched.

Dixie lifted a dark eyebrow. "But we are out of wishbones, deary. So that's going to have to be a question for him."

CHAPTER 12

*C*onnor joined his mother on the piano bench, where she sat strumming the keys. She wasn't playing anything intentionally, just a soft melody in the background of the melee of the family room. He'd seen Kendra and Dixie disappear with Faith in tow and figured they were upstairs doing their wishbone thing. Every year, they did it. Every year, they extracted secrets from one another.

He wondered what secrets Faith got out of them, if she'd won at all.

Now she was on the floor, playing with his two nephews, a cup of coffee on the table next to her. It was getting late, the boys were tired, Dixie was yawning, and Tad was brooding since his team lost. Connor halfheartedly cheered alongside him, but by halftime, they both knew it was over.

Roger was asleep in the recliner, his snoring buried under the melody of his mother's song.

Connor kissed her on the cheek and stood. "I think we're going to get out of here. Thanks for having us."

Abruptly, she stopped playing and stood. "Sure thing, sweetheart."

"Cupcake, you ready to go?"

Kendra snapped a glance from Faith to Connor and chuckled. "Cupcake? Oh, I bet there's a story behind that one."

Faith didn't miss a beat, rising to her feet and saying, "Better luck next year on the wishbone break."

At her words, he felt a pleasant pressure in the middle of his chest. Faith here next year sounded pretty damn good to him. As she said her round of good-byes and hugged his sisters, and mother, that pressure in his chest increased—and not in a bad way.

He took her hand as Evelyn walked them to the door.

"Pie, sweetheart," his mother said, large plastic container in hand. "For both of you." Her eyes flicked from Connor to Faith. "For later."

"Shopping tonight?" he queried, taking the container. His mother never missed Black Friday for as long as he could remember.

"Yes. Dixie and Ken are dragging me out at one a.m. One!" Her gaze went to Faith as if considering inviting her, then back to Connor. She pressed her lips into a smile. It was a good call. Black Friday was time she reserved with her daughters. Dix and Ken taking Faith up to the attic was one thing, having her interlope on their girls' day another. Besides, he was looking forward to having Faith to himself.

"G'night, Mom." Another kiss to her cheek, then he was out the door, calling, "Tell Dad in the morning I said 'bye.' " Roger would sleep in that recliner through the night. Not for the first time, he considered he was a lot like his old man. Sleeping in a chair.

God.

On the silent drive home, Faith mostly looked out the window. There was no snow, but the night was brutally cold. He guessed she had a good time—didn't seem to be the kind of girl who'd fake something like that.

In her parking lot, he left his Mustang idling. She'd been surprised to see him show up in the burnished gold vintage automobile, but he explained there was no way he'd cart her around in his work truck for a night out. She was flattered. She should be; he'd meant it that way.

"Want to come up?" she asked, eyes lowering into a slow blink. Sexy, those navy-blue eyes. In a house full of browns and hazels, Faith's eyes were the most stunning.

"Have to. You have half my pie." His face split into a wicked grin, making sure she knew he'd meant that in the filthiest way possible.

With a laugh, she reached for the door handle and he stayed her movements with one hand.

"Just once, Faith," he said in the quiet confines of the car, "let me treat you the way you should be treated."

Her movements paused and she folded her hands into her lap. He came around, pulling open the Mustang's door and bracing himself from the wind. She stepped out and shuddered.

They hustled to the stairs, his arm nestled around her back as he led her up to her apartment. At the door, he pulled his key from his pocket and made short work of letting them inside.

Inside, her place was quiet, a small nightlight glowing

in the hallway, the alarm silently blinking. He keyed in the code and shut the door, locking it behind him.

Faith slipped out of her coat, making a point to walk to the hallway to hang it before disappearing into the bedroom. In her kitchen, he put the pie on the counter and opened the cabinet to find a bottle of wine.

"Drink?" he called.

"Ugh, I'm too full," she called back.

"Me too," he lied. He'd be chowing down the leftovers Mom packed in a grocery sack at three in the morning. He'd left them in the car. Since the temperature was roughly the same as a refrigerator, he figured they were safe out there.

Sighing, he shut the pantry, feeling restless and wondering what he was doing here. It'd been a long time since he'd brought a woman around his family. What possessed him to take Faith was a mixture of things. One, she'd never had Thanksgiving and he was not lying when he told her missing out wasn't right. It wasn't. And he knew his family and their tradition of stuffed turkey and Nan's cranberry sauce, and Dix and Kendra's harebrained wishbone thing they did in secret would not only give Faith a sample of tradition she longed for, but maybe cure her of ever wanting it again.

"Okay, don't laugh," her soft voice floated in from behind him.

He turned around and every thought of his mother, sisters, family, and dinner promptly exited stage left. If there was one thing Faith could take to the bank, it was that he wouldn't laugh. She wore a strapless, tiny rectangle of clothing that could only be described as a dress. There was a slit high on her right thigh, and those legs kept going and going and going down to a pair of shoes with tall heels being held together by two thin straps apiece.

"Not laughing, Cupcake," he croaked out of a very dry throat.

She quit wringing her hands and smiled. "I bought it the other day and I was so excited and loved it so much, part of me was dying to wear it to your parents' house. Luckily for you, I do have some sense of decorum." Her teeth bit into her bottom lip. "And it is not a warm dress. I just wanted you to know I can look really nice if I want to."

He didn't know if it was her dress or the tender lilt of her voice in the quiet confines of her apartment, but she drew him in. Looked like she was making her move. He'd always known he only needed a crack to infiltrate her defenses. And this was way more than a crack.

She'd kicked the damn door open.

He went to her, hands out, and slipped them around her waist. "I think you look beautiful no matter what, Cupcake, but you seriously rock this dress."

She smiled up at him, proud. He could see her pride in the deep breath lifting her chest. Her hair was curled tonight and spilled down her back, tickling his forearms.

"I managed not to kiss you tonight," she said.

"Tonight's not over," he said, lowering his lips.

Against them, she whispered something he'd never forget. "I want you."

Simple. To the point. And yeah, he could relate.

Closing his lips over hers, he didn't let her say more, but let his kiss answer. He tucked her lithe body against his, tilting his hips into hers when she pressed into him. He hardened in a second, doing his level best not to grind his cock into her thigh, and doing a damned fine job of resisting, in his opinion. Her sexy, lean body plastered against his was not an easy thing for any member of his anatomy to resist.

She tugged her head back to smile at him, looking relaxed and happy, and like a woman he wanted in bed. Now.

"That feels like a yes." She winked at him.

Winked.

Right fucking now.

"Lead the way."

She did. Taking his hand and drawing him down the hallway, they made the short walk to her bedroom. A lit candle stood on the dresser. Her room was spotless, the bed made, closet door boasting a full-length mirror. He made mental note of where that mirror lined up on the bed and where he'd have to line her up on the bed to see them doing what they were about to do.

Smoothing his hands up her arms and over her bare shoulders, he traced his fingers along the bodice of her dress over the small swells of her breasts. This was the first time, the only time, Faith had ever flinched under his touch.

He tipped his head. "Cupcake. Talk to me."

"I should warn you...I—there's not a lot of, um..." She scrunched her eyes closed and said, "My boobs are really small."

* * *

Oh, Lord. Had she seriously blurted that?

There had to be a better way to tell him that every

man's favorite part of a woman—boobs, *obvy*—was not her strongest suit.

Way to sell it, Faith.

Connor was still looking at her like she'd lost her mind, and maybe she had. She was bringing baggage to her bedroom, from Michael, the bastard, and much as she didn't want him in her bedroom, he was there.

Licking her lips, she continued digging a hole. "This dress makes me look like I have more than I do. But I don't. And the pushup bra I'm wearing isn't helping matters, either." She squeezed her eyes shut again. "I mean, it is helping, but...well, I'm just saying there is some false advertising going on about what is beneath the material of this dress."

She opened her eyes to find Connor subtly shaking his head. Then he grinned, his shallow dimples making a rare appearance. Rather than tell her it was okay and strip her of her clothes anyway, he took her hand and walked her out of her bedroom.

Out. Of the bedroom.

Right about then, her heart dropped to the soles of her very sexy shoes. She told him what to expect, and he took them sleeping together off the table. Guess he was more of a boob man than she'd suspected.

Not that she could fault him. She understood. She did. But it didn't mean his rejection hurt any less.

In the living room, she stopped following and their arms stretched out between them. "I could use that wine, now."

He faced her, hand still in hers, looking amused as he paced to where she'd stopped advancing. "Cupcake, I need you to hear me."

Oh no. This seemed bad. Like, *bad* bad.

"I'm a guy."

She couldn't argue that fact. Every line of his body from broad shoulders to wide chest to sturdy thighs to the sexy way he rocked worn jeans, henleys, and the leather jacket he'd tossed over her kitchen chair said that he was a guy. No, a *man*. Which made her feel worse. Because yes, she was a girl, but she wasn't a voluptuous girl, and most men wanted voluptuous.

She'd never achieve voluptuous even if she ate a Devil Dog a day.

"When a guy sees a woman naked, he is rarely evaluating every part of her. Mostly, we're just fucking stoked to have her naked."

Fair.

Keeping hold of her hand, he drew her closer. "I take it from your *warning*, you are trying to prepare me for something that bothers you a great deal. But know this, Cupcake. The size of your tits does not bother me."

"Until you see them." Biting down on her lip hard, she chastised herself for saying that. She kind of couldn't believe she did. But then again, what did she expect? She had a leak in the vicinity of her mouth this evening. Unfortunately, the rest of what should've been an inside conversation spilled out of her mouth, too. Maybe because she needed to say it out loud, or maybe because she thought it only fair for him to hear it.

"I know I shouldn't mention him, but Michael requested I keep my bra on any time we were...together." Wow, there really was no elegant way to say this. "I just...I didn't want you to get my dress off and wish you hadn't. Gotten it off." She winced, feeling her face go warm with embarrassment. "Michael likes big breasts"—

like Cookie's, came the errant thought—"and the bra I'm wearing makes my boobs look big. And I didn't want you to be upset because I've been promising you something that is not a reality."

She trailed off when she noticed Connor's expression turn severe. Definitely an inelegant time to mention Michael. Right. So, basically, she'd botched her chances in getting Connor McClain in bed tonight.

Bummer.

She fanned her hand in front of her, attempting to move this evening forward. "You know what? I feel like this is going in the wrong direction. And maybe we should—" This time, he cut her off.

"You don't know me, Faith. It's occurring to me I don't know you all that well, either."

Because she'd false advertised her boob size?

"We know each other," she said, her voice small. "We've worked together for over a year."

"I didn't know this shit was going on." He gestured to her generally.

"That's why I am letting you off the hook. You can chalk it up to my drinking too much wine."

"You're sober."

That was also unfortunately true. The staggering amount of food she'd inhaled at the dinner table guarded against alcohol being able to impact her system.

"Which tells me that when you invited me to your bed, you meant it." He lifted his eyebrows. "Am I right?"

Not wanting to lie to him, she nodded.

"Good. Now the part of this you didn't expect was that I'm not going to throw you down on your bed and have my way with you with this shit going on."

She sort of couldn't get past the idea of him throwing her onto her bed and having his way with her. That sounded... Gosh. Lovely.

"That's not going to bed with us tonight."

"No?" The hope in her voice was prevalent.

"Not while you're this mistaken about who you think I am." Those big rough hands covered her hips and pulled her close, and his smile broke through his severe expression like the sun after a storm. "Couch, Cupcake."

She turned her head to the right and looked at the couch a few inches away. It was facing the TV and they were standing at the back of it. So she would have to skirt around him to sit on it. He got out of the way and let her do just that. She clipped in her tall, strappy heels to the front of the couch and plopped down.

Connor joined her on the couch and she sat to face him, expecting him to say more. Instead, he picked up the remote and began flipping through channels. She looked to the television, then back at him. He stopped on a movie, one she didn't recognize, and he held out an arm. "Scoot in. Gonna warm you up." He said this without looking over and she obeyed, sliding in.

His warm hand hit her chilly shoulder, and a second later, he retrieved the blanket from the back of the couch. After a few minutes of watching an action flick she'd heard of but never bothered to rent, she asked the question burning her brain.

"What's happening?"

He didn't move his head, just his eyes. And those eyes slid to hers, making her stomach feel funny and her arms pull the blanket tighter around her shoulders. "Why don't you relax?" Then those eyes went back to the television.

It took her two commercial breaks to relax, but relaxation did come. She was leaning fully on his shoulder, had kicked off her uncomfortable shoes and folded her legs beneath her, covering them with the blanket. She was not lying about the dress not being warm enough for winter. It was barely warm enough for summer.

In the middle of nowhere, Connor said, "That is what I like to hear."

"What?" she asked, thinking he was talking about something in the movie she had missed.

"You breathing deep. Sounds like you're finally chill." He turned his head, bringing his lips just over hers. "Now, you can kiss me, Cupcake."

Unable to resist the invitation, Faith rested her hand on his chest, stretched her chin up just a little, and put her lips on his. He reacted immediately, turning his body toward hers, sliding the arm that wasn't wrapped around her shoulders to her back, and pulling her in. His mouth slanted over hers, his tongue pushing past her lips. She drank him in, making out with him for long minutes, savoring his flavor and the way he kissed her. Controlled yet wild. She'd never been kissed the way Connor kissed her. His lips were perfect, sealed over hers but parting to let her take in a breath, preventing her from getting too far away.

Next, she felt the blanket being ripped off her body and tossed to the back of the couch. The chill in the air didn't matter; the heat between them would keep her warm.

Pulling his lips from hers, he left her mouth to say, "Climb up."

She looked at his legs. "Sit on your lap?"

"Straddle me. I want you on me."

Wow. Just hearing him say how he wanted her turned her on. Worried just how turned on she might be if she crawled onto his lap, she had half a mind to ask him to lay her on her back. But on the other hand, she really wanted to do what he wanted her to do. Which was a departure from her goal of independence. Then again, woman-on-top screamed of independence. Dominance.

She liked that, too.

Her dress was so short she didn't even have to hike it before she threw a leg over his thighs and settled over his fly. When she was there, he tilted his head back to take in her height.

"Whose lap are you on, Faith?"

How to answer that question? "Um... yours?"

"And I am..." he prompted.

"Connor McClain." She felt her lips smile down at him, her fingers twist together behind his neck. What was he getting at?

"Good." His hands went to the back of her dress, finding the zipper easily. "Don't want you to mistake me for that asshole who broke into your apartment."

Mistake Connor for Michael? Not possible.

With one swift move, he had the dress unzipped and she felt the bodice give. She pulled in a deeper breath than before now that the tightness was no longer wrenching her ribs. Peeling down the top of her dress, his fingers glided along the strapless pink bra, over the lace covering her nipples, or what would have been her nipples if there hadn't been several inches of padding in the bra.

He reached around behind her back and grasped the bra strap, and that's when she snapped into reality. Her hand went to his wrist to stop him.

Again, he asked, "Who am I, Faith?"

Oh.

Right.

Now she got it. She wasn't giving him a chance. A chance to prove he wasn't anything like her ex. Maybe he was, maybe he wasn't. Maybe he would get her bra off and be completely disappointed, or maybe he couldn't give a shit.

Only one way to find out.

She released his hand and closed her eyes as he expertly undid the strap of her very padded, high-end, lace bra. It made her A-cup a solid B bordering a very small C. It was her favorite bra *ever*. When cool air hit her flesh, she felt a blush steal her cheeks. She never hyperventilated before, but thought she might as the rough pads of his fingers slid over her shoulders and down her arms.

"Cupcake, I need you to open your eyes."

When she did, she saw Connor's eyes not on hers but on her chest. His hands encircled her rib cage, his thumbs gently stroking the sensitive flesh between the valley of her breasts. They rose and fell with each nervous breath she took as she waited for him to say or do something.

For an agonizing amount of time—could have been a few seconds or a few months (it felt like the latter)—she just breathed and waited and worried.

Then his thumb brushed a nipple and she canted her hips, pushing down onto the erection pressing into her core.

"Sensitive," he noted, and still, she could not tell if he was happy about that discovery or not. He rolled the same nipple between his thumb and forefinger, and a shock like a lightning bolt shot straight to her panties, leaving

her damp and wanting him desperately. She swallowed
thickly as his other thumb repeated the motion of the
first one. First, the brush, then the pinch. Ending with her
bucking against him again.

He shook his head and finally met her eyes.

"No good, honey," he said, and there was such evident
disappointment in his eyes, she felt as if tears might pour
down her cheeks any second now. Then he added, "Your
nipples are incredibly sensitive. A man making you keep
them hidden, not giving them the attention they need."
He shook his head and a smile crested his firm, delicious
mouth. "Damn shame."

"But—"

Cutting her off mid-sentence was his MO, evidently.
Connor closed his lips over one of her nipples and suckled, and every last syllable of what she might've said
vanished into the air between them. Cradling the back
of his head, her fingers kneaded his skull through his
short hair as her hips continued sliding back and forth
over his lap.

He continued assaulting her nipple until she felt the
tension coiling inside her. My God! He was right. She
was so sensitive she was about to climax from this alone.
Was that pathetic or fantastic? *Fantastic*, she thought as
he pulled his lips from her and traced her nipple with his
tongue. He brushed the damp bud with his thumb and she
jerked.

"Yeah, honey. You're going to go over like this.
Ready?"

She nodded and he latched on to her, working her
with his hands, sucking her with his tongue. Her hips,
so greedy for her release, continued moving back and

forth over his thighs and Connor continued his wet, slick assault on her—up until now, apparently—least utilized erogenous zones.

Opening his mouth wide, he took her breast into his mouth, sucking her deep, and her hands clenched on to the back of his head. A second later, she was pulsing, spasming, and collapsing all at once, her hands pulling at his hair, a soft mewing sound coming from her throat she'd never in her life heard before. She'd been brought to orgasm, yes, but never like this. Never this gently, this thoroughly, and never from the A-cups men often skipped over.

He pulled his amazing lips from her body and cupped the back of her head, kissing her as deeply as he'd suckled her and holding her against his big body. "Now."

"Now?" Every muscle in her body barely worked, so it was a wonder she pushed her voice past very weak lips.

His grin was predatory, heady. "Now you can have me in your bed."

$\mathcal{C}$HAPTER 13

$\mathcal{F}$uck, but the girl came like a rocket.

Every inch of him—including the hard-as-steel inches in his pants—wanted to lay her down and work her into another orgasm like the last. Faith came hard, but she came quiet. Hitched breath, adorable, muffled pants of pleasure, and this high, keening sound that sounded half like she was laughing and half like she was crying.

He did that.

Disintegrated her into this quivering, long-limbed woman who lacked the strength to climb off his lap.

"Making me feel studly," he announced as his hands cupped her bottom.

"Mmm."

Incoherent. Fuck, but he loved that, too.

He leaned forward and stole a kiss. "Hang on, gorgeous."

She latched on to his neck and moaned one of those

sweet little noises in his ear. A shudder nearly buckled his knees, but he managed to stand, her ass in his hands, those long, long legs locked around his hips.

This needed to happen and happen soon.

Preferably before she stopped quivering against him. One orgasm on top of the other would render her loose and sleepy, and that was how he wanted her.

In her room, he sat on the edge of her bed, her still in his lap, still dressed only in half of the tiny black dress she'd paraded into her kitchen to show him.

He moved her to her back on the bed and Faith covered her eyes, but her mouth was smiling from beneath her hands.

"Something funny?" He smiled back, not that she could see him.

"Ugh."

Grinning now, he pulled his shirt off and unbuckled his belt as he kicked off his shoes. "Not thinkin' that is a true sentiment, Cupcake."

She peeked those flooring blue eyes out from between parted fingers. "Was that a pathetic display of how easy I am?"

"No. It was an awesome display of how talented I am." He unbuttoned his pants and slid them to his ankles.

Her smile vanished. "Commando."

"You knew that the day you eyed my ass through my torn jeans."

She blushed. He liked it way too much.

"Shimmy out of that dress, Cupcake. You have a condom handy, or do I need to grab one from the 'stang?"

"You have condoms in your Mustang?"

"Yup."

She gestured to the nightstand.

He raised an eyebrow. "Who bought 'em?"

"I did."

"Why?"

"Because the kiss over the ice cream bowl turned me on so much."

Honesty. The honesty floored him as much as the pair of navies zeroing in on his hard-on now.

With a grin, he yanked open the drawer, snatched up a packet. Sheathed, his cock hard and ready, jutting straight up, he watched as she shimmied out of her dress and revealed lace panties.

"Those for me?"

"Yeah. I thought you'd like them."

"You're right, Cupcake," he said. Though "like" wasn't a strong enough word for the barely hidden promise of what lie beneath the flimsy material. "Still shuddering from earlier?"

"I think I recovered."

Hmm. No good.

He climbed over her, lowered to his forearms and ducked his head. Then he took a nipple to his tongue and her entire body bowed.

* * *

Her second orgasm was nipple-induced and this time she didn't feel pathetic. She felt *incredible*.

While she was still pulsing out her release, her knees together as her hips bucked, Connor latched on to her thighs and pulled her legs open.

"Ready, Cupcake?" he asked, nudging her entrance.

"Please," she said, or wheezed. Something. Her vocal cords were as weak as the muscles in her legs.

He slipped inside of her and her legs found new strength, drawing up to cradle him between her thighs. He fit there, big as he was, probably because she was tall, her legs long. She accommodated him perfectly.

And oh, the feel of him *inside her*, hot and thick. She was clamped around him, absolutely soaked from when she came a second ago. He pushed in to the hilt and paused, and at the same time they both breathed out, "*ohhh*."

It felt that good.

He buried his face into her neck, nuzzling her head to the side as he kissed and stroked her with his mouth.

"Giving it to you hard," he announced. "You want it different, you'll have to be on top."

"Hard," she agreed. So sated from him pleasing her twice, her body was primed and ready for him. Ready for him to pound into her, every inch of him. Repeatedly.

He slid in and out, making good on his promise of hard, each thrust hitting her so deep that, unbelievably, she was about to come again. His every movement was smooth, wrapped up in a big body that should have been less agile and more clumsy.

But there was nothing clumsy about this man, she was learning. Every thrust found its intended mark, and she felt herself coiling, tensing in preparation to give herself to him all over again.

By the time a loud growl reverberated from his lips over a pulse point on her neck, she threw her head back and came with him, surrendering silently, unable to give voice to the earth-shattering climax electrifying her body.

Long after his release, he continued moving, pushing into her deeper, harder, still working. He did this for her, she noticed. Making sure she was good and thoroughly satisfied. When her arms fell limply from his neck, he stopped the exquisite torture.

He pressed a kiss to her lips and she responded feebly, barely able to pucker. He slid his tongue along her lips and down her throat, then slipped out of her. Again, in unison, they both grunted "*uhhhh*" at the disappointment of being unjoined.

That's how intense it had been.

That's how perfect it had been.

* * *

Leftover pie was good.

Leftover pie post-sex with Connor McClain was *perfection.*

Faith moaned around her fork and didn't miss the sly smirk on his face. He looked damn pleased with himself, and pretty damn hot, considering he stood in her kitchen wearing naught but a pair of well-worn denim.

He'd hauled her out of bed, and when she protested to being naked, wrapped her in the comforter, carried her into the kitchen, and plopped her onto the countertop. Then he retrieved the container of pie and proceeded to fork bites into her mouth, then his.

She'd never sat on a countertop and been fed pie before. She liked it.

Another bite, another moan.

Another smirk from him. "I do enjoy that sound."

Pulling the blanket over her body, she refused to

acknowledge what he was inferring and instead asked, "Aren't you cold?"

His bare chest was a sight to be seen. A dusting of light hair between his pecs faded until the line below his belly button. Yeah, she knew exactly what treasure lie at the end of that trail.

"Not cold, Cupcake." He took a bite three times the size of the bite he gave her, then licked the fork and discarded the container. At her whimper, he grinned, yanked open the blanket, and positioned himself between her legs. "Second thought, I am cold," he murmured against her mouth. She kissed him and he pushed his big body against her smaller one. He wasn't the least bit cold, emitting heat like a furnace.

Mmm, tonight had been so decadent. The overeating, the dessert. And she didn't mean the pie. Yeah, the dessert she was thinking of was the naked kind. The kind where he'd treated himself to her breasts like they were parfaits and then slid into her body and rocked her world.

As she was coming down from her sex high and sliding into her sugar high, she'd begun to consider he probably shouldn't stay the night. They hadn't talked about it, and he hadn't offered, but she felt like that was an obvious upcoming discussion. Although a round two in her room was far from the worst thing she'd have to endure, him staying, being close…well. She had to draw the line somewhere.

If independence was the ultimate goal, then Connor in her bed with her curled around him was in defiance of that goal. Snuggling seemed the invisible line he shouldn't cross. Maybe because he'd crossed over a plethora of others. The more he was around, the more her boundaries blurred. She'd drawn those lines in the sand to protect herself. Protect herself from ever finding another fiancé in a clinch with a woman on the living room rug.

Even as she thought it, she couldn't imagine Connor betraying her. But she also wasn't willing to erase every boundary between them. And she sure couldn't go back to the way things were before. There had been no stopping what happened earlier... what was about to happen again if she had to guess by his roaming fingers.

Those rough pads came around and brushed her nipples and she let her mind go hazy. Never had she known she was this sensitive to a man's touch *there*. Before Connor, she'd been too consumed with worry over whether the man touching her there was judging her small breasts to really enjoy what he was doing. Not so with this man. He gingerly plucked and pulled while sipping her lips and dragging his tongue along hers.

She kissed him back, hand ringing the tribal tattoo looped around his bicep, and threaded her other hand into his short hair. His mouth. She'd never be able to stop him once he kissed her. And the beauty of it was...

She didn't want to.

* * *

Papers fluttered to the floor as Connor backed Faith against her refrigerator and knocked magnets off its surface. The kissing on the counter had intensified, and after he'd disrobed her—or de-blanketed her, as it were—she'd attacked him. Hopped off the counter and pushed his back to the stove. Then into the opposite counter. He'd spun her and pressed her against the fridge.

His hands covered her slim, delicate body. Never in his life had he felt skin so soft. Smooth. Like silk under his touch. She moved like water against him, undulating, bending, bowing as his hands raced to catch the next wave. Hand encircling her wrist, he pulled her away from his fly. She'd been stroking him pretty good, and he was hard as iron and primed and ready to be inside her.

He'd planned ahead, pulling the condom from his pocket before dropping his unzipped jeans to the floor, not letting loose her wrist. Swiveling her to the wall, he pinned her hand over her head and watched as her dark blue eyes darkened further, those swollen pink lips being wet by a pink tongue he wanted to feel on every inch of his body.

"Cupcake," he growled, letting her go to roll on the condom. And the sentiment sounded almost humorous in his gravelly tone.

"Yeah?"

"Do not lick your lips."

A foxy little smile graced her mouth. "Why not?" The tip of her tongue touched the corner of her lips and swept back into her mouth.

Rather than answer, he gave her a torturous kiss, wanting her mouth, wanting her. Bending, he lifted her by the hips and pressed her against the wall, anchoring her there with his body, holding her there with his eyes.

He lined up, slid inside, and in tandem, they both groaned long and low. She laughed, her breath warm against his lips as he repositioned her. She locked her legs around his lower back and pressed hers flat on the wall. "A move we both appreciate."

"Nothing feels this good." It was the truth. And he

didn't just mean being inside a woman, he meant being buried inside Faith.

"I've never been taken against a wall before."

"Lot of firsts for you tonight," he managed between thrusts. So wet. So warm. So, so good.

Her fingers traced his ear and gently, she leaned in and kissed him. It was so heartfelt, so sweet, it nearly halted him.

"Thank you," she whispered.

There was no talking after that, simply him moving the way she needed him to until she bowed her back and thrust her pert, petite breasts out. He bent and took one on his tongue, savoring the feel of her channel clamping on to him as she dragged another climax out of him, no less intense even though they'd finished not long ago. Face in her neck, he kissed her pulse, savoring the scent on her skin—God, what was that?

"What are you wearing?" he asked into her neck.

Another sugar-sweet laugh, then, "Nothing?"

He extracted his face from her neck, her hair clinging to the stubble on his cheeks. She brushed it away, her delicate fingers moving over his skin like a breeze. So fucking soft. "Perfume or something."

"Oh, oh yeah. It's jasmine. I think."

"Jasmine, you think," he murmured, inhaling her again. Heaven's what she smelled like. "Gonna let you down, Cupcake." He drew back and her arms tightened around his neck.

Watching her intently as he slid out of her body, they both sighed at the loss of contact, the sound coming up from deep in their bellies. He'd noticed that in her bedroom, too. They were in sync.

Never. Never had it been like this. Seemed he'd experienced a first, too. *Her.*

Once she gained her footing, she moved past him and down the hallway where he heard the bathroom door shut. He made do with disposing of the condom in the kitchen trash can, then pulled on his jeans.

Snatching the comforter from the countertop, he took it into her bedroom and spread it over her sheets. Rumpled, twisted sheets. He smiled, remembering what they'd done to rumple and twist them. As the air collapsed out of the comforter, Faith stepped in behind him. She smiled over her shoulder as she opened a dresser drawer and pulled out a long gray nightshirt. Basic cotton and she still looked elegant.

"So." She looked suddenly modest propping one foot on the other and dragging the hem of her nightshirt down. "I'll be at the mansion tomorrow."

Tomorrow. He hadn't thought past the here and now.

"Yeah, me too." He gestured at nothing. "Decorations or whatever."

She smiled, a big smile, then rolled those dark, stormy blue eyes toward the crappy plaster-stomped ceiling overhead. "*Whatever.* Just *Christmas* decorations."

Her tone had definitely changed. The air sizzling between them all night seemed as if it'd been sucked out of the room.

"So tired." She yawned. "I'll sleep well."

Two rounds and done. He wanted to argue, but he didn't. He'd been damned lucky as his night had gone. His henley was on the nightstand, half thrown over the lamp. He pulled it on at the same time he toed on his boots, not bothering to tie them. "Sure you can keep warm without me?"

She crawled into bed, tugging the thick blanket up to her chin. Long, fair blond hair scattered across her pillow. The breath she took was deep as she sank into the bed. He could understand why. It was nearly two in the morning. It'd been a long day all around.

"I'm not only warm, I'm completely relaxed." He could see her eyes had grown heavy. "Thanks to you."

Leaning over the bed, he placed a gentle kiss to her lips. "I'll lock up."

Eyes closed, she returned, "'kay."

Okay. He set the alarm, pulled on his coat, and left.

Halfway home, his sex-buzz had thoroughly faded into the cold rain pelting his windshield. The prospect of sleeping on his recliner, or even in bed at his white-walled, cardboard-box-filled apartment sounded not as good as turning around and crawling into bed with a warm, sleepy Faith.

But she hadn't asked him to stay. A thought that creased his forehead in frustration as he recalled their last conversation.

In her own way, she'd asked him to leave.

Damn.

Another first for him. But this one, he didn't like. Ridiculous as it was, it made him feel kind of...used.

Inside his apartment, he glanced from the kitchen table piled with work orders and invoices, to the completely clean and gleaming surface of his countertops.

He threw his Thanksgiving leftovers into the microwave and groused at the plate spinning inside. Yeah, he didn't like the way this night had ended, even though he should have been beyond satisfied overall.

CHAPTER 14

*F*aux pine garland interspersed with real pinecones, red ribbon, and holly berries draped the wall behind the bar, along each long wall, and over the threshold of the double doors. With the sconces glowing—also adorned with pinecones and red ribbon—the ballroom was beginning to look a lot like Christmas.

Faith pulled in a deep, appreciative breath, settled her hands on her narrow hips, and smiled at her handiwork. She loved this time of year. In spite of all her mother had done (or hadn't done, as it were) to make it the least favorite time of year, Faith's hope endured.

There was something about the crisp, downright cold air, the first hint that the gray skies would bring snow, and the festive music pouring out of every speaker in every store in town that made her want to make a roaring fire, stir marshmallows into hot cocoa, and pull on her wooliest pair of thick socks.

Resolutely, Connor banged a nail into the wall and hung another wreath. They were nearly done prepping the ballroom for the toy drive. They were expecting the rental company to fill the room with tables and chairs, but not until the day before. For now, she and Connor simply had to set the stage.

"Not bad for a guy who hates Christmas," she teased as he climbed down the ladder. His booted feet hit the carpet silently, and he let the hammer slide through his hand until the metal part rested in his palm.

Who knew that move was sexy?

"I don't hate it." He didn't hesitate to cross the room and stand really close to her. And she didn't hesitate to lean forward and accept the kiss she assumed he wanted to give her. After they parted, his eyes roamed her face. She wondered what he would say—had been wondering what to say herself since last night's incredibly amazing sexual experience had sent her to La La Land with nary a care in this world.

Maybe that's why she'd skipped into the mansion this morning, donning now her gay apparel, and ready to deck the halls in red, green, silver, and gold.

Silver and gold, silver and gold, her head automatically hummed.

But last night's not-all-that-spontaneous sex left her wondering what to do with today. What to do with every day following. Would he come to her place tonight? Should she invite him? He'd left last night without argument, which was good. Did him not staying over set the stage for their future encounters, or would they have to outline it next time? And the time after that…

Oh, she hoped there'd be a next time followed by a time after that…

She wasn't exactly accustomed to sleeping with a guy she wasn't seeing in any sort of formal capacity. Though, if Connor and she were technically "seeing" each other, their first date was a *doozy*—meeting the family on the second biggest holiday of the year followed by a few rounds of mind-blowing, toe-curling, thought-numbing—

She didn't realize she sighed aloud until Connor's brow dented. "Cupcake, somethin' on your mind?"

To lie or not to lie, that was the question.

"Yes." Not lying, it was.

"Tonight," he guessed.

She blinked. "Yes, actually."

"Your place. After I run an errand." He was talking about Jonas, she now knew. The "errand" who had saved his life overseas. Her eyes wandered the expanse of his sure chest, currently not filled with shrapnel or bullets thanks to this mystery man.

"Was that what you were wondering?" he asked.

When she bit her lip, he leaned forward to kiss her again. She did, as unable to keep her attraction for him at bay as she was unable to resist a Devil Dog in its white, crinkly wrapper.

"Tonight," he murmured against her mouth, "and each night after. As long as you want me, I'm there."

Her heart ka-thumped against her rib cage in a combination of worry and excitement. As long as she wanted him.

"And if I stop wanting you?" she ventured, half-teasing, half-serious.

"Not gonna happen. I'll see to it." His grin was downright predatory.

He tweaked her chin with his thumb and forefinger and

strolled across the room to the toolbox he'd toted in here. Bent in half, he dropped the hammer with a *clank* and she watched his jeans mold around one of the finest male asses she'd ever seen in her life.

As long as she wanted him.

She could work with that.

* * *

"Food and sex go together, that's *why*," Faith was arguing. Again, she was perched on her countertop, wrapped in her comforter. Connor, dressed only in jeans, stood next to her, eating handfuls of cereal from the box.

He crunched, then smiled and spoke around a mouthful of Cocoa Puffs. "Yeah, but for you, food is like foreplay."

"Well they're kind of the same," she said, digging into the box and coming out with a few puffs for herself. "Both fill you with this sense of ecstasy"—she popped the cereal into her mouth—"and after you're through, you feel like sleeping."

He swallowed his bite before taking a guzzle of almond milk from the container. He eyed the carton again with a shake of his head. "I have to tell you, this shit's pretty good."

"Thanks." He offered her the carton and she followed his lead and guzzled a drink from the spout. When a trail of milk slid down the corner of her mouth, he caught it with his thumb.

"Sex and sleep," he said after he sucked the droplet of milk from his thumb, "now there are two things that go well together."

She laughed.

"Two things that, as soon as I finish doing them, I want to do again right away."

Lifting an eyebrow was a talent she'd taught herself in the mirror, arduously, over days and days when she was twelve years old. She so wanted to be Vivien Leigh after she'd seen *Gone with the Wind*. She canted that brow now, hoping to look mischievous and take-charge.

She didn't know if she succeeded, but something about the expression worked because next, Connor pulled the blanket off her, baring her shoulders. He cupped her breasts in his large hands.

"Can't believe you don't like these as much as I do," he commented, kneading and pulling at her now erect nipples. "So perfect. Round and perky. Not too small, and the pale pink-peach color...*Perfect*."

She'd be lying if she said she wasn't beyond flattered that the most attractive man she'd ever seen—let alone had taken to bed—was complimenting her aforementioned least desired asset. But, her issue was her issue. He was turning her on, though, so it was through a veil of lust she muttered, "Well, when the boys tell you constantly your boobs are small, that kind of thing sticks."

"Because they knew you'd never go out with them," he said, continuing his exploration. He met her eyes and stepped between her legs. She widened the space between them to accommodate him. Closer now, he lowered his voice. "They knew there was no way in hell you'd go out with them, so they lashed out."

She pulled the blanket up and over them both, closing it around his shoulders. "I went out with you."

"You're smart."

"You're cocky."

"True story."

She tipped her head back to laugh and when she did, his lips landed on her neck. He tongued and kissed her, his hands leaving her breasts to close over her back and pull her to him. Being in Connor's arms, in the bubble they were in, made her feel so very safe. Or maybe it was simply him who made her feel safe.

So she told him, "You make me feel protected. Not alone."

"That's a good thing, Cupcake." He kissed her jaw, leaned closer to her ear.

"You can't stay," she blurted.

His mouth froze at her lobe, then his head pulled back so he could look at her.

"I'm sorry. I just feel like I should tell you. As long as we are sleeping together, I can't have you sleeping over."

Now he was frowning. His hold loosening.

"The sex is still on the table. Trust me. On the table, the countertop, the bedroom, the couch. The balcony if you want," she sort of joked. "But the sleeping here, the closeness is too…"

He'd drawn his head back farther to watch her, and now his lips were pursed and he definitely looked unhappy.

"I know it's no big deal to you, but I wanted to say it and, there. I've said it." She tipped her head to the side. "You can continue kissing me now." When he didn't, she straightened her head and blew out a breath. "What? Talk to me."

"You want me to leave."

"No! I mean, yes, but you know…when we're done."

Ugh. That sounded awful. Even to her. She thought of her mother and her man-friends. Maybe she should have asked Linda Shelby for pointers on how to have a meaningless fling. But that was the problem, wasn't it? Connor wasn't meaningless. He was a good man, a good soldier, a good son and brother. He'd saved her, stood up for her, and he'd made love to her with a single-minded dedication the likes of which she'd never experienced.

And that was the problem, quite frankly. He had the potential of becoming a permanent fixture, and she didn't need anyone *fixturing* themselves in her life. Especially when the potential fallout was soul-consuming.

"Not gonna happen, sweetheart."

She blinked. "What's 'not gonna happen'?"

"You want me, you get me. I'm not climbing out of your bed and going home to my shithole apartment unless you're with me."

"You are, actually." This was her place, and he couldn't tell her he was staying if she said he wasn't.

"Okay. Been fun." With that, he stepped away, wrapped her tightly in her comforter, and strolled through her apartment toward the bedroom. When she shuffled in there, balled in her blanket like a turtle, he was threading his belt through his pants and had pulled on both his T-shirt and sweater.

"What are you doing?"

"Going home."

"You don't have to go…yet."

He gave her a look of complete disdain. "No? You're not through with me yet?"

"That's unfair."

"I agree."

Heat infused her cheeks. She had to be glowing like Rudolph right now.

Stepping into her personal space, he lifted her jaw with his palm. "Look, Faith"—him using her name was almost impersonal and she didn't like it—"I get that the assbag cheated on you. I get that you're nervous. I get that you think you're cursed. I also get that if I reminded you I was younger than you, you'd freak out, so I haven't."

She felt her chin jerk. "What?"

"I get you. That's the point."

"But what... what does this have to do with your being younger than me?" Even as she downplayed it, she felt sweat prickle her underarms. Suddenly, the cozy blanket was stifling.

His eyebrows lifted. "I don't miss much." Which was not an answer. Before she called him on his evasive maneuvering, he lifted her, blanket and all, and sat on the edge of her bed with her on his lap. "Your mom dates younger men. You do your level best to be nothing like her. I tell you I'm younger, you find another ridiculous reason to push me away."

Every extremity in her body began to tingle as she thought back to Sofie's "Cougartown" comment. Faith was supposed to be lazily floating down denial, so was shocked to hear the question, "How much younger?" leave her parted lips.

"You're proving my point."

He was right. She was. She didn't want to sleep with a younger man because her mother had made a hobby of it. "You seem... mature."

More mature than her at the moment.

"Yeah," he replied drily. "Been cutting my own food

for a whole year now." A sigh, then, "Michael was older than you, right?"

"By a few years." Her mind spun at the shift of subject. What was he getting at?

Connor put his lips on her ear, his rough voice sending chills down her spine. "Did he make you feel like I do?"

Undeniably sexy, womanly, and wanton? No way, José. She shook her head.

Connor drew back, a small smile tucked on his mouth.

"Don't you want to know how old I am?" she asked.

"I only care how I make you feel."

So he wasn't going to answer her. She took the sight of him in. He was close. So very close to her since he was cradling her on his lap. Faint lines fanned out from the sides of his eyes, smile lines visible even when he didn't smile. There were even a few dents in his cheeks for those on-occasion dimples that flashed when he really, really smiled.

"You don't look under thirty," she muttered, unable to let it go, apparently.

"Afghanistan," he said. "Like visiting the surface of the sun."

She touched a smile line currently not in use.

"You fearing someone breaking into your place," he stated, "is a normal fear. You fearing me sleeping next to you, or fearing getting involved with me because I am younger than you, or fearing I won't like your tits because they're small. Faith, baby, those are not normal fears."

Stiffening in his arms, she tried to get up. He didn't let her. Those big arms had big muscles and she wasn't going anywhere. "Let me go."

"Forget it."

Fine. He wanted to play this way? She could play this way. With as much dignity as she could muster dressed in nothing but bedclothes and being held captive in his lap, she tried to cross her arms over her chest. She ended up with them sort of curled against her body.

"I didn't ask you to deliver me from my fears," she said. "In fact, my entire goal in life is to be independent. I will not rely on a man to take care of me, to tuck me in at night, to—"

"But you would like one to make you come so hard you cry."

His brash words stunned her silent. Mainly because they were true. Okay, now she was pissed. "Are you suggesting I'm...using you?"

"Are you?"

"I thought this was mutual."

"Mutual means me in your bed, and not only while we screw."

"Charming." She elbowed him as she scrambled out of his lap and surprisingly, he let her. In a huff, and not caring that she was nude, she tossed the comforter onto her bed. He helped her straighten the corners of the blanket, holding up an edge so she could crawl in. She climbed in the opposite side and turned on her belly, pulling the pillow under her cheek. She was seething. She was pouting. Angry he would dare suggest she was using him! Even though...she kind of was. Still. *Still*, he didn't come clean about being younger than her...or by how many years, until it was way too late for her to back out. Which was a lie by omission. The nerve of this man, who—

Air hit her legs as the blankets were drawn up. Firm lips hit the back of one knee, then the back of the other.

When she went to move, those hands clamped down on her legs, holding them down. Because those damp lips felt so good on the backs of her legs—another place she had no idea she liked to have kissed—her traitorous body began to relax. As his lips climbed higher, decorating her legs with soft kisses, up to her thigh, just under her bottom, she went from relaxed to squirming.

When he parted her legs, she didn't fight even a little. He hadn't visited this particular part of her body with his mouth yet, and she'd be lying if she said she didn't want him to. He granted her unspoken wish, his hands opening her to him, his tongue slicking along her already damp center.

A muffled moan sounded from her throat and she buried her face into her pillow. He lifted her hips, continuing to draw his tongue up, over, and around. By the time he ducked his head lower and swept it gently over her clit, she was on all fours, the pillow muting her sounds of encouragement.

Fingers replaced his tongue, assaulting her by spreading the wetness and causing her to moan more. He inserted one, then two, and she felt her knees grow weak. In a flash of purple, the comforter was thrown off the bed and she was being flipped onto her back.

Connor hauled off his sweater and T-shirt, mussing his short hair in the process and pegging her with eyes that were filled to overflowing with lust. He took each of her ankles in his hands and tossed them over his shoulders, lowered his face, and continued the project from the front he'd started from behind.

Oh.

Oh.

If before felt good, now felt *spectacular*. He licked and twirled before sucking, his movements intentional, slow. A hand on her pelvis held her captive, while his other moved under her bottom and tilted her hips up.

Then he hit his stride.

Gauging her reactions, he sped up when she cried out, knowing he'd found the spot that would make her come. And she did. The intensity was so consuming, she had smashed a pillow over her face to cry into it, not surprised in the least when she emerged to find tears dampening the corners of her eyes.

Damn. He was right. She did cry when she came.

She peeked out from under the corner of the pillowcase down at him. His big shoulders parted her thighs and he wore a look of intensity on his face. Watching her, he drew his tongue along her most sensitive spot again. She thrust upward, he dove deeper.

"You have another in there," he instructed. "I can tell." Then he set a course to lay waste to her again.

After he'd given her three—or four…hard to tell—more orgasms, Faith lay limp, pillow over her face, arm over the pillow. She felt his firm mouth glide from her thighs to stomach to breasts and linger briefly before he kissed her neck.

He took the pillow from her face and tossed it off the bed. Hovering over her, he asked, "Done with me, Cupcake?"

At least he was calling her Cupcake again. An improvement. "This your way of teaching me a lesson?"

"No. This is my way of showing you what you're missing if you kick me out of your bedroom."

"Bribery." The word was more of an observation than

an accusation. If she wanted Connor, for as long as she wanted him, she got all of him. That's what he was saying. She couldn't pick and choose. Didn't stop her next petulant question.

"Why do you want to sleep here so badly?" she barked.

"Because I like the idea of watching over you while you sleep. I like the idea of you not being alone."

"You don't like to be alone?" Did he? She had no idea.

"Do you?"

She answered with a deep breath.

He climbed off the bed and pulled his hands through his hair, currently ruffled in the pattern of her wandering fingers.

"This isn't how I do things," he announced.

"What *things*?"

Agitated, he groused down at her from the edge of her bed. Shirtless, it was hard not to appreciate how fine he was—even seething.

"I like you, Faith. I'm not doing anything with you I don't want to do. And I don't want to leave you." He lifted his arms and dropped them as if helpless. "Either we do this thing, you in my bed, me in yours—all night— or we don't, and I try to find a way to like you without burying my face between your legs and making you scream until you cry."

Blunt. Wow. Also, sexy. Which made no sense. Who knew she had a thing for crass?

She blinked up at him, unsure what to do with a man who wanted her—all of her, in an uncompromising way. After being with a man who was ambivalent, who would have gladly accepted half-measures, Connor's offer was a little jarring.

"And if we do this thing…" she said, picking the hem of the sheet. When neither of them finished her sentence, she hazarded a gaze up at him.

His hard face softened, and the transformation from military badass to buff landscaper happened before her eyes. It was a subtle shift. One was a hometown boy who called ladies "Ma'am" and offered to help the elderly cross the street; the other was a man who would stand by his honor and Code no matter what, rigid and uncompromising when he set his sights on a goal. Apparently, his sights were set on her. And apparently, in bed, Connor McClain was a touch of both.

"If we do this thing," he said. "We do it. We don't do this back and forth bullshit where you want me, you don't want me. You want me, Faith, you got me. We don't have to advance to a wedding or a life together, but as long as we're together, we are going to continue being friends, continue working on the mansion, and continue wearing each other out in the bedroom."

And really, when he put it like that, it sounded completely appealing.

"You know what I want," he said. "Up to you to accept."

Boundaries didn't get much clearer than the way he'd set them up. Accept or throw him out. He hadn't left when she suggested it earlier, but she guessed he'd leave now. A gauntlet had been thrown.

"Guess you'd better get undressed and crawl in here, then." Her voice was small, but she meant what she said.

For a few scattered seconds, all he did was watch her down the sharp edge of a perfect Roman nose. "Yeah?"

She nodded.

He dipped his chin. "Checking the locks. Back in a sec." Before he left the room, he chucked the comforter onto the bed in a wad. She was straightening it over the mattress from her position on the mattress—she couldn't exactly move her legs just yet—when he came back in.

He undressed silently, throwing his clothes over a chair in the corner of the room. He crawled into bed wearing not a single article of clothing. She turned to look at him. Arm thrown over his head, he lay staring at the ceiling.

"I don't want to fight with you," she said in the quiet dark of her bedroom.

"Then don't." He put his arm around her body and hauled her close. She rested her head between his shoulder and his chest as his hand curled around her back. Cold, and definitely unaccustomed to sleeping naked, she shuddered.

"I should put something on. My feet are like ice." To prove it, she stuck cold toes on his legs and heard him inhale sharply.

"God, woman!" he said on a laugh. When he looked over at her this time, the traces of hard had evaporated from his face. His warm smile, the one responsible for those lines around his mouth that belied his real age, had returned. Dipping his face, he kissed her nose. "We're doing this."

It wasn't a question. But she agreed anyway.

"We're doing this."

CHAPTER 15

*C*onnor didn't so much jolt awake as he surfaced. And unlike most nights his eyes popped open in the wee hours, the last thing on his mind was war. A feat considering he'd visited Jonas before coming to Faith's. Sometimes his visits brought that awful day to the surface. Now, it trembled in the distance, wavy, like he was seeing it through the desert's scorching hot air.

Not hard to figure out what changed. What woke him was not a thought about the living nightmare of his past, but Faith's fantastic mouth sucking him deeply.

Drawing a sharp breath, he knifed up, his hand finding her head, now bobbing up and down over a hard-and-getting-harder part of his anatomy.

God in heaven, Lord above.

There were no words. Only the pattern of his chaotic breaths.

Her tongue swirled, causing him to tense. He pulled

his hand from her head, not wanting to force her back down. Well, *wanting to*, but not wanting to discourage her from continuing. And, *oh please, Jesus*, he wanted her to continue. Was it okay to pray for a blowjob? He wasn't sure. He didn't *care*. Her fingers drifted up his chest and over his belly, her nails raking down his abs.

One more downward motion, and she released him with her mouth but held his shaft in her palm. "Did I wake you?" came her sultry voice in the dark.

"Yeah." His voice was comically ragged. Deep and barely working.

"Relax."

With her working him into a lather? Not a chance.

"I mean it," she challenged. He could make out a lifted eyebrow in the streetlight shining through her bedroom window. "Lie back. Relax."

Easing down onto the pillow at his back, he tried his level best to do what she was asking. He closed his eyes and focused on the tongue and mouth distributing zings of pleasure that shot off like firecrackers up his spine.

When the head of his cock tingled, he sat up again and pulled the blond vixen with the magic tongue off him. Wordlessly, he flipped her onto her back, sprawled over her, and held himself up on his forearms so he didn't crush her to death.

"Let me go. I'm not done," she protested.

"Feisty."

"You were enjoying it."

"Hell yes I was." But he didn't want to waste it pumping into her mouth. Revved up as he was, he'd like a shot at turning her inside out. "Your turn."

"I had a turn earlier tonight."

"Your turn again."

He slid as far down as her breasts and took those sweet nipples onto his tongue. After a few minutes of torture and her pawing at his head, he pulled her legs apart and worked his hips between her supple but slim thighs. He slid to the hilt, drawing a breath from Faith as well as from him.

Their lungs deflated in unison.

"Connor. We didn't…you didn't…"

"Shit." The condom.

He froze, pulsing, his head clearing from the fog he was mired in a moment ago.

"Wasn't thinking."

"I'm clean, you know. Got tested after my engagement ended." Her fingers raked into his hair. "And you remembered pretty quick."

True. But he wouldn't hold out long, not without a barrier between them.

"You feel good. Too good," he managed, reminding them both, "birth control is important."

"I am in agreement." She laughed as she said it, which was a good sound.

"Honey, you scramble my brain." He pulled out, or tried, but a pair of long legs clamped around his hips.

"Don't." It was a whisper. Damn near a plea.

"I get you, babe, I do." He pushed his fingers into her hair and kissed her lips gently. "But I can't hold out with nothing between us."

"I'm on the pill. I just…until now I wasn't sure if we…"

"It's okay, Cupcake. We can still use a condom." Not that he wanted to, but he understood. This was closeness in a different way. He drew back but her heels dug into his ass as she pushed him deeper inside her. He welded his teeth together and concentrated on his breathing. She was tight and hot and he could not, repeat, could *not* hold out if they continued much longer.

"Don't want you to." Fingers sifted into his hair, pushing it this way and that. "I like how you feel."

"I like how you feel," he admitted, dropping his chest to hers and brushing against her breasts. Unable to keep from it, he began to move. Slowly, intentionally. When she threw her head back, it was in silent agreement he wasn't going to leave her until they both finished. Her mouth dropped open, but the sounds she made were like before. Quiet, muted, like he'd stolen her very voice.

He loved every second of it.

When she shuddered her completion, he was right there with her, pumping deep, rocking into her, kissing her. Breaths intermingled, tongues sparred, and when he drew out of her tight body, again, they expelled the same bated breath.

"Every fucking time," he said against her mouth, kissing her.

"I know." She did know. She *had* to know. They were in sync in the bedroom—had been from the beginning. Gauging from his past experiences, this was not typical. The thread of connection deeper than bodies joining in a room. Deeper on a level neither of them claimed to want in the daylight.

Especially Faith.

"I'll be back," she told him.

They came apart and Connor rolled onto his back, hand resting on his chest. She kissed him lightly on the side of the mouth as he closed his eyes and tried not to think.

But it was no use. He thought.

He thought about how things had been with Maya when he was too young to know anything about anything. How things had been on the handful of encounters he'd had with women since. Women who knew the deal. Knew he was military and he would leave. Women who, while they cared about his general well-being, had no interest in being there for him when he came back. Women he didn't want more from than a night, maybe a few nights. Women who didn't want any more than that from him.

Those relationships were nothing like the nights he'd spent with Faith.

And when he thought about what he'd experienced overseas, what he'd experienced here during the interim, and what he'd experienced so far with the blonde about to crawl back into bed with him, he knew. This was different. What they had wasn't something to toss to the side.

She wasn't someone he'd soon forget.

Again this brought thoughts of Maya. How deeply embedded he'd been. How she'd broken him in two, both body and soul. Shattering his heart to the point he couldn't bear to be in the same country as her, so he'd enlisted in the army. She'd betrayed him in the worst possible way.

"All yours." Faith gestured toward the bathroom, her long, lean body gliding across the room like she'd floated in instead.

All mine.

She had been through the same thing he had. No, there wasn't a pregnancy involved, but her dipshit ex had betrayed her in the worst possible way, too. She didn't feel the same way Connor felt about it—so lost she ran away. Instead, she'd dug in. Decided to become tough and deal with the unavoidable things right in front of her. Where he'd spent years pretending Maya didn't exist. Prioritizing basic needs. Food, shelter, water. Fighting and defending himself from enemies who'd sooner kill him than look at him. Fearing he might die and watching his friends die. All those years spent apart from anything good and pure and whole made him an expert on what was.

That's why his landscaping business thrived. That's why he knew to savor each moment. That's why he knew what he and Faith had, and what they had wasn't something he could find just anywhere.

Heavy.

He was accustomed to his thoughts being heavy in the middle of the night. But usually they were locked on a memory. Now they were locked on the woman next to him.

"Gonna grab a bite to eat," he told her, kissing her forehead. "Want anything?"

"Bottomless pit."

In the dark, he grinned. "Sex kitten."

"Mmm." Her smile faded as she breathed deep.

Connor pulled on his jeans, made his way to the bathroom, then to the kitchen. He didn't end up going back to bed. His mind was too full to think.

* * *

That next week flew. Faith and Connor with the help of Sofie and Donovan, who were back in town, finished decorating the mansion. Every square foot (all umpteen-thousand of them) was draped either in twinkle lights, pine garland, red ribbons, or mistletoe.

Faith had gotten acquainted with the mistletoe in the dining room repeatedly. Connor grabbed her every time she passed through the doorway.

Donny had walked in on one mistletoe kiss this morning and pointed out that "payback was hell" before walking back into the kitchen. Connor had smiled, then deepened the kiss and pressed her against the wall for good measure. Yeah, he was A-Okay with PDA.

She tried not to question whatever this was they were exploring. She had promised to be all in, and after he'd made it clear how important that was, she refused to re-think it.

They'd been taking turns staying at her apartment or his. Save for tonight—Friday—they'd agreed to sleep in their own beds. For one, he had his mysterious "appointment" he had not explained the origins of, and she happened to have her own appointment this evening.

He'd kissed her good-bye at the mansion—under the mistletoe, no less—saying, "Have an errand. See you tomorrow, Cupcake."

Tonight was wine night with the girls. But tonight, they weren't going to Charlie's house with the fabulous porch or Faith's apartment. Reason being, Gloria Shields was in town and had rented a cabin. And by "cabin," Faith saw as she pulled into the driveway, Gloria must have meant "mansion."

The huge house was perched upon Peak Point, one wall completely glass, the rest of the structure concrete and modern lines. Firs, pines, and maples tucked around the house, making the glass wall almost private. A light dusting of snow had fallen today, but the brown grass poked through the meager accumulation. They'd been lucky so far. Normally, winters in the Cove were harsh, dumping inches upon inches and burying the residents in a mountain of white.

The toy drive was next weekend, and the girls agreed, they all needed a break from the planning. Since Gloria had flown in for the occasion, they opted to get together here before the formal event.

After everyone had arrived, Glo gave the grand tour. The spacious, clean layout on the inside was as impressive as the outside. Finishing the tour, they reconvened in the kitchen where Faith took the familiar position in front of a bottle of wine, corkscrew in hand. "Now this one," she said, "I have been saving for a special occasion."

She craned an eyebrow at Gloria, handing her the floor. Glo had an impish smile on her full, red lips. The literary agent represented both tattoo artist/illustrator Evan Downey as well as rock god/writer Asher Knight and their children's book phenomenon. Based in Chicago, Glo had clients scattered throughout the country. She had even represented Charlie a few years back when she sold a few photographs to *Rolling Stone* magazine.

"Special occasion?" Sofie raised her eyebrows, propped a fist on one rounded hip, and fixed her bright green eyes on Gloria. Her eyes fettered to Faith, briefly, as if she'd been betrayed.

"I know nothing," Faith said as she twisted the screw. "Only that there is news." When Glo texted her to invite her over, she'd asked her to bring a special bottle of wine for some secret, special news.

"She's right. I didn't tell her details," Glo said as the cork popped from the neck of the bottle.

"Did you sign someone famous?" This from Charlie, who accepted her glass of wine. She looked pretty today, dressed in a thick sweater, jeans, and knee-high leather boots.

"Ohhh, good guess." Sofie snapped her fingers, then accepted her glass of wine. She wore a similar outfit to Charlie, save the fact her boots were black, not brown, and had heels. Impractical, but pretty. Kind of like Sofie herself. She raised her glass of red. "Cheers to signing Beyoncé!"

Faith chuckled as she poured her own glass.

Gloria, cheeks full of red wine swallowed and licked her lips. "Not Beyoncé, sorry."

"Jay Z?" Charlie guessed.

"No," Glo answered.

"I think they come as a set," Faith put in.

"The news"—Gloria interrupted their banter, rubbing her hands together, her expression both nervous and excited—"is that the Cove is about to have a new resident."

"Who?" Charlie's eyes grew wide.

Glo raised her eyebrows.

"You?" Charlie squealed, ran to the other side of the breakfast bar, and wrapped the other woman in her arms.

"Oh my gosh, I am so excited!" Sofie ran over to Gloria next and threw her arms around her.

After they let her go, Faith took her turn giving her friend a hug. Gloria wasn't in town very often, but every time she was, the girls tried to get together with her. Glo was blunt, sassy, and downright fun to be around. She had a hard edge that Faith admired. An edge she wished she could replicate. It'd be easier to protect her heart if she had that edge. Glo was bulletproof. Enviably bulletproof.

"What made you decide to move here?" Faith asked.

"Well..." Gloria let go of Faith and filled her wineglass, which was not all that *unfilled*, and took a sip before answering.

"Oh, should we sit?" Charlie pulled out a high-backed chair.

Gloria gestured into the living room, filled with white and black leather furniture. "Let's go in there. Get comfortable." After they were settled on the cushy furniture of her rental, she continued. "I have lived in Chicago for a long time. Built my career there. Made friends"—she gestured at nothing—"you know Kimber."

Kimber Downey had married Evan's oldest brother, Landon, and they had a son, Caleb. She'd crashed a wine night once before, as well as came to the charity dinner last year. Faith liked her. The redhead was spunky and sharp—no surprise she was Gloria's bestie.

"I travel a lot more with work than I used to," Glo said. "Kimber is busy with the kiddo and her two stores. I want out of the city. I want to be based where I feel at home. Much as I love Chicago, it feels too busy for me lately." She wrinkled her nose and Faith could tell she was about to be funny. "Do you think I'm getting old? Needing to settle down?"

Sofie spoke first. "No. I think you want to be around your friends. And we are all your friends. I, for one, am thrilled beyond belief to have you here. Are you going to work out of your home?"

"Do you have a home?" Charlie's brow creased with concern.

"Much as I like this place, I'm not sure it's my style." It was true. The place was opulent but almost in an off-putting way. "And I'm not sure the owner would go from rental to sale. But, I have been looking. I'm hoping to make a decision within the next six months."

"Six months?" Faith felt her eyebrows rise. "You are really doing this. You are moving to Evergreen Cove."

"I really am." Gloria's smile was genuine and relaxed. She wanted this. Good for her. Recognizing something wasn't right was one thing. Changing it was another. Faith wondered if she wasn't failing in those endeavors for herself.

"Have you considered renting a storefront down-town?" Sofie asked. "I think the space for Make It an Event is open."

"I thought an accountant moved in there," Charlie said.

"He did," Faith put in. "But only for a few months, then he left."

"Okay, I have sucked up enough of the attention for the evening," the no-nonsense agent said. "Everyone tell me what you've been up to."

Charlie regaled a tale about her ten-year-old stepson, Lyon. *Ten*. The last few years had flown by.

Sofie talked about the upcoming toy drive (proving herself incapable of truly taking a day off) and the very, *very* wealthy people who had RSVP'd. "I must have re-minded Donny nine times the event is black tie. He wants to wear jeans."

"Of course he does." Faith snorted. Their guys were jeans guys. All there was to it. She took a hearty sip as she realized she'd just thought of Connor as "her guy." Hmm.

"I can't imagine him in a tuxedo," Sofie said.

"I can." Glo trilled her tongue. But her smile was warm when she said, "You two really worked things out, didn't you? I knew it. There's something about him I really like."

"His ass?" Charlie asked wryly, and the room exploded with laughter. Since she had married Evan, her comments had become cheekier. So to speak.

"He does have a great ass." Sofie raised her wineglass and they drank to Donovan's great ass.

Glo lifted her chin. "What about you, Faith? You have been quiet this evening."

"She went to Thanksgiving dinner with Connor." Sofie waggled her eyebrows, happily ratting her out.

"Sexy military landscaper," Gloria said with panache. "Those arms. That chest."

"And he's funny," Sofie added diplomatically.

"Also, great ass," Charlie lifted her glass.

"Great ass," the rest of them chimed in unison.

Charlie climbed out of the chair she was lounging in. "More wine, anyone?"

"More wine, everyone!" Sofie called after her, then pegged Faith with a meaningful stare. "So...spill."

Under her friends' scrutiny, she didn't know quite where to start. "He found out I never had a traditional Thanksgiving dinner and he invited me to his parents' house. That's it."

"Never?" Glo sounded surprised. "My childhood was totally fucked up and even I had a few traditional holiday dinners."

"My mom and traditional don't really go together," Faith said. Understatement of the millennium.

"Connor's older sisters kidnapped her and shared a family secret of some sort." Sofie sipped from her glass.

"You had better spill, sister." Gloria looked serious. Faith knew better than to challenge the raven-haired agent when she was serious.

"Okay, fine."

"Wait for me!" Charlie scuttled into the living room with a fresh bottle and filled everyone's glasses while Faith told the story of "Wishbone Attic," then at Glo's further prompting, she told of Michael's break-in, Connor's insistence to watch over her and keep her safe. How they kissed over ice cream. Then kissed in the indoor greenhouse...

"Mm-hmm, Donovan told me he caught you guys. Serves Connor right." Sofie chuffed. "He's overheard plenty where Donny and I are concerned."

"You two still can't keep your hands off each other," Faith accused.

"Me? Connor has pulled you under the mistletoe more times than I can count!"

"So is he bossy in bed?" Glo's smile was deviant. "Slap your ass? Order you around?"

Faith bit her lip but couldn't hide her smile. "No, he's not bossy. Well, he's kind of bossy. He wouldn't go home."

"You wanted him to go home?" Charlie looked as concerned as she sounded.

"I..." How should she put this? "I didn't want him to go home per se, I just didn't want to become overly reliant on him since we're just... we're just..." She waved a hand, trying to think of a delicate way of putting it.

"Screwing," Glo said. Indelicately. "Makes sense to me." She'd put on her serious face again. "I didn't make it a habit to cuddle with Asher after, and it's a good thing I didn't since he banged that skank."

Charlie winced.

Glo pointed at her. "Don't."

"I didn't say anything." But Charlie sure looked like she had something to say.

"I know Ash and Evan are bros, and I know Ash has a story about that night, one that makes him sound like he was an innocent bystander, but you can't tell me he didn't take advantage of a chick crawling in his window." Glo had gone from serious to seriously perturbed.

Charlie pressed her lips together before murmuring, "I believe him."

Gloria's frown intensified. The room was silent for a few awkward beats.

"Sorry. We don't have to talk about this." Glo polished off her wine in a few generous chugs, which had to have burned her throat, then reached for the bottle and topped off her glass. "So after Connor wouldn't leave, what happened?"

Hoping to smooth over the previous conversation, Faith said, "He made me see stars. I mean it, entire cosmos exploded behind the lids of my eyes."

"Oh, that's the best," Sofie put in wholeheartedly. Tipsy now, her eyelids drooped to half-mast.

Charlie sighed, the sound wistful. "I love young love."

Gloria wagged her finger. "You and Evan are an exception." Before Sofie could open her mouth, Gloria turned that wagging finger at her. "And I don't even know what to make of you and Donovan Pate. You have some sort of Fate thing going on that surpasses space and time. When are you two getting married anyway?"

"Soon." Sofie went a pretty shade of pink. "Probably soon."

"And she plans weddings now. So that's convenient." Faith winked and Sofie smiled at her lap. She loved how happy her friend was. Loved how things had worked out for Charlie and Evan, too. But in this foursome, she definitely had more in common with hardened Gloria than her other two floating-on-air friends.

Glo, clearly done being serious, lifted her glass. "To Connor and his massive man parts." She cocked her head at Faith. "I assume *all* of his parts are massive?"

Faith didn't know whether it was the wine or the fact that she kind of liked being envied for her fine taste in men, but she lifted her glass in cheers and agreed, "*Massive.*"

"This calls for more wine," Charlie announced, and stood from her chair again.

$\mathcal{C}$HAPTER 16

$\mathcal{C}$onnor was able to convince Jonas to come with him to the mansion instead of hanging out in his bleak apartment. The women were staying at Gloria's rental house, so Donovan was having poker night.

When Connor challenged him—Donovan didn't play poker—he admitted the poker was an excuse to drink. Deck of cards optional.

Evan had not only brought a deck of cards, but also classic poker chips. Heavy resin instead of cheap plastic, one side of each chip was engraved with—of all things—dogs playing poker.

Jonas wore his poker face, as well as sunglasses, and lazily stroked the dog's head. Gertie seem contented to get an ear rub, and didn't give any of them a clue as to what was in Jonas's hand. Shame. Connor had a lot riding on this hand.

"Call," Donny said, throwing in the remainder of his chips.

Evan, who'd folded about ten minutes ago, eyed the pile representing real cash and muttered, "Damn."

"Me too, I'm in." Connor chucked in the rest of his chips, figuring what the hell. At this point, he needed to see if what Jonas had in his hand outweighed Connor's three of a kind.

Jonas tossed his cards on the table.

Fuck if it wasn't a full house. A round of curse words lifted into the air.

A horrible winner, Jonas promptly patted himself on the back while scraping his spoils to his side of the table.

"Unbelievable." Donovan shook his head. "You lucky son of a bitch."

Briefly, Jonas's eyes flickered over to Connor. Connor knew his buddy well, and he knew that he did not consider himself lucky at all. He'd lost his family after the war—lost everything after the war except for his person, which was intact. On the outside, anyway. On the inside, Connor wasn't so sure.

Over the last couple of weeks he'd been getting worried about his friend. Jonas was a bit of a shut-in as it was, but he had been insistent Connor didn't have to come over. "What with your new girl and all," he'd said.

Connor ignored him and visited anyway. Faith was a big part of his life right now, but he could split his time with her and the man who saved his life.

"Beer?" Evan stood from the table. They'd set up in the great room, where Faith and Connor had draped every surface in gold- and cream-colored everything. Ribbons, flowers, garland…Right now, the lights were off, the corner next to the rebuilt stone fireplace cleared for the trees Connor was picking up this weekend. They'd decorate those to match, he imagined. He couldn't stop a small smile from pulling his lips. This frilly stuff may not be his style, but watching Faith's eyes light up whenever she was decking the halls had him warming to the idea of the upcoming holiday.

"Switching to whiskey," Donovan muttered, eyeing the pile of chips he'd just lost. "That's going to leave a dent."

"I only take cash," Jonas said, grinning.

Donny grinned back. "Ev, whiskey!" he called to Evan, who disappeared out into the foyer.

"Mess with the bull, get the horns, gentlemen," Jonas was still bragging. "But next time—"

Voices raised in the foyer—one Evan's, one Connor did not recognize. What followed was the sound of the heavy front door banging the wall. Without thinking, he leaped to his feet, turning over his chair. He was vaguely aware of Jonas jumping to attention and following him out of the room.

In a flash, Connor was in the foyer, shoulders back, eyes alert, fists balled. Then he spotted the reason for the ruckus and felt himself relax.

Self-proclaimed rock god Asher Knight stood in the open doorway.

Evan had him wrapped in a hug, lifted him, then dropped him to his boots. "The hell are you doing here?"

"At ease, soldiers." Donny's hands slapped both Connor's and Jonas's shoulders. He slipped past them and held out a hand to Asher. "Dickhead must have heard me say the word 'whiskey.'" Ash hugged Donny, clapping his back as he did. When they parted, Donny said, "You're early."

"Wanted to surprise you." Ash turned and pulled two bags from the front porch. "I didn't check in anywhere yet. Have room for one more in this mansion?"

"So happens I do."

Bags in hand, Ash nodded as he passed by. "Connor."

"Good to see you, man." Connor patted his shoulder. He'd be the first to admit the rock star—dressed all in black, his lean body suggesting he drank more than he ate—was a tad immature, but he supposed immaturity came with the job description.

"Maybe we should relocate to the bar in the ballroom," Donovan suggested. "Fully stocked." He raised a dark eyebrow at Connor before leading Asher up the stairs to show him his temporary digs.

"I'll take my money and run," Jonas said. "But thanks for having me."

"You good to drive?" Connor asked.

"Yeah, absolutely." His eyes were clear. Connor nodded.

Evan pulled out his wallet. "I'll cover Donny's since I'm bottoming out his booze tonight."

"I'll hit you later," Connor promised, then walked Jonas to the door. Once he was gone, he turned to face Evan.

"Shots?"

With his buddy good to get himself home, and his girl safe and sound at Gloria's, Connor figured why not. It'd been a while since he tied one on.

"Shots."

* * *

Asher, rings covering fingers latched around the rim of a glass half full of whiskey, leaned on the bar top, and narrowed his eyelids conspiratorially. "I have something to say."

They'd been hitting the bottle pretty hard for the last hour plus, by Connor's estimations. He was now nursing a beer and feeling like he might topple off his seat. With great effort, he leaned in. "So say it."

The rock star's gaze met his, but he looked like he was having trouble focusing. "None of you can tell your girls."

Evan muttered, "Fuck man, out with it." Far as Connor could tell, Ev had been matching them drink for drink but was nowhere near as plastered. How'd he do that?

"Especially you." Ash threw the shot back and slammed the glass. "Charlie and Gloria are close and I don't want her saying anything."

"Sounds serious." Donovan, playing the part of bartender, downed his whiskey and pushed the bottle across the bar.

"You either." Asher refilled his glass, then pointed at Connor with the bottle. "And you don't say anything to Legs. Promise? It's big, guys."

Though inebriated, Ash did look uncharacteristically solemn.

"Promise," Connor vowed. Whatever Ash's secret was, he doubted it'd come up in casual conversation between him and Faith.

"Promise," Donovan said.

When Ash turned to Evan, he nodded. "Yeah."

Ash took a deep breath. "I have a son."

The only sound in the room was Asher spinning his glass on the wooden bar, eyes locked on the amber-colored liquid. This went on for a minute, maybe two, before he spoke again.

"I have to verify he's mine, but she claims he's about a year and a half old. And I'm the father. Math works out," he announced, his tone glum.

Connor felt the world drop out from under him. Asher's story was a hell of a lot like his own. Maya coming to him pregnant, telling him she was having his child. He'd uprooted his entire life for a baby he later learned wasn't his.

"Who?" Evan asked.

Asher didn't look up from his glass. "Jordan."

"*Fuck.*"

"Who's Jordan?" Donny asked.

"One-night stand," Evan answered. "The girl who busted into his cabin the year I moved here."

Donovan's turn to swear. "Shit, man."

Asher lifted his head. "This is why I don't want it getting back to Glo."

Connor had heard the story trickle down from Sofie to Faith at some point or other. Bits and pieces he'd put together. When Ash was in town for the Starving Artists Festival a few years back, he slept with a chick who was here on vacation. Then he and Gloria hooked up. After that, Ash claimed he was loyal only to her, but Glo stopped by his place one night and the same girl— Jordan, apparently—answered the door dressed in very little.

"You'll have to tell her eventually," Evan pointed out.

"If the kid's mine," Asher said.

"Still," Donny said.

"It's his story," Connor interrupted. All heads swiveled to him. He looked at Asher. "It's yours, Ash. You need to be the one who tells it. I won't say anything." He exchanged glances with Donovan who likely knew right where his head was. Back on Maya. The day the dumbass biker showed up in his parents' driveway. The day she turned to tell Connor she was a liar and he wasn't going to be a husband or a father.

Connor had demanded proof, too. Hurt, angry, he requested a DNA test, but Maya had already had one and provided proof not a day later. Life as he knew it came crashing down around his ears. All his plans—quitting the restaurant, starting his HVAC classes, laboring for his father when it ranked right up there with having dental work—were for nothing.

In a flash, Connor realized he'd mired himself in a job he hated and was back living at home. A sudden desperation to leave overtook him. He had nowhere else to go since Donovan—his former roomie—had moved to New York by then. So, Connor enlisted, and deployed, beginning the four-year journey into welcome oblivion shortly after.

"Sure that's the only kid you got out there?" Evan asked, breaking the tension around them with a lazy smile.

Asher leaned on his barstool and hooked an arm over the back. "You're an asshole, you know that, Downey?"

But he was smiling. Covering, if Connor had to guess.

Donny refilled their glasses and they lifted them in cheers. For what, no one said.

Connor guessed each man had his own reason for drinking.

* * *

Three live evergreens were hauled into the mansion on Monday morning. Connor, Donovan, and Asher dragged them through the house one by one. Faith convinced Sofie to take a quick break to stand in the doorway of the office and watch.

Sexy men dragging trees around was not a sight to be missed.

Once the trees were in their respective metal stands, the fun part began. The decorating. The girls had gone shopping earlier in the day and therefore had an embarrassing amount of garland, lights, and ornaments. Sofie was also pleased to find a few boxes marked XMAS that had belonged to Donny's late grandmother hidden in the basement. Boxes that somehow had been missed when he'd donated truckloads of junk to the thrift store last year. Along with all the new decorations, there were some antique ornaments to put on the tree as well.

First, though, Sofie asked Donny if he thought hanging them brought bad juju. Faith knew his childhood was one full of abuse and neglect, and in this house, no less. Even though his father and grandmother were no longer alive, Faith had to admit, she had half a mind to toss even the most precious antiques into the trash.

But Donovan didn't feel that way. When Sofie had

asked, his eyes zeroed in on hers, then he brushed her lips and said, "You are my good juju, Scampi."

Seriously. So stinking sweet.

By mid-week, they were done with everything, including the toy shopping Faith and Connor had to do for their own donations to the drive. Being in a toy store, hand in hand with the man she was sleeping with, definitely made her feel as though things had become way more serious than she had planned. But then she reminded herself that she'd agreed she was all in. And "all in" included toy shopping at the moment.

Afterward, she and Connor ate dinner out, then returned to her house to wrap their gifts. The three large shopping bags in her living room took up most of the free floor space.

"Wonder if you could have bought any more Legos?" she teased, unshouldering her purse and pulling her coat off.

He caught the coat before she had it all the way off and strolled to her closet in the hallway. She watched as he hung their coats side by side, which also made her think things may have advanced without her permission. She quickly shut the train of thought down. Any kind of relationship with Connor would mean not overthinking every little thing. Plus, this time of year tended to be a nostalgic time of year for her, even though she'd never really experienced a Christmas in a traditional sense, so it was best she didn't put too much thought into anything.

"Legos are timeless." He closed the closet door. "Perfect for all ages."

"I wanted to do something tonight…" And since he was here, she would have to do it with him.

He came to her and rested his hands on her waist. "I

want to do something tonight, too. Three guesses what it is. First two don't count."

"You won't like it." She shook her head and peered at him through her lashes.

He frowned but he was teasing her, she could tell. "Is it candle wax? I had a bad experience with hot candle wax once, but it won't stop me from trying it again. Whatever your brand of kink, Cupcake, I'm in."

Lighting her on fire with his kisses was something he did on a near daily basis, so she wasn't surprised when his lips covered hers, then covered them again. When he gave her room to breathe, she palmed his face.

"*It's a Wonderful Life*," she said, giving him one more brief smooch.

He grinned. "It ain't half-bad."

She laughed, loving the sound, the feel of it rolling around in her chest. So carefree. How come, ever since he'd come into her life, her worries had erased?

"I mean the movie. Every year, I watch classic Christmas movies." She dragged her fingernails along the bottom of his head, through the short hair trimmed neatly at his neck. "Except for this year. I haven't wanted to force-feed you holiday spirit, so..."

"Because I won't go away, you can't watch your holiday fluff?" A smirk curved the corner of his lip.

She kissed it. "Right."

"Okay, Cupcake. But if I get bored, we get to make out during."

He didn't get bored. And what was more surprising, given how traditional his family seemed, he had never seen the movie. He claimed Kendra and Dixie watched it, so he always thought it was a girl movie.

"You are not helping relieve this assumption," he told her when she started to sniffle.

The credits rolled, and Faith wiped the tears from under her eyes. "It's full of hope. I guess that's what this entire season is about for me." She sniffed again, unable to help herself. "Hope." She rolled her eyes at herself and started to get up from the couch. "Sorry. I get sentimental."

He pulled her onto his lap, pushed the length of her hair over one shoulder, and kissed her neck. "I like you sentimental. Seeing you happy makes me happy." He placed another light kiss on her neck, then pointed at the tree on the other side of the room decorated in red and green. The miniature fake pine may not be much, but it was enough for her.

"That. Is an embarrassment."

"I know, I know." She felt her eyes roll. "Christmas trees. Bah humbug."

"No. *Fake* Christmas trees. Bah humbug. Should've let me bring you a big fat fir."

"And put it where?" She gestured around her meager apartment. With her couch and love seat, entertainment stand, and end tables—and now shopping bags—the room was packed.

"Just saying, you deserve a really big tree. You deserve a perfect Christmas."

She turned and wrapped her arms around his neck. "Why, Connor McClain, I do believe I'm making you sentimental."

Pressing her hip onto a certain hardening part of his body, he put his lips against hers and said, "I do believe you're making me something. Sure as hell isn't sentimental." With that, he tilted the back of her head and slipped his tongue past her lips.

They made out, the music from the movie fading into the background, the soft lights from her tiny Christmas tree illuminating the corner.

Life really was pretty wonderful.

CHAPTER 17

"You're pushing it," Connor said from the stove in his apartment.

Faith, clattering around somewhere in the back of his house, promised, "You'll like it."

Like it.

He grunted as he glanced over at the potted rosemary, shaped like a Christmas tree, then to the white and red poinsettias on his kitchen table, their pots wrapped in shiny red foil. Faith had insisted on bringing some Christmas cheer to his apartment since they were staying at his place tonight.

He'd gone to see Jonas for their normal guys' night but being in his friend's apartment had not been very uplifting. Jonas hadn't decorated for Christmas, either. And the fact that Connor had noticed the absence of it proved the effect Faith was having on him.

He left her at his place, and she promised he would

find her where he left her, in his bed, a sweet, satisfied smile on her face, wrapped in his dark blue sheets. Looking back, he would admit it was not easy to leave her there. But it was sure easy to come home to her.

When he walked in, he did not find Faith in bed, but bustling around his apartment. He found plants instead, which she insisted was one of the reasons he didn't like being home.

"How is it you love plants and have no plants?" she'd accused. Good point. He supposed to him, this apartment was never really home. Thankfully, she didn't buy him a midget Christmas tree and decorate it. But, she did buy a singing Santa Claus on the stand. Motion sensor. It started its repetitive *ho-ho-ho*-ing and Connor found the off switch and shut it down. That thing was going in the trash at the first opportunity.

Try as he might to be a Grinch, he couldn't be upset about any of this. Faith's smile lit up her entire face. She buzzed around here on a mission, thrilled to share things with him she had never shared with anyone else.

When he asked about her douchebag ex and their Christmases, she told him she and the jerk-off had decorated their shared house. Faith admitted she had always felt like she was doing everything wrong. Evidently, Michael was incredibly particular about his "environment," and she wasn't permitted to have any say in the decorations without expressed written consent. That being the case, even though Connor knew he wasn't a dick like her ex-fiancé, he was further incentivized to allow her to do whatever she wanted to do to his apartment.

Singing Santa included. Maybe he wouldn't throw it out.

"Almost ready!"

"Take your time." He'd come home from Jonas's house starving. While he waited he scrambled up some eggs. Leaning at the counter, he shoveled them into his mouth and waited for his girl to surprise him with whatever she was doing in his bedroom. In his bedroom without him.

Better be good.

Taking the orange juice from the fridge, he drank from the carton, then looked around his living room at the plants, the Santa…and silver garland draped over the TV stand. Damn, she was wearing on him. He didn't even mind the fact that there were Christmas decorations in his house. Not that he hated the holiday, by any means. He always bought gifts for his siblings, his nephews, and his parents. He went to his mom and dad's house and ate honey-baked ham. Eggnog was something he enjoyed with his brother-in-law, Tad. But Connor never bothered decorating his place for the holidays. Hell, he hadn't bothered unpacking yet. He never decorated his place, period.

Looking around now, he realized Donovan was right. This apartment was a crash pad. And Jonas lived much the same way. Minimal furniture. Boxes that should have been unpacked years ago still taped up. Like they were both squatting until something better came along.

Connor polished off the juice and dropped the carton into the recycle bin. When the container hit the bottom of the bin, he realized something better had come along. Faith had come along.

"Have a seat. I'll be right out!" she called from the bedroom.

No stopping the smile that inched across his face, so

he didn't bother trying. He moved through the kitchen to his small living room, but before he could collapse into his recliner, he froze solid.

The bedroom doorway was directly across from the living room, and since she had just opened the door, he could see what she'd been up to.

She strolled out of his bedroom wrapped head to toe in two things: red lace and multicolored lights. When he managed to drag his eyes from her see-through bra, to the scrap of panties barely covering her, he spotted the pair of tall, black high-heeled shoes. Those long legs got longer as she took steps to meet him. Then stood eye to eye with him. Eye to fucking eye. No need to move his head down even the few inches that normally separated them. Just her navy blues and the glow of red, green, and white bulbs against the surface of her very smooth skin, highlighting every inch of her perfectly toned, slim body.

She grinned at him, pleased with herself. She should be. He was going to have to excuse himself to pick his jaw off the floor. She'd tied her hair into a braid, and the length of it lay over her shoulder like a rope. The end of it was decorated with a red ribbon. He lifted the end of the braid and fiddled with the strands.

"I wanted you to associate the holiday with something positive," she said, her voice husky. "So…"

"So." It was the only syllable he could get out of his clogged throat. He dropped the braid and palmed her back. Instantly, she put her arms around his neck. He liked that. Liked that she liked to touch him. That she'd done this *for* him. That she was here and had decorated his drab apartment—and herself—like a Macy's department store window. He was a lucky guy.

Softly, her lips brushed his and his eyes sank closed. Then he pushed her a few inches away from him. "Much as I wanna touch you, Cupcake, you gotta let me look." His voice was gravelly and low.

She backed up a step and held out her arms. Draped in light, nipples peaked and nearly punching through the scant amount of material that made up her bra...God. Gorgeous.

He shook his head. All he wanted to do was look at her. Well, look at her and touch her. Touch her and feel her undulate beneath him like silk in the wind. Come together the way they always did, in a crush of expelled breath and unrivaled intensity.

But first. The lace. His eyes returned to her bra.

"I like you in red."

"Yeah?" She beamed, and not just because she was dressed head to toe in Christmas lights.

"Yeah. Come here."

Obeying, she clipped over to him and suddenly the setting was wrong. His apartment, a cold backdrop for the warmth he felt for her. Well, they'd have to make their own heat. Raising her arm, he began uncoiling the strands she'd worn for him.

"I decorated your bedroom."

He kissed the inside of her wrist and, for the first time, looked past her into his room. His bed was made, his black comforter pulled over the sheets. The headboard was strewn with white twinkle lights bound with red ribbon at the posts.

That was where she belonged. Beneath those lights. Spread across the blanket, the darkness a contrast to her beautiful pale skin and fair hair. Careful not to tangle her more, he pulled the strands of lights from her arm, from around her slim waist, from around the small swells of her thighs. He bent to his knees to slip the lights from around her legs and pull off her tall shoes. When she lifted one foot, he kissed the inside of her knee, teased the delicate flesh behind her knee with his tongue.

She sucked a breath through her teeth, sensitive to his touch.

"Ribbon on the bed's giving me ideas," he admitted, his voice hoarse.

"Me too. But I don't guess you'd let me tie you down."

He stood, skimming his palms up her silken legs the entire way. Heaven help him. They went all the way to her throat. "No, Cupcake, I tie you down, not the other way around."

She clamped on to his shirt and tugged his mouth to hers. "Kinky." She gave him a kiss, hard, forcing her tongue into his mouth. He accepted, spearing his fingers into her hair and destroying the braid she'd bound it in.

"Later," he managed, pulling her mouth from his. "Tonight, I want your hands on me. Cupcake, what I'm about to do to you..."

Her eyes went dark and wide, her mouth dropped open, not in shock, but in thrill. She wanted that. Wanted him. He scooped her into his arms, tossing the remainder of the lights to the floor and carrying her to his bed. He dropped her onto the bed with a bounce. She laughed, head tossed back, cheeks rosy, lips pink.

Damn. How'd he get so lucky?

Without removing a single piece of her clothing, he sank onto the bed, pressed his lips to hers, and kissed her long and slow. Kissed her until her fingernails abraded the back of his neck, until her breathy moans filled his mouth, until her hands began tugging at his shirt.

She wrestled with his belt buckle next as he continued torturing them both with deep, slow, wet kisses. On a breath, she whispered his name.

"Yeah, Cupcake," he said, giving her a break from his assault.

Fingertips slid down his jaw. "You're teasing me."

"Yeah. We're not rushing." He slid a finger over her bra and traced her nipple through the lace. Her back arched, eyebrows pinching as she squeezed her eyes closed. "You're my present," he told her, tracing the nipple again. She emitted a soft "ooh." He grinned and whispered against her lips. "I'm taking my time unwrapping you."

Those navy eyes popped open, something undeniably sweet in their depths. Like he'd flattered her by suggesting she was a gift. Rather than say more, he put his face against her neck and began his descent there.

Licking, nipping, and kissing every inch of her until she squirmed and begged and pleaded. Even then, he didn't stop.

* * *

She might hyperventilate and die. Yes. Possibly die.

The word "please" had left her lips about twelve times. Her body was damp, her skin chilled from the open-mouthed kisses Connor had left on every inch of her body. From the trail he'd forged from collarbone to pelvic bone with his mouth. He shoved her panties to the side and delighted her with his tongue, sweeping it along her center and making her claw at the comforter and beg some more.

This would not do.

"How many you want?" Mouth at the sensitive flesh on her inner thigh, his breath was hot, his voice muffled.

"I want you inside me."

"Not what I asked."

Dragging his lips over the lace panties, he bit the material and let it go. She was so ready, so swollen with need, even that slight snap made her buck. His fingers clasped onto the skinny straps at the side of her panties and dragged them over her hips, past her thighs, to her knees. He unhooked one leg and dropped the other over his shoulder, leaving the scrap of material dangling from her ankle.

"Mmm," he said, close, so close now to touching her. She was utterly bared to him. Open. And she wanted his mouth on her, wanted the release he promised. "How many?" He slicked his tongue over her center in the softest way.

She cried out, unable to keep from lifting her hips. He released her and she managed, "One. One is fine. Please."

What had he done to her? She had never in her life begged for a man to be between her legs, but Connor, who prided himself in his abilities—and good night, nurse, did he have a lot of bedroom abilities—was so good at taking her up and over, she'd become shameless.

"Connor, please, I'm dying." See? Shameless.

His chuckle reverberated over her and she squirmed again. "Not yet you're not."

Just as she was about to argue again, he buried his face in her most personal place and tore an orgasm out of her in record time. The release felt so good, she opened wider to him. When she did, he devoured her with renewed commitment, dragging a second, then a third climax from the depths.

As she pulsed and twisted beneath him, his lips left her. He climbed her body and, before she could open her eyes, sank his cock in to the hilt. Nothing felt better than him inside her. *Nothing.* Wrapping her legs around his back, she admired his bare chest, unsure when he'd taken his shirt off. She ran her fingers around the tat on his bicep, grasped the sheer strength of his arms, his muscles popping as he held himself over her and slid out and in again, deeper than before.

The man was a god. Therefore, she cried out the name.

He kissed her neck, suckling the sensitive flesh there and driving into her with so much force, she pulsed again immediately. This time when she came, it rocketed through each of her limbs, causing her to pinch her brows together and scream out, mouth open, breath ragged.

Screaming orgasm. A first for her.

His release was on the cusp of hers, and he wasn't much quieter than she'd been. Low, guttural, sexy male groans sounded in her ear and were drowned in her hair. When he stopped moving, he dragged his mouth down her chest, yanked back the bra she was still wearing, and pulled a nipple onto his tongue.

Her hands went to stop him, unable to take another attack on her very sensitive nerve endings, but he stayed inside her, continued suckling, then reached up and pinched her other nipple. Unable to keep a last orgasm at bay, her cries overtook her. He plunged deeper, suckling, pinching.

Voice lost, she gasped, shuddered so much she feared

she might fall apart. Only then did he let up, did he move that hand from her nipple to her throat, where he tugged her neck to his waiting lips. Their breaths eased, mingling in the silence of the room.

He kissed her skin one last time, nipped her earlobe, and spoke. "Say it with me, Cupcake."

When he pulled out, they emitted a moan in tandem. Every time he entered her, every time he exited her, they were together. Right there. On the same wavelength, bodies and souls intertwined. Shared breath, shared everything.

Like the world stopped and started on their marks.

Propped on his forearms over her, he stayed in that position for a long while—lips resting on her neck, fingers stroking her hair at the temples. He raised his head finally and watched her. She picked out the flecks of green and gold in his eyes, glinting in the twinkle lights over her head.

With a gentle shake of his head and a twitch of his mouth that might have been a small smile, he left her and wandered down the hallway to the bathroom.

Faith rolled to her side, put a fingernail into her mouth, and chewed.

Something happened just now.

Something big.

Something she was not ready for.

CHAPTER 18

"I know I'm supposed to be your calming force in the face of the pressure of the toy drive at your house but I'm not very calm right now and I kind of need you." Faith said the words in one long breath as she blew into the library office at the mansion.

Sofie, with barely any time to react, lifted her head as her pen halted over her desk calendar. Her mouth formed a perfect "O." After several seconds, she blinked. "Honey, what happened?"

Faith stuck her head out of the doorway of the library, saw no sexy men traipsing through the foyer, and shut the door. She wrung her hands and collapsed on the red velvet couch in the center of the room. Sofie joined her.

"This is not normal sex," Faith whispered. "Sex should be like...like...like any other body function. Like breathing. Inhale, exhale. Or…or, like that runner's high people who exercise say they feel."

Sofie quirked her lips. "I never feel that. Though, I don't run."

"Me neither." Head leaning back on the sofa, Faith turned to face her friend. "But you know what I mean. Your body is meant to act, then react. It should act, then react *appropriately*. Sex is a physical act. It should be limited to your body's physical presence." She sat up, put her elbows on her knees, and dropped her face into her hands. Her next words came out slightly garbled since she was pressing her palms to her cheeks. "He makes me feel things in parts other than my physical parts."

Sofie's hand landed on her back and begin to circle. Rubbing, consoling.

Faith lifted her head. "Don't tell me what I think you're going to tell me."

"Okay. I won't tell you I think you are falling in love with the sexiest landscaper I've ever met."

"I can't, Sofe. I cannot *even*." Faith felt her chest hollow out at the words. She stood and held her arms around her waist, pacing in front of the crackling fireplace, the flames low but warm. "You know Michael destroyed me. You know what believing in a future did to me."

The only way to safeguard against that kind of bone-deep hurt was to live in the now, not the future. Being independent meant counting on no one other than herself. At one point, she'd had a vision of her future. Not just the wedding, but growing old with someone at her side. She was determined to live in the "now," but Connor was making it difficult to stay in the present. If Faith let herself, she could easily start having all those future thoughts about him.

Sofe shook her head. "I don't see a woman who looks destroyed, honey. I see a woman in a great pantsuit—Ann Taylor?"

"Calvin Klein."

"Nice." After a nod of appreciation, her friend continued. "I think he makes you happy. And I think he is probably as gone for you as you are for him and neither of you will admit it."

That couldn't be true. Faith couldn't *let* it be true. "It's the holiday. Or the fact that he's really good in bed."

"How good?"

She delivered the truth like it was bad news. "Unparalleled."

Sofie pursed her lips. "Hmm. Well, okay…you know what?" She stood from the couch with such determination, Faith knew she had a solution she wouldn't strangle her for offering.

"What?" She clasped her hands together so tight her fingertips went numb. "Tell me. What?"

"Enjoy it, Faith. You said he told you to be 'all in' while you're together. So stay in the present. Be 'all in' in the moment. Doesn't mean you have to move in together or get married or have babies."

"That's essentially what he said." Faith's laugh was a little weak, but she'd admit to relief.

"Remember what you told me last year? You told me the power to walk away is all the power I needed."

With a sigh, she reminded Sofie: "You didn't stay away."

"No. I didn't. But I could have."

Back at her apartment, Faith thought about what Sofie said as she got ready for the toy drive. The same hollow-chest sensation returned. *The power to walk away.* Was that what she had? She wasn't feeling all that powerful at the moment.

Standing in her bathroom, she was digging for a bottle of perfume in the linen closet when she knocked over a box of tampons. While scooping them back into the box and cursing herself for being clumsy, that's when it hit her. When was her last period? She frowned as she stood, closed the linen closet door, and bit her lip.

A...while.

A little while.

Nothing to be overly concerned about—her cycle wasn't like clockwork anyway. She pushed the thought to the back of her head and continued getting ready for the massive soiree that was the toy drive tonight.

Her new black dress awaited, and a new coat and scarf. And new lingerie. Also in black. Black *lace*. Though she did opt for padding in her bra tonight. She knew Connor didn't care either way, but for the dress to work, she needed the help.

Yep. That's all she was going to think about the rest of the evening. Her sexy underwear, her hot date who would be wearing a tuxedo tonight, and the fact that she was living in the now. In the moment.

Not in the past, where she may have missed her period. Not in the future, where she'd probably start anyway and not have to worry.

Only now.

* * *

The First Annual Evergreen Cove Toy Drive was just about to begin. Connor had not seen Faith yet, and he'd been here for about half an hour. The majority of the Cove's upper crust was in attendance and had congregated in the ballroom.

Donovan strolled into the foyer from that direction, eyes wide with alarm. He was dressed in a black tuxedo, similar to Connor's, a bow tie knotted at his neck. "Did you know Mayor Thompson is here? The mayor. In my house."

"You've come a long way, man." He thumped his buddy's shoulder solidly. Donny had once toilet-papered the man's house. "Hey, where is Sofe? I haven't seen Faith yet. I assume they're together."

"They disappeared upstairs an hour ago. I haven't seen her since. She left me in charge of all of the bigwigs." He shook his head. "Not a good idea. I'm not exactly a people person."

Connor repressed a chuckle. His friend may not have been much of a people person before he reunited with Sofie, but as the owner of a thirty-five-room historical mansion that was often the site of charity functions as well as an annual summer campout for abused kids, Donovan was starting to look a lot like a guy who was the very definition of "a people person."

"I need a beer," Donovan said. "Only thing in there is champagne. Nasty."

"No whiskey shooters being served?"

"Too highfalutin for that."

Connor opened his mouth to say what, he didn't even know, because a flash of bright pink drew his attention to the top of the stairs. And to Faith—the one who was dripping in a sea of pink. She looked . . . God.

Sexy. Elegant. *Incredible*.

"It's not too much. You look beautiful." Sofie's voice echoed down the stairs.

"I just don't know what I was thinking when I bought it," Faith replied, her hushed tone drifting down the stairs. "It's like a prom dress or a—"

"Look at you," this came from Donovan, who sounded at least half as awestruck as Connor felt.

Connor had yet to unhinge his tongue from the top of his mouth to say anything.

"Faith," Donny said with clear appreciation, "you look stunning. Almost as stunning as my wife-to-be."

Sofie's easy laugh carried down the stairway as she took the steps. Donovan met her halfway and took her hand. The big-hearted brunette was in a floor-length black dress, her hair pulled back, curls around her face, but that was all of the details Connor took in before his eyes tracked back to his girl at the top of the stairs.

Taking a cue from his buddy, who had apparently become a gentleman over the last year or so, Connor took the stairs next.

"You got her?" Donovan asked him.

He scaled a few more steps, his eyes glued to hers. "Yeah, she's mine."

He felt a smile grace his mouth, grateful any words made it past his lips. His girl was a knockout. A vision draped in a sea of shining pink.

Faith looked too scared to move, her hand wrapped tightly around the banister, a worried look on her face.

"Why didn't I buy black?" she asked as he joined her.

Eye to eye with her again, he suspected in thanks to a pair of tall shoes hiding under her dress, Connor pressed his lips to hers, heedless of the glittery gloss being transferred to his mouth.

When he pulled back, her worried expression had faded. She lifted her thumb and brushed his bottom lip. "I really need to not wear lipstick around you."

"I agree." He leaned in and stole another kiss. "Why are you thinking you should be wearing anything other than what you have on? You are going to steal the show down there."

"That's what I'm concerned about." She twisted her fingers with one hand. "I thought black tie meant very formal, not literally wear black."

"I'm sure some of the other ladies are wearing colored dresses. Anyway, what do you care? Your only concern should be what I think. And I think you look like you need to be loaded into a stagecoach drawn by horses."

"Thank you." Her smile was almost shy as she looked at the floor. Her long blond hair appeared a little bit shorter than usual, every piece of it wound in big springy curls covering her shoulders and pouring down her arms.

"Although, if you really want to get out of that dress…"

Not missing his meaning—and how could she when they tore one another's clothes off at every opportunity?—she swatted his arm.

He offered his elbow. "Come on, Cupcake. You may look good enough to eat, but I'm saving that for later. We'll dance instead."

They took the stairs one by one. "You dance?"

"Well."

"You are a man of many surprises, Connor McClain."

He glanced at her as they stepped into the foyer. "I

hope you're not saying that because you are easily impressed, Faith Garrett."

There was a kid—probably not a day over twenty—dressed in a smart black suit manning the door. When the bell rang, he pulled it open and ushered in from the cold a shivering Gloria Shields.

"Oh my gosh, could it be any colder here? I'm from Chicago and I'm freaking freezing."

The kid's face flinched into a smile, and Connor didn't miss when the guy's eyes dipped to Gloria's assets the moment she slipped out of her long black coat.

"Oh, thank God," Faith breathed, pressing a hand to her chest. "You wore purple. I could kiss you."

The kid at the door lifted his eyebrows in a look that said, *I'd pay to see that.*

Not Connor. Faith was all his. He didn't want her lips being kissed by anyone, male or female, ever again. Faith scuttled over to Gloria and while they complimented each other and laughed, he stood statue still as that last thought echoed in his mind.

He didn't want Faith to be kissed by anyone other than him. *Ever again.*

After they'd made love last night, he had determined there wasn't another word for it. Sex was one thing, screwing was another. But being in her bed, under her gaze, wrapped in her arms and legs, sharing the same air...

It was a done deal. Faith was it. Too soon to tell her, but he did not have a problem showing her. He wasn't going anywhere.

"Glo, you'd better let me escort you." Connor offered his free elbow to Gloria, when Faith took his other arm.

"I can't let you walk around unchaperoned looking this beautiful."

"I got her."

Asher Knight, out of his required uniform of torn jeans and a threadbare black T-shirt, stepped into the foyer. His tux was black, his shirt was black, and he had even worn a bow tie.

Connor felt Gloria's hand tighten around his forearm as Asher's eyes clashed with hers. He knew that look. It was the way Connor looked at Faith. Difference was, Faith didn't recoil from him the way Gloria was recoiling from Asher now.

Fuck if he could blame her. Ash had not only slept with a girl shortly before he and Gloria started their thing, but he'd gotten the girl pregnant. Maybe. Connor wondered how soon Ash would find out if the boy was his.

"Come on, Sarge." Asher offered his hand. "We can be professional. We are here on business."

Stubborn as she was beautiful, Gloria lifted her chin in defiance. Her sleek black hair slipped over her shoulder as she regarded Connor with earnest blue eyes. Earnest, but hard. She struck him as a woman who had seen a lot of hell. Maybe not as much as him, but this wasn't a contest. Hell was hell depending on who the person was. And Connor guessed some of that hell was hell Ash put her through.

Helping his buddy out, because quite frankly everyone made mistakes, and Asher struck him as a guy who was at least trying to make up for them, Connor jerked his chin at Gloria. "Go with him. He gives you any trouble, I'll beat his ass."

To his surprise, the normally sharp-tongued, smirking

rock star nodded his agreement. "I accept those terms. Sarge?"

Loosening her hand from around Connor's forearm, Gloria slipped her hand into Asher's palm. He tucked her arm into the crook of his, turned with her, and walked through the foyer. As he did, he dipped his head and whispered into her ear.

A shiver overtook her shoulders in the strapless purple gown she wore, suggesting Asher affected her on a far deeper level than she would ever admit.

"Ready?" Connor asked his date.

Faith took her eyes off her friends to look over at him, a sentiment in their depths suggesting she had not missed what happened between Gloria and Asher, either. Question was, was she going to continue avoiding her feelings in the same way after Connor admitted his?

Too soon, part of him warned. He may be younger, but he was wise. He had a lot of life experience. Experience that made him more mature than he should be. Still, if she couldn't see what was between them now, part of him wondered if she ever would.

"Ready," she confirmed.

He breached the few inches separating them and caught her lips in his. But he noticed she leaned in and kissed him a little bit longer than was polite. He noticed because the kid at the door cleared his throat.

Connor didn't care. Her leaning on him was a good sign. He'd like her to lean on him a bit more.

A lot more.

CHAPTER 19

Connor was not kidding about being able to dance. She'd noticed before he was both big and agile, and as he spun her around the dance floor, she became more convinced that his agility was somewhat superhuman. Even when the beat picked up, he was able to hold her tight, lead with confidence, and avoid stepping on her toes.

The bright fuchsia dress she had worried about wearing, while yes, beautiful, was an eye-catching garment. She didn't think she had met a single person in the room who didn't compliment her on it. Fitted at the bodice, it hugged her small curves from chest to knee, where the mermaid-style skirt flared subtly into a pile of pink fabric that just brushed the floor.

A slit up the side allowed her to walk normally, in the long-legged stride she was accustomed to. Every time her leg poked out of the material, Connor looked at her with such heat she wanted to drag him into a closet and show him what was underneath her skirt.

What was it about him that turned her into a horny teenager again? Come to think of it, when she was a teenager, she wasn't horny. She'd been reserved. Probably due to the fact she couldn't have sneaked much past her mother. Oh and speaking of which, look who was at the bar...

Faith had pointed out Linda Shelby's arrival mid-dinner to Connor, who commented that she was beautiful. He was not wrong. Linda was stunning. Both Faith and Skylar had their mother to thank for good genes.

"Wine, Cupcake? I'm parched." Before she could answer in the affirmative—she did need wine, and a lot of it—he leaned down and took her lips in a very intimate kiss. "Although, I do believe I could subsist on you and you alone if pressed."

She tore her gaze from the sexy smile decorating his face, her lust fizzling as she met eyes with her mother. Linda stood across the room, giving them both the evil eye. Connor took Faith's hand and started for the bar—toward her mother.

"Uh"—Faith stopped him by bracing her hand on his arm—"maybe we could drink the water at our table instead."

He didn't miss a thing, his gaze going over to her mother. He lifted a hand to wave. Reluctant, but bound by the rules of polite society, Linda raised a manicured hand and wiggled her fingers.

Connor lowered his arm. "She can't be that bad."

Faith let out a choked laugh. "Oh, yes she can."

He threaded his fingers in hers as they walked across

the room, his stride confident. Faith watched as Linda's chin drew higher and higher. Faith's height was the one thing she did not get from her mother. Like her younger sister, Skylar, Linda was petite and several inches shorter than Faith.

"Well, well," Linda said when they reached her. "My daughter moves out of my house, I hardly hear from her, and the next time I see her"—she tilted her chin down to take in their linked fingers—"she is with a man that is definitely a different man from the one she thought she might marry." That derisive glare slipped over to Faith. "What are you wearing, dear? Did you need attention so badly that you'd put on the equivalent of a fluorescent road sign?"

Connor tensed. Well, Faith had tried to warn him. Ignoring her mother's insults seemed to be the best plan of attack, so she plastered a smile on her face and said, "Mother, I would like you to meet Connor McClain. He is a professional landscaper, and he returned recently from Afghanistan."

"A soldier." No telling if Linda was impressed by this fact, though she did utter a practiced, "Thank you for your service."

"You're welcome." He didn't offer his hand for Linda to shake. Instead he held on to Faith and said, "I was wondering when I would get a chance to meet you, Mrs. Shelby."

Faith noticed he didn't say it was *nice* to meet her. Probably because it wasn't.

"*Mizz,*" Linda said, heavy on the *Z* sounds. "Shelbys do not marry. You have a living testimonial of that fact hooked on your arm."

Before things got ugly, Faith needed to get him out

of the snares of this woman. Faith had thirty-one years of learning how to deal with world-famous, best-selling author Linda Shelby. He'd only had a few minutes. But before she could interject, he spoke.

"I assume, given the beautiful creature hooked on my arm," he said smoothly, "that Shelbys do dance."

"Oh yes. We dance. I saw you two twirling over there." With the lift of one fair brow, Linda said, "Light on your feet for a big boy."

Lord help her. Her mother was flirting with her boyfriend. Or...whatever he was.

"She had to learn it somewhere." He let go of Faith's hand and offered both of his to Linda. "I'm guessing from you."

Eyebrows rose high on Linda's Botoxed brow. "Surely, you don't mean to take me out there."

"I have a feeling you and I have a hatchet to bury. May as well do it civilly."

Where. Had. This guy come from? She knew Connor was smooth with her, but the way he handled her mother was...well, it was impressive was what it was.

Faith watched with disbelief as her mother accepted. Before he swept Linda onto the dance floor, he turned, palmed Faith's jaw, and dropped a kiss onto her mouth. "I'll be okay, Cupcake. I'm a trained professional." That delicious mouth of his quirked into a smile, then he went to the dance floor, taking Linda's fingers gingerly with his. Faith watched in silenced awe as her mother swayed to the rhythm and gave him what appeared to be a genuine smile.

"What is going on *there*?" Sofie asked, appearing at her side. And, thank God, with a glass of champagne.

Faith accepted it, guzzling down half its contents. "Connor McClain, Linda Shelby Whisperer."

Sofie laughed. "He is a smooth operator, I will say that. I didn't know that woman was capable of being charmed."

"Yeah well, he's in the right age bracket for her."

"Nah. He's far too mature for your mom."

"Fact." They watched the dance floor a moment longer.

"He's been through a lot," Sofie said introspectively. "Life has a way of aging people unevenly."

Those words were still rattling around in her head when he finally came back to her. Linda didn't appear to be completely tamed as she swept in the direction of the bar, but she wasn't bucking in her saddle any longer.

The evening winding to a close, Faith didn't feel badly about allowing Connor to lead her out of the ballroom.

"My feet hurt," she grumbled.

"Let's get those shoes off." Again, he gave her a look like she was made of melted chocolate and he wanted to lick her off his fingertips. She quivered. They walked from the ballroom, only to stop in the hallway. Raised voices were coming from the opposite end.

Asher and Gloria.

"We should go back..." she whispered.

"No, I have plans for you. Their drama is not my problem."

Hoping that Gloria heard her heels on the parquet floor, Faith clipped down the hall alongside Connor. She didn't mean to overhear, honestly she didn't, but it was kind of hard to miss the conversation. She clucked her tongue, pained by what she'd heard.

Connor pulled her closer and promised, "They'll be okay."

She wasn't so sure. She didn't know the details of Asher and Gloria's affair a few years back, but she did know Glo found a half-naked woman in his house in the middle of the night. As a woman who had experienced firsthand the pain of a cheater, Faith couldn't side with Asher on this no matter how much she wanted to.

Hand in hand, Connor and Faith moved from foyer to the great room. Immaculately decorated in gold and cream and with white lights strung everywhere, the room was elegant in its simplicity. Since this was where guests brought the presents, it was filled with wrapped packages of all shapes and sizes. A few oddly shaped gifts weren't wrapped: basket- and soccer balls, a hockey stick, and a pink bicycle standing in one corner.

There were so many donations, the packages wrapped around half the room. And, like its name suggested, the "great" room was sizable, which meant lots of presents. The drive was a success.

The double doors clicked closed behind her and when she turned, Connor was flicking the lock.

"What are you doing?"

"I need a minute alone with you." He came to her in three steps and caught the back of her head gently. Then he kissed her, and like she always did, she leaned into him, putting her hands on his crisp suit jacket.

"You look so handsome tonight," she said, resting her forehead on his. "Never thought I'd see you in a tux."

His eyes, filled with heat and wicked intent, perused her silk-covered body. "Never wanted to tear a dress to shreds before."

She laughed as his palms squeezed her hips.

"With my teeth." He caught her next laugh against his lips, and she hummed as she fell into him again.

"I'm in. Whatever you want to do in here. Under the tree? On the couch? That table looks sturdy." She shrugged one eyebrow into a come-hither lift.

Palm splayed across her back, he pressed his lips to hers. "All of the above. But first, we need to talk."

* * *

Faith's dark blue eyes popped wide the moment he said they needed to talk. He realized belatedly he may have scared her by that announcement. No good ever came of those words.

"Linda Shelby," he said, and he watched as her shoulders relaxed.

"Oh man. I thought it was something serious. Okay, hit me. What did she say to you?"

"It wasn't what she said to me that matters. It's what I said to her."

Her thick black lashes blinked. "What did you say?"

He pushed the length of her blond curls off her shoulders and took her face in his palms. "She told me you were cursed."

A smile that was almost a smirk lifted the corners of her pink mouth.

"And she said if I ever wanted to be married, I'm wasting my time with you."

The smile was gone. He kissed her top lip. And, very carefully, said, "I told her I did want to be married and I didn't believe in curses."

"Connor." A whisper.

"I wanted you to know exactly what I said so she couldn't turn it around." He let go of her.

Faith's eyes swept to the side and her hands clutched together in that nervous habit she had. "She's not wrong."

"She is." Linda was very wrong. Faith was the girl he should be with. She may not know that yet. He couldn't say he was ready to march down a white aisle right this second, but that possibility was not out of the question. For him.

"You have such a big, beautiful family. And mine..." She shook her head, her empty stare locked across the room in dismay.

"Cupcake, look at me."

She did, reluctantly.

"I didn't mean I want to get married today. We're seeing what happens. We're all in for as long as you want. Don't jump off a bridge, okay?"

"Okay."

He smiled. She was gorgeous, even frowning. "Okay."

"I have to get something off my chest."

"Go." His turn to feel a sharp stab of fear radiate through him.

"Your sisters play this...game. That's what they took me off to do Thanksgiving night."

"Right. The wishbones. The truth-telling thing."

"You know?"

He chuckled. "Cupcake, you think they have been sneaking into the attic for the last decade and a half and I didn't find a way to listen at the vents? Hell, I put a tape recorder up there one year."

She laughed—much more rewarding than her frown. Unable to keep his hands off her, he took her fingers in his. She bit her lip, looked half-nauseated.

"Tell me."

After a beat, she did. "I asked about you. I asked about where you went on Fridays."

He figured that would come up. All he'd ever told her was he had an errand, or had to visit someone. Respectfully, she hadn't asked more. Now he saw why. She *knew* why.

"I know it's an invasion of your privacy, but they told me about Jonas. About what happened. About the mother and child…" Her brows bent into a look of concern, her eyes blinking rapidly as if she was fighting tears.

"Faith." He put his hand on her nape and kept his hand there while she continued.

"I'm so sorry. I can't imagine how you feel. What it was like to see something like that. What it's like to owe someone your life." She shook her head and her hair tickled his forearm. "They told me if it ever came up, I should tell you what I knew. Kendra said you don't like to be lied to."

Kendra knew him well.

"I was waiting for you to bring it up…but I didn't know how far to push. What the boundaries are…with us, I mean."

Very serious now, he came closer and held her eyes with his. "Listen to me carefully. You don't worry about boundaries with me. Not ever. You have something to tell me, you tell me, honey. I'm glad you know. It's not easy to talk about. Not something I bring up in casual conversation. Reason being"—he put a fingertip in the tiny dent between her eyebrows and smoothed it out—"I don't want you to hurt for me. Not ever. I can handle this."

He could handle her, too. He could handle having her

caring about him, looking at him like she needed comforting, like she needed his strength. He'd been at it for a few months now—trying to get her to trust him, to lean on him. To let go of this ridiculous idea she had to be tough all on her own.

"I'm here for you, Connor. I just wanted you to know that."

Damn. Now that was sweet.

Afraid to acknowledge the feeling spreading across his chest like wildfire, he erased the gap between them and took her lips with his. She responded as passionately, pulling him by the lapels and ruining her lipstick yet again.

Backing her to the sofa, he reached for where he was sure there was a zipper. She continued kissing him as he fumbled with the tab, then there was a gap and his hand was brushing against her bare back beneath the strap of her bra.

"There's a hook and eye," she murmured against his lips.

"A what?"

Giggling, she turned around and lifted her hair.

Oh. A hook. He undid the pesky piece of metal and when she turned, she dropped the front of the dress, peeled it down her lean form, and stepped out of it. Now she was dressed in only black lace and a pair of tall, bright pink shoes. And stockings.

"God help me." It was a very real prayer. The stockings were black with seams running up the backs, thigh-high, and covering those mile-long, gorgeous legs he'd had the privilege of having wrapped around his back on a near-nightly basis. When he wrenched his gaze from her legs, he noticed straps and a matching lace garter belt.

"You like?"

"*Like* is not the word, Cupcake." He reached for the snaps on the garter, never having seen one in person before. What woman dressed like this? None he'd ever known. Faith was so painfully feminine, she made him ache. *Throb.* Yeah, that was going on currently. Figuring out the clasp wasn't hard. He flicked it and the plastic tab let loose like a rubber band, snapping her flesh.

Her mouth dropped open and she inhaled a short, sharp breath.

He felt his eyebrow lift.

"Stings," she whispered. And it was not an objection.

He undid the other three snaps, releasing the stockings and allowing the elastic to lightly sting her. He palmed her perfect ass cheeks, pulling her close and kissing her again and again.

She yanked at his jacket, pulled at his belt, and tore a button off the rented tuxedo shirt, losing it somewhere in the deep rug they stood on. Finger on the bow tie, she grinned at him, something naughty but nice glittering in her navy eyes. "I'd like to see you in just this."

"Just the bow tie?" He craned an eyebrow, amused.

"Yeah."

Lifting the tie, he popped the collar, wiggled the stiff tuxedo shirt out from under it, and pulled it off his arms. When he was dressed from the waist up wearing only the strip of tied silk, she raked her fingernails down his chest, over each nipple and to his abdomen. His muscles clenched at the feel of her fingers on his skin. So soft, so light.

So fucking perfect.

She yanked the leather belt out of the loops and unzipped his pants, sucking in a breath when they dropped to the floor. "Commando."

"I don't like to be restricted." He grabbed her up and in a flash of movement unhooked the bra at her back. Then he tore it off her arms and tossed it over her head. "You done with the bow tie?"

"Not quite." She tugged the bow, undoing it and slithering it from his neck. Desire flared in her eyes.

She wrapped the length of it around his wrists, but he was on to her, and no way was she doing what she was thinking of doing. He snatched the silk from her hands and lashed it around her wrists and, working quickly, tied her hands together with a knot she wouldn't be able to undo.

"You want to be taken, sweetheart, I'll take you. But you're not going to be in charge of anything other than coming with my name on your lips." She gasped and he lifted her wrists, bent his head, and took a nipple onto his tongue.

"They'll hear." The hitch in her breath encouraged him further.

"Yeah." He flicked his tongue over the peaked bud. "They will if you're not quiet." Pushing her onto the gold sofa, he laid her on her back and shoved her bound wrists over her head. Tied up, spread from end to end of the couch, she looked like a sacrifice waiting for whatever he wanted to do to her.

And oh, he had plans.

Without giving her a chance to say more, he reached for her panties. They gave, the flimsy lace tearing from her hips with a satisfying *rip*. Another gasp came from her lips, but when he looked up at her, her eyes were dark and wide, her mouth open, her chest and face flushed.

"Now you go commando, too."

"Is this bad? I mean, doing it in a room full of gifts for children?" Her mouth split into a smile, suggesting she liked the idea of being "bad."

"Yeah, sweetheart. It's bad. Not nearly as bad as it's going to be when I bring you to the brink and you have to try and keep it down." He dropped her legs over his back and settled between her thighs.

"Can I touch you?"

A scant inch away from tasting her, he smiled from between those creamy thighs. "Cupcake, we talked about this. You can always touch me."

She put her bound hands on top of his head, and he didn't need further encouragement before he took her onto his tongue.

CHAPTER 20

$\mathcal{S}$parks burst behind Faith's tightly shut eyes as she did her level best to keep from crying out. Not only had Connor stayed between her legs long enough to make her every muscle tighten and loosen to the point of being unusable, but then he'd slid inside her and continued moving until she orgasmed for...

She had no idea how many times.

Her wrists, still tied together, were hooked around his neck as he drove deep, pressing her hips and back into the cushions on the couch. Earlier, someone had tried the knob on the door and she'd nearly shot out of her skin. Connor assured her whoever wanted to come in could wait. "But you can't," he'd said, thrusting again.

"Tighter, honey," he said into her ear, his teeth nipping the fleshy lobe and letting up. Using her inner muscles, she clamped down on him, spent but willing to do whatever he asked. He went over a moment later, his low groans buried in her hair, his breath cascading down her neck.

They lay there after, breathing, recovering. Simply enjoying what had passed between them again. When he regained his strength—she liked how she stole it away whenever they were together—he gently lifted her hands linked around his neck and tore at the knot of the tie with his teeth.

Stripes pressed into her skin from the material. He pressed his lips to one of the faint marks. "Tell me I didn't hurt you," he said, continuing examining her as he held the weight of his body on his free arm.

With a deep, satisfied, utterly sated laugh, she said, "You did a lot of things to me, Connor McClain, but not a single one of them hurt."

He grinned down at her, that certain something hovering in the air between them again. She knew the emotions were dangerous. Faith didn't dare think the "L" word, but the affection they felt for one another was impossible to ignore. Every time they made love, he rattled her to the absolute core. Now, more than ever, she needed to remember her advice to Sofie last year. Faith needed to maintain her independence, keep her power. If she didn't, there wasn't a prayer she'd escape without getting hurt.

The man had the potential to destroy her. They were in the beginning stages of what they shared now, but after six, eight months, after a year or two, this part would fade. Then there would only be arguments about what was his and what was hers. Financial discussions, family drama, arguments that would erode and chip away at who they once were and all they'd once had.

When she left Michael, she had not left intact—and the scariest part was, the only reason she'd left was because he cheated on her. If she had stayed, she'd have been the same repressed woman she'd become with him. It was like she'd morphed into him over the years, forgetting who she once was. She could not allow that to happen again.

Maintaining her independence was about more than just being independent. It was about keeping her personality, her sense of self. Her strength as an individual. That was too much to give away to any man. Even a man who turned her inside out and then looked at her the way Connor looked at her now.

"Cupcake, you should not be frowning."

"I'm not." She smiled.

"You were."

"I...was worrying people noticed we went missing. What if whoever knocked needs in here?"

To her surprise, he didn't argue. "Valid." He kissed her wrists again, kissed her mouth, then pulled out and left her prone on the couch.

"Oh, I could so sleep." Her eyes grew heavy. After an evening of dancing, smiling for the crowd, handling her mother, and having mind-blowing, semi-kinky sex, Faith could sleep for *days*.

"We'll get you home, Cupcake. Get dressed." He pulled on his tuxedo pants, leaving his chest gloriously bare.

Home. Her home or his? Either way, they'd be together. Regardless of what happened in the future, there was no doubt their lives had merged, had seamed together so tightly there wasn't much space in between. Part of her warned of the danger ahead—how much harder it'd be to pull back the closer she got now, but another, larger part of her basked in the idea of snuggling into Connor's solid presence and sleeping the night away.

He held up the scrap of lace that used to be her panties and stuffed them into his pocket. "Keeping these."

With a laugh, her worries washed away. She sat up on the couch and redressed, watching as Connor tucked the wrinkled bow tie into his other pocket.

* * *

Christmas Eve came on a Thursday. Faith took the rest of the week off. She'd been sleeping at Connor's place, and was proud that not only had she brought in some decorations, but had also convinced him to unpack a box. One in a sea of many, but still. Progress was progress. The box he'd chosen was filled with some of the things he had from his time spent in the army. Letters from his sisters, care packages including drawings from school-aged kids, as well as handmade cards from his nephews.

She also found a frame with a group of very attractive, fit men wearing camouflage in front of a scorching hot, colorless desert backdrop.

"Look at you." She'd pressed a finger to the glass, over Connor's scowling face. "Hard."

"As nails," he'd commented, taking the frame from her. She asked him to point out Jonas and he did. The man was shorter than Connor, with dark hair he appeared to be at the start of losing. He didn't fill out his tank top nearly the same way Connor did, but without a doubt had an attractive, friendly face. Connor had named off the other guys, too, going quiet when he pointed to a dark-haired Hispanic-looking man. "Marco. Lost him."

Lost him. Those two words filled her heart with pain.

She'd consoled him, but not in an obvious way, just a touch. Placing her hand on his cheek as she cuddled with him on the recliner. He'd held her, eyes on the frame, mind on his friends. Then he hugged her close and she kissed his temple, and they made love right there on his living room floor, slow and sweet.

The man was a deep well. Maybe that's what scared her the most. She'd only scratched the surface of who he was, what he knew, but already, she wanted to climb into the bucket alongside him and descend to the bottom of that well. She wanted to know everything about him.

And she didn't want to, at the same time.

"Mom," he said into his cell phone now. He was laid out on her couch, arm behind his head, legs crossed at the ankles. His shoes were kicked to the floor and the television was on mute, but the weatherman on the screen was saying the same thing he'd been saying for days: A blizzard was coming. Right in time for Christmas.

"We can get there. Getting there's not a problem." He rolled his eyes when Faith smiled down at him. Leaning her elbows on the back of her couch, she watched the forecast and listened to his conversation with half an ear. "We'll get snowed in, that's why. Yes. Yes. Do you and Dad have what you need for the next few days?"

She glanced down at him and he winked at her. Sandy-brown hair mussed, strong arms, thick legs, and dressed in the killer combo of jeans and a henley, the man was sex on a stick. She smiled again.

"I'm going to stay with Faith. Make sure she's good." Taking her hand on the back of the couch, he linked their fingers. She tried to ignore how warm it made her feel to know he wasn't going anywhere. As a resident of Evergreen Cove, she was no stranger to the winters here. She'd been snowed in once before, and there'd been plenty of days she wished she were snowed in so she didn't have to go out in it. Knowing Connor would be here with his giant-ass Ram truck to help her get out if she needed to was a relief.

"We'll come see you after the storm blows over. Christmas dinner after Christmas. That can be a new McClain tradition." He finished his phone call with a "Love you guys. Merry Christmas" and a promise to call and let her know he was okay and not frozen to death. He dropped the phone on his chest. "Evelyn McClain has decreed there will be no McClain tradition of celebrating a holiday after the holiday, but since the advice of the mayor is for everyone to get where they're going and stay there, she will accept us for a post-holiday dinner and a gift exchange."

She held her smile in check; afraid he'd see the fear in her eyes she felt in her gut. Christmas with Connor's family was a big step. Bigger than Thanksgiving dinner. "I hate to interfere with your family time. I mean... I don't know."

He stroked her thumb with his. "You don't have to go."

She licked her lip and bit down.

"I get it."

But did he? She wasn't sure. He turned his head and watched TV, dropping her hand. She felt like she should comfort him, but before she did, her cell rang. She crossed to the kitchen counter, yanked it from the charger, and answered.

"I am so excited I can't see straight," came her best friend's excited voice.

"Do tell."

"A snowed-in Christmas and I'm in a mansion."

"Rub it in, why don't you?" she teased. "What about your family?" No doubt, the Martins—Sofie's mom and dad and two sisters—would want to see her.

"We went last night instead. Mom freaked out about the weather and called everyone in early."

"That's a good idea."

"What about you?"

"Oh, uh"—she stole a glance over her shoulder at the man on her couch who had unmuted the television but was likely listening to her talk—"we're here. No plans until after the weather blows over."

"I'm glad to hear you say that."

Uh-oh. What was about to happen?

"We want you and Connor to hole up here for the storm."

"Sofie—"

"I know. You two are doing it like rabbits, but I swear we will give you your privacy. This house is massive. Have you not noticed? And we have a master bedroom cleaned and completely stocked."

"What? Don't you two want to spend Christmas alone? You can run around naked and not worry about anyone seeing you."

This got Connor's attention. He sat up and cocked a curious brow her way. She waved him off.

"We do that all the time. It's always us here. And the ballroom, the great room, the dining room—everything is still decked out for Christmas. Seems like a waste if no one can enjoy it."

"Sofie..."

Connor's cell rang and he lifted it to his ear. "Donny."

"Your future husband just called my...uh, Connor."

"Your Connor. I like that."

So did she. A little too much?

"Donny will talk him into coming. Connor lives for home-cooked meals. Plus he'll want to look in on his babies while he's here," Sofie said of the room filled with lavender.

Sure enough a second later, Connor lowered his phone and called out, "Pack your shit, Cupcake, it's gonna be a Pate mansion Christmas."

* * *

Abundance Market was teeming with shoppers young and old who'd flocked to the grocery to stock up on food for the "big storm." In all likelihood, the storm would strand people for a day or two before salt and plow trucks came to dig out the residents.

Faith skirted around a woman with an overflowing cart. No one needed *that* much food.

When they set foot through the doors, Connor had palmed her back, spotting Michael rushing around looking harried. She'd seen him, too, but he hadn't seen her yet.

"You sure?" Connor asked, his concern evident.

"I'm sure. Divide and conquer is the only way we will get out of here before Christmas. He's too busy to notice me anyway." And if he did, what was he going to say? Nothing. There was nothing to say. He was engaged to be married to the girl he'd left her for, so really the potential of Michael striking up a conversation with Faith was pretty slim.

Connor kissed her on the lips, gave her a handled plastic basket—keeping one for himself since the carts were all in use—and rushed off in the opposite direction. He was tasked with picking up breakfast stuffs for the two of them, lunchmeat and cheese from the deli, and Faith was in charge of chicken breasts and frozen veggies, and wine. Sofie and Donny promised they had plenty of food, but Faith refused to show up empty-handed. She and Connor could wrangle together a meal or two during the long weekend without a problem.

After her basket was half full, she traded hands, wishing she could have found a cart. Food was heavy. She veered toward the wine aisle to see if Layer Cake Primitivo was in stock. She nabbed the last three bottles. The wine did not help lighten the load.

Next to the pharmacy, she put the overflowing basket on the floor and shook out her hands. There was a long line, mostly elderly people, and an awkwardly positioned stand to the side offered the appropriate combination of condoms and pregnancy tests.

Hmm.

She didn't have her period yet and was starting to legitimately worry. Maybe picking up a test wouldn't be a bad idea. If it came back negative, she could drink the wine in celebration. If it came back positive, she'd let Sofie drink it for her.

Sofie would help her through this. Faith would need a friend to wait outside the door while she found out if her fling had resulted in a child or not.

A baby.

God. *Terrifying.*

And sort of exciting, if she were being honest. But mostly exciting in a terrifying way.

She and Connor were friends, great friends who had great sex, but an entire life spent shuttling kids back and forth...? No thanks. A pregnancy would not a marriage make. She refused to get married and make it work "for the kids." For one, she was cursed, and she was not attempting to walk down the aisle in the name of a baby. She was raised by a single mom without a dad around. And while he wouldn't bail—she knew him well enough to know that—she also knew her child would be fine being raised by parents who weren't wed.

So really there wasn't anything to worry about.

Except having a baby with Connor.

She felt a presence behind her and for a heart-stopping second feared Michael had found her, or Cookie, and here she was, staring at prophylactics and pregnancy tests. Well, she could lie and say she was shopping for condoms. Way less embarrassing.

But then a rough, but gentle voice cut through the din of rushing shoppers. "Cupcake."

She turned to find Connor's brow dented with concern. His eyes went from the rack to her face.

"Basket got heavy. Just needed to rest a second."

He nodded, lifted the basket in his free hand. His basket had to weigh a ton, too. She spotted cereal, a carton of almond milk, orange juice, eggs, peanut butter, and bread, and that was just what she could see.

His eyes went back to the rack. "Something else you need to get?"

"Nope." She smiled brightly but he wasn't buying it, his expression one of frustration mixed with worry.

"Talk to me, sweetness."

Unable to deny him the truth—he'd never lie to her—she talked to him. "I'm late."

Hazel eyes hit hers and held.

"Like, really late," she said, her voice almost a whisper. "The timing is bad to find out, isn't it? Why add worry to a weekend spent with friends?"

He took a deep breath, his chest expanding under his leather coat. She held her breath, waiting for his response. At last, he said, "Grab two, Cupcake. We need to be sure."

Swallowing thickly, she nodded, pushed past a cart standing between her and her future, and plucked two tests from the rack.

Connor lifted his basket and she threw the boxes in.

Wordlessly, they made their way to a register with the shortest line, and he put the baskets at their feet. While she chewed on her fingernail, he pulled her close and kissed her temple.

There was no need to say anything. As usual, they were completely in sync.

She might be pregnant. If so, they needed to know.

If so, they would handle it.

CHAPTER 21

*Y*ou have got to be fucking kidding me." Getting out of the grocery store had taken thirty minutes, even after he and Faith had stepped into line. The cashier ran out of change, then ran out of paper bags, then the lady in front of them had to write a check but didn't have any form of ID.

He'd kept his cool throughout the very frustrating wait, kept his worry in check when Faith told him she might be pregnant with his child, but now, crawling through town while the sky dumped piles of snow at record speed was trying every last ounce of his patience.

"Should we go back?" she asked worriedly from the passenger seat of his truck.

"No, babe. The entire town is behind us. No way we can turn around and get anywhere." He glanced in his rearview mirror. Cars were barely visible through the blowing snow. They were closer to the mansion than either of their apartments anyway. "This was stupid. We should have stayed at your place."

"We'll get there." She clasped his hand and for another forty-five minutes, he rolled at snail's pace through the ever-increasing snow pile, finally determining one thing for certain.

They were not getting there.

A cruiser sat at the intersection of Lee and Smith Streets, the officer dressed for the cold in a fur hat and thick parka gesturing in one of two different directions. Connor didn't need to hear what the guy had to say because he could see a huge pine lying across the road through the blur of white.

"Road's closed. There's no way to get to Donny's."

"What? Why?" She craned her neck and must have spotted the mass of branches and limbs blocking the way because next, she slumped in her seat. "What do we do?"

"We turn back for your place, we can fight traffic, get there in an hour or two." The car that had pulled out of line before him spun in the snow before getting traction and lurching forward a few meager inches. "Maybe."

"Two hours," she mumbled, despair in her voice.

Or they could go around the tree, hang a left on Linden. The road would not take them to the mansion, but behind it. And Connor knew his way to the back of a certain friend's property.

"Have an idea."

Since Donovan had asked him to work on the cottage, Connor had been over there a few times. If the electric was out, there was a generator. And a fireplace. He'd cleaned the flue, so it wasn't like there was a family of raccoons living in the chimney or anything.

"Where are you going?" Faith asked as he swung out of the train of cars.

"Around." Putting his beast into four-wheel drive, he gave the officer—who was not Brady Hutchins, he noticed—a wave as he skirted around the line of cars. Then he turned and followed the snowy back roads to the cottage.

When she worried aloud they might get stuck, he assured her they wouldn't. What they needed to do was get off the damn road before they were wedged in between cars not fit for this weather. If that happened, most people would be abandoning their vehicles and heading for the nearest shops to take refuge. No doubt the hotels were full for the holiday.

Sorry, but Faith was not spending her Christmas in a hotel or a store. *Their* Christmas.

Our first Christmas.

By the time he was bumping along the snow-covered driveway leading through the trees to the cottage, she caught on. "Hey, I know this place. Sofie showed it to me once. How smart are you?"

"Very. Just ask my ninth-grade biology teacher."

Her soft laugh permeated the cab of his truck. He stopped in front of the cottage, relieved beyond measure they'd made it down the snowy drive.

He turned to her and smiled. "Food, shelter, and heat in a few. Stay in here and keep warm while I get a fire started."

"I can help."

"Cupcake."

"I'm not going to sit here and let you do everything. Are there blankets in there?"

"Think so. And if the electric isn't out, we may be able to get hot water. Furnace, not so much."

"I'll call Sofie. Let her know what happened."

"You do that. Sit here a minute. Let me at least clear a path for you to walk." She didn't argue. He leaned over and kissed her softly. "I got you."

He climbed out of the truck and landed in deep snow. Then he waded to the shed where he knew there was a shovel, pulled it out, and started to dig.

I got you.

A smile tipped his mouth and he let that idea warm him. Hell yeah, he had her.

* * *

"In his truck, waiting for Connor to shovel a walkway for me," Faith told Sofie over the phone. She felt sort of guilty sitting here while he dug, but the snow was shin-deep, and she had on a pair of tennis shoes *not* made for traipsing through the snow.

"Donny said there is no way to get out to you until it stops snowing."

"Yeah, I'm sure if there was a way for Connor to drive over the fields and through the woods to your mansion, he'd have done it already."

There was a pause on the line before Sofie said, "Unless you don't want us to come get you."

Faith would be lying if she said that thought hadn't crossed her mind at least three times already.

"You have groceries enough for a day or two, right? And firewood. And even if the power is out, there is a generator…"

"Sounds rustic," Faith said, not sharing her true feelings. What it sounded like was romantic. Spending the weekend in a cozy cabin, fire burning, sipping red wine...well, if the pregnancy test was negative. Wow. No way was she sharing that news over the phone.

"Not a bad way to spend Christmas."

Christmas. Faith thought of her apartment at home, the gifts under the tree, the lights she'd draped over her bookshelves. The stockings hung by the patio door. She'd miss being surrounded by cozy decorations. She sighed.

Sofie must have heard her sigh. "Honey, you don't need fancy decorations to make Christmas with Connor special."

"Mind reader."

"Call us if you need us. Donny was halfway out the door to do what, I have no idea, but I stopped him."

"He'd probably start digging a trail and not stop until he got here."

"Yeah, him and Gertie with a little barrel around her neck."

They laughed at the visual and then Faith noticed Connor coming for the truck. "Oh, I have to go. Here comes my landscaper in snow-covered denim."

"Have fun."

She shoved the phone in her coat pocket when he pulled open the passenger door. "Turn off the engine, Cupcake, and grab your purse."

She did as she was told and he lifted her off the seat and carried her in his arms to the covered front porch. Firewood was stacked against one wall, an ax speared into a log.

When they got to the door, he put her onto her feet. His

cheeks were red, cold, and his breath was coming out in visible vapor between them.

"Front door service," he said with a smile. Despite the effort he'd expended, he looked happy.

"You're in your element, aren't you?" She brushed some of the snow off his coat and grinned at him. He'd pulled on a navy-colored knit cap, and his hazel eyes looked almost blue beneath it.

"I don't love winter. But nature is nice. I'll give you that." He lowered his face and kissed her, a cold-lipped kiss no less delicious than any other before it. "You're nice." He opened the front door for her and they walked in. The inside of the cottage was nearly as cold as it was outside.

"Oh my frostbite!" She clutched her arms around her waist. Because it was *glacial* in here.

"I know. Fire first. Electric is out."

"What?" *Great*. Rustic was right.

"I'm going to start up the generator, but it'll take a while to heat the water. Might be able to get a warm shower tomorrow. Go to the loft, pull out all the blankets you can find, and pile them on the couch. We'll sleep in front of the fire."

She turned her head and saw the loft, wooden railings, stairs, primitive but meant to look that way. It was a nice place, if freezing. "Okay. The groceries?"

"I'll get 'em."

An hour later, Faith wouldn't say she was warm, but they were a lot closer to getting there. A monster-sized brown couch sat in front of the fireplace—Connor had shoved it there rather than leave it against the wall. He'd built a fire and started the generator while she put the food in the now-running refrigerator.

The bags they'd packed were also in the living room, and thankfully, the bathroom was in working order, even if the water coming out was icy and the toilet seat made her yip when she'd sat on its frigid surface earlier.

She was plating some cheese, turkey, crackers, and grapes for dinner when he slipped behind her in the kitchen. He was still in his coat. So was she.

"Will it ever get warm in here?" she asked through chattering teeth.

"I'll keep you warm, Cupcake." He wrapped his arms around her waist and tugged her back against his body. He was warm, in spite of being outside more than he was in. "Wine."

"Um…" Her eyes went to the unopened bottles. She wasn't willing to drink alcohol until she found out for sure if there was a baby in her uterus.

Before she could think of how to put that delicately, Connor said, "Go find out and then either we will share that bottle or crack open the orange juice instead."

She tried to smile, honest to God. But a smile wouldn't come. He turned her to face him and she went, needing his strength, needing his comfort. Some independent woman she'd turned out to be.

His palms tipped her face and he pressed a sweet kiss on the center of her lips. "Go."

"What if—"

"We'll deal with 'what if' when you find out." He tipped his head in the direction of the lavatory. "Go."

Snatching up the plastic bag holding the two tests, she thought maybe he was right. Better sooner than later. Better to know than not know.

Before she got out of the kitchen, he snagged her hand.

She saw a plethora of emotions on his handsome face—worry, she thought. Maybe concern. Maybe hope. They matched her feelings so well, she almost didn't want to acknowledge them.

He squeezed her fingers with his, then let go.

She went to the bathroom, tests in hand, courage teetering on the brink, and shut the door with a soft *snick*.

* * *

He had no idea how long these things took, and purposefully didn't look at the time on his phone when Faith went into the bathroom with two pregnancy tests that may or may not change their lives forever.

Instead, he stoked the fire, added a few more logs, and arranged the pile of quilts on the couch. The cottage was drafty. Yes, the generator was on, but the furnace wasn't an option. He'd had issues with it before and wasn't wasting good energy trying to fix it now. HVAC never was his thing. They'd have to make do with sleeping on the couch in front of the flames this weekend.

Of all the things he'd readied in here, insulation hadn't been top priority. Still, it was better than being trapped in traffic or having to hole up in a store on Endless Avenue for the night. They'd gotten several more inches of snow since he'd dug his way to the front door of this cottage.

Not exactly how he'd planned on spending his Christmas Eve. Last year, he'd spent it with a bottle of whiskey and Jonas. Then Christmas with the fam the next day. It'd been fine, but he'd had a hell of a hangover. Still, was always fun to see his nephews open their presents. He'd finally gotten around to getting a signed book from Evan

and Asher. That gift went to Drew, the reader. Corran was
the builder. Worked with his hands best.

When Dixie had her kids, Connor had been overjoyed.
He loved those boys. Loved his sisters. Tad was okay. Not
a bad guy, but not exactly up his alleyway. Aware he was
occupying his mind with anything but Faith, he stood from
the couch and paced to the kitchen. Maybe he'd open that
wine anyway. Have a glass or three while he waited.

Halfway across the room, the bathroom door opened.
He froze, watching the gap grow wider. Then she looked
up, her eyes red and leaking tears. Without hesitation, he
rushed to her. A moment later, he was holding her against
him, her cheeks wetting his neck as her fingers clawed
into his shirt. She wasn't sobbing, but she was definitely
having trouble pulling it together.

"Let's sit down, sweetness," he said against her hair.
He stroked it over her shoulder and started to pull her in
the direction of the fire. She didn't move, pulling his hand
until he was standing in front of her. Eye to eye with those
beautiful blues.

"Negative," she whispered. She gave him a watery
smile. "I don't know why I'm crying. I thought I'd be relieved."

Palm to her jaw, he smiled back as gently as he could.
"Not a simple thing, Cupcake."

"I just...the timing. It's wrong. And we...I mean, we
don't..." She shrugged, not knowing how to relay what
she was thinking.

"We don't have any plans to stay together. This was a
life sentence," he guessed.

"Yeah." There was more she wasn't saying. He could
see it.

Threading his fingers into her hair, he said, "But it doesn't sound like a bad life sentence."

"It sounded almost..."

"Wonderful," they said at the same time.

The same fucking time.

He lowered his lips and kissed her. Soft turned to deep. Deep turned to hard. Soon hands were pulling and pushing, kneading, and roaming. Unable to stand in the center of the living room and kiss her, he lifted her up and carried her over by the fire.

Then he laid her down on the pile of blankets covering the couch, stripped her bare, and made love to her slow and long and until they came in unison.

Came the same way they did everything—together.

* * *

"So much wine," Faith mumbled. It was cute.

His girl wasn't quite loaded, but she was feelin' no pain. After he poured her a glass of wine—and himself a glass—she'd had a moment where she felt bad for drinking it.

"Is it like we're celebrating?" she'd asked, frowning at the red liquid.

"Cupcake, it's Christmas Eve. Of course we're celebrating. Two paths, sweetness. One didn't pan out. That's it."

He hated seeing her sad. Up to him, she'd never have that forlorn, lost look in her eyes again. He got it, though. He may be the one bucking up for her benefit, here, but he'd been pretty rocked by her tears.

There had been a second he was certain—a million percent certain—that she was crying because she was pregnant. Which would have meant she was freaking out. Which he could live with. It was a big announcement. He knew, he'd been on the receiving end of it once before.

"I never told you about Maya." He kept his eyes trained on the flames.

Ever so softly, she spoke. "You didn't."

"Here goes."

She moved closer, snuggling against his side. They'd gotten dressed after—too damned cold to sit here naked. She had pulled on his henley and he'd tugged on his T-shirt. She looked cute in his shirt. He had his back to the arm of the couch and was stretched out with room to spare. The couch was huge. Faith's breasts were pressed against his ribs, her arm thrown over his shoulder, wine-glass aloft in one hand he couldn't see because of the length of the sleeve. She may be tall, but she was still a woman, and she was swimming in his shirt. He liked that just about as much as he liked everything else about her. Liked the way she looked at him when he talked. Liked how much she cared. Liked how she responded to him when he told her what to do, or when he wanted something from her. He liked how she kissed him, liked the way her hands felt on his body . . .

No. He didn't like it.

He *loved* it. He loved her. Sure as he was of anything on this planet, he knew that above all else. He had fallen for Faith Garrett. Sank like a stone.

Too soon to lay the news on her, he knew. Not after her dealing with the news today. Not during the holidays when she might think he's saying it for sentimental reasons. Wasn't like him to hold back, but he couldn't put that on her back along with this, the timing, and the fact he was just now confessing about Maya.

He loved her too much to do that.

"Back in the day, Donny left for New York and I stopped squatting in his apartment and moved in with Mom and Dad," he said. "I was nineteen. Stupid. Thought I knew everything."

"Nineteen…"

"Don't do the math. You'll freak out."

She spared him a smile. "I always forget we worked together."

"No reason for you to have noticed me."

"Hard to believe that. You're the sexiest man I've ever seen."

Flattered, he paused in his storytelling to kiss her. She tasted like wine, so he told her so. She offered her glass to share. He sipped and continued. "Maya and I would break up for months at a time. I met her in high school and we had this on and off thing. You know how you do."

"I did that with my high school boyfriend. Kid stuff."

"Yeah." He shrugged his eyebrows. "She didn't out-grow it, apparently. She came to me, belly round, told me she was pregnant and that it was mine. Timing was right, so I didn't even think. Just reacted. Went to my parents, told them immediately. Asked my dad how soon I could start working for McClain's Handyman Services, how to get certified, asked if he could hire me full-time so I could get insurance for both Maya and me."

"You were going to marry her."

He nodded. He was. Would have been an absolute dis-aster.

"So that's how you got your start as a repairman."

"Necessity." He'd hated the work. Hated the electrical classes, hated HVAC, hated installing cabinets and fixing sinks. Hated the process the entire way. But he'd have done anything to be there for his future child. For the woman he'd convinced himself he loved. "Maya moved in. One month later, she moved out."

"A month."

"The guy she'd been sleeping with after we broke up—or, God help me, probably during—pulled into the driveway one day and told her he'd changed his mind. Big, dumb redheaded guy on a motorcycle. Lee was his name. Skinny, mean-looking. Put her right on the back of his bike. I tried to stop her, tried to stop him. There was yelling, there was swearing. There was my dad coming out to the driveway to hold me in place. Lee flipped us off, left with Maya, and I never saw her again."

Faith placed her palm on his chest. It warmed him through the soft cotton of his shirt. "Connor."

He emptied the wineglass down his throat and put it on the floor.

"You flipped your whole world upside down because you believed you were going to be a father." Her eyes flicked to the side in thought. "If I would have come out of the bathroom and said I was pregnant..."

"We'd still be here on this couch." He cut her off, refusing to let her finish her thought. "You'd just be more sober."

Her teeth speared her lip. She watched the flames for a minute before locking on to his gaze. "I would never trap you."

Too late.

"I know, Cupcake."

"I mean it."

He brushed her nose with his. "I know." He sat up, throwing the pile of blankets off his body and putting his feet on the floor.

"Where are you going?"

"You want more wine?"

"Sure."

He stood, pulled on his pants, then sat down and tugged on his socks and boots.

"Seriously. Where are you going? We have plenty of firewood, don't we?"

"I"—he grabbed his sweater from the back of the couch and jammed his arms into it—"am getting you a tree."

"A...tree?"

His head popped through the neck of his sweater. "A Christmas tree. It's Christmas. Almost. You need a tree. We're not getting out of here tomorrow, either, I'll bet."

It was still coming down out there. Fast, too.

"You can't be serious. There's a blizzard outside." Her eyes were wide with concern, but he could also see she liked that he offered. And he liked that, a whole helluva lot.

"Cupcake." He leaned over her on the couch, eyes on the henley she wore. He could just make out the shapes of the pink confections that were her delicious nipples. He dragged his eyes back to her face. "You'd better find something to decorate with. Be creative."

Then he kissed her lips, and because there was no resisting the call of those breasts, dropped to his knees, lifted the hem of the shirt, and took a taste of them as well.

CHAPTER 22

*F*aith had amassed a pile of, erm…*unique* tree trimmings, when Connor finally busted through the front door with a very large, very snowy evergreen tree. He turned and gave the branches a shake, dumping piles of snow on the threshold.

"Grab that for me." He tipped his head in the direction of a metal something-or-other sitting on the porch.

She lifted the contraption, mouth dropping open when she recognized it for what it was. "You found a tree stand?"

He didn't answer, grunting as he hauled the tree across the room and to the corner. She swept some of the clods of snow onto the porch with her shoe, then shut the door against the wind.

It was still snowing, and blowing. Blustery, frigid weather and he'd gone out and chopped down a freaking tree. That said, she couldn't stop the smile from lighting her face. He went outside. And cut down a tree. *For her.* As romantic gestures went, this had to be at the top.

Holding the trunk with one hand, he held out the other. He was as snow covered as the pine leaning against the wall, stretching almost to the ceiling. She met him in the corner and handed over the stand. With her help, they wrangled the tree into place, knocking more snow to the ground, onto her, soaking through her sweater and Connor's henley she wore underneath.

She fetched a few towels to clean up the hardwood floor, but by the time she did that, there was only water, the fire having done its job at melting the snow.

Breathing regulating, he propped his hands on his hips and craned his head. The treetop stood about a foot or more over his head. He pulled off his knit cap, revealing messy hair, and sniffed, his nose red from the cold. He had to be freezing.

"Thank you." To show her gratitude, she kissed him. He kissed her back, taking his time, his lips cold but delicious.

When they pulled away, his eyes went to the pile of stuff on the floor she'd gathered to decorate the tree. Then his eyes went back to hers, thick sandy-brown brows rising high on his forehead. "Really?"

She studied the rather crafty, in her opinion, decorations she'd chosen and grinned back at him. "It'll be pretty."

"Love the way you think."

Something warm unfurled in her chest like a length of ribbon. Like twine wrapped around kraft paper packages. Whiskers on kittens...Connor had quickly become one of her favorite things, she realized. And the look in his eyes, the sound of his words...

He'd paid her a lot of compliments over the months they'd spent together, but he never said he "loved" anything she did. Always liked. Never loved. Figuring she was getting swept up in the sentimentality, the emotions—and the Primitivo—she shook her head to dislodge the thoughts currently nesting there.

"Gimme one of those blankets," he said.

She handed one over and he put it under the tree. "That'll take care of the melting snow and double as a tree skirt."

"Now we decorate."

"First, more wine," he instructed. "And I'm starving."

* * *

It was nearly two a.m.

The last two hours were split between the kitchen and decorating the tree and finishing the third bottle of wine.

Faith hiccuped, then giggled, satisfied when it was answered by a deep rumble of laughter at her back.

Connor was happy. She was happy.

Life couldn't be better. Even here, in a barely heated cabin, buried beneath inches of snow, cobbling together dinner as best they could. The stove was gas, so she guessed they could have made it work, but instead they'd slapped ham and cheese onto bread with no condiments.

"Needs mustard," Connor had replied glumly.

"Mayo," she'd argued.

After choking down their late-night dinners, without chips she might add, they opened more wine. Because, why not? Bellies full, they decorated the tree, laughing as they did, because honestly, the décor was kind of funny.

"Our Christmas tree is turning me on." His voice reverberated off her rib cage. They'd fed the fire and returned to their blanket pile on the couch to admire their handiwork, her against his chest, him holding the wineglass they were sharing.

"I think it's festive."

"The red one is." He kissed her temple and pointed at the lacy bra strung over two branches. "Red one's my favorite."

Yes, she'd adorned their Christmas tree with her underthings. They were pretty and delicate, and in the absence of garland and tinsel, she had to think of something. Thongs and bras it was. But he'd contributed, too.

"I think the spoons are a nice touch," she said.

The silverware—and she used that term loosely—in the drawers of the kitchen had to be the cheapest flatware on the planet. While they were preparing their dinner, he lifted one of the spoons up and bent it in half with his thumb, then lifted an eyebrow.

"Do it," she'd said. "We'll replace them with something nicer. Just save a few to eat with."

Now, bent spoons and forks hung on branches, catching the light from the fire and winking at them conspiratorially. The finishing touch was on the top branch. One of her black pumps, with a very tall heel and red sole, acted as the angel on their naughty yuletide tree. She'd brought the shoes with nefarious plans in mind. Wearing nothing but them, for example.

When she confessed her intentions, he'd smiled approvingly and told her, "Gonna take you up on that, Cupcake."

She smiled at the eyesore on the side of the tree—where a few branches had snapped during the drag indoors. Other than sacrificing one of their couch pillows, there was nothing doing for filling the hole. "Looks like someone took a bite out of the tree."

"Hey, you go chop a tree down and see how easy it is," he teased.

"No way."

The arm he'd wrapped around her was solid. He squeezed her gently. "It's not perfect."

"It is, though." She rested a hand over his and interlaced their fingers.

"Yeah," he agreed quietly. "It is."

They sat, snuggled together in their couch-and-blanket fort, and listened to the soothing sounds of the logs crackling in the flames. After a minute or two had passed, she turned her head and caught his lips. "I'm so sleepy."

He snagged one more kiss. "Me too, Cupcake. Let me get rid of the glass."

Before he sat up, she stopped him. "No, you've done everything. I'll get it." She climbed over him and out of their makeshift bed and took the wineglass. In the kitchen, she did some light cleanup, rinsing the plate they'd shared, tossing the paper towel into a paper grocery sack acting as a trash can. When she returned to the living room, she found Connor, eyes closed, mouth open slightly. The firelight lit the sharp planes of his face, the full set of his mouth.

He was so very attractive. So deadly gorgeous. Her eyes went to the tree. He was also sweet, so sweet she ached with longing. She was beginning to think he'd do anything for her. She was beginning to think he'd do anything for *anyone*. Like take care of this place when he hated handyman work because Donovan asked. Or start working for his father when his girlfriend came to him needing a *baby daddy*.

A deep sigh worked its way from her belly and blew out of her nose. There was something about him being willing to do anything for her that made her feel as if she was leaning on him too much.

If that pregnancy test had been a plus instead of a minus, he would have made things right for her. But was it because he did what always needed done? Because he had a strong sense of duty? Or because he genuinely wanted to help?

Did Connor do what he *needed* to do or what he *wanted* to do?

Was he with her because he wanted to be? Or was she just so needy he responded to her neediness with service.

Tread lightly, girl, her heart warned.

He was giving her everything she wanted...but what about him? If he was shortchanging himself, he'd realize it eventually. And then she'd be in the same position she was with Michael.

That was something she couldn't risk. Not ever.

The negative pregnancy test was a blessing. Because Connor, whether he'd admit it or not, was now free to go whenever he wanted.

And so was she.

* * *

Faith was fast asleep when steam from a coffee mug curled into her nostrils. Connor watched her eyes flutter open, thinking she might be the most beautiful he'd ever seen her.

Hair everywhere, flowing like a blond fountain over the blankets, pillows, and his shirt she'd slept in. Her lips tipped into a cute smile, her eyes blinked again, heavy and groggy.

"Mornin', Cupcake." His voice was craggy from waking too early. He'd been restless come sunlight. Christmas morning hadn't been a morning he was anxious for in years.

Until this year.

She had changed him. In a short time, and for the better. Watching her love of the holidays, her genuine, childlike excitement for a time of year that typically fed his soul nothing but depression, he had opened his eyes this morning excited for the first time in years.

She'd done that for him. And for that reason, he wanted to make her morning the most special one she'd ever had.

"Where did you get that?" Her eyes were wide and filled with gratitude, focused only on the mug.

"Wouldn't you like to know?" He'd looked for a coffeepot and coffee—though it would have been some ancient, nasty coffee he'd bet—but found nothing. So he had to start looking elsewhere.

She sipped and closed her eyes, then smiled. "You found my stash."

He grinned back at her. "I did." Instant coffee. Just add hot water. Hot water, thanks to a gas stove and copper-bottomed saucepan, he'd managed.

"Bless you."

He sat on the edge of the sofa and snagged the cup from her grasp. "You have to share. There was only one packet left."

She pouted.

He winked at her, took a drink. Mmm. Good for instant. He was impressed. Handing back her cup, he kissed her temple then stood. "Merry Christmas, sweetness."

"Merry Christmas, beefcake."

With a chuckle, he strode to the kitchen. "I'm making breakfast. Hang tight."

* * *

The sight of Connor walking away from her had one very big advantage. *Dat ass.*

She grinned in the wake of that swagger. His butt was snugly gripped in denim, along with his other, and her most favorite, appendage. And, man, could he use it. The man was sex on legs, and if that wasn't impressive enough, he'd excavated into the depths of her purse to find her last packet of Starbucks Via and made her a cup of coffee.

Curling her hands around the mug, she took another precious drink. Caramel flavored and he'd even poured in a splash of almond milk. And now, he was making her breakfast.

Something about him being a keeper flitted through her brain, but she pushed it out again. Dangerous thought, that.

The sun came out from behind the clouds, pouring in through the open curtains, and she turned to squint outside. Drawn to the window by the bright, almost blinding amount of white, she carefully kicked the blankets off and went to see what the day looked like.

A long stretch of land dotted with trees—both evergreens and those without any leaves—was covered with piles of fluffy snow. Unmarred by animal prints, or human shoe prints—not even Connor's from last night. The early hours must have brought more snow and filled in his tracks. The wind had drifted a white curve like a wave over the window's edge. Snow weighed down the pine bows and maple tree branches, and settled several inches on a wooden slat fence standing on either side of the driveway. Connor's massive truck was buried, snow almost to the wheel well.

Unable to keep her feelings in about how gorgeous the landscape was outside her window, she muttered, "Wow."

"Nature's majesty," she heard behind her. Big arms looped around her waist as he relieved her of her coffee mug and took a drink. His front warmed her back, and she enjoyed the luxury of leaning against him, of being totally folded against his body. "Been a while since I've been snowed in," he said. "Eighth grade, maybe."

"It's beautiful here." She sighed, grateful they had nowhere to be.

"It is."

"Why do we live in apartments?" she wondered aloud. She hadn't expected an answer, and was surprised to get one.

"Don't know."

"Especially you. You must love being out here, surrounded by this landscape. Imagine it in the summer. Green, full trees, the field out there covered with high grass."

"Not hard to imagine considering I've been caring for the land for a year now."

"Really?" She didn't know that. As he talked about the

tasks of clearing felled trees and thick brush, she could hear the excitement in his voice.

"If not for the paperwork," he grumbled.

"Mmm. I saw the pile on your kitchen table," she said. "I cleaned it up as best I could the night I...decorated myself for you."

His arms squeezed a little tighter. "Like how you decorate."

Like. See? Maybe everything was back to normal.

"You should get a handle on your invoicing. There are a lot of write-offs for a business, you know. I've learned a lot from Sofie."

"Bet you have," he said noncommittally.

It was on the tip of her tongue to offer to help him get his business in order, but then, that wasn't really on the table, was it? They were doing...well, each other, quite frankly. So it wasn't like she should meddle in his business affairs. But part of her called her a liar. Because since she'd stepped out of that bathroom with tears in her eyes, things between them were way beyond "doing each other."

When that thought settled uncomfortably in the pit of her stomach, she opted to change the subject. "Tell me your favorite Christmas memory." Outside, the sun glistened on the snow, making it glitter in the golden light. A breeze shifted the pines and flurries swirled in the air.

"Hmm." His low timbre vibrated pleasantly along her ribs. "Probably the Christmas I spent with Donny. Christmases with my family when I was a kid were nice—the way you get gifts and favorite toys. But the time I spent out on my own, doing things my way, was the best. And it was the only Christmas I spent like that. Then I was back home with Mom and Dad."

"Maya."

"Yeah. Maya."

"What was special about yours and Donny's Christmas? That you got to drink way too much?"

He chuckled and she liked how happy and relaxed he sounded. She drew a deep, satisfied breath.

"I made him get a tree."

"Drag it in from the out-of-doors, did you?"

"Basically. I did go to a tree farm to pick it out, but it was last minute and it was a sad, sorry-assed tree. You know, like the one at your apartment."

She elbowed him gently. It was like elbowing a brick wall. His laugh was soft and low and warmed the center of her chest as well as any cup of coffee.

"Anyway, it was a scraggly tree. You think we're having a Charlie Brown Christmas? You should've seen that collection of twigs."

She smiled at the idea of two bad boys cobbling together Christmas. "And then you two, what? Roasted chestnuts?"

"Nah." His voice went quiet and he handed back her mug, then wrapped both arms around her. "We talked about family. About girls. He told me bits and pieces of his past. I told him about Maya. We'd been split up for a while, but I was missing her. Or not her, but someone. I didn't know what the hell I was doing back then."

"I don't know what the hell I'm doing most of the time," she admitted. She didn't. She was firmly planted in adulthood and she still felt under-qualified to make major life decisions.

"I think that's normal."

"You seem to have it together." He had his family,

his friends, his own business. Sloppy paperwork aside, he seemed to be doing a hell of a lot better than most people twice his age. She felt as if she'd latched on to everyone she knew. She worked for her best friend, her mother had let her move back home last year, and now she was relying on Connor to taxi her around, to take care of her on Christmas...

"Trust me, Cupcake. I am figuring things out, too. I didn't even unpack my shit until you made me."

"Just one box."

He was quiet for a bit before asking, "What about you? Favorite Christmas?"

She chewed her lip, stared into her light brown coffee, and drew in a deep breath. Then she told the truth. "This one."

"Faith."

"You've turned something potentially awful into the best holiday I can remember." Eyes focused on the glittering snow outside, she smiled.

"Sweetheart." His hands left her waist and palmed her hips.

"It's true, Connor," she said to the window.

He moved her hair with his chin and kissed the side of her neck. She helped him out by tilting her head, giving him enough space to continue the exploration. He did, turning her so he could glide his tongue along her collarbone, to the hollow of her throat, back up until it curled around her earlobe.

A sigh drifted from her lips.

Earlobe in his teeth, he groaned into her ear. "Have an idea."

"You do?" she asked on a gasp. His mouth was intoxicating. Her body was already going pliant as she leaned into him.

"Xmas nookie."

Her eyes flew open and she laughed, loud. She smiled at him and he smiled back. "Charming."

"You prefer eloquence?" he asked.

"Are you capable of it?"

Mock surprise colored his features. He stole her mug and put it on a nearby side table. "You kidding? Full of it."

"You're full of something."

He flattened his hands on her back and tugged her closer. "I'm full of you."

Breath hitching in her throat, she tried but couldn't make light of that statement. Like she'd been honest with him when she told him this was her favorite Christmas, she could see he was being just as honest. His eyes were sincere. His gaze intense.

He didn't let up.

"My life is full with you in it, Faith," he said, his voice low, his eyes glued to hers. "Been a lot of years since I've felt anything but hollow."

Sensing something big was coming, she felt her body go from pliant to tense.

"Especially in the winter." His eyes slid to the side. "Everything dies. Different season than Afghanistan, but it has the same effect. Over there everything is dead because it's so freaking hot. Here, it's dead because it's colder than a witch's tit."

She wanted to tease him about his lack of eloquence, but couldn't. His face was too serious, his eyes lost in memory.

"Whenever I was home for the holidays, my mood was

shit. The indoor greenhouse Donny let me build in his house last year helped. He knew I needed it. Having my hands in the soil, having a project, made the winter more bearable. But this year, hell...I didn't have to bury my hands in the dirt to find life." He focused on her. "I found it in you."

Oh. Oh, wow. She wanted to say something to ease the tension between them, but her mind was a blank. Her heart beating fast, her mind trying to process what he was telling her.

"Watching you with my family"—his brow creased as his eyebrows drew together—"watching you light up when we decorated the mansion for the toy drive...I've never seen anyone in my life get so excited over lights on string. And the way you smiled when we sat down to *It's a Wonderful Life*, listening to the way you laughed when I teased you. Can't get any more life into the moments I've spent with you."

Her eyes were burning with unshed tears. She blinked frantically. It was the season. Christmas made everyone softer, drew people together, made them more sentimental. Maybe he meant what he was saying, and maybe he didn't. She wouldn't allow it to penetrate her heart. She couldn't.

"Wasn't going to tell you this last night because I was afraid you would think I was feeling the holiday spirit—"

Oh no.

"But I can't not tell you the truth, Cupcake. You deserve it. Regardless of the crap timing, the holiday, or the two negative pregnancy tests in the bathroom trash can."

"Connor, don't do this." It was a plea. Her eyes on his, she begged with them, too.

"I don't care if you feel the same way or not, but you need to know—"

"Connor."

"I'm all in, babe. I fell for you so hard, my head's spinning. I know it in my gut. The way I knew overseas when danger approached. That pit of my stomach certainty I can't deny."

But he hadn't known about the terrorist that almost shot and killed him, she thought automatically. His focus had been on the mother and child. On something beautiful, something pure. His attention had been elsewhere, not on his gut.

She shook her head, sure she shouldn't say *that*.

"Quit freaking out and kiss me."

"Connor." It seemed to be the only two syllables she was capable of speaking. He didn't care.

"I love you, Faith. Kiss me." The pressure increased on her back. His hand left her to snag the coffee mug. "Or else I'll drink the rest of it, I swear."

The tension broke and she laughed, a few stray tears leaking from her eyes.

"Ah, there she is." His smile was so pure, so genuine, she returned it. His lips came closer to hers. "This is as good as it gets, baby. Give me a kiss and tell me Merry Christmas."

He stole her lips and she went, careful not to spill the precious coffee he'd bribed her with. Pressing into him, she enjoyed his strength, his arms, his heat. She kissed him and decided for today, for now, in this peaceful, perfect landscape where they were together, she would allow his words into her heart.

Just a little.

It was the best kiss of her entire life.

When they parted, his eyes were heavy, his gaze hot.

"Merry Christmas," she whispered.

He handed back her coffee.

"Breakfast," he reminded them both. "Almost forgot."

"I almost forgot my own name," she joked.

He shook his head, smiled, and turned, walking to the kitchen. She watched him go, but this time didn't admire his attractive form. This time, her mind was latched on to three words she hadn't expected to hear from any man ever again, let alone this man.

I love you.

He'd really said it. Blurted it out like it was the truest thing in the world. And she hadn't returned his sentiment. Because she felt a lot of things for Connor, but love...love was dicey.

Love left her in shambles, practically at the altar.

She agreed what she felt for him was an intense emotion, but in her experience, love wasn't intense. Love was an emotion that was sure and strong, but subtle. The way she loved her sister, Skylar, or her best friend, Sofie.

Maybe what she felt for Connor was lust. Okay, no maybe about it. What she *definitely* felt for Connor was lust. And what he felt for her? Probably the same thing.

By the time she turned to study the snow outside of the window again, her coffee had gone cold.

More proof that the longer things go on, the less appealing they become.

$\mathcal{C}$HAPTER 23

$\mathcal{T}$he phone calls and texts started as they sat down to breakfast. Connor made omelets, loaded with ham and cheese. They were incredible.

Sofie started texting first thing in the morning, right around the time Donny called Connor. Faith was sure Donny's call had everything to do with a reconnaissance mission to dig them out, whereas Sofie's back-and-forth texts were an attempt to extract sexy details out of her.

Not long after Sofie promised to let her get back to Connor, Skylar called and encouraged her to call Linda Shelby. So, at her sister's prodding, Faith hung up and called her mother. Linda may not celebrate Christmas, but she was glad to hear her eldest daughter was "alive and well" as she put it. She nearly made it off the phone without mentioning Connor when the man stood, lowered his lips to the phone, and said, "Merry Christmas, *Mizz* Shelby." Then he winked at Faith while she rolled her eyes and did her level best to answer her mother's prying questions.

One thing was certain: Somehow, he'd won over her mother on the dance floor.

Connor's mother called next, and he told her he needed to finish eating his breakfast, then handed off his cell to Faith. Lyn wished her happy holidays before passing the phone to Kendra who tried to pressure her to come over for post-Christmas dinner and gifts. Faith didn't say yes, but she didn't say no, and the only reason she got away with that was because Pennsylvania-based Dixie was not in town yet. Ken jokingly wished her a Merry Christmas with "my stupid brother," then ended the call.

Faith slid his cell across the table while he finished his omelet in two big bites.

She'd seriously never seen him as at ease as he was right now—even in bed—and she'd seen him plenty at ease there. Something shined in his eyes—something relaxed and easygoing. He thought he was in love. In love with her and enjoying his first Christmas in a long, long while. And she'd made that possible for him.

She wanted more than anything to let go of fear and jump off the cliff with him. He'd catch her. Probably.

"What are you thinking so hard about?" he asked from the sink as he rinsed his plate. "I smell something burning."

"Ha-ha."

"This morning, I'm guessing," he said.

He really wasn't going to let this go. Further proving her point, he came to where she was sitting and knelt in front of her chair, scraping the metal legs when he pulled her around to face him.

"Told you, Cupcake, you don't have to reciprocate. You just keep doing what you're doing. You keep being your sweet self, keep smiling at me, laughing at my jokes, and screwing my brains out."

Shocked, she drew a hand back and slapped one rounded shoulder. Her hand stung. She swore. The man was solid rock. Except for his gooey center. Gosh. He'd fallen for her. She loved the idea of that. Falling. As if he'd had no control. He was so much braver than she was.

In her mind, she clung tighter to the crumbling edge of the cliff.

"There she goes again," he muttered. His hands went to her pants where he flicked the stud of her jeans.

"Excuse me, what are you doing?"

He undid her zipper. "Don't worry about it."

She gestured to her half-full plate of food. "I'm trying to eat."

"So am I," he said, tugging at her jeans.

She'd walked into that one. He untied her tennis shoes, then her jeans were off and he tossed her shoes, followed by her pants, over his shoulder.

"Legs, Cupcake." He pointed at his shoulders with both hands. "Now."

"I thought you were eloquent."

"I thought you were ready to come ten times."

She bit down on her lip and her hips jerked. A totally involuntary reaction.

"See? I know you." He did. Already, he knew her. Her body and, most of the time, what she was thinking. It was unnerving. He pointed at his shoulders. "Cupcake. Legs."

Giving in, because who could turn down this offer? Not her, that was for darn sure. She propped her sock-covered feet on Connor's shoulders. He slid down, his width parting her legs wider and wider as he lowered his face between her thighs. He hummed in the back of his throat, and she felt that hum on her most private part, before the hot slick of his tongue was dancing over her skin.

Then she forgot about her breakfast, dropped her head over the back of the chair, and tilted her hips toward his exploring mouth. She didn't count ten. She didn't count at all. She just let each and every electric shock tear through her body as she endured the assault of his incredible mouth.

When he told her to touch herself, she obeyed. Impervious to the chill of the house, she took off her shirt and tugged at her nipples while she watched the man who had fallen for her work to delight her in every way imaginable.

* * *

He supposed it was a cheap shot to continue convincing Faith to do things his way via breath-stealing orgasms. Cheap, but sure as hell was fun. He could tell she was hesitant ever since he'd let her have it this morning. But he wasn't the kind of guy to keep things in, timing or no. Her body was willing. Her brain, however, was resisting him.

Well. She'd come around. Hell, she was about to come now, he thought as he lifted her hips the slightest bit and increased the pressure on her clit with his tongue.

Instantly, she shuddered out another climax. He drew away from her, leaning his elbows on the seat of the chair, and watched her. Her thumbs and forefingers were locked around her nipples, her eyes squeezed shut, and her cheeks a flaming pink. He reached down and adjusted his erection, pressing painfully against the confines of his jeans.

"Mmm," came a satisfied sound from the spread-eagle blonde in front of him.

"Cupcake," he said, his eyes going back to her small breasts. "Could watch you do that all day."

Her eyes opened. She licked her parted lips. "I could do it all day." She rolled her nipples between her fingers and thumbs again.

God help him.

He took her hands away and replaced them with his mouth, suckling each nipple gently while she squeezed her legs around his torso. Her fingers went to his cropped hair, massaging his skull. He could tell she was close to going over again, and for that, he wanted to be inside her.

He stopped tonguing her and kissed her lips. She was panting, which made him very pleased. Nothing stroked his ego like pleasing a woman. And he pleased this woman repeatedly whenever he touched her.

"Up, babe," he instructed. "Bend over the table."

"That sounds..." She smiled. A sated, and heaven help him, drop-dead gorgeous smile.

Eyebrows lifted, he waited.

"*Naughty.*"

What a word. He shook his head. "Oh, here we go."

She grinned. "And nice."

"I sense a theme."

"Well, it is Christmas. And for my present this morning, I want to be on top. I'm guessing we'll break the table if we attempt that."

He took one look at the wobbly legs. "Probably."

"Chair, then."

"Not much better, Cupcake."

She stood, pressing her small breasts into his face where he stole another kiss or three. Then she stood and pulled at his hands until he stood with her. She instructed him to sit. He did, pushing his throbbing erection to one side of his fly.

"Dying here," he let her know.

"Don't move." Wearing only her socks, she pranced out of the kitchen. "One second!" she called. He heard her rustle around in the living room, heard what sounded like a few utensil ornaments hit the floor, followed by a solid *thud*. When he figured out what she was doing, a smile pulled his mouth.

Sure enough, she clicked into the kitchen a moment later. Gone were the socks. Now, she was dressed only in the tree topper, and its mate: two black high-heeled shoes that pushed her tight little ass into the air and made her legs go on forever.

Her body shifted and she propped a hand on one delicate hip, her curves gentle but downright lethal. "Mr. McClain, did you order a holiday lap dance?"

If this wasn't proof she loved him, he didn't know what was. His grin got bigger. Along with other parts of him.

She approached, her hair cascading over her shoulders and brushing those pointing nipples, her lithe body moving like she knew how to use it. And she did. Moving over him, she straddled him and he lifted his palms.

"No touching," she whispered against his mouth. "Or I'll stop."

He lost her in a blur of lashes when he narrowed his eyelids. "No deal." He palmed her ass and pulled her close.

"You're terrible at being submissive."

"Damn straight. Undo my pants, Cupcake. Skip the dance. I want inside you."

He helped her with his jeans, standing and kicking them off. She tugged at his shirt, which he helped her with as well. Naked save for his socks, he sat on the chair, and Faith, every inch of her long and lean body, straddled him. She lowered onto his length, and his hips rose to meet her.

Hands on her ass, he plunged her downward, and when she was encased, and he was pulsing deep inside her, they both let out a helpless breath.

"Every time," he said against her mouth, his eyes sinking shut.

She kissed him and said no more, but there was no need. He guided her, hands around her hips, up and down, kissing her mouth the entire time. Her fingers played at the back of his neck, stroking his jaw and sliding up into his hair and back down and over his shoulders. As if she was memorizing his body with her touch.

"Gonna be fast," he informed her, pushing into her again. Lightning fast. He couldn't—

Faith settled her ass against his thighs and leaned back into his hands at her back. She put her fingers to her nipples and tugged, moaning for his benefit or hers, he wasn't sure. Also: It didn't matter. Watching her turn herself on while he continued slamming into her was enough to cause his release to build in record time.

Her moans got louder, her fingers plucking her nipples as she rose and fell to meet his every thrust.

Incapable of words himself, he increased the speed of his thrusts, and she arched into him, her moans now for her and not only for him. He watched her exquisite face pinch, her mouth drop open, and her hair fall over her face as she hunched forward. What he felt was better—her clamping around him, tightening and letting go over and over as her climax took her. He followed, holding her against him as he buried his face in her hair and rode out his release.

She laid her head on his shoulder and he held her, their bodies shuddering, a faint sheen of sweat where their skin touched.

* * *

One wide palm held her close where she collapsed against Connor's shaking body. They were both breathing heavily, sweating and spent. He didn't let her boss him around, instead grabbing on to her and slamming her down onto his rigid length with a force that almost had her coming on the spot.

Seriously. How many more times could she orgasm? With the man currently inside her, she was beginning to think there was no end in sight.

He slid his palm to the back of her head and pressed a kiss to her temple. He did that a lot, she noticed. Could do the most mind-blowing things to her, talk dirty to her, then offer the sweetest, softest press of his lips and make her feel precious.

"Love those shoes," came his low, rocky voice in her ear. *Love*.

"Not because they're fine Italian leather, I'm guessing," she teased, rolling her head to the side and kissing his throat.

"Leverage, Cupcake."

"I love...these shoes, too."

"Tease."

She blew a laugh through her nose. He was never going to let her get away with her private thoughts. Lifting her face from his neck, she asked, "How do you know everything I'm thinking?"

"Because I'm observant." His hazel eyes twinkled. "And you're easy to read."

"Am not."

He put her face into his hands. Still closed around him, the moment was as intimate as it got. Especially when he locked his eyes on to hers. "Beautiful, yes you are. And I love that, too." He pressed a kiss to her nose. "Have a surprise for you. At first you'll hate me for it, then you'll get into it and thank me repeatedly for hours afterward."

She felt her eyebrow lift in curiosity.

"Yes or no."

Unable to turn down a promise of thanking him repeatedly, she said, "Yes."

The unmistakable heat in his smile made her tingle all over.

"Okay, but you asked for it."

* * *

A long, low groan worked its way from the soles of her warm feet, up to the heated center of her chest, and through her throat. Her breath came out as steam, mingling in the cold air threatening to frostbite her nose.

"Thank you," she said, her voice barely audible over the sound of Connor groaning from his side of the hot tub. "Thank you, thank you, *thank you.*"

His rumbling chuckle shook his shoulders. Eyes closed, he lounged on the far side of the Jacuzzi, arms out, steam curling off his broad shoulders. "Told you."

He had told her. And he'd been right. When they bolted, bare-assed naked across the snowy porch wearing only towels, she'd cursed him high and low. But then he threw open the top covering the four-person hot tub and helped her with her shoes. She'd climbed in and sank into oblivion. And thanked him repeatedly.

"I had no idea this place was equipped with a hot tub," she told him now.

"Got it up and running a while back. All I had to do was slip out here and turn up the heat. Then get you to join me."

"I thought you meant sex. This might be better."

He opened his eyes to slits and took her in. Steam lifted into the air between them. "Wait'll we have sex in here. That's next. But first, recovery. You wear me out."

"Me? I don't have any *oomph* left in me after that session."

"Waiting for a 'no,'" he said, his eyes sinking shut again.

"I'm serious. I'm spent."

"Still not a no."

Dammit. He was right. Because she wouldn't say no to what he was offering.

"Fine, but give me a minute or ten."

"Take ten, Cupcake. I'm in no hurry."

* * *

The snow was officially done falling according to the weather reports. There was no television in the cottage, but remarkably, he had a signal on his phone and was able to check the weather.

Connor had made a call to his buddy later in the day to talk logistics. He needed to get a plow down here, and stat. Donny assured him once he got out of his own driveway, he'd be down to help dig them out. The drive stretched a long, long way into the woods, and even if Connor could get his Ram up and over the piles of snow back here, they'd likely get stuck before making it to the road.

Donny agreed and offered to give Connor as long as he needed. "You have plenty of food?"

"Yeah, we're not gonna starve."

"Yeah, I bet she's keeping you warm," Donny had said with a chuckle.

He'd laughed it off, called his buddy an asshole, and hung up with a "Merry Christmas." Donovan was not wrong, though. Faith had warmed him, body and soul. And the hot tub earlier. Lord. She'd be the death of him.

They hadn't attempted sex in there after all, but they had let their hands wander under the bubbles. She'd stroked him, her hands magic, her tongue in his mouth turning him inside out. He didn't realize how lonely he'd been until today.

Until just now, actually.

"Gin!" Faith shouted, holding both fists into the air in triumph. "McClain, you suck at this game!"

She'd found a deck of cards in a drawer in the kitchen, and after determining all fifty-two were there, sat down and revealed her competitive side. Gin Rummy. She owned his ass in this game.

"Who knew you were such a bad winner?" he grumbled.

"Who knew you were such a sore loser?"

"Three out of five. I'm just getting warmed up. Unless you want to switch it up. Strip poker?"

She grinned at him, but refused. They went from cards to dessert. She had slipped a package of cookies into her Abundance Market basket. Paired with almond milk, they were not half-bad.

"They're no Devil Dogs," she commented, shoving the rest of the chocolate chip cookie into his mouth. "But they'll do."

He swallowed and licked his lips, taking another two cookies from the plastic tray. "You are addicted."

"I don't see you resisting the pull of sugar, either."

Or her, he thought to himself.

"You're wearing off on me." He meant it in more ways than one, but illustrated by shoving an entire cookie into his mouth.

She took a bite and chewed, her gaze focused on her lap. "What's . . . I mean. I'm just curious. What's next? For us?"

Way to ask him that when his mouth was full. He swallowed, guzzled down a drink of milk. He knew getting out of this cottage wasn't what she meant, but he went with it anyway. "Donny's coming to help dig us out tomorrow after the plow trucks come by."

She nodded. Still wouldn't look at him.

"We have enough to eat for breakfast and lunch tomorrow. You worried?"

A tiny frown pulled her lips. "No. Not at all."

He waited for her to fish, but she must have decided against it. Either that or he wasn't as good as reading her as she'd accused him of being.

"I have a surprise for you," she blurted, climbing off the couch. She went to her suitcase leaning against the wall. He turned his head to watch her rummage, curious. And he admired her slim curves, the graceful way she bent down and stood again.

Then she came to him with a wrapped package. Red with silver polka dots and a silver ribbon wrapped around it. "Here."

"You bought me a Christmas gift." He was … flattered. She didn't have to do that. He didn't get her anything, unsure if they were to the exchanging gifts portion of their relationship. Other than the kinds of gifts that turned them each inside out and made them shout one another's names.

"It's not a big deal."

He patted the couch where three big blankets were piled. The fire was doing its job, however, and so did the hot tub. It was toasty in here. "Sit with me."

She did, sitting on the sofa and folding her knees to her chin. "Really, it's nothing."

"It's something. And I didn't get you anything."

"You did."

He paused with his finger under the tape to look over at her.

She pointed at the tree, decorated in her frilly undergarments and the cheapest flatware imaginable. His back still ached from sawing that fucker down.

Smiling, she said, "You made sure I had a tree."

He smiled back at her, feeling his chest swell with pride. "You love Christmas. You can't have Christmas without a Christmas tree."

"I could have."

"I didn't want you to."

She uncurled and put her knees on the cushion, leaning close and kissing his lips. He moved his present to the side and feathered his fingers into her hair, kissing her back.

When she drew away, she whispered, "I know" followed by, "open your silly present."

"How silly could it be?" He tore at the paper, revealed his gift, and promptly laughed. Laughed so hard, his stomach hurt and tears pricked the corners of his eyes. When his vision cleared, and his laughter ebbed, he looked up to see Faith smiling, too, and looking pretty proud of herself.

"Cupcake." He held up the box. "You bought me a Chia Pet."

"Like it?"

"No."

Her smile faltered the least little bit.

"I love it." And he loved her. But he was going to ease off that topic for a while. Until she realized the same thing about him. And she would. He knew what they had wasn't normal. Wasn't typical. Wasn't the kind of thing you could overlook and ignore for long. "Get over here."

"I can't have any more sex today," she said, crawling to him like he asked.

"Not what I want," he said when she nestled into the crook of his arm.

"What do you want?"

Arm around her shoulders, he gave her a light squeeze. "This."

"Hmm. This is nice." She picked up the box holding his topiary-to-be. It was terra-cotta in color and in the shape of a dog. The chia seeds would sprout into the dog's fur. "I figured you liked to grow things. And I figured you'd have room for it in your apartment."

"It's the most thoughtful thing anyone's ever given me," he admitted.

"That's how I feel about our tree of cutlery and camisoles."

Another deep laugh echoed in his chest and made him wipe his eyes. Seriously. Had he been this happy in…ever? Sure, he'd laughed. Yes, he'd had great times with his family and friends, but this easy, relaxed, carefree feeling? He'd never had this with Maya. Never had this when he'd lived with his family. And he sure wouldn't use the term "carefree" when describing scorching days and nerve-racking nights in Afghanistan.

"Forks and frills," he said as she leaned against him and they admired the tree.

"Silver and…skivvies." This time she laughed, and he'd be damned if it didn't echo the way he was feeling at the moment. Light. Relaxed. But then didn't she echo the way he was feeling most of the time?

He leaned back against the couch and closed his eyes. "Christmas nap, Cupcake." Suddenly, he was beat. It'd been a fun, but long, day.

Snuggling against him, she laid on his chest. He pulled her into him and she arranged her arms and legs until she was fused to his side. Not for warmth this time, just because she wanted to be there.

"Pine needles and panties," he murmured against her hair, and felt her shake with laughter again.

He slid into sleep seconds later.

$\mathcal{C}$HAPTER 24

$\mathcal{F}$aith had never been so tired in her life. After a holiday packed with sex with Connor, and sleeping half on him, half on a sizable but not that comfortable couch, she needed a night in her own bed. A night where she slept for twelve to fourteen hours straight. She also needed coffee.

Lord, how she needed coffee.

So when her best friend in the whole wide world showed up in the freshly plowed driveway—*thank you, city of Evergreen Cove*—with a thermos full of coffee, Faith launched herself into Sofie's arms.

"Will you marry me?" Faith asked, cradling the coffee thermos to her chest.

"You're too late," Donovan commented as he and Connor brushed snow off Connor's Ram with brooms.

"We'll be back." Sofie laughed, then took Faith's elbow and led her to the cottage.

"I want some of that, Cupcake!" Connor called after her.

"Thought you had some of that," she heard Donovan mutter.

Sofie clucked her tongue. "Boys, I swear."

But Faith found herself giggling. Like there had been any doubt in anyone's mind what happened over the holiday.

Sofie entered the cottage and gasped, and Faith instantly realized why. The tree. Thankfully, she'd already taken down her underthings and stowed them into her suitcase. The flatware, however, still dangled from the branches. Without the lace, or the lit fire glowing in the room, the tree looked pathetic and sad.

"We'll replace them," Faith explained as Sofie fingered one of the forks bent over a branch.

"Don't you dare worry about that." Her friend's eyes grew warm. "He cut you down a tree?"

She lifted a shoulder and dropped it. "Yeah."

"Oh my gosh." Sofie's eyes were wide. "He likes you."

If she only knew. Connor told Faith he *loved* her. And they'd shared several special, intimate moments no one would understand unless they were here and saw them play out.

"*Really* likes you," Sofie repeated, looking up at the massive tree.

"I like him, too." Faith went to the kitchen and rinsed the mug she drank coffee from yesterday. When he had surprised her with a cup of coffee from the packet he'd found in her purse.

Faith could feel her curious presence in the kitchen, but her best friend said nothing.

After she'd poured half the steaming coffee into the mug, Faith turned. "What, Sofe? What are you thinking?"

With a blink of her green eyes, Sofie walked over and rested her hands on the countertop. "I know you went through hell with Michael. And I know you are afraid to trust again. But what I know for sure is if this is real for you and Connor, the way it is for Donovan and me, the way it is for Charlie and Evan—"

"This isn't that." It couldn't be that. What her friends had with their guys was…well, it was a long-term relationship with intertwined pasts. Faith may have known Connor in passing for a minute several years back, but they had no real history to fall back on.

"But if it *is*," Sofie continued, "then you owe it to yourself to open up and let him in." She held up her hands and backed a few steps away. "That's it. That's all I'm saying. I've said my piece."

"It's not like I haven't been thinking about…everything over the last couple of days, you know." She screwed the top back on the thermos Sofie brought and lifted Connor's mug. "Not like there's a lot to do in here."

"Mm-hmm. I see that." Arms crossed over her chest, her friend slid her eyes to the floor under the kitchen table before pegging Faith with a smug smile.

One of Faith's shoes—one of her very fancy shoes—rested on its side on the linoleum. Shoes she had no business wearing in a cottage covered in snow unless she'd put them on to prance around for Connor's benefit. When she met Sofie's eyes, she was still grinning.

"Okay, there were a few things to do." She lost the battle and returned her friend's smile.

Sofie bit her lip—to keep from laughing—but Faith wondered if she wanted to say more. Probably wanted to remind her how things had started out hot and heavy with her and Donovan and ended up with the two of them completely in love.

But that was Sofie's story. Not hers. Faith had given the road to *Blissville* a shot with Michael, and it hadn't worked out. Even though she didn't mind hanging out with Connor, or sleeping with him—come on, who wouldn't like that?— love and marriage and kids were a whole different ball game.

An entirely different sport.

The honeymoon would end eventually. Faith hoped Sofie and Donovan lasted. Hoped when they encountered strife, they made it through the hurdles that always came and found their way back to happiness. Charlie and Evan seemed to have hit their hurdles early, and passed the test without incident. Those two were a matched set.

Again, Faith pictured Gloria and Asher, and how very hurt they were whenever they were around each other. They were proof things didn't work out for everyone. There was a fifty-plus percent rate of divorce in this country, for Pete's sake. It wasn't like Faith wasn't being realistic.

"Can I say something else?" came Sofie's small voice as Faith headed for the front door with a filled mug for Connor.

She felt herself deflate. "Can I stop you?"

Sincerely, Sofie said, "Yes."

"I love you but I'm not sure if I can handle any more truth." The truth from Sofie's view of things—her pie-in-the-sky worldview.

"Fair enough." She could tell it was hard for her friend to keep her opinion to herself. And honestly, Faith had not kept her opinions to herself, either, when Sofie was going through her stuff with Donovan. But right now, Faith was feeling so...raw. Vulnerable. Another slash of truth might be the blow that drew blood.

Outside in the sunny but frigid weather, she handed over half her coffee to the man occupying her present and, possibly, her future. Before tasting the steaming drink, he kissed her, pressing his cold nose to her cheek. "Thanks, Cupcake."

When she turned, she caught Donovan's eye. His lips pulled, his expression uncertain. Faith wondered what he and Sofie talked about when it came to their best friends. Did Donovan share Sofie's hopefulness? Or did he see trouble coming? Did he see, because he and Sofie had a seven-year break, that maybe Faith and Connor would not work out until some time had passed between them?

Or maybe not. Maybe she was simply in the way of a task two really good-looking men were trying to complete. That seemed safer, so that's what she chose to believe.

"I'll let you get back to it," she mumbled, and scampered back into the cabin.

* * *

At her apartment, Connor pulled her suitcase out of his truck and walked with her up the stairs. He used his key to let them in and turned off the alarm on the wall.

Faith stepped in behind him, taking in a deep breath. She felt like she hadn't been home for a week, though they were only gone a couple of days. Her little Christmas tree sat in the dark, looking sad, even with presents still under it.

A switch clicked, and her tree blinked to life.

"Technically, it's still Christmas. Dinner at Mom's

tonight." He walked through the hallway with her suit-case, calling behind him, "They probably bought you something, but you don't have to reciprocate. They won't expect it, anyway. So no feeling bad about it."

She twisted her fingers together and chewed her lip. The very last thing she wanted to do today is go to his parents' house and be around his entire family. Just thinking of Kendra's and Dixie's penetrating stares was enough to make her want to crawl into bed and hide there.

Everything she and Connor had shared these past few days, the intimacy, the aloneness, had been perfect. But now, back in her apartment, surrounded by her things—by reality—she was feeling out of sorts.

"Tonight," she said quietly. "I forgot about that."

"Yeah?" He stood in front of her and palmed her jaw. "You're probably beat. I sure as hell am."

"Exhausted." She hoped he took the hint. "All I want is a hot shower and my bed." Smiling, she added, "Maybe watch *A Christmas Story* three or four times."

"Sounds like the perfect day." He studied her a little too closely, and for a moment she worried he might argue with her, or try to make her go with him tonight. She bristled for the possibility, but he surprised her. "You should stay home if you don't want to go."

"Really? You don't mind?"

"Not like you're excited or anything, are you?" His lips twitched, amused.

"It's not that I don't want to see everyone." Even though it kind of was. "It's not that I don't appreciate the invitation..." Embarrassed, she looked down at her fingers.

"Cupcake, I get it. It's a big family thing. You don't

have big family things. Besides, they aren't dating you, I am. Long as you let me back in tonight when I come over, you won't get any argument from me."

She tipped her chin, said nothing.

He ducked his head and looked into her eyes. "That okay? If I come back?"

It wasn't like him to ask. What an odd juncture. "Of course."

"Good. Call me if you need anything." He gave her a soft, brief kiss, and headed for the front door. Then he left. She watched the deadbolt click and heard him call through the panel, "Alarm, Cupcake."

Obediently, she strode over and set the four-digit code. She blew out a breath and closed her eyes, and without thinking of one other thing, walked to the bathroom and pulled on the shower.

* * *

Gifts had been opened, and his nephews were in the other room playing with their new toys. Connor's father was lounging on his recliner in front of the television, paying the rest of the family no mind.

Dixie and Mom were looking at old photo albums. That left Connor, who was palming a beer and standing in front of the family's Christmas tree under the pretense of walking down memory lane. But it wasn't the ornaments from when they were kids that held his attention. The only thing on his mind was Faith.

"Okay, where is she really?" This came from Kendra, who was also holding a bottle of beer and doing her impression, dead-on, he might add, of a prying older sister.

"I wasn't lying, Ken. She's at home, beat. Probably scared her off with that Thanksgiving voodoo ritual the two of you perform in the attic every year."

This earned him a punch in the arm. She squeezed his biceps when he didn't flinch. "Good God. I remember when you used to be little. You are a monster, you know that?"

"I'll take that as a compliment."

"If you don't tell me what happened, then I'm just going to guess."

He gave her the side-eye. "Don't know what you're talking about."

"Oh, come on. I'm not as clueless as Mom. And I'm not as wrapped up in myself as Dixie. The last time I saw the two of you together, I could see you were enamored with this girl. Now I see you without her, and I have to tell you, baby brother, you look kind of heartbroken."

He took a pull of his beer and rolled his eyes. "Kendra, I am not heartbroken. She's at home. She's expecting me tonight. We're good."

"But it's not advancing the way you'd like it to?" she guessed. *Accurately.*

Why? Why didn't he have brothers?

"No complaints on my end," he told her. "It's good." Sure, he may have dropped the I-love-you bomb a little early, but Faith knew he wasn't going to push her on this. And, proving he wouldn't, he had let her stay home without forcing her to come here. He bet if he'd kept on her about it, he could have convinced her to come, but that wasn't what she wanted. He respected that.

"You do realize the last girl you brought home for a holiday was Maya, right?"

He sighed and walked away from the tree. Kendra followed him.

"I like Faith," she said. "I think whatever stuff you're dealing with, maybe you should let her in. Maybe you should share things with her. Tell her about Afghanistan. Tell her you've been lonely since you came back home. Tell her…"

Getting that his sister wasn't leaving him alone anytime soon, he spun on her. Keeping his voice down, he used a sharp tone to get his point across. "Tell her I love her?"

"Oh, Connor." Kendra's mouth snapped shut. Then her eyebrows bent in concern.

He pulled a hand through his hair, frustrated. While he would've liked to blame his frustration on his sister, he suspected this was his delayed reaction over Faith's reaction to his heartfelt admission. Over her *non-reaction*.

"I told her about Afghanistan," he said to the ugly wood paneling in the room. "She told me she got the truth out of the two of you first."

Kendra winced. "Yeah, sorry about that…"

"I don't care about that," he said honestly. "I want her to know. Just like I wanted her to know about Maya. Just like when I realized that I was falling for her, I thought she should know." He shrugged. "We were snowed in at this little cottage. I cut her down the Christmas tree. We shared meals, wine…" *A pregnancy scare.* "I know it's fast. I didn't expect her to jump in and tell me she loved me, too. I still don't expect her to." Another deep sigh. But he'd like to know there was a possibility for a future.

Kendra's hand wrapped around his arm again, showing support with the gesture. "Hey, it's only one family dinner, right? There'll be plenty more McClain meals she can attend. And it sounds like you two have shared a lot with each other. I'm sorry I brought it up. I guess I assumed—"

"You assumed your baby brother wasn't dealing with his shit. Thought you'd come over here and set me straight."

His sister's mouth curved into a sardonic smile. "All right. I'll give you that."

They clanked the necks of their beer bottles together and drank.

"Your turn," he said. "Tell me who you're dating. And why he isn't here."

"He." Her eyebrows went up and her mouth quirked. "That's a big assumption."

His lips twitched. Ken and her secrets. "I see you have more to talk about than I first assumed." He dipped his chin at her now-empty beer bottle. "Refill?"

"Refill."

Connor dumped their empties in the recycling bin and walked to the garage to get two more beers, looking forward to getting to talk to his sister. To chill out with his family. To enjoy the holiday the best he could without his girl on his arm. But that was okay, he reminded himself. Because he'd be at Faith's place in a few short hours and crawl into her bed.

Or so he thought.

When his cell phone rang an hour later, his plans changed in a heartbeat.

* * *

How long did family Christmas functions last, anyway?

Faith had emptied the bottom of her wine bottle into her glass and frowned at the red liquid. When she opened the wine an hour or so ago, she assumed she would be sharing the bottle with Connor.

Of course, she realized it was ridiculous to be jealous of him spending time with his family when she had elected not to go with him, but it didn't stop her from being upset he wasn't here.

When her glass was again empty, and her eyes grew heavy, she found herself getting almost angry she hadn't heard from him yet. It was midnight. Surely, Dixie and Tad had put the kids to bed by now. Surely Kendra had gone home and his parents had retired for the night.

She picked up her cell phone and cleaned the screen with her sleeve. In the background, *A Christmas Story* played on DVD for the umpteenth time, the chant of, *"You'll shoot your eye out!"* having lost its novelty the third time around.

Maybe she could text him. A simple "good night :-)" would be a good way to let him know she was not waiting up for him, but also wouldn't be too aggressive. Just as she was keying in the message, her phone rang.

Connor. His instinct on the nose, as per his usual.

She smiled and answered with, "About time. I was beginning to wonder if your sisters had a Christmas ritual that involved gagging you with ribbon."

"Faith, it's Kendra."

"Kendra?" It took her a second to regroup when Connor's sister's voice came over the line. And she sounded scary serious. "Everything okay?"

"No. We are at the hospital…"

Her entire world narrowed into one small circle. Her brain stopped processing the meaning behind Kendra's words. The only thing reverberating through Faith's mind was the word *hospital*. Connor was in the hospital?

"...Not looking good. I thought you should know. Connor is pretty torn up. I offered to call you, and he let me."

Wait...

"I'm sorry, Kendra. I think I missed something. Did something happen to Connor?"

"No! No, oh my gosh, I'm sorry if I wasn't clear. I bet I just scared the life out of you."

She had. Faith's hands were shaking. Her everything was shaking.

"It's Jonas. His friend from the army? He attempted to take his own life late last night. His ex-wife happened to be in town and stopped by with his daughter. They found him..." Emotion clogged Kendra's throat, and her next words came out quiet and garbled. "Oh, Faith. It was awful. Anyway, he's lost a lot of blood. He's in intensive care now."

Jonas. *Blood*. What had he done? Faith lowered herself to the couch, her hand gripping the arm.

"I can't come to the hospital," she said vacantly. "I drank an entire bottle of wine."

"It's okay. I don't think this is a place you want to be. Just thought you should know that Connor isn't going to be coming over to your house tonight. He didn't want you to worry."

Tears began streaming down her cheeks. Well, she was worried. Not because Connor wasn't showing up at her house, but because his best friend was fighting for his life in an intensive care unit.

"Can you please tell him to call me as soon as he can?"

"Yes. Absolutely."

Faith thanked her and hung up the phone, then stared at the screen until it went dark. If she hadn't drank as much as she did, she would be in her car heading over to the hospital right now.

More than anything, she wanted to be there for him. But then again, didn't Connor have enough people there for him now? And, she had the selfish passing thought that if he really missed her, he would've called himself. It was nice of him to ask Kendra to call, but didn't couples who meant something to one another tend to call in person during emergencies?

She dropped her phone and closed her eyes, pressing her palms to her face. That was the wine talking. Using her feelings of inadequacy to salve over her worries. Suddenly, she couldn't sort her emotions. She was feeling angry and sad and nervous and overwhelmed all at the same time. Maybe it was better that Connor hadn't called. Who knows what she would have said?

Kendra promised to have him call her later. Faith would be here for him when he did.

* * *

Connor had met Jonas's wife and daughter once, right before his wife split. He and Jonas had both been on leave, back in the Cove, and as far as Connor knew, Mindy was perfectly fine and dandy. Sure, she was rigid. Flat line of a mouth, straight dark hair, leading down to her waifish figure. She was thin, but unlike Faith, too thin.

She appeared to be thinner since the separation. Jonas's

daughter was staying with Mindy's parents who also lived in the Cove. Mindy stayed at the hospital overnight, her cheeks sunken into hollows, worry present on her pale face.

He found himself torn between being pissed off and feeling sorry for her for leaving Jonas, which was probably why he kept his mouth shut when she had broken down in his arms.

"This is my fault," she had cried.

He had said nothing, mainly because there was a large part of him that agreed with her. If she and their daughter, Emily, had stayed, Jonas never would've tried to kill himself with a pistol. So in a way, yes, this was Mindy's fault.

Correction, Connor had reminded himself numbly as burning hot tears pressed the backs of his eyes. Jonas never *would have* killed himself with a pistol.

The doctor had come out early the next morning to deliver the news. Mindy broke down. Connor's sister, Kendra, who had stayed the night there, too, hugged him close and cried as well. He felt his emotions shatter in his chest, the shards cutting into vital organs, but he did not cry.

It wasn't a case of letting himself cry or not. He just... didn't. He felt the loss. The loss for Emily, who would never see her father alive again. The loss for himself, because his friend had checked out of the game.

That feeling of loss and grief covered him for the next two days. Through the visitation at the viewing—closed casket due to Jonas's fatal injury. The feeling stayed through the funeral. Through the tense phone conversations he'd had with Faith.

He didn't go to see her. He didn't want her to see him like this. Broken. Empty. Like someone had scooped out his insides. She was understanding about it, apologizing and offering, more than once, to attend the funeral with him.

Connor had asked her not to, though he knew she would have come. Faith didn't know Jonas or his family. She didn't need to dive into the pool of grief with others wading around—flailing around. They were all at a loss right now. No one knew what to say, or how to comfort one another. Everyone's face simply reflected the same question. A question that would not soon—if ever—have an answer.

Why?

After the funeral in the freezing, blowing wind, after the pastor droned on over the casket, there was a gathering at Jonas's parents' home. Connor kissed Jonas's mother on the cheek, hugged his sister, and even hugged Mindy and patted little Emily on the shoulder.

The guilt finally hit him when he climbed into his truck. Connor and Faith had been snowed in, which kept Connor from showing up for his and Jonas's weekly visit. That thought had started out as an angry swirl in his gut after the doctor delivered the news Jonas had not lived. By the time Connor convinced Kendra he was okay, climbed behind the wheel of his Ram, and left the hospital, that anger had morphed into an ominous black whirlwind, sucking up everything in its path.

The winter roads were colorless, coated in piles of snow. Like the landscape in Afghanistan, Evergreen Cove was all the same muted color, the road and trees and land before him washed out—only in shades of white and gray instead of orange and brown.

Death. So damn much of it. It was one of the reasons

he'd most looked forward to his tour being up. No more looking over his shoulder, or finding one of his friends' lifeless bodies.

Apparently, that was something he could not run from.

It was like the cold from the winter had seeped into his bloodstream. He felt nothing. Which was not good, because he should feel something. When his best friend, the man who saved his life, put the muzzle of a gun to his temple and pulled the trigger, Connor should feel fucking *something*.

At home, he walked into his apartment and looked around at the blank white walls. The muted furniture, the stacks of cardboard boxes. What was he doing? Living half a life. Living like Jonas had lived.

He dropped his keys on the kitchen counter, lifted a knife out of the block, and cut into the tape on the first box he saw. No more was he willing to wait for his life to start. Every one of these boxes marked a time in his life when he was stagnant. Unsure about what he wanted. Living in between decisions.

That wasn't him. He was all or nothing. Jonas had chosen nothing. Connor refused to join him.

Tape sliced open, he found T-shirts and other articles of clothing in the depths of the box. Some of them were salvageable; others destined to relocate to Goodwill. Either way, they needed washing. He stomped through the hallway to his utility closet, yanked open the accordion doors. He opened the washer's lid, banging it against the wall, and tossed in the box of clothes. After laundry was started, he reclaimed his knife and tore into a second box.

Books.

He cut the tape off of a third box.

CDs. Movies.

Chest heaving, knife in hand, he looked around his sparse living room. Recliner. Television. Not a shelf in sight.

He needed a couch. A new chair. Bookshelves. Artwork. Stuff that made a "crash pad" into a home. This was not a home.

Since his parents' house, he had never made a home for himself. The closest he'd come was setting up the indoor greenhouse at the mansion. But even that wasn't his own space. It was his buddy's space. A space he was invading.

He tossed the knife onto the counter, went to the refrigerator, pulled out the carton of orange juice, and drank. Then he sat on his recliner, carton in hand, elbows resting on his knees.

This shithole would never be home. It had never felt like home. It never would feel like home. This was the place he'd lived while waiting to find a home.

In that moment, orange juice container in hand, staring blindly at the frayed rug at his feet, he realized he'd already found a home. A place nestled in the woods with a hot tub on the back porch and a missing tree from the side yard.

Missing because he sawed it down and propped it into a corner next to the fireplace on Christmas Eve.

Lifting his cell, he dialed the one man who knew all about finding a home when you don't have one of your own. He answered on the second ring.

"Donovan," Connor said in greeting. "I need to talk to you about the cottage."

CHAPTER 25

$\mathscr{F}$aith's mind was not on the planning of Gloria Shields's party. It should be. Their friend and soon-to-be resident of Evergreen Cove would be moving here within a month.

Gloria had found a house and rented the former Make It an Event storefront on Endless Avenue. She'd hired Sofie and Faith to plan a welcoming party for her clients as well as potential clients. Since the Cove had a lot of wealthy residents, and quite a few who made their living via creative endeavors, it was a great idea.

"Are you sure you want to be here doing this?" Sofie appeared in Faith's field of vision, leaning over her desk in the office in the mansion. "I feel like you should take the week off."

Faith looked away from her computer and met the concerned gaze of her best friend. "I'm fine. Why?"

"With what Connor is going through, maybe he..."

needs you. I don't want to keep you from being there for him."

"You're not." That was the clincher, wasn't it? Connor *didn't* need her. He was dealing with Jonas's death on his own terms. Despite his proclamation that he had fallen for her, despite the days they'd spent together over the holiday in each other's arms, he'd done a complete one-eighty. "He needs time alone."

"No, he doesn't." Sofie's eyebrows slammed down, her tone impassioned. "Donny spent seven years handling things on his own. It didn't help him."

Gently, but forcefully, Faith stated, "Connor isn't Donny."

Sofie straightened from the desk. Some of the severity went out of her expression. "I know. But he shouldn't be alone right now. He's been through a lot."

"Yeah. He's going through something and won't share what it is."

"He will. I can't tell you how I know, but he is going to come to talk to you soon. If you go to him"—her eyes flicked around the room guiltily before landing on Faith again—"maybe you could speed up the process?"

Faith cocked her head to one side in suspicion. "What do you know? You have to tell me."

Sofie pressed both hands over her mouth and shook her head. Then for good measure walked out of the office. Well. So much for having a best friend. Best friends were supposed to share all their secrets, but apparently, hers was keeping one to herself.

Faith finished out the workday without asking any probing questions about what Sofie might or might not know. Frankly, she was tired of hearing what everyone else thought she should do. She was also tired of not hearing from Connor. Yes, he called, but only to relay the most basic of information. He was fine. He didn't want her to worry. He'd see her soon.

The last thing she wanted to do was put herself in the middle of friends and family she didn't know to attend Jonas's funeral, but it would have been the right thing to do. It stung that Connor hadn't wanted her to go. She should have gone anyway. She never should've let him talk her out of being there for him.

In her apartment's parking lot, the asphalt was cleared, but high, plowed piles of snow encircled the light posts. As she took the steps up to her apartment, it was hard to believe just a few months had passed since Connor dogged her every step, followed her home, and insisted on sleeping on her couch to protect her from the bogeyman.

And when the bogeyman ended up being the very man she almost married, Connor still didn't back off. And when she'd insisted on being independent, he didn't back off then, either.

But now, in the face of losing his friend, and the moment where she felt like he should turn toward her and not away, he was nowhere to be seen. That was her last thought before she unlocked her front door and found him in her kitchen, twisting a cork out of a bottle of wine.

Forgetting her earlier pithy thoughts, she dropped her purse onto the kitchen table and raced across the room. He caught her in his arms, palm to the back of her head, and held her tight.

"I'm so glad to see you," she mumbled into his sweater. "I've been worried."

"Told you I was okay, Cupcake." He kissed her temple and drew her away enough to look into her face. She didn't need to see his slight smile to know things were going to be all right. She knew the moment he called her by her nickname. "I didn't want you to worry."

"I know I said it over the phone, but I feel like I should say it in person." She held his eyes. "I'm so sorry about Jonas."

He kissed her lips and thanked her, then turned back to the wine. "Mind if I pour you a glass?"

She snapped her gaze to the bottle, then back to him. "Sure."

By the time she hung her coat in the closet and kicked off her boots in the bedroom, Connor had two glasses poured and was gesturing for her to sit on the sofa.

She did, sitting next to him and accepting the glass. The nervous butterflies in her stomach beat her rib cage without mercy. Sofie had hinted that something was up, and if proof wasn't sitting on her couch elevating a glass of Layer Cake Primitivo, she didn't know what was.

"When I was done with the army for good," he said, studying the red liquid in his glass, "I knew it would take time to transition back into my life. I estimated a few months, tops." Subtly, he shook his head. "Was wrong about that. It's been a few years. Just now getting my business off the ground, finally transitioned away from Dad's handyman business, but I'm still living out of boxes."

She reached for his hand and he held her fingers against his palm. He looked at their linked hands for a moment. "Was," he muttered. "Was living out of boxes." He met her eyes. "I'm not doing that anymore."

"That's good." Despite her spoken sentiment, she felt

as if the other shoe was about to drop. The tension from the realization tightened her grip on his hand.

"Remember when I told you this thing with us, you were all in or all out."

And here it came. She nodded.

"I have a Christmas present for you. If it's not too late for you to accept it."

Oh. That was sweet. "You didn't have to do that. You did get me a tree."

His smile was small, the sadness from Jonas's death still radiating through his flat stare and slumped shoulders. He put the wineglass down, reached into his pocket, and came out with a key. Turning over her palm, he pressed the silver key into her hand. "I bought a house."

She stared at the key, speechless.

But he wasn't done. He took her wineglass and set it on the coffee table next to his, then erased the space between them, palming her face and forcing her gaze to his.

"The cottage where we spent Christmas. The fireplace where we ate dinner. The kitchen where..." His smile turned both loving and sinister. "Where you wore the shoes."

"Connor..."

"It's yours, Faith. Ours. I'm no longer living temporarily. I'm no longer living apart from you."

She thought she might hyperventilate. He...bought a house. Bought a house for them to live in...*Together*. What Connor was offering, what he was *doing*, was generous, slightly crazy, and way, *way* too soon. She just moved in here. She'd barely had a chance to make it her own. Heck, he'd spent more nights here with her than she'd spent here alone.

Yet his gesture was also the sweetest thing anyone had

ever done for her. It had come from the heart, but she knew the heart was exactly where he was having trouble at the moment. His heart had been recently broken, was filled with grief over Jonas.

Unsure how to react, she managed, "This is unexpected." She licked her lips nervously and plinked the key onto the coffee table, swapping it for her wineglass. She drank down a few greedy sips.

"Yeah." He leaned back on the arm of the sofa and rubbed the side of his index finger under his bottom lip, looking very much like he did the very first night he'd stayed with her. "Jonas," he said, confirming the direction of his thoughts. "After...Everything snapped into focus in an instant."

"Because of how you are feeling," she blurted before she could stop herself.

His eyebrows met over his nose. He didn't look angry, more upset. And like he wanted her to explain herself. She could do that.

"What I'm trying to say is sometimes when we get caught up in the feelings of a moment and, um, we are unable to see what's really going on in front of us."

His eyebrows went lower, and his mouth pressed into a firm, angry line.

Trying again, she cleared her throat and continued, "Like when Michael and I got engaged. With that big happy occasion hovering out in front of us, I missed all of the signs he might not be as happy about it." Except that wasn't really the way it was. She rolled her eyes at her own inability to relate to Connor. "Not that I was happy about getting married. It was more like something happening because it had to. Because I needed it to."

Now she was frowning. Was that true? Had she simply needed a wedding to prove to herself she was capable of being married? In the middle of her epiphany, Connor interrupted her.

"In or out, Faith." He was still frowning.

She blinked at him.

"In"—his frown intensified—"or out."

Her mouth was frozen open, unable to continue making the point she was not doing a very good job of making. "It's too soon for me to—"

"Too soon." His voice had no tone.

"For us to get a house."

"But not to have sex. Have a baby."

"I'm not pregnant."

"No. Guess it's a good thing, too, since you're half out already." He stood and she put down her glass and stood with him.

"That's not fair," she said as he darted down the hallway. She would have moved in with him if she found out she was pregnant. Maybe. She bit her lip. Maybe not.

When he reappeared in the living room he was pulling on his brown leather coat over his big shoulders, and looking none too happy about it. "Better I know now."

She snagged his arm. He shrugged her off.

"Excuse me," she said, suddenly angry. "You can't expect to come in here and tell me we're moving in together and me just...comply. I do reserve the right to say no." Her heart was thundering in her ears. She didn't like being on this side of his angry expression. Seeing Brady under it, seeing Michael under it, had been thrilling. Being the recipient of that fury...not fun.

"Yeah, you do." He stood several inches away from

her, and she didn't like him not touching her. Didn't like the fact that he wasn't giving her two seconds to think...to react. To...anything. His eyebrows went up. "Well?"

"N-now? I can't...I can't decide now."

"I decided a long time ago." Finally, his rough voice softened. His eyes went gentle. He took a step toward her and relief flooded her chest.

"I know." Licking her lips, she clutched her hands together.

He dipped his head the few scant inches between them to meet her eyes. "I told you I loved you."

He had.

"You also told me I didn't have to reciprocate," she reminded him quietly.

He drew away from her, almost recoiling, his face going as hard as stone. "I was wrong. You're not halfway out."

Her heart thrashed against the walls of her chest, but still she said nothing.

"You're all the way out." He said this with a sort of macabre acceptance, and she felt her hands begin to shake.

"I'm not out." She wasn't. She liked Connor. She liked being with him, talking to him, eating and drinking with him. "But I'm not going to move in with you."

Nodding, he looked to the door.

"Out, out," he murmured almost to himself. "There were only two choices, Faith." He faced her and it shook her to the core to see his eyes glistening with unshed tears.

"Connor." She took a step toward him.

He stepped back, his voice calm but his words harsh. "What the fuck do you want from me?"

She blinked, stunned by the question. "I don't want anything from you."

He walked to the door, yanked it open, and paused. Before he left her apartment, and left her to pick up the pieces from this evening, he shattered her with one final question. "Know what I want from you?"

Her heart stilled in her chest. She didn't have an answer. But he did.

"Everything." He didn't slam the door, didn't stomp down the stairs, didn't run across the parking lot. Simply pulled the door closed as he said, "See you later, Cupcake."

She went out on the balcony and watched him swagger to his truck, that sure strong gait walking away from her while she stood mute in the cold, her hair whipping around her face and stinging her cheeks.

"I did the right thing," she whispered as he climbed into the driver's seat and started the engine. But when he pulled away, and the cold penetrated her skin and seeped into her bones, she wondered.

Did she?

Was there really only one option for her and Connor? Move in together? Make this thing between them permanent, or else he'd go away for good? And if so, why had she chosen the latter?

When the wind blew cold, and her teeth began to chatter, Faith went back inside. Then she sat on the couch, looked from her wineglass to his, and decided to drink them both.

She would finish the bottle. She would fall asleep

on the couch. Then she would call off work tomorrow. Maybe she'd call off the day after that, too. Maybe she'd quit altogether. Move back in with her mother. Stay away from the mansion. Stay away from Connor completely. Hide like the coward she was.

But she could never do that, could she? Connor was a friend of her friends. He worked with and for her friends. He was involved in her life in so many ways. He was all around her. She'd have to deal with him, whether she was *with* him or not.

And that, she realized as she refilled her glass and stared at his, may be the truest test of her strength there'd ever been. Because independence was now hers.

Thrust upon her, maybe because she'd been fighting for it this entire time.

She was victorious.

But the only thing she felt was lost.

* * *

"Pivot," Donovan said from the doorway.

"Don't make me laugh." Connor lifted the edge of his plastic-wrapped couch, using the muscles in his legs and arms to haul it a few inches higher. "Push," he managed.

Donny pushed, and miraculously—finally—they got Connor's first piece of furniture he'd bought in...ever... into the cottage. They settled it on the floor in front of the fireplace. He'd already hauled out the old couch. Frankly, he couldn't look at the makeshift bed where he and Faith had spent Christmas another second.

"Beer?" Connor offered.

"Yeah." Donovan sat on the couch, plastic crinkling.

He delivered, and they twisted off the caps at the same time and drank.

"So."

Nice try. "I'm not talking about Faith."

Donovan tipped his head, sending his black hair sliding over one eye. "You sure as shit are."

He glared over at his buddy, who leaned an elbow on the arm of the new leather sofa.

"I recall you making a phone call to me when I was being an idiot about Sofie."

"This is different."

"I know. You're being an idiot about Faith."

"She doesn't want me." Embarrassing to admit. But true.

"Boo-fucking-hoo."

He clenched his jaw. "Dammit, Donny, I'm not doing this shit. I've been through enough."

"You need to man up, McClain." He took another pull from his beer. "Take it from one idiot to another."

"I'm reenlisting."

That shut his friend up for a second. But only one. "Why?"

Connor shrugged, but he knew why. He was a man who served. Who liked to feel as if he were doing some good. Here…here, he was no good. Faith didn't need him. He hadn't been able to be there for Jonas.

"Much as I honor and admire the fact you put your ass on the line for the betterment of our country," Donny said, holding his gaze steadily, "I'm going to have to respectfully disagree."

"Not asking your opinion."

"Sure you are. And I think you're running away from Faith like you did Maya."

"Fuck you." He paced the room.

"Don't take it out on me, man. You need to face her. Face what you're avoiding. The real issue. And the real issue here, brother, is not me."

Connor felt his nostrils flare. Mainly because Donovan was making a point he couldn't deny. His friend wasn't the issue. The issue was that Connor had thrown down the mother of all ultimatums and the gamble hadn't paid off.

"Nailing Faith down to a house, to a commitment with you, isn't going to ensure she won't leave you later," Donny continued.

He felt his frown intensify and the confusion set in. "That's what you think this is about?" Was it? An epiphany tingled on the edge of his brain. He wanted to ignore it, but his "friend" wouldn't let him.

"After Maya left, you lost a shot at fatherhood. You lost a shot at marriage. You were so messed up over her taking away your future, you went over the big blue ocean to get away from her."

"What do you know?" he grumbled, only halfheartedly lashing out at this point. "You weren't around."

Donovan stood and plunked the beer bottle on the side table by the window. "Not doing this with you. I don't have your patience." He grasped the doorknob.

"Hang on."

He turned, black eyebrows raised. "Now he listens?"

Connor crossed his arms over his chest. "I need you to help me haul in my dresser before you go."

Donny shook his head but dropped the knob.

Quietly, Connor said, "I'm listening."

Then he faced his friend and did just that. Listened. Listened as Donovan explained that Faith was in the same place Connor was way back when. And explained how it'd taken years for Connor to get to the place where he could open himself up to someone else again. To buy a house. To start thinking in terms of love and family and a future.

Much as he hated to admit it, his buddy was making sense.

"Faith's had, what? A year or so to recover?" Donny reclaimed his beer and gestured around the cottage with it. "She won't move in here with you because she's still shut down."

"Yeah, well, that's her choice. I told her in or out. She opted for out."

Donny took in this new information, but surprisingly, didn't berate Connor for it. Instead, he offered the simple observation of, "Convince her to let you in."

Connor didn't look at him, instead at his boots, now damp with melted snow.

"Or wait for her."

"I don't do that."

"Start," Donny said. "Or you'll lose her for good."

Connor raised his head and met his friend's pale blue eyes. Donny was a lot of things to a lot of people. Honest and blunt were two things he was with everyone.

His friend popped the door open and headed outside. "Let's get the dresser."

Connor followed, the uncomfortable conversation knocking around in his head. He didn't want to wait. He didn't want to put himself in a position where the waiting turned into her leaving. Maybe that was unfair. The only other option Donny had suggested was Connor convincing her to let him in.

As he gripped the corner of his dresser in the back of his truck, he found he couldn't decide which option he liked less.

* * *

"Okay so for tonight's party, we have about a dozen people coming. Pretty small." Sofie handed over a Cup of Joe's mocha and sat down on Faith's couch. "I want you to come."

Faith, who had yet to shower (again), shook her head. "I don't want to go to a party."

"I know."

"Connor will be there."

"Probably. He practically lives in our backyard."

The house. *Our house.* Faith wanted to cry, but she couldn't. For some reason, the tears wouldn't come. "I'm not in a partying mood."

"You know"—she sat—"New Year's Eve is a time for magic. A kiss at midnight, resolutions. Your whole life could change tonight."

"Or maybe it won't." Maybe she and Connor were as in sync with this breakup as they had been with everything else. They were both hurt, both unwilling to budge. Maybe that was a sign in and of itself. "I'm not rushing things just because he thinks I should. Just because I hurt when he's not here."

Just because her chest was hollow and her nose was dry and her eyes were scratchy from unshed tears. Just because his being gone made her feel like life would suck forever.

"What's stopping you?" Sofie asked gently. "What's stopping you from taking the leap?"

"I don't want to need anyone ever again. I never want to be to the point of marriage, or…a baby." At that, her breath clogged, voice choked, and she let out a sob, releasing her pent-up tears.

Sofie put down her coffee and moved to the side of the couch. Faith collapsed into her. Then she told her. Everything. The negative pregnancy tests, Connor saying he loved her, how scared she was. How terrifying it was to feel so much for someone so soon. That she wasn't even sure if she could trust what she felt.

Pushing her hair away from her face, Sofie held Faith's face in her hands. "You listen to me, Faith Garrett. Connor is not Michael. If he says he loves you, he means it."

"He meant it with his ex, too." She sniffed. Here it was, the crux of her fears. "He wants to be needed. He wants to provide. What if…what if I'm convenient for him? What if this is more about him slaying his demons than really loving me?"

Sofie dropped her hands. "Honey."

Since no argument came, Faith guessed she'd made a point. Damn. She was hoping to be wrong about that.

"You should ask him." Sofie's green eyes were sincere. "Just…ask." Like it could be that simple.

"Yes," Sofie said without hesitation. "Come tonight. And if Connor doesn't show up, you can go to the cottage and corner him. You need to know. It's a new year, Faith. Make it matter rather than sit here and wonder."

Make it matter.

New year. New her. New start.

"Okay." She pushed herself off the couch. "Dress code?"

"Come as you are."

Faith held out the T-shirt she was wearing. One she

snagged from Connor that was three sizes too big. Under-neath was a pair of yoga pants and bulky socks. "Really?"

"Well. Come as you'd like to be seen by our friends." Sofie's smile faded slightly when she added, "And Connor." She stood and walked for the front door. "Either we'll toast to your success, or drink to your failure. But you'll know. And knowing is better than not knowing."

How true.

With a wave, her friend vanished out of her apartment and Faith went into her room to find something decent to wear. And practice her speech.

The speech.

The moment she embraced her courage and confronted her fears.

Did Connor love her for her? Or was he trying to make good on his unresolved past? She had to know. Or there'd be no hope for them at all.

CHAPTER 26

"Hey, sweetheart." Gloria Shields swept over to Faith dressed in tight, black jeans, heeled boots, and a big cowl-neck red sweater. With her painted red lips, long sheet of black, silky hair, and stunning blue eyes, she looked amazing.

"You look incredible. I had no idea you'd be here." How about that, Faith was smiling, and it felt genuine. Maybe she'd be okay regardless of how tonight went. She pulled Gloria into a hug. "Oh, and you smell good."

"Keep it up, I'll go home with you tonight." She winked long black lashes. Then Glo's smile vanished. "Sofie mentioned trouble in paradise with you and the grunt."

"It's..." She shook her head. "I don't know. I'm going to talk to him tonight."

"Good luck with that."

She knew Gloria meant the statement sincerely. "Thank you."

Shouts rose from the bar on the other side of the ball-room and Glo and Faith turned from the cart of desserts from Sugar Hi to see Asher walk through the double doors, arms spread.

"I'll never be rid of him," Glo growled, her voice low and unhappy. She finished her champagne. "It's nearly eleven thirty and I'm just now loosening up. But there is no one here to kiss." She lifted and dropped an eyebrow. "Everyone is annoyingly coupled off."

It was true. Even Officer Brady Hutchins had brought a date when he was here earlier. He left not long ago. Probably for the best Connor didn't find him here. *If* he showed.

"Well, I think Scott Torsett is still single, but Donny sort of hates him."

Gloria chuckled. "The lawyer? Was that the guy Sofie dated?"

Faith nodded. "Yeah. Donny didn't like seeing them together. So he threatened to break his hand and escorted him out of Salty Dog."

Glo was laughing, but then her smile faded as she locked eyes with Asher Knight. Faith could see the heat between them—how much they both wanted each other. How much they were both fighting being together. It was hard to watch.

Were Faith and Connor doing the same thing? Were they denying themselves to protect their hearts?

"Is there any saving it?" Faith wondered aloud.

Dragging her gaze from Asher, who had turned his at-tention to Donovan and ordered a drink, Glo looked at Faith now. With a shrug of her small shoulders, she gave her a sad smile. "No. Sometimes there's not."

"I'm sorry. I can see it, you know. How hurt you are."

Glo, usually stoic and rigid, pursed her lips and looked down at her empty flute glass. "He hurt me." She snapped her blue eyes back up. "Being left for another woman..."

"There's no other betrayal like it," Faith finished for her. She had nearly forgiven Michael for it, for one insane second last year. In this very mansion, in fact. But then, she'd walked away from him... and went to Connor.

"I have a military man to question," Faith said. "Is it cliché to find him at the stroke of midnight?"

Raising one black manicured eyebrow, Glo joked, "No. It's cliché to run out at midnight, and lose one of your shoes on the stairs."

She laughed—actually laughed. Maybe she'd be okay tonight no matter what happened. Until she heard the whoop come from the guys on the other side of the room again. This time, they were applauding Connor, who strode in dressed in his usual outfit of battered jeans, lace-up boots, and a navy blue henley. It'd only been a couple of days since she had seen him, yet he looked different somehow. It wasn't like he'd aged, or his hair had gotten longer. But after seeing him every single day, not seeing him for a while made him look completely foreign.

God. She missed him.

He sent her a perfunctory glance, then tipped his chin in a nod, before taking Asher's hand in a hearty shake and settling at the bar. Donovan poured shots and Evan materialized, Charlie in tow, who lifted a shot glass as well.

"Now's your chance," Gloria said. "Go tell him you love him."

"I never..." Faith shook her head.

"Take it from me, toots." Glo winked, looking very much like a classy Hollywood star from the era of black-and-white movies. "You love him."

* * *

"Ten minutes!" Sofie announced, sliding behind the bar and wrapping her arms around Donny's waist. Beside him, Connor was aware of Charlie leaning on Evan's shoulder.

"It's obnoxious around here," Asher muttered under his breath as he lifted his refilled shot glass. Connor noticed his own glass had been filled as well. Asher clinked his glass against Connor's. "The single women are standing by the cupcakes ignoring us."

Cupcake. Connor downed the liquor and hoped it would numb the ache that word held. No such luck.

"Sucks."

He looked at the rock star.

"I know you think I'm an asshole," Asher said. "Arguably you are right." Donovan and Sofie, Evan and Charlie, and a few other friends were leaned on the corner of the bar chattering loudly, ignoring their conversation.

"I don't think you're an asshole." Immature, maybe. Misguided, definitely. But Ash was not a dick. He cared about his friends, obviously, or else he wouldn't be here.

"She won't hear me out about the girl I had in my cabin years ago." Asher sounded grim. Connor faced him and found him looking grim, too. Tired eyes met his. "When she finds out about my son, she's going to hate me

more than she does now." He lifted a sardonic brow. "And
that's sayin' something."

Shit. The kid. "You had the DNA test."

He nodded. "He's mine. I had sex one time with that
girl and we have a son." He reached for the whiskey and
poured a shot for himself. When he offered one to Connor, Connor shook his head. Asher drank his down, then
blew out a breath. He sounded beat. Looked beat. "I'm
not going to quit trying with her."

"The mother?"

Asher winced. "No, man. Sarge," he said, his nickname for Gloria. "She's it. She's stubborn and feisty and
she hates me. I have a way to go." He held up a finger
as if making a point. "Oh, and I have a child with the
girl she thinks I cheated on her with." He shook his head.
"Stacked deck."

Connor had to admit, his odds were not good.

"What about you and Legs over there?" he asked.

"What about her?" Changing his mind, he refilled his
shot glass after all.

"She's looking at you like I look at Gloria. Pining."

He felt his heart lift even as he shook his head. He was
not having this conversation with Asher Knight. The man
had no idea how to handle women. Or himself half the
time.

"I know." Asher gestured to himself. "Asshole. But listen to this asshole. You guys are salvageable. You're still
here, not in another state. And she's at this party looking
at you like she wants you. Glo looks at me like a cock-
roach just skittered into the room."

Connor had seen firsthand that wasn't true. Gloria
looked at Asher like he'd crushed her heart under his

cowboy boot. But the guy had enough to deal with without being enlightened further.

"Unless," Asher continued, "you let some half-dressed groupie into your house over the last few days"—he stopped speaking and grasped Connor's shoulder—"You didn't, did you?"

"No, of course not."

He blew out a breath, visibly relieved, and pulled his hand away. "Well, then if you didn't do that, buddy, she's about to have you back."

Connor stole a glance over his shoulder, caught Faith looking at him. She turned to Gloria, ignoring him again. "How the hell do you know that?"

"One thing I know." He spread his arms. Leather jacket, black tee, black jeans, cowboy boots hooked over the rung of the stool he sat on. "Women." With a grin, he refilled his shot glass and banged on the bar top with the flat of one palm. "Whiskey, boys! All around. Why am I drinking alone?"

Everyone joined in on the next round, and Sofie called out, "Five till midnight!"

Connor passed up the shot, opening a bottle of water instead. When he turned to catch Faith's eye again, she was no longer standing by the dessert cart. And Gloria was slipping behind the bar to pour herself a shot of tequila.

"Sarge," Asher greeted.

"Asher." She threw back the shot and gestured to the door with her glass. To Connor, she said, "She's outside. Chickening out."

He swallowed thickly, wondering what that meant. Then he decided to find out for himself.

As he slipped off the stool, he heard Asher say, "Atta boy."

* * *

Nope.

She was still a coward. It was nearly midnight and Faith couldn't possibly say everything she had to say to Connor before the ten-second countdown and then there would be kissing and if he was still angry with her like she suspected...

Well, she couldn't stand and stare at him as the ball dropped and wait to see if he kissed or didn't kiss her. How awkward would that be?

It was freezing out here, but the cold felt almost good. She wrapped her coat tighter and snuggled her nose into her scarf. The patio was clear, but there was a clean bed of snow stretching out across the back of the house, un-marked save for Gertie's paw prints.

The door opened behind her and even all the way out here, she could hear the party inside roaring. She didn't have to turn around to know who'd followed her out here. Gloria probably hadn't wanted to stick around for the awkward midnight tradition, either. Well, at least there was strength in numbers.

"Not going to kiss Asher when the ball drops?" Faith asked.

"He's not my type," came a low voice.

Connor.

Her breath puffed out in front of her face. She wanted to turn around, she just...couldn't. A plate appeared in front of her, on which was a shiny, chocolate-coated Devil

Dog from Sugar Hi bakery. Her eyes traced the fingers, the thumb, the whole of Connor's strong hand. A hand that had consoled her, protected her, turned her on. Helped her stand, held her face.

"I know how you like to indulge when you're upset," he said. She still hadn't turned around. And now there were tears pushing against the backs of her eyes, and she was pretty sure she didn't want to.

She did anyway.

The wind kicked his short hair up in the front, the sandy brown mess she'd fallen in love with from the first morning she'd woken up in his arms.

Hmm. How about that. She had fallen in love with his hands and his hair.

And him. Gloria was right. Faith did love him.

"Maybe we could share." He glanced at the cake in his hand. "I'm having a horrible start to my new year."

From the ballroom, she heard the shouts. They rose onto the air, the words clear in the silent night.

Five! Four!

"This isn't how I wanted to do this," she said quickly.

Three!

"Me neither."

Two!

His lips closed over hers as the shout of "Happy New Year!" rang from the house. He pulled her against him with his free hand. It felt so good to be close to him again, all she could do was close her eyes and lean in. Lean into his solid chest, his sturdy warmth. His arm wrapped tightly around her back, as his lips lifted away from hers.

In tandem, they sighed.

"I have missed that," he muttered, his eyes still closed.

Face-to-face, she admired how long his lashes were, those sharp cheekbones, and his firm mouth. She had missed him, too. So very much.

He opened his eyes and pegged her with his green-gold gaze. "Gloria said you wanted to talk to me. Said you came out here because you chickened out."

A dry laugh echoed in her throat. "She was right."

But then again, Gloria knew of what she spoke. There were plenty of things unsaid between her friend and Asher. In her own way, Gloria was chickening out, too.

"Let's have it," Connor said.

No time like the present, she supposed. "I guess . . . You were wrong. I am a coward."

His eyebrows drew together like he wanted to argue. He didn't. So she continued.

"I'm afraid maybe you don't love me as much as you love the idea of having someone near. Someone who won't leave. Someone who was almost pregnant with your child."

His nod was tight, but it was a nod. "That's fair."

She didn't mean to look surprised, but she could feel one skeptical eyebrow lift. He noticed and swallowed a smile. With one finger, he pressed her eyebrow down.

"Continue," he instructed. "I'm listening."

Wow. Something had changed. She couldn't get him to listen to anything she had to say in her apartment a couple of days ago.

"Okay," she said. "I'm also afraid to feel what I feel for you. Because the last time I opened myself up, I lost . . . everything." But had she? Even as she blurted that out, she wondered if it was true. Looking to the side in thought, she shook her head. "No, no, that's not right. I didn't have everything with Michael. I had the idea of everything. The ring, the engagement, the shared living quarters." Her eyes made their way to his, where she focused on the flecks of gold in a sea of brown and green. "With you I have everything else."

She did. She had his heart, and though he didn't know it yet, he had hers. Shrugging, she went for it. "I'm tired of being afraid. There are things I want and I'm not going to be scared of wanting them anymore."

His Adam's apple bobbed when he swallowed thickly. Turning, he put the Devil Dog on a small iron table covered with snow. Then he came back to her, grasped her jaw in his hands.

Cold fingertips against her warm face, he trained his gaze on hers. "Tell me what you want."

"I want to lean on someone."

"I have big shoulders," he said.

"You do." She smiled. "I don't want to be alone."

"You're not."

"I want to spend the rest of my life laughing and crying with the right person." He didn't interrupt this time. "I want every day of my life to feel like the Christmas we spent together."

His eyes were severe, fierce. As if by boring into her head, he might extract her thoughts. He was looking for the answer to the one question she knew he would never ask her. So she'd have to tell him.

"The truth is," she said, her voice quiet, "I love you and I'm afraid to say it out loud."

His mouth dropped open, a breath blowing out, visible in the cold air. He took a step closer to her and lowered

his forehead to hers. She closed her eyes when his face
went blurry, but his voice surrounded her.

"Say it again, Cupcake. Please."

It was the *please* that made her smile. "I love you,
Connor."

His hands went to her head and he pulled her close,
tightening his hold around her body as he hugged her.

"Shit," she heard him whisper.

She pulled back to look at him—after trying twice, he
finally let her—only to find him wiping his nose and eyes
with the sleeve of his coat.

"Cold's making my eyes water," he said, sniffing. A
nervous laugh shook his shoulders. He turned those red-
rimmed eyes and rosy cheeks to her now. Snow had begun to fall and was sticking to his hair. Levity gone, he
took her hands and warmed her fingers in his. "Let me in,
Faith. You won't be sorry."

"I know."

"You're not Maya."

"I know."

"I wanted that pregnancy test to be positive but it had
nothing to do with my past."

That, she didn't know. And it was oh, so good to hear.
It was also her turn to share something private. Her chin
shook as she felt her eyes fill.

"Me too." Freeing her hand, she swiped her eyes.
"God, we're crazy."

"Promise me," he said, drawing her attention.

"Promise you what?"

"Promise you'll let me love you and I promise no more
ultimatums. Whenever you're ready, we can do the house
thing. Or not. Whenever it's good for you."

She nodded. Grateful for the promise. Grateful for him. Grateful for second chances. And her moronic ex-fiancé who, by attempting to gain entry into her apartment, had given her the man in front of her.

"Happy New Year, by the way." Connor nodded back, the covenant struck.

"Happy New Year to you." Eyes sliding to the abandoned plate, she asked, "Can I have that now?"

"There she is." He grinned. "Let's go in and eat it, yeah? Freezing out here."

"Yeah."

He took the plate and her hand, and led her inside. They didn't go to the ballroom, but instead, to the indoor greenhouse where she'd first come to him. When she knew what she needed but was afraid to trust her instincts. She didn't want to doubt herself ever again.

"Like it?" he asked when they walked in.

She almost asked what he was talking about, but then she saw it. The Chia Pet, in the center of his lavender garden, green shoots starting. Throwing her head back, she laughed. "That's ridiculous."

"This really sexy girl gave it to me," he said, lifting the cake off the plate. "She is a sugar fiend. Legs up to her neck." The cake came closer to her lips. "She wears the sexiest underwear I've ever seen in my life. And her nipples—"

She pressed her fingers over his lips. "I get the point."

Kissing her fingertips, he lowered her hand and closed in on her with the Devil Dog. "With this bite, I promise I will fulfill every one of the dreams you spoke about outside, for as long as you let me."

Had anything ever torn her eyes away from a

chocolate-dipped, cream-filled cake before? She didn't think so. But she took her gaze away from the tower of chocolate perfection to meet Connor's face. Sincere, genuine love shined from his eyes.

"You can lean on me," he said. "I won't ever leave you alone. You can spend the rest of your life laughing and crying with me, and I will do my damnedest to make every minute with you from here on out just like our first Christmas together."

He went blurry in front of her as tears filled her eyes again. She blinked them back. There was nothing to cry about now. Instead, she leaned in and took a very large bite out of her most favorite dessert.

He chuckled and she knew why; she could feel the chocolate dotting her lips, the whipped cream on her nose, the crumbs tracking down her chin. She covered her mouth to chew the oversized bite and gestured to him. He crammed the cake into his mouth, his bite twice as large as hers, and reminded her of the day, in this very room, when he consoled her. When all he wanted in the world was to make her laugh.

She did that now as she cleaned off her face with her fingers. He swallowed the bite and his tongue came out to take a bit of cake from the corner of his lip. Then he dropped the cake on the plate and licked his fingers. Never in her life had anything looked as sexy as Connor McClain licking his fingers after taking a bite out of a Devil Dog. A Devil Dog that was so much more than a shared dessert.

Kissing her, he wrapped his arms around her and she melted into him like she always had. He was here. He was *hers*.

Arms around his neck, she leaned close to his ear and whispered, "I promise, too. All of those things."

They held each other until Faith made out Sofie's voice through the vents saying something about where "those two disappeared to." Gloria's muffled but pronounced voice answered, "I'm sure they're fine."

After that, Faith didn't hear much of anything, other than Connor's suctioning lips on her neck, and the promises he whispered into her ear as he turned her inside out with his amazingly talented hands.

She was in the right place. Finally. And better yet, embracing her courage, and her future.

A future, as it turned out, which included Connor.

EPILOGUE

$\mathcal{A}$ row of cheery pink and yellow tulips lined the side of the cottage. The brutally cold winter had finally given way to spring, and Faith was so glad to see the sun, if she could hug it, she would have.

At the door of Connor's cottage, she took another look around at what he'd done to the place. Since "The Thaw," as they'd been referring to it, he'd cleared out a few trees at the side and back of the house, had a large, decorative outdoor fireplace (built by the talented Donovan Pate) added to the side of the driveway, and was now clattering around in the shed off to the side of the house.

Or so she guessed by the loud curse coming from that vicinity.

"Hey! Beefcake!" She held the gift bag in her right hand aloft when he poked his head out.

His smile never failed to make her smile back.

After the New Year's kiss and shared Devil Dog, she promised herself she would not rush headlong into anything until she was ready. Come February, however, she was over at Connor's new house almost exclusively, promising she'd stay "a few more hours" before she retired to her own apartment. He always insisted she give in and stay the night, and honestly, he'd won that argument nearly every time it came up. Anyway, it was silly to draw a boundary they'd never had before.

The boundaries continued being pushed when she'd started helping him with his abysmal accounting system. If Faith was one thing, she was organized. Invoices, billing, and receipts had been something she'd been overseeing for C. Alan Landscaping as soon as he'd allowed her to get involved. Which was basically, *immediately*.

In relationship matters, however, he had promised he wouldn't push her, and she had promised she was all in. So far they'd both kept those promises. Until this morning, she had no idea how "all in" she was. Her fingers curled around the handles of the bag. All in, as it turned out, was now, *all the way* in.

He stepped out of the shed wearing a tight navy blue T-shirt and distressed jeans smudged with oil or dirt from whatever he'd been tinkering with. He was, as always, drop-dead gorgeous.

"Love that smile, Cupcake," he said now, returning her grin with one of his own. "Come for some afternoon delight?"

"You wish," she said as he tracked over to her. "I brought you a gift." She lifted the black bag, stuffed with a ridiculous amount of pink tissue paper. When he reached for it, she pulled it away. "Ah, ah. Kiss first."

He snatched the bag from her hand before she could stop him and hauled her against his body, no doubt smearing whatever was on his jeans onto her light gray pantsuit. She was about to take him to task for it when his tongue entered her mouth, leaving her breathless. Dry cleaning worked wonders, so she decided not to worry. There were bigger things in life than fabric stains.

"That's more like it," he rumbled against her lips.

"You are really terrible at being submissive." Her eyes narrowed.

"Maybe you're really terrible at being dominant." He let her go and pulled a handful of pink tissue paper out of the bag and chucked it into the fireplace. Pulling out another large handful of paper, he muttered, "What's this for, anyway? It's not my birthday. Valentine's Day has passed. And I thought we agreed—"

Whatever he'd been about to say froze on his tongue. She took him in, memorizing this moment—the look on his face in this moment. His eyes were on what was in the bag, his mouth open, a wad of pink tissue paper crinkling in his hand.

"I bought two," she said. "Just in case."

Blinking up at her, his fist closed around the paper. "And they're... You already..."

"Took them?" she finished for him. "Yes. They both say the same thing."

Visibly, his throat worked as he swallowed. He dropped the paper into the fireplace, pulling out the two plastic sticks before he tossed in the bag, too.

"Pregnant," he read off one of the sticks. "Pregnant,"

he repeated, reading the other one. Then her big guy seemed to lose the ability to stand, and collapsed onto a concrete bench.

She sat with him. "There's one more thing."

He took his eyes from the tests, his expression dazed.

"Connor McClain." From her pocket, she pulled a sprig of lavender and held it up in front of him. "When I first met you, I thought you were an overly confident, broad-chested man with a great ass."

A hint of a smile tilted his lips. Lips surrounded in enough sexy stubble to make her knees weak. Good thing she was already sitting.

"Now I know better."

He took her hand with his free one, still holding the pregnancy tests in one fist.

"Now I *know* you're an overly confident, broad-chested man with a great ass," she teased.

He shook his head in warning, his tentative smile widening.

"You are also the man of my dreams." Her grin faded, done teasing. "The man who let me in and taught me how to be brave. Like you." She turned over his hand and put the lavender in his palm.

She sought his eyes, noting they were suspiciously damp.

"Marry me," she said.

He blew out a deep sigh. "You ruin everything."

"What?" Her mouth dropped open. "I do not."

His tongue darted out to wet his lips. "Your engagement ring is in my top dresser drawer. I was going to ask you this weekend."

"Really?"

"Really."

"So I didn't have to get pregnant to snare you?"

Losing his ability to hold back his laughter, he chuckled, low and deep. Leaving a mark on her heart deeper than the one he'd left there before. This man had her. Body, heart, and soul.

"Cupcake"—he embraced her—"you snared me a long time ago."

When she lifted her face from his, she found him smiling.

"A baby."

"Our baby."

His grin was undeniably big. No doubting how he felt about her news. He was as overjoyed as she was.

"So?" she pressed, lowering her voice to mimic his. "You in or are you out."

"In." He kissed her, long and hard, and until she melted right into him and almost forgot what she'd asked.

"Yeah? You're going to marry me?" Happiness bubbled in her chest like a fizzy drink.

"I'll do more than that to you." He stood and lifted her off the bench, carrying her to the front door and informing her she now had to move in. Then he carried her up to the bedroom loft and gently laid her on the very large bed she often slept in beside him.

"Really, really terrible at being submissive," she commented a second before his lips covered hers.

Proving he wasn't the least bit perturbed by her accusation, he peeled off her pantsuit piece by piece and got down to turning her on. They made love the way they always had: joining on a shared exhalation and parting on a guttural sigh.

Round two had rendered her practically useless. Since she'd closed her eyes in the hopes of sinking into a blissful sleep, it took her a moment to realize there was the cold sensation on her breast. She opened her eyes to find a gold engagement ring encircling her nipple.

Lifting it, she looked through the circle at the man lying on his stomach on the bed, looking at her through the other side.

"Connor."

"Yeah, Cupcake?"

She slid the ring onto her finger, unsurprised at the perfect fit. Feeling the weight of this moment, she flicked her eyes back to his. "What about the curse?"

"Lifted," he said, kissing her finger and the ring at once. He placed a kiss on each of her nipples, then her lips. "You'll make it down the aisle, Cupcake." He pressed a kiss to her bare, and for now flat, belly. "The three of us will make it, period."

In her heart, in her gut, she knew he was right. If anyone had the power to lift an age-old Shelby curse, to make Faith have, well, *faith* in love and marriage again, it was the overly confident, brave, bare-chested man lying next to her.

On a smile, she said, "Thank you." Because without him, where would she be?

"What was that?" She could tell by the arch of his brows he was teasing her. Luckily, she caught on quickly.

"I said . . . I love you."

"That's what I thought you said." He kissed her once more on the lips. "Love you, Cupcake." Then he moved quickly, placing himself between her thighs, where he instructed. "Legs. Shoulders. Now."

Obeying her bossy soon-to-be husband, she lifted her legs and deposited them onto his shoulders. He craned an eyebrow. "Good to see you're all in."

Yeah. She was all in.

And soon, so was Connor.

FROM THE DESK
OF JESSICA LEMMON

I couldn't resist including a recipe to pay homage to Faith's favorite dessert! Actual chocolate-dipped Devil Dog cakes are a bit complicated, so I deconstructed them into their simplest form. And how appropriate are cupcakes since "Cupcake" is Connor's nickname for Faith? With special inspiration from master bakers Erin McKenna and Chloe Coscarelli, here is the recipe I came up with. They are amazing!

Devil Dog Cupcakes with Red Wine Chocolate Sauce

Makes 12–14

Cupcakes

- 1 ½ cups flour
- 1 cup sugar
- ½ cup cocoa powder
- 1 teaspoon baking soda
- ½ teaspoon salt

- ½ cup coconut oil (melted)
- 1 tablespoon apple cider vinegar
- 2 teaspoons vanilla
- 1 can coconut milk

Directions:

1. Preheat the oven to 350° Fahrenheit. Line a 12-cup muffin tin with cupcake liners.
2. Whisk flour, sugar, cocoa powder, baking soda, and salt into a large bowl.
3. In a separate bowl, combine oil, vinegar, vanilla, and coconut milk.
4. Add wet ingredients to dry and stir until just combined. Do not overmix.
5. Fill cupcake liners about two-thirds of the way full. If you have leftover batter, line a few cups in another tin, or just eat the batter. (That's what I did.)
6. Bake 16–20 minutes or until toothpick comes out dry.

Vanilla Frosting

- 1 cup non-hydrogenated vegetable shortening
- 2 teaspoons vanilla
- 3 cups powdered sugar
- 3–5 tablespoons nondairy creamer (or milk)

Directions:

1. Using beaters or a stand mixer, beat vegetable shortening and vanilla, adding powdered sugar a cup at a

time. When mixture becomes dry, add non-dairy milk one tablespoon at a time.

2. Continue adding sugar until all three cups have been added. Scrape down the sides with a rubber spatula as needed.

3. Spoon frosting into a large plastic bag (or a frosting bag), twist and cut the corner off. Set aside.

Red Wine Chocolate Sauce

- ¼ cup nondairy creamer (or milk)
- 1 cup chocolate chips
- ¼ cup red wine

(I couldn't resist adding wine to the chocolate sauce. I mean, this recipe is in honor of Faith, after all! If you don't want the wine, simply swap out for extra creamer. Leftover chocolate sauce will solidify in the fridge but will melt in a few seconds in the microwave.)

Directions:

1. Warm the creamer or milk over the stove until simmering (but not boiling) and add to a bowl.

2. Stir in chocolate chips to melt (it takes time, so be patient), while warming the wine on the stove to simmering. Once wine is warmed, add to the chocolate mixture.

3. Continue stirring until smooth. If the chips are not melting, pop bowl into the microwave for 15 seconds

and stir. Repeat if necessary until sauce is smooth and glossy.

To assemble:

1. Once cupcakes are cooled completely (good luck—I ate one warm), unwrap from cupcake liner and put on a plate.
2. Pipe a generous mountain of frosting on the top, then spoon on the chocolate sauce. Top with a tiny bit of frosting and a maraschino cherry.
3. Enjoy with a fork and a smile...preferably at your next Girls' Night Out.

After a family tragedy, sexy tattoo artist Evan Downey moves to Evergreen Cove to escape the past. But a beautiful woman he once knew may be his new chance for a future...

Please see the next page
for an excerpt from

*Bringing Home
the Bad Boy.*

CHAPTER ONE

He'd heard the stress of moving was like dealing with death, but since Evan Downey had dealt with a lot of death, it was with a fair amount of authority he called bullshit.

There wasn't anything particularly *fun* about packing, selling, and leaving behind the house. He and his wife, Rae, had purchased the place together when they first got married—the only home their son had ever known.

The house had been a place of love and promise, but now painful memories poisoned the good ones. He would miss the door frame where he and Rae had scribbled Lyon's height each and every year. Their walk-in closet where Evan had laid Rae down and made love to her the day they moved in.

What he *wouldn't* miss was the hallway where she'd staggered, hand on her chest, and collapsed, never regaining consciousness despite his and the 911 operator's attempts to keep her heart pumping until the paramedics arrived.

Moving didn't compare with the living nightmare of losing someone he'd expected to be around when he was old and gray.

At the very least until their son entered elementary school.

As he watched the house dwindle in the side mirror of the family SUV, he calculated he should be rounding the acceptance stage of grief right about now.

About damn time.

"Bye, house," his son Lyon, age seven going on seventeen, announced from beside him. Gone was the Superman action figure he'd clung to last summer. Now his sidekick was his iPad. He had one earbud stuck in his ear and one dangled onto his chest, as per their agreement that Lyon not completely shut him out. Though the music wasn't loud enough for him to hear—another of their agreements—Evan knew it was tuned to classic rock.

Definitely his kid, he thought with a smile.

With 1417 East Level Road behind them, he turned his attention to the city that lay ahead; the city he'd called home since he'd married one beautiful, sassy woman named Rae, the curvy black girl who'd busted his balls about nearly everything since they were teenagers.

God, he missed her.

She'd built a life alongside him, settling into her nursing career while he set up his tattoo shop.

Before striking out on his own, he'd been under the tutelage of tattoo master Chris Platt; a hippie to rival all hippies, with a heart of gold and a head full of titanium. By the time Evan had packed up his things and gave notice, Chris let him know under no uncertain terms that he believed in him and his abilities. And that he'd succeed.

He had.

"Bye, Woody," Lyon piped up.

Evan turned his head as they drove by his shop where Woody had worked for years, and as of three months ago, had purchased outright. Woody had stepped in the year Rae died, when Evan's concentration revolved around breathing in and out, and keeping a three-year-old boy alive. It was no small feat and, at the time, had taken everything he had.

"Will you miss it, Dad?"

He threw a glance into the rearview, but there was no need. He knew the shop's façade as well as his own face. The crack on the sidewalk out front that sprouted dandelions every spring, the brick crumbling on the southeast corner. The black marquee done up to look like an old-fashioned apothecary that read LION'S DEN. Rae's idea, and in honor of their one and only offspring. Save for the fact their lion was a *Lyon*, which she insisted suited Evan's rebellious, go-against-the-grain demeanor.

She was right.

An image of her shining brown eyes, huge smile, and that horribly ugly sea foam green bathrobe she insisted wearing on her days off popped into his brain, and he felt his smile turn sickly.

"*Dad.*"

"Yeah, buddy," he finally answered, his throat dry as he watched Lion's Den grow tiny in the rearview. "I'm gonna miss it."

What he wouldn't miss were the memories of his late wife assaulting him everywhere he turned in this city.

"What about Leah?" his son asked as they pulled onto the highway. Evan ground his back teeth together.

Leah had been one of his, for lack of a better term, "friends with benefits" for the majority of the year. And though he arranged to keep his dates secret from his son, she'd "stopped by" unannounced last month when she saw the SOLD sign go up in the yard.

Angry tears had shimmered in her eyes while her hands gripped her purse like she might brain him with it. He hadn't understood why. A long time ago, they discussed that what they had was about the physical and nothing more. She'd insisted on arguing with him, in front of Lyon no less, and Evan had to do the unfortunate business of dumping her—when they were never really dating—on his front lawn. It was a dick move, but then, so was sleeping with a woman on a tit-for-tat basis.

No puns intended.

Speaking of tat, his eyes zeroed in on the sparrow on his right forearm, the string of hearts snapped free, the broken heart drifting. That one was for Rae. The roses on his arm were for his mom and his aunt. A lotta death. Too much, too soon. They said bad things happened in threes. For his and his son's sakes, he hoped the adage continued staying true.

"*Daaaad.*" Irritation lined his kid's voice when he didn't respond right away.

"Sorry, buddy, I was thinking. No, I won't miss Leah," he answered honestly.

Another dick thing to admit, but she hadn't meant all that much to him. Them in bed, *cordial* would be the best way to describe how he'd treated her. As awful and uninspiring as it sounded. That's what they'd both settled for, which was equally awful and uninspiring.

He bit back the grimace attempting to push forward on

his features. Rae wouldn't like who he'd become if she could see him now.

But she couldn't see him now. She hadn't been able to see him since the moment she'd collapsed four years ago and he hadn't known he'd been five minutes away from losing her forever.

He wished he could remember their last conversation, but he'd been distracted. Not listening.

"Me either," Lyon said, snapping him out of his reverie. "Leah was mean."

Evan blew a breath out of his nose, as close to a laugh as he was gonna get, and considered that Lyon was the only reason he hadn't spiraled into a whirlpool of depression.

Settling in for the drive north to the lake town they would now call home instead of Columbus, Evan once again reminded himself that this venture was a second chance. For him and his son. A place to create new memories, be closer to Rae's parents and Rae's best friend on the planet, Charlotte Harris.

"Excited to see Aunt Charlie?" he asked Lyon.

Charlie had been "Aunt Charlie" since she walked into the hospital room the day Lyon was born. Rae had held up the blue blanket Lyon was wrapped in after she'd sworn her way through eighteen hours of labor, and Charlie, with tears in her eyes, had taken him into her arms and said, *"Hi, Lionel Downey, I'm your aunt Charlie."*

She'd been a fixture in Lyon's life always.

Since Rae had passed, she'd become more of a fixture. Charlie was a dear friend. A constant, a solid person he and his son could count on. A light in a dark place.

Whenever she visited them, she dragged out photo albums, sometimes bringing new photos of her own to add to the pages, and sat Lyon down to tell him stories of his mother.

Charlie insisted on never letting him forget her. While he agreed this was best for his son, Evan did better when he wasn't confronted with Rae's smiling face as he walked down the hallway. Or her still one, a vision that woke him in a sweat more often than he cared to admit.

For that reason, he'd left the photos in the albums, had tucked the picture frames of the two of them away. But there was no escaping the spot of carpet in the hallway where she'd collapsed, or the other side of the bed, its emptiness as real a presence as Rae had been when she was alive.

Moving to Evergreen Cove would not only get them away from the house choked with her memory, but would bring Lyon closer to the things that meant most to him.

Charlie was one of those things.

"I can't wait!" Lyon said, a very real light shining in his eyes.

Kids were so resilient. Especially his kid. Through the process of packing and moving, Lyon had been both apprehensive and excited. Evan saw the sadness in his eyes when he talked about not seeing his friends at school anymore, but Malcolm and Jesse, the two boys who were his best buds, visited the Cove in the summer. Lyon had been appeased with the promise of hanging out with them.

Plus, the new house offered the attractive package of swimming in the lake, a new house with a bigger bedroom, and Charlie nearby. Evan hoped that might make up for some of what they'd all lost.

Not everything, because God knew he couldn't replace Rae, nor would he try.

But he'd sure as hell take whatever reprieve he could get.

* * *

The pain in the voice at the other end of the phone sliced through Charlotte Harris like a shard of glass. Three seconds ago, when she'd seen her best friend's name pop up on her phone, she'd answered with a chipper, "hi!"

Her greeting was met with a beat of silence, followed by a deep, male response. One hollow, broken syllable; the nickname he'd given her a year ago.

"Ace."

Her heart dropped to her stomach, her extremities going instantly cold in spite of the warm nighttime air. There was something registering in his tone that sent fear spilling into her bloodstream.

"Evan?"

A beat of silence, then, "Yeah."

She stood from the chair she'd been lounging in and paced to the three steps leading from her porch down to the inky, still surface of the lake. In the background, a pyramid of pine trees climbed the hill in the distance.

"What is it?" This from her boyfriend, Russell, who stood from the porch swing behind her.

She held out a finger to tell him to wait a minute.

"What happened?" she asked into the phone.

Something. She and Evan were friends, but not call-each-other friends. If he was calling her now, it had to be because there was a problem. With Lyon, or—

"Rae." *His voice cracked, a painful sob shattering the airwaves and sending an adrenaline rush through her bloodstream. He drew in an uneven breath.* "Jesus, Ace."

Unable to hold herself up any longer, she sank onto a step and issued the understatement of the year. "You're scaring me."

"She's gone, Ace." *His voice went hollow, into a dead tone she never wanted to hear again as long as she lived.*

"Gone…" *False hope she'd recognize later as denial leaped against her chest, borne of desperation to find a reason other than the obvious for this almost-midnight call.*

Maybe Rae went shopping. Maybe she and Evan had a fight and Rae went to her parents' house. Maybe—

"Gone," *his whisper confirmed.*

That's when the tears choking her throat pulsed against her eyes. That's when Russell took the phone from her hand. And that's when she knew.

Rae Lynn Downey, her very best friend, more like a sister than her actual sister, wife to the long-ago besotted Evan Downey, and mother to a dimpled three-year-old Lyon Downey was… gone.

It took five days for that fact to settle in.

For her to see Rae's physical body in the casket, for her to notice Evan's formerly bright eyes weary and bloodshot, for her to witness firsthand the dev-

astation of Rae's parents and the somber expres-
sions on Evan's family's faces.

For her to accept what "gone" meant.

Gone was permanent. Gone was forever.

Gone was unfair.

Standing over her body, Charlie vowed to Rae
she'd watch over her family. She kissed her fingers,
placed them on her best friend's cold cheek, and
whispered to the woman she'd never see alive
again, "Sorry, Rae."

Wheels crunched along the gravel outside her house, bringing Charlie out of the memory clouding her head and back to her living room. She dropped the open magazine she'd been staring unseeing at for the last however many minutes and swiped a single tear from her eye.

Then she cleared her throat, closed the magazine, and bucked up. Because Evan and Lyon couldn't arrive and find her mourning Rae. There was no reason to darken this occasion with melancholy. Them moving here was a good thing. The best thing for them all. Their coming here had reminded her of the promises she'd made, the pain they'd gone through. The loss they'd endured.

She peeked between the curtains and confirmed the tires on the gravel did not belong to Evan's SUV. Releasing a pent-up breath, she watched a blue pickup climb the hill and vanish into the trees.

Not them.

Evan had texted her—she checked her phone, then the clock—forty-six minutes ago, to say they were ten minutes away and since then she'd sat anxiously by the front window. Knowing him, and she did, he probably stopped at Dairy Dreem for an ice cream the moment they set foot in town.

She snapped up her iced tea, frowning at the ring on the coffee table. Where was her head today? She swiped the water ring with one hand and turned for her back porch, pausing first to slip on a pair of flats.

Charlie's house was the most modest on her street— she liked to tell herself it was because the house was built before Evergreen Cove had become a vacation destination. She and her boyfriend, Russell Hartman, had purchased the small, white clapboard because of its view of the lake and the fantastic porch. At the time, she believed that buying a vacation home as a couple was a sign of permanence.

Wrong.

But she had no regrets about the house. Since she worked from home, she'd outfitted the family room facing the lake at the back to hold her desk, computer, and a few shelves for her supplies. She'd kept the couch, and yes, the television, in the room. Her office connected to the kitchen where she had a small table and chairs, but the real prize of her home was the porch. The wide, covered expanse, befitting of a Georgia plantation five times her home's size, was where she ate most of her meals, entertained, or just sat and enjoyed the view.

Rather than stare out the window for the arrival of the Downey boys, she tracked out back to the swing hanging by a pair of chains, smoothed her dress, and sat.

Resting the tea at her feet, she sucked in a breath and took in the view. While the front of her house offered up traffic and trees, she preferred the back—the lake and the hill that rose behind it, a jagged skyline designed from pointed pine trees. This view was why she and Russell had purchased on the private beach.

When he left her two years ago, he'd kept the huge new-build with the cherry tree in the backyard. Rae had always told her a man who was unwilling to marry her was a man who would walk away. At the moment when he'd delivered her morning coffee in the enormous white kitchen with gleaming granite countertops and told her he was leaving her, Charlie thought of Rae's words first.

Sad, but true.

He let her keep the vacation house in Evergreen Cove, and the Subaru they'd recently paid off. "I'd pay alimony if we were married," he'd told her, assuaging his guilt. "The house at the Cove, the car, it's the least I can do."

The very least, she thought bitterly at the time, but now she didn't feel bitter. She considered herself blessed things had ended before she'd thrown good years after bad into a relationship doomed to fail.

Russell was a software developer, a pragmatic thinker, and ten years older than Charlie. She met him at a wedding—prior to her photography career, so rather than the photographer, she'd been the bridesmaid at this particular event. A guest of the groom, Russell had sought her out, danced with her, and practically begged her to take his phone number.

After several dates she learned he didn't want to be married, and he didn't want children. She had always wanted children and assumed children were the natural path following marriage. But when it became clear they were serious, she'd decided both marriage and children were things she could live without. With the right person, sacrifices were unavoidable. Forever would be worth it.

But her relationship didn't last forever, making the six-year compromise she'd made much harder to live with now.

After the kitchen conversation over coffee, he'd arranged for movers to extricate her from the house and then Russell had *eloped* with a woman with *three* children. One going into college and twin boys in the sixth grade. He gave no explanation for what changed his mind, but she knew. The other woman, Darian.

Darian had changed his mind.

Which had the unpleasant side effect of making Charlie feel like she hadn't been enough.

She'd taken what was behind door number two and moved on as intact as she could. Some nights, the hurt and the fear of being alone lingered. The fact she'd been unable to achieve the seemingly simple goal of having a family and settling down had haunted her enough that on those nights she became practically nocturnal.

Taking in a deep, humid breath, Charlie centered herself on the here and now. June was nearly July and the hot and sticky had both settled in at the Cove for the long haul. Sunlight danced on the surface of the lake, sending waves rippling in the wind. Behind the lake, in the sea of evergreens lining the hills, there were a few hidden homes, but that was too "deep woods" for her taste.

From her coveted porch—yes, even her fancy neighbors with their large, enviable homes admitted to coveting her porch—a patch of grass gave way to shore and led into the water. Her aquatic neighbor, Earl, stepped out onto the deck of his beaten houseboat off to the left where it was anchored in the deep, and raised a hand to wave. She could make out his pipe, handlebar white mustache, and sunglasses from here. He was tanned and brawny and made the best clam chowder she'd ever tasted.

Murmuring from the side of her house brought her to her feet as the smile spread her mouth.

Finally!

The voices grew louder as they closed in and she strode across the porch to meet them. She couldn't make out the exact words, but she knew the boy's voice as if he were her own.

"Aunt Charlie!" Lyon appeared around the corner and burst into a run. Before she had a chance to take the three steps to the grass to meet him, he bounded up them and straight into her arms. She caught him against her, savoring how small he was, knowing it was a battle with time she'd lose, and bent to kiss his head. His tight curls had grown out some since she saw him last. They tickled her nose.

Pulling away, she flattened his hair with both hands. It sprang up again, refusing to be tamed.

"You need a haircut," she teased.

"I *knoooooow.*" He rolled his green-blue eyes. Lionel Downey was a stunning kid. He had Rae's chocolate-brown skin, a touch lighter than hers had been, and her genuine, full smile. He had his father to thank for his eye color: ocean blue so striking against his dark features.

"That's a tired subject, if you can't tell."

Her eyes went to Evan, who'd crossed his bare arms over his chest and leaned a hip into the column at the bottom of the steps to watch their interaction. His presence wasn't overbearing or intimidating, but easy. Evan matched his laid-back, live-and-let-live attitude with a lazy swagger that was anything but. He'd worked hard his entire life and as a result, confidence oozed from every pore. The thinning pair of Levi's, the casual T-shirt hugging his chest, his array of tattoos, and devil-may-care smile he showed to the world were him through and through, but Charlie knew Evan ran deeper than his outer layer.

Her eyes tracked along the tattoos decorating his arms to the new one. His latest patch of artwork was a series of evergreen trees, their dark blue-black bases circling his wrist and branching up his arm, their tops almost reaching his elbow. Each tree was a different height, and knowing his attention to detail, each one had some significance. The whole of the pictorial on his arm had a big one.

His moving to Evergreen Cove.

Unable to keep it from happening, her heart reverted to the state it'd been in at age fifteen, somersaulting in the wrongest way imaginable. Before he was Rae's, oh, how Charlie had pined for Evan Downey. Must have been seeing him back here, or maybe her earlier thoughts about her life, that caused the mini-backslide.

But she couldn't backslide. She'd made a vow to herself, to Rae's silent body, to care for Lyon and Evan.

"Did you guys eat?" she asked.

"Yeah. Dairy Dreem," Lyon confirmed.

She knew it. She tilted her chin at Evan in reprimand. An accidentally sensual smirk crooked his mouth, surrounded in a one or two days' worth of stubble.

"We didn't *only* get ice cream."

"Yeah, we had French fries," Lyon added, earning a headshake from his dad.

"No loyalty." The smirk slid into a grin and if that didn't cause her heart the subtlest flutter, the wink would.

And there it was, one blue eye closing and opening again—a flutter in and of itself—the blue so bright, it was nearly electric.

Was it any wonder he'd been on her radar when she was a vacationing teen visiting the Cove? There'd been three "bad boys" she and Rae had noticed whenever they sunbathed at the beach. Evan Downey, Donovan Pate, and Asher Knight. For Charlie, Evan stood out the most.

Evan only had eyes for Rae.

At first she was heartbroken, but Charlie had kept that fact to herself. Teenage crushes were a dime a dozen, and predictably, she outgrew it in a few summers. Rae and Evan had been designed for each other. By the time she stood at Rae's side as her maid of honor, there wasn't a bone in her body not overjoyed that her best friend had found the love of her life.

After Rae's death, Charlie had become a more consistent part of Evan's and Lyon's lives. Russell hadn't liked it. More than once, she wondered if her decision to care for Rae's family rather than prioritize him had ultimately led to their demise.

Staying in touch with Evan had been easy when she and Russell lived close by. After the breakup and relocation, however, her trips to Columbus became less frequent. Once she was settled and had a job, Charlie did make an overnight trip down to visit, and she ended up babysitting for Lyon.

She hadn't minded the babysitting part. Not at all. But the fact that Evan had gone on a date with an incredibly beautiful blonde, then come home around three in the morning smelling of perfume and sex, had hurt her heart in a way she hadn't known possible.

When he'd passed her in the hallway, Charlie had ducked her face into her palm to stifle a sob. Evan abruptly turned on his heel to wrap her in his arms and comfort her, and she had just lost it.

Him giving himself to a harlot who didn't appreciate the things Rae had fallen in love with: his huge heart, his bottomless love for his family, was awful to witness.

Rae and Evan were supposed to live happily ever after. Lyon was supposed to grow up, get married, and dance with his mom at the reception. And Charlie...well, her life hadn't turned out the way she'd planned, either.

Unable to voice the real reason for her crying jag, she'd blamed her emotions on her breakup with Russell, rather than the way it punched a hole in her chest to see the way she and Evan, Lyon, and Rae had all been short-changed.

Life didn't heed plans and dates. Life went on, and left whomever it pleased behind in the wreckage.

The memory caused her heart to ache, and her gut to yearn for what could have been. She flicked her eyes heavenward and sent up a mental, *Sorry, Rae*.

"Can I go inside?" Lyon pulled away from her and grabbed the handle on her sliding door.

"Knock yourself out," she answered. "One more hug, though." He acquiesced, giving her a halfhearted squeeze. She'd take what she could get. Soon, he'd be at an age where he wouldn't snuggle with her any longer and she thought that might be the day she started crying and never stopped.

Evan pushed out of his casual lean, uncrossed his inked arms, and stomped up the three steps separating her from him. "Missed you, Ace."

Him being close made her feel better instantly. "Missed you, too."

He slid the door aside and motioned for her to go in, but when he ran a hand through his shaggy, mussed bedhead, she felt her heart kick against her chest in the slightest show of appreciation.

And for that, she should be ashamed.

Sorry, Rae.

Fall in Love with Forever Romance

A BAD BOY
FOR CHRISTMAS
by Jessica Lemmon

Connor McClain knows what he wants, but getting Faith Garrett into his arms this holiday is going to require more than mistletoe...

SNOWBOUND
AT CHRISTMAS
by Debbie Mason

Grayson Alexander never thought being snowbound in Christmas, Colorado, for the holiday would get so hot. But between working with sexy, tough Cat O'Connor and keeping his real reason for being there under wraps, he's definitely feeling the heat. And if there's one thing they'll learn as they bring out the mistletoe, it's that in this town, true love is always in season...

Fall in Love with Forever Romance

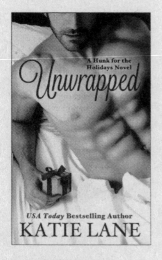

UNWRAPPED
by Katie Lane

Contractor Patrick McPherson is deeply committed to his bachelor lifestyle. But as the Christmas season approaches, he still can't quite forget his curvalicious one-night stand. Then Jacqueline shows up unexpectedly, and all holiday hell breaks loose. Because this year, Patrick is getting the biggest Christmas surprise of his life...

PLAYING DIRTY
by Tiffany Snow

In the second book in Tiffany Snow's Risky Business series, Sage Reece must choose between bad-boy detective Dean Ryker and sexy power-player Parker Anderson. Caught between a mobster out for revenge and two men who were once best friends, Sage must play to win—even if it means getting dirty...

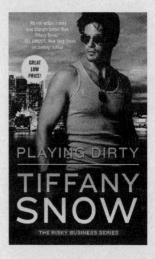

Fall in Love with Forever Romance

THE TAMING OF MALCOLM GRANT
by Paula Quinn

The beautiful and blind Emmaline Grey risks everything to nurse the mysterious Malcolm Grant back to health. But can she heal his broken heart too? Fans of Lynsay Sands, Karen Hawkins, and Monica McCarty will love the next book in Paula Quinn's sinfully sexy Scottish Highlander series.

VISIT US ONLINE AT

WWW.HACHETTEBOOKGROUP.COM

FEATURES:

**OPENBOOK BROWSE AND
SEARCH EXCERPTS**

•

AUDIOBOOK EXCERPTS AND PODCASTS

•

AUTHOR ARTICLES AND INTERVIEWS

•

**BESTSELLER AND PUBLISHING
GROUP NEWS**

•

SIGN UP FOR E-NEWSLETTERS

•

**AUTHOR APPEARANCES AND TOUR
INFORMATION**

•

SOCIAL MEDIA FEEDS AND WIDGETS

•

DOWNLOAD FREE APPS

BOOKMARK HACHETTE BOOK GROUP
@ WWW.HACHETTEBOOKGROUP.COM